Manda Scott is a veterinary surgeon, writer and climber. Born and educated in Scotland, she now lives in Suffolk with two horses, two lurchers and too many cats.

Manda Scott first made her name as a crime writer. Her debut novel, *Hen's Teeth*, was shortlisted for the Orange Prize. Her subsequent novels are *Night Mares*, *Stronger than Death* and *No Good Deed*, for which she was hailed as 'one of Britain's most important crime writers'.

Dreaming the Eagle and *Dreaming the Bull*, the first and second books in the Boudica series, are also available in Bantam paperback.

D0550244

MANDA SCOTT

BOUDICA
DREAMING THE HOUND

BANTAM PRESS

LONDON · TORONTO · SYDNEY · AUCKLAND · JOHANNESBURG

TRANSWORLD PUBLISHERS
61–63 Uxbridge Road, London W5 5SA
a division of The Random House Group Ltd

RANDOM HOUSE AUSTRALIA (PTY) LTD
20 Alfred Street, Milsons Point, Sydney,
New South Wales 2061, Australia

RANDOM HOUSE NEW ZEALAND LTD
18 Poland Road, Glenfield, Auckland 10, New Zealand

RANDOM HOUSE SOUTH AFRICA (PTY) LTD
Endulini, 5a Jubilee Road, Parktown 2193, South Africa

Published 2005 by Bantam Press
a division of Transworld Publishers

A catalogue record for this book is available from the British Library.
ISBNs 0593 052625 (cased)
0593 052633 (tpb)

Typeset in 11/13½pt Sabon by
Falcon Oast Graphic Art Ltd.

Printed in Great Britain by
Clays Ltd, St Ives plc

1 3 5 7 9 10 8 6 4 2

Papers used by Transworld Publishers are natural, recyclable products made from wood grown
in sustainable forests. The manufacturing processes conform to the environmental regulations
of the country of origin.

For Debs, with love and thanks

ACKNOWLEDGEMENTS

Thanks to my editor Selina for her continued resilience, patience and acuity of thought – and for understanding the nature of dreaming. Continuing thanks also to Nancy and to Deborah for outstanding copy-editing throughout the series, to Kate Miciak for holding faith on the far side of the Atlantic, to my agent Jane Judd for rock-solid support, and to H. J. P. 'Douglas' Arnold for keeping my Roman thinking in line.

Particular thanks to Jonathan Horowitz and Chris Luttichau, both excellent and inspiring teachers, for sharing their understanding of the dream in its many forms, and to all those who attended the dreaming workshops of 2004 for their courage and willingness to trust the process.

Thanks to all of those who made horse-ownership a possibility, particularly Tessa, without whom it would never have happened at all, and certainly would have failed at the first hurdle.

Finally, heartfelt thanks to Gigha, mother to the kittens, who came home to die during the editing process and altered again my understanding of the boundaries, or lack of them, between life and death; you were a bright star in the days and I miss you.

CONTENTS

WESTERN EUROPE

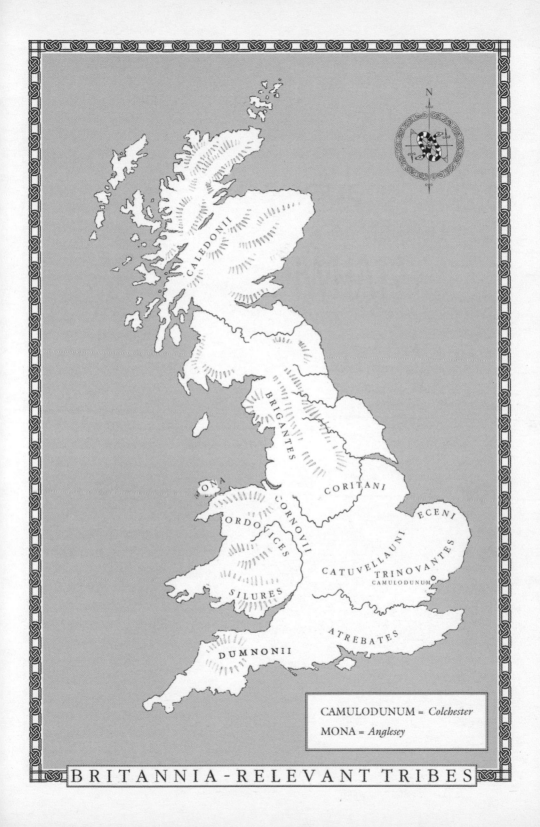

BRITANNIA - RELEVANT TRIBES

CAMULODUNUM = *Colchester*

MONA = *Anglesey*

LISTEN TO ME. I AM LUAIN MAC CALMA, HERON-DREAMER, ONCE of Hibernia, now Elder of Mona, adviser and friend of Breaca, who is the Boudica, Bringer of Victory. We are in a time of great peril; if you do not understand the past, you cannot come to understand the present, and without it, the tribes of Britannia have no future. Here, tonight, by the fire, you will learn what has come before. This is who we were; if we win now, this is who we could be again.

It is fourteen years since the Emperor Claudius sent his legions to invade our land. Then, we were a diverse people, of many tribes and many gods, united only in our care of our dreamers: the men and women who came here, to the gods' island of Mona, to study for a dozen years in the great-house under the elders. Warriors, too, came to learn the arts of honour and courage that might lead later to acts of heroism in battle. We fought against each other for show and thought each skirmish a mighty battle.

Then Rome came, with its legions and cavalry. The men of Rome do not fight for honour or to hear their names sung in the hero-tales at winter. They fight for victory, and when they have made a land their own, they do not leave it.

The tales of how we fought have been told in other places; the battle of the invasion lasted two days and will be told for ever round the fires. A thousand heroes lost their lives and those few who emerged alive did so through the sacrifices of others. It was then that Breaca, once of the Eceni, then Warrior of Mona, led the charge to rescue Caradoc and earned the name by which we know her: Boudica, Bringer of Victory.

Breaca and Caradoc were amongst those who, on the orders of their elders, left the battlefield. They did so with reluctance, fleeing only to continue the war against Rome, and to protect the children, who are precious above all else. They brought them here, to the gods' isle of Mona where warriors and water hold safe all that is most sacred; where dreamers, singers and warriors of many tribes come to know themselves in the full gaze of the gods, that they may take that knowledge, and the wisdom it brings, back to their people.

From here they fought for ten years, preventing the Roman legions from gaining any foothold in the west. Thus the Romans built their first fortress in the east at Camulodunum, which had been the stronghold of Caradoc's people.

In the early years of the occupation, thousands of warriors and dreamers died in the east; whole villages were slaughtered in reprisals for rebellions, real or imagined, and it was declared illegal for any man, woman or child to bear a weapon.

The legionaries who broke the swords of our warriors were led by an officer, Julius Valerius, who rode a pied horse. More than anyone else he was hated, for he had been Eceni once, and had sold his soul to Rome and its gods. He fought for Mithras and for the emperor and both thrived on Eceni blood.

Breaca and Caradoc had a son, Cunomar, and then a daughter, Graine. Shortly after her birth, Caradoc was taken captive by treachery and made prisoner in Rome. Captured with him were his son Cunomar and his elder daughter, Cygfa, a warrior of high renown.

The family were taken to Rome, to die at the whim of the Emperor Claudius, only that Airmid, the dreamer who is the other half of Breaca's soul, found a way to bargain with the oldest and most dangerous of the ancestors and was able to prevent their death and, much later, to bring about their freedom.

Caradoc was tortured and maimed beyond repair. He was well enough to bring his family to the coast of Gaul, but not to go beyond it. He could not have returned as a warrior to Mona – his injuries were too great for him to wield a weapon as he had done with such success before his capture and he would not inflict on his warriors the pain of seeing him brought low by Rome. Thus he stayed in Gaul and word was sent that he gave his life to save his children as they boarded the ship that would bring them back to Mona.

That was three years ago. Breaca mourns Caradoc, but inwardly. Outwardly, she has given herself heart and soul to the battle against Rome. In summer, she leads the warriors of Mona to keep the legions from reaching our island, and to push them back as far as she can from the mountains of the west. Through winter, she hunts alone, taking men singly or in pairs, and they have come to fear her, as if she were a spirit of the mountains who feeds on their souls.

One other returned on the ship from Gaul, who was not expected: Julius Valerius, the once-Eceni cavalry officer who had led the oppression of his people. By the will of the gods, he was called back to Rome by the ailing Claudius to undertake a final duty: to escort Caradoc's family to the Gaulish coast and thence to a ship that might take them to freedom.

Claudius died before the family could reach freedom and Nero, his successor, required that they be returned. Valerius could not go against an oath sworn in the name of his god, and thus was named traitor, and forced to flee.

I would have brought him to Mona, for reasons that are not only my own, but Breaca forbade it and she is not only the Boudica, whose word holds sway with the warriors, she is also Breaca of the Eceni, sister to the man who was once Bán and became Valerius, an officer of the legions.

These, then, are the ones who have fashioned our pasts: Breaca, who hunts legionaries in the mountains of western Britannia, and her brother Valerius who is in exile in Hibernia, where he drags out a living as a smith. Neither can continue at this for ever. The world changes and they must change with it, or die.

Meanwhile, the children, and the dreamers, wait on Mona, watching a world that grows more brutal by the year. Rome seeks revenue from its provinces, and Britannia is not the rich vein of silver and gold that Claudius believed it to be. Nero was made emperor in his place and Nero is ruled in turn by his advisers.

13

These are men without pity, for whom a land and its people mean nothing, unless they have gold or can be made to yield it.

This is the future we fear and against which we fight. Mona is safe now, under the care of the gods, but if it is the gods' will that it be no longer safe, then all that is sacred will continue in the hearts and minds of those who hold the lineage of the ancestors. We are those people, you and I. Dream now, and know that in the dreaming is your future and all that we believe to be true.

PROLOGUE

MARCUS PUBLIUS VINDEX, STANDARD-BEARER OF THE SECOND century, third cohort of the XXth legion, stationed on the far western frontier of Britannia, drank wine sparingly when on winter foraging duties and never took unnecessary risks. When the late-night need to urinate became overpowering, he stepped away from the watch fire only for a moment and told his armourer where he was going and why. Passing between the tents, he whistled the tune of the ninth invocation to Jupiter as evidence that he was still alive.

At the margins of the firelight, where the rain became silver and the sound of it hammering on the tent hides was too loud for his tune to be heard, Vindex called out to the armourer and was answered. The stream of his urine cascading on rocks made a good counterpoint to the rain. There was a cold satisfaction in pissing on the base of the mountain; for as long as the sound of it lasted, he was solid in his victory over the weather, the sucking mud, the lack of game and of corn and, best, over the native warriors who grew out of the dark and left the unwary dead to be found in daylight. He shouted as much to his armourer, slurring only slightly.

The last word had barely crossed to the fires when a hand caught his chin and dragged his head back and up. He did not feel the slice of the knife across his throat, the blade was too sharp to create pain, but it cut down to the bones of his spine, severing the soft tissues in its path. The tidal wave of his life surged out to earth.

The standard-bearer died surprised, and his ghost, surprised, did not know itself dead, only that the night grew suddenly bright, as if noon had come, and that, impossibly, where once had been fire-warped shadows, now one of the native warriors knelt in plain view by the fallen body of a man carving a curse mark on the forehead.

Vindex had lived through too many battles to waste time in questioning the impossible. His sword had already stabbed at the exposed neck of the enemy before he had thought to question the identity of the corpse lying so close to his feet. As his body lunged after, he gave all his breath to a shout that would rouse the entire camp.

His sword, his arm, and the full weight of his weightless body passed through the crouching warrior. His shout, which could cross a battlefield, raised no armoured men to his aid although a decurion of the cavalry, drinking wine by the fire, pulled his cloak tighter and stamped his feet, cursing the sudden cold.

Vindex opened his mouth to shout again and then stopped as the part of him that reasoned realized at last that the men of his watch had not noticed him at all.

'They can't hear you. Your people choose not to hear the cries of the slain. It's your strength and your greatest weakness. You'll never live safely until you learn to listen to your ancestors and your newly dead.'

The voice that filled Vindex' head had a different quality from those of the men he had left at the fire; it spoke to his soul, not his ears. The enemy warrior finished carving the curse mark and, rising, turned round.

Thus, for the first time, in the darkest part of the night, with no sun and rain clouds covering the moon, the standard-bearer of the XXth saw the face of his enemy. He saw rain-damp hair the colour of a fox in winter with the warrior's braids left loose in mourning and the quill of the single crow's pinion woven in at the left dyed entirely black, for one who has severed all connections to family and tribe to hunt alone; and thereby perhaps to die alone. He saw the blood-wet knife, recently used, saw the sling hanging at the belt beside the pouch of river pebbles and knew with a soul-knowing beyond vision that each stone was painted black, that it might more surely kill those against whom it was sent. He saw the sign of the serpent-spear carved on the brow of the body – his body – and, because he had seen the same mark on the brows of other men eight times in the last three days, its meaning was already carved on his liver.

By the cumulation of these, finally, Marcus Publius Vindex, son of Gaius Publius Vindex, knew the identity of the woman who had killed him and thus came to understand that he was dead.

Feeling foolish, he lowered his sword. From the fireside, the armourer shouted a new question with an edge of concern in his voice. The silence which, living, the standard-bearer should have filled stretched too long.

The Boudica rose slowly, sheathing her belt-knife. 'Whom do you worship?' she asked. Her mouth did not move but the words became part of the night.

In the same way, Vindex answered, 'Jupiter, god of the legions, and Mars Ultor, for victory.' Then, appraising, 'You should leave. They'll come soon to look for me. You cannot stand against so many and live.' The quality of his care surprised him. Dead, he discovered that he harboured neither the hatred nor the terror he had in life.

'Thank you. I'll go when I have to. Your men have not yet lit a torch and I have never yet met a Roman who could see well in the rain.'

She grinned and Vindex read no fear in her eyes, only the exhilaration of battle, beginning to wane. He had known that feeling, and the boundless peace that followed it, and knew that it was for these he had fought, far more than the silver he had been paid, and that he was not alone.

Moved by his new compassion, he said, 'You will never win, fighting as one against many.'

Amused, the Boudica raised a brow. 'I have heard that before. Not everyone who says it is Roman, but most have been, and all of those were dead.'

'Then you should listen to us. We bear you no ill will, but can see some things more clearly.' It was true; the concerns of his life were melting away leaving behind a clarity Vindex had sought throughout his life and never found. 'I offer you this as a gift, from death to life: if you do not rouse the east of the province to battle, the legions will win and Rome will bleed your people dry.'

The Boudica finished wiping her hands on the turf. She nodded, thoughtfully. 'Thank you. I will consider your gift in the morning, if I am alive to do so.' She was no longer smiling, but she did not hate him, either. 'You should go home,' she said. 'Your gods will know you in Rome. They cannot reach you here.'

The armourer shouted a second time, and was not answered. A legionary emerged from the safety of the tent lines and his terror at the sight of the body was far greater than Vindex' had been. His cry brought the armourer and he, finally, called for torches. Men ran as they had been trained and if the light behind the tents did not blaze for them as bright as noon, it was enough for the fox-haired warrior to be seen.

She did run then, fluidly and with no great urgency, like a deer that has not yet heard the hounds. The armourer of the second century was a clear-thinking man who abstained entirely from wine. He had also, for three years, been his cohort's champion spear-thrower, honoured for the speed and accuracy of his casts. He called afresh and five men ran to bring him spears, passing each one new to his palm as the last took flight. Ten were thrown in the space of a dozen strides. The foremost of the torch-bearers saw the eighth one strike and shouted to the armourer and to Mars Ultor, claiming a kill. Vindex, seeing with different eyes, knew that the Boudica was wounded, but had not joined him in death.

From beyond the margins of the camp, her voice filled his head. She sounded breathless and disjointed and he was unable to tell if it was pain that afflicted her, or an overwhelming need to laugh.

'Go home,' she said again. 'The journey to Rome is faster in death, I promise you, and the land is warmer. Why stay here in the rain where you're not welcome? The legion no longer owns you when you're dead. You can go where you want.'

The thought had occurred to Vindex more than once in life. In death, joyfully, he understood himself free. Passing through the walls of the officers' tent and the insubstantial matter of his centurion, he began the not-so-long journey back to Rome.

At the place where he had been, three more men of his watch died in a hail of black-painted river pebbles. The armourer was the last of them.

I

AUTUMN AD 57

THE WATER WAS COLD, AND MADE BROWN BY PEAT AND RECENT rain.

Breaca of Mona, known to all but her family and closest friends as the Boudica, leader of armies and bringer of victory, knelt alone at the side of a mountain stream and washed her face, hands and the bleeding wound on her upper arm in the torrent. The water ran briefly pink where she had been. She cupped clean water in both palms, rinsed her mouth and spat out the iron after-taste of blood.

A blue roan mare dozed in the shelter of a nearby beech thicket, the end result of a lifetime's breeding and better than anything Rome could offer. She was haltered but not tethered and came to call, her feet bound in soft leather to dampen the sound of her progress. Mounted, Breaca travelled north and a little east, moving up into the mountains, keeping to rocky trails where Coritani trackers, paid by Rome, would be least likely to find signs of her passing.

If she had scaled the peaks, she could have looked west past further mountains and across the straits to Mona, but she did not. The standard-bearer's warning echoed, disturbingly, with the muted footfalls of her mare and would not be made silent. *You will never win, fighting as one against many*. Vindex was not the first to have warned her of the dangers and futility of fighting alone, or even the second, but he was the enemy and she did not have to trust his opinion.

It was harder to ignore the warnings of those who cared for her; the elders and dreamers of Mona, who watched over her children through her long winter absences, and could not tell them where their mother was or if she had died yet, at the hand of a standard-bearer who was not quite as drunk as he might have looked.

Luain mac Calma, the Elder of Mona, had been first, quietly, to say that the Boudica's life was worth more, and vengeance for one man's life worth less, and he had been followed by a succession of others who claimed to love her and hold her best interests at heart. Only Airmid, dreamer and soul-friend, had always understood why Breaca needed to hunt alone as she did and had never spoken out, openly or in private, against the black feather braided into the Boudica's hair and the winter killings that it foreshadowed.

Airmid was on Mona and Mona was another world and Breaca chose not to look at it and thereby not to think about it, or its people.

She passed upwards, and the track became rockier. Grey stone lined either side of the tracks, marbled by swirling lichens. She dismounted after a while and unbound the mare's feet, that they might grip better on the wet stones. The rain became less; it had belonged to the night. Clouds on the eastern horizon parted to show the first knife lines of light. Lacking any binding, the wound in her arm slowly ceased to bleed and ached only a little. The officer whose spear had caught her had kept his weapons scrupulously clean, for which she was grateful.

Half a day's ride to the south, at the overnight campsite where a standard-bearer, an armourer and two junior officers of the XXth legion had died, a wisp of greased smoke rose at an angle to the sky. Crows roused and called and began to drift towards the scent of burning men.

The thick-set, grey-haired man stooped over the neck of his horse with his attention fixed on the trail did not appear to notice either of the two slingstones that cracked on the rocks near his head. His horse, noticing both, shied a little, throwing him off balance, and he clutched ineffectually at the saddle. The care of his gods kept his head from cracking on the stones of the path as he fell and a

cushion of heather gave him safe landing but he did not rise afterwards, even as Breaca knelt at his side.

'Where are you hurt?'

He flicked dry, cracked lips. 'I have the flux. You shouldn't touch
me; you'll be tainted.'

'Maybe, but the harm is done now.' Breaca pushed her good arm
under his shoulders and levered him to his feet. She would have
given him water but carried none. In its absence, she used the sick
man's horse for support, wedging his shoulder against the saddle.
He swayed and made himself stand.

His accent, his horse and the weave on his tunic were all of the
northern Eceni. A mark worked in ink in the skin below his
collarbone showed the falcon and running horse linked. Breaca ran
her forefinger along from horse to falcon and felt the small nodule
of amber buried under the skin beyond the falcon's wingtip that
verified the mark's authenticity.

'Are you from Efnís?' she asked, and when he nodded, 'Why
were you following me?'

'I wasn't. The mountains are alive with Romans and I would
deliver my message from a living mouth to living ears if the flux
does not kill me first. I was trying to reach the forests near the
coast to take shelter there before crossing to Mona.'

Breaca shook her head. 'You won't reach them in time. The men of
the fifth cohort are stationed near the coast. The third cohort lost
four men last night: the signal fires have been lit since dawn, waking
every other legionary into action; they will have ringed the forests
long since. I know of somewhere closer that may be safe if we are
permitted to enter. Can you ride another two dozen spear throws?'

'If there's shelter at the end of it, yes.'

The cave mouth was a vertical crease in the cliff face set by the
gods at such an angle that it was invisible unless approached
exactly from the south-east. The hound-sized rock placed by the
ancestors to guard the entrance was patched with damp moss and
hidden by the grasses that had grown up around it. In years past,
it would have been scoured clean when the ancestors were
honoured at each old moon and the carved marks swirling on its
surface would have been made bold again with red ochre and white
lime and ash. In the bleak new world of Roman occupation, those

who should have done so were either dead or had taken refuge on Mona and the rock and the cave mouth behind it were blurred with neglect.

Breaca had only passed the cave once, and that the previous winter, but had seen then what others might not, committing its location to memory without any real intention to use it. She probably would not have attempted it now, had not her need driven her to it; the risks of entering such a place without a dreamer were far greater than the risks of death or capture by Rome.

Standing alone before the hound stone, Breaca said, 'I offer greetings to the oldest and greatest of the ancestor-dreamers. I will clear your dwelling place as I leave, I swear it. For now, the weeds are my protection as they have been yours. Will you permit me to enter and to bring one other with me?'

A voice beyond the range of hearing said, *Who asks?*

'I ask, Breaca nic Graine mac Eburovic, once of the Eceni, once Warrior of Mona, hunting now under the black feather of no-tribe. My mark is the serpent-spear which was yours before me and will be yours again when I have gone.'

The ancestor-dreamer said, *So. I endure and you may not. It is good you remember that. Have you come to ask my aid in your vengeance, as you did before?*

'No.'

She was the Boudica, who led thousands into battle, and her palms were sweating. She wiped them on her tunic. It was far easier to face the legions in the rain and the dark armed with nothing more than a knife and a pouch of river pebbles than to speak to an empty cave mouth in daylight. She remembered Airmid, and the fear in her voice when she had last faced the ancestor-dreamer: Airmid, who feared nothing and no-one.

Breaca looked back down the path to where the dying messenger waited out of earshot. He had dismounted when she did and stood leaning against his horse. As she watched, he slid slowly to his knees, and then toppled sideways to lie curled like a child, breathing harshly.

If she had been alone, she would have taken her chances dodging the legions and stayed out in the open. If she waited, she would be alone before too long, but the dying man was Eceni and from Efnís and he had given his life to bring a message to Mona. She could not with any honour leave him to die on a mountain path within reach of the legions when there was shelter at hand.

Touching the hound stone as much for courage as for luck, Breaca said, 'We are two, one wounded, one assailed by flux. We ask only to enter into your protection, bringing our horses, nothing more. The Romans who seek our lives are close behind; I saw them enter the valley as we climbed the mountain. It is my belief that their trackers will have no knowledge of your dwelling place, and that if they did, the legionaries would not dare to cross the threshold. Even they recognize the sacred when they meet it.'

Or if not the sacred, then the simply dangerous. The ancestor's laughter was the slide of a snake over winter leaves, a sound to erase all peace and the hope of peace. *They know I will pierce their dreams, waking and sleeping, and they will die as did their governor, slowly and in madness. They may not fear you enough to abandon the land, Breaca once-Eceni, but they fear me enough to make offerings in secret to quell my wrath.*

Breaca had seen the twists of corn and broken wine flasks and, once, the rotting head of a doe as she led the horses up the trail. She had not known them as offerings to the serpent-dreamer and even now could not confirm it. She said nothing. A lifebeat of waiting passed. Then, *Yes, you may enter. I, who may yet destroy you, give you leave.*

The cave was not as fully dark as Breaca had expected. The horses walked willingly into the entrance and were made safe in a chamber open to the sky, three spear lengths inside. Here, bird lime streaked the walls in layers of white and caked the floor, cushioning the sound of hooves. Hollows in the rock held water and the recent rain had made them clean.

Further in, the sky could not be so clearly seen, but grey light leaked for a while from the towered heights of the roof. On the floor, the skeletons of small beasts cracked underfoot where they had fallen, unwilling sacrifices to the ancestor and the gods. The walls pressed inwards so that the pathway became a tunnel and rock snagged Breaca's tunic at both shoulders.

'We should stop.' The Eceni messenger could barely walk. He tugged on Breaca's sleeve.

'Not yet. There's a turn ahead and then the floor opens into a chamber with a river running through. We can rest there and you can drink the water. You need it.'

He held on to her, staring. In the failing light, she could see the widening whites of his eyes. 'Have you been here before?' he asked.

'No, but I know of it.' She did not tell him that the serpent voice of the ancestor-dreamer drew her on, whispering, nor that it had spelled out the time and manner of his death.

The chamber they entered last was too broad for Breaca easily to map the margins, and entirely without light. Working by feel, she laid and lit a small fire. Orange shadows drew monsters from the dark, casting ghost-flames on the small river flowing through the northern corner of the cave. Echoes of water thickened the silence. The sound was pleasanter by far than the sibilant hiss of the ancestor.

At the river's edge, Breaca tended the dying messenger. She folded her cloak and his and laid him on both on a bed of flat rock. He had brought his own water skin, long empty, and she filled it and let him drink and then washed his face, neck and hands with what was left.

'You should not,' he said, less certainly than before. 'We were three; two brothers and a sister, each charged with the same message. We had ridden only two nights when the flux took us. It passes from one to the other faster than a cough in a winter's roundhouse.'

Breaca said, 'If I am to die, this place is as good as any; the legion's inquisitors won't find us here to wrench what we know from the last breath of our lungs. If I am to live, then you can rest tended in safety. What happened to your brother and sister?'

'I don't know. We took separate roads when we met the legions. Each of us was to ride for Mona. With three, there was hope one would live to reach the ferry and deliver our words.'

Ask him his message. The ancestor's voice cracked off the walls. In her own place, she sounded far louder than the dying man.

'When he has peace.' Breaca spoke aloud and the messenger was too near death to notice.

She had tended the dying times without number on the battle-field, but only rarely with other sickness, so that it took some time to do what was needful. She bent over him, trying to see past the tallow-grey skin to the life and the mind beneath. His face shrank onto the bones of his skull. His eyes had fallen deep into the folding flesh of his face and his hair was slick with sweat and the water with which he had just been washed.

Ask!

Touching her palm to his forehead, she said carefully, 'This is your resting place. Briga will take you from here and the ancestor will guide you safely to the lands beyond life. I will return to Mona when it's safe to travel. Is it your wish that I carry your message with me?'

'It would be, but I can't give it while not yet on Mona.' The man grimaced, trying to rise, and failed. 'I'm sorry. It would kill both of us if I tried. Efnís laid a geas on all three messengers. If I tried to speak, my tongue would swell in my mouth and block my breathing before the words were out. More, the one to whom I spoke would die, if not as suddenly, then as surely. If caught, we were permitted to say that much to whoever tried to press the question.'

Breaca smoothed the hair from his brow and poured on a little water to cool it. 'Efnís is wise. If you had been captured, it would have been good to die swiftly, knowing your message safe and Rome's interrogators condemned to a slow end.'

The man struggled with that, frowning. 'But not so good now when I am dying in the company of a warrior and friend. I will take my message safely into death and Efnís will never know of my failure.'

'He will. No-one passes to the other worlds but the dreamers know of it. Even so, I may have an answer. Would I be right to believe that your message was to be given to the Elder of Mona, Luain mac Calma, or, failing him, to Airmid of Nemain, and that it concerned the Boudica?'

It was a risk. Neither of them knew the margins of the curse. The messenger smiled faintly and tested his answer silently twice before, nodding, he said, 'You would be correct.'

They both waited. In the moments that followed, his breathing was not impaired, nor did his tongue swell any more than the flux had already swollen it.

Breaca let out a breath. 'So then if I were to tell you that my daughter, second child of my heart, soul and flesh, is called Graine after my mother and that my father was Eburovic, smith and warrior of the Eceni, would your mouth remain unblocked and your tongue unswollen as you delivered to me your message?'

His eyes had fallen shut and did not open when she finished. Waiting, Breaca did not know if he slept, or if the shock of her identity, however obliquely revealed, had carried him beyond speech.

The relief when he reached out and gripped her hand left her without words. He opened his eyes and tears wavered on the rims, cast in copper by the firelight. His voice was a fine thread, drawn tight by pain and effort. 'You are the Boudica? The Warrior of Mona?'

She nodded, smiling. 'Yes.'

He shoved himself upright, wheezing. 'Why then are you here, unbraided, wearing the black feather of no-tribe and hunting alone in lands held by Rome?'

She had not expected his anger, nor the sudden energy it gave him; he knew nothing of the soul-stripping meetings between the Boudica and the dreamers she served, of the battles fought amongst friends with words the only weapons. He did not choose to hide the accusation in his voice or the hurt in his eyes. He laid himself down again, but his gaze, challenging hers, could have been mac Calma's, or Dubornos', or Ardacos', or any one of her children's.

Rising, Breaca laid a fistful of heather roots on the fire. Fresh flames sparked green and a violent blue where the earth burned before wood. Staring at the colours and not the man, she said, 'I have been killing Romans, as you saw. The four dead of the third cohort were my kills, and two the night before last.'

The messenger was an intelligent man. Watching her, he said, 'So you hunt alone because the risk is too great to expose others to the danger and Briga will take you into death when she feels the killing is enough. Do the elder dreamers of Mona consider that a good risk?'

'Not at all.' Breaca smiled, surprising them both. 'But it is not for them to forbid it. My life is my own and I believe it is a good risk. It's nearly winter; the time for fighting is over but the legions must still forage far beyond their forts for food and firewood. There's more damage done to their minds with four men dead in the night than with forty dead on the battlefield in open warfare. Each death leads to desertions and those left behind dream of a time when they can leave and sail for Rome. An army that comes to the field without heart fights to lose, you know that.'

'I do. And a people lacking the leadership of the gods does not fight at all.' An old anger flickered, and a more recent fear. Each died away, leaving only the fatal weariness that had cloaked the messenger when he first fell from his horse.

Carefully, Breaca said, 'The Eceni do not lack leadership.'

'They do now.'

He was dying fast; both of them could feel it. Words unspoken weighed on them, sucking breath from the air. Choosing the path that offered least damage, Breaca asked, 'Can you tell me in what way your people and mine are leaderless?'

'I don't know. Saying that much might kill us both.'

He gathered himself and then, against her protests, pushed himself to sitting. His gaze devoured her face and then moved down to the reddening wound on her arm. The spear's head had not, after all, been so clean. Blood seeped a little from the gash, but the arm around was angry and hot, and had begun to smell unclean. He reached out to touch it and they both felt the flesh twitch under his fingers.

He said, 'Perhaps Efnís was wiser than either of us knew and you are dying anyway.'

Breaca sluiced water over the wound. 'Perhaps. I have felt closer to death than this, but they say Briga often comes when least expected.'

'Not for me.' He smiled and the shape stayed on his lips long after his mind had gone elsewhere. In a while, he said, 'Efnís crafted his words for Airmid, dreamer of Nemain, but the tales have always said that she holds one half of your soul and Caradoc the other. If that is true, then it may be that, in the gods' eyes, I am speaking as if to Airmid and I can speak to you safely. I am willing to try, but my death is certain. I have nothing to lose. You could have many more winters of hunting Romans alone. Will you risk the loss of that, to hear my message?'

Breaca closed her left fist, feeling the brush of pain in her palm that was the memory of a sword cut. It did not ache to warn her of danger. The spear wound in her upper arm throbbed alarmingly, but other wounds had been as deep and gone as bad and she had not died of them.

She looked across the fire into the darkness of the cave but found no help there; the ancestor-dreamer was uncharacteristically silent. As at all the most important decisions in her life, Breaca was alone. There was a freedom in being so.

She said, 'There is not so much pleasure in killing Romans that I would want to miss a message from Efnís that has cost the lives of three warriors. Yes, I will share your risk.'

II

'YOUR SISTER IS DEAD.'

    'I have no sister.'

    The air in the smithy was dense with the smoke of scorched metal and loud with the clatter of beaten iron. Sun streaming in through the smoke hole cast a puddle of light on the floor, missing both the stoked fire and the anvil. Neither was a mistake; the smith of Hibernia liked the red shadows of his work-world and had no desire to meet the exposure of daylight, particularly not in his current company.

    He played his hammer down the arm's length of cooling metal that would one day soon become a sword blade and felt the rhythm rock pleasingly through his bones. Doing so, he ignored the visitor standing on his threshold. Quite deliberately, he did not invite him to cross it.

    Luain mac Calma, once of Hibernia, now Elder and foremost dreamer of Mona, was not used to being ignored. He had rarely been denied entry to the home of another and never when he had travelled ten days to bring news of some moment.

    Nor did he need light to see the body and soul of the man he had come to visit; a dreamer spends a great deal of his life in half-darkness. Standing on the threshold, he studied the straight, blue-black hair, grown to shoulder length when once it had been cut short to please the legions, the lean lines of the body, once

31

battle-fit and kept almost to that by the work of the forge, the sculpted cheekbones and high brow of a man whom the gods had spun far away from his life's course, and not yet cast back. There was anger there, and a stubborn pride, and neither of these quite covered the fear, or the effort being made to hide it.

All of this, he compared to what he had last seen of this man, and was not disappointed; three years' peace and solitude had healed more than mac Calma had thought possible. His doubts, which were many, rested on the condition of the smith's heart and soul.

He drew a breath and let it out, slowly. Over the pounding clash of the hammer, he said, 'You are Bán mac Eburovic, Harehunter and horse-dreamer of the Eceni, and I am growing very tired of your fictions. Your boy tells me—'

'He is not my boy.' The hammer missed a beat and, stammering, found it again. 'He calls himself Bellos, after the Bellovaci who were his people among the Belgae. I may have bought him as slave but I have returned to him his name and his freedom. Nevertheless, he hates me. He remains here only because his fear of the Hibernians is greater than his hatred of me. Their menfolk are not gentle in the expressions of their affection towards well-favoured youths with gold hair and eyes the colour of the summer sky. He's safer here than anywhere else and he knows it, or he'd be gone long since.'

Mac Calma let one brow rise to the top of its flight. 'He looks on you as a father.'

The smith shrugged. 'A man may despise his father and still be his son. Look at Caradoc.'

'Or at you.'

The hammering ceased. The silence after was hard on the ears.

With exquisite care, the smith laid aside his hammer and, with his tongs, lifted the still-glowing blade on which he had been working. By the blood light of its shine, he spoke quietly and distinctly, as a man might who offers an invocation to his gods in the quiet of a temple.

'Listen to me, mac Calma. I will say this only once. Who sired me is not my business and I will not allow it to be yours. Eburovic of the Eceni raised me and cared for my childhood. Corvus of the Quinta Gallorum taught me to fight and to love and gave me

32

the name that I use. These men I value and respect, but that does not give them ownership of my life or my soul, nor would they claim it. I did not leave the Eceni by choice and did not by choice commit treason against Rome and my emperor. Both have happened and so now I belong neither to the legions nor to the tribes. For the first time in my life, I am free. I intend to stay that way.'

'Are you so?' The dreamer nodded. 'And who is it, who is so free?'

'What does a name matter? Here in Hibernia, I am who I make myself to be. I am Valerius to those who favour Rome and wish my aid in improving their Latin. To the rest, I am simply the black-haired smith on the hill who can mend their blades and their brooches and sometimes help their women in childbirth. If you have issue with that, Elder of Mona, take your complaint elsewhere. I have nothing of yours.'

The smith, who had, in his past, been both Valerius, decurion of the Thracian cavalry, and Bán of the Eceni, was shaking when he finished. Three years without wine or ale had not taken from him the tremors of their excess. Blessedly, the unfinished sword he held did not shake with him. Even so, Luain mac Calma watched him too closely for comfort.

The smith was stripped to the waist. The scars of war shone white in the rivers of his sweat. Given sufficient time, a man who cared enough might read a history of the taking of Britannia on the map of his injuries. Two men had cared so and both lived now out of reach of heart as well as mind. If he chose to let them, the memories of either could cripple him. He lowered the blade into the vat of water standing by the anvil and let the steam erase his past.

He was not wholly successful. He might as well have named aloud the two men, and the hurt of their loss, so profoundly did mac Calma's face change. Through the thickening white, the Elder said, 'I'm sorry. I should not have come to disturb your sanctuary. I thought only that you should hear the news.'

Your sister is dead. He would not ask to know more. Even that was too much.

The steam cleared slowly through the smoke hole. By the time the smith could see again, mac Calma had already gone. His voice reached back lazily from the daylight, speaking to the Belgic boy, Bellos, who was no longer a slave but nevertheless held the guest's horse outside as if it were his duty.

'The red Thessalian mare standing in the paddock was to be my guest-gift. She is elderly and not fit to be ridden but was once of high value. She is in foal to a Pannonian battle horse and if the foal takes on the merits of both sire and dam, it may be of some worth. I have business with the dreamers of Hibernia and it would inconvenience me greatly to have to take her back. Perhaps if you could . . . ?'

Luain mac Calma had trained for three decades with the best minds of Mona; oration was a tutored skill, layered over the gifts of his birth. When he chose, he could raise the inhabitants of an entire great-house cheering to their feet with the first line of a tale, or whisper a sick child to sleep so that it would heal before morning – or touch the soul of a man who thought to make himself invulnerable, and prove to him that he was not.

The smith stepped away from his anvil. 'Who have you brought? Where did you find a red Thessalian mare?' He was at the door, in full daylight, forgetting that he preferred the dimness of the forge. The cooling sword hung useless from his hand.

In answer, the dreamer stood back so that his guest-gift could be seen. The mare stood in the small paddock at the side of the hut. She was more than elderly, she was ancient, an elder grandmother among horses, and she had not been well cared for. Her back was swayed from the bearing of too many foals. The weariness of travel and of living hung around her as the first taste of death. Her coat was red, the colour of cut liver, with white scars on her flanks. An old brand showed indistinctly at the base of her neck.

Once, long ago, when the mare was in summer coat and groomed to perfection, the brand had been clear: Leg VIII Aug; a cavalry mare of the VIIIth Augusta, she had been given to a boy of the Eceni who had known of her from a dream.

It had been so very long ago. One might hope that a summer of shared joy with a battle at its end would have left as strong a memory with the mare as it did the boy who rode her, but her eyes lacked hope and met the smith's without recognition. Hoarsely he said, 'She's too old to be in foal.'

'I think not. It will be her last, but she will do it well. Would you rather she foaled it under the care of another man? I can take her back to Mona if you wish.'

Mac Calma knew all the ways to a man's heart and did not

disdain to use them. The smith did not trust himself to speak, but nodded when Bellos looked at him and then watched as the boy ran to the mare and offered her a lick of salt that he kept in his palm. It was not the first he had given her; Bellos had been a slave once, and knew intimately the hurts of slavery in another, and how to assuage them.

Finding his voice again, the smith said, 'Her heart is broken. What is left of it, she has given to the boy.'

Mac Calma did not disagree. 'But her foal will give his heart to whomsoever trains him for battle. Airmid believes it will be a colt, black and white with a shield and a spear on its forehead. I have no reason to disbelieve her.'

The smith let his gaze rest on the horizon a while before he trusted himself to speak. 'It was a mistake, clearly, to speak aloud the dreams of my childhood. I was young then, and over-trusting. But that dream is long dead and cannot be revived. It died when Amminios made me a slave and took my battle mount into his breeding herds, and if Breaca is dead, then the dream can never be brought alive again; she was the biggest part of it.'

'Did I say that Breaca was dead?'

They were a sword's length apart. Valerius, once-officer of the cavalry, still held the half-made blade in his hand, alive with the first stirrings of the weapon it would be. With no clear effort on his part, the tip rose to the level of the other man's throat. Very quietly, he said, 'Don't play with me, dreamer.'

Mac Calma stood side on to the sun. His shadow, impossibly, took the shape of the heron that was his dream. He shook his head. 'I would never play with you. I did not intend any misunderstanding. It is not Breaca who is dead, but Silla, your younger sister, the only one of the royal line to remain in the lands of the Eceni. She died bearing a child for Prasutagos, whom you knew as 'Tagos, who has named himself king of the entire Eceni nation. He is a supporter of Rome and there is nothing now to check him. If he is not removed, the Eceni – who were your mother's people, even if you claim they are no longer yours – will become enslaved to Rome in ways we cannot break.'

It is not Breaca who is dead . . .

Valerius heard the rest and did not care. That single fact wrote itself in his mind, repeating. He held his new sword too tightly.

Ridges of half-formed metal gouged into the meat of his fingers. The tidal wave that rocked him was neither relief, nor anger, nor grief, but a mix of these, made ugly and unclean by the manner of the telling.

Late in the chaos, he remembered that Luain mac Calma stood nearby and that there were fictions he still wished to preserve.

He said, 'You forget what I have been. If the Eceni lack weapons and the will to fight, it is because I have broken them. Knowing that, do you seriously wish me to weep for the fate of a defeated tribe?' An unknown, unpetitioned god allowed his voice to seem to him normal.

Mac Calma's smile was unreadable. 'Not at all. Your mother was of the royal line and you carry her blood, however unwilling. I had hoped you would agree to come east, to raise the Eceni in war against Rome in your mother's name so that Breaca might have remained in the west where she is needed and might have led her warriors against an army divided. I understand now that you will not. I have already apologized for disturbing your peace. It will not happen again. I wish you well with the mare and her foaling.'

Luain mac Calma may have been a dreamer but he rode with a warrior's skill. His horse, galloping, cut crescents in the sodden Hibernian turf that remained long after the grey of his cloak had become one with the mist and the sky.

Valerius watched until a squall of gulls cast high over the coastal hills and broke the horizon. Turning, he found the boy, Bellos, watching him with the same mix of fear and care that he had shown since they first came to Hibernia.

Suddenly, newly, Valerius wanted the boy to feel safe. He said, 'Do you like the mare? She was mine once, when I was your age. I rode her in battle and she made my first kill for me. Afterwards, when Amminios captured her, she gave birth to a black and white foal, the Crow-horse; the one you have heard of.'

They had talked a little of their pasts; Bellos knew fragments of Valerius' own time in slavery, and of Corvus, who had freed him, and a great deal of the Crow-horse, who had made it possible. The horse had come to assume mythic proportions between them. Often – almost always – it was easier for both to talk of beasts than of men.

The boy's eyes widened. 'This mare is the dam of the Crow-horse?'

'Yes. She was everything he is, but that she did not carry his hate in her heart. If I asked it of you, would you care for her?'

It was a gift, and Valerius did what he could to hide any pain in the giving. Bellos knew him better than mac Calma, but was kinder. If anything showed, he did not acknowledge it. Instead, he grinned, brightly, and his gaze lost its wariness and he reached into his belt pouch for more salt and held it up so that she could lip it from his hand.

A thought made him frown, and then smile again. He said, 'I will take her, and treat her as she deserves, but the foal is brother to the Crow-horse and must be yours. Promise me you will take him and keep him?'

Valerius had not known that the boy was listening, nor that he could understand Hibernian sufficiently to follow mac Calma's arcane turn of speech. He did not want the foal, but he wanted the boy to feel safe with him more. He said, 'Of course I'll keep him. The Hibernians are good people, but they would not know how to raise a battle horse if it fell from the sky into their paddocks.'

He ran a hand over the mare and felt her flinch beneath his touch. Thinking aloud, he said, 'She's too thin now to do a foal well, and she has been treated badly. We'll need hay and corn to feed her and you'll need to spend time with her daily so that she comes to trust you. That way she will help us when the foal comes.'

They spent the day planning and the afternoon bringing fodder by cart from the village on the coast. Bellos became less shy in that one day than he had in the three years of their companionship. Valerius watched it and cursed himself for needing mac Calma's false solicitude to show him what to do.

When they retired for the night, he did his best not to sleep, but the blackness caught him, and the dreams within it, which were the old dreams, of loss and destruction and the litany of those he had killed.

He woke early and found Bellos had woken earlier, and had left by his bed, by way of a waking gift, a platter with cheese and an apple saved from the harvest and a beaker of well water, and he was grateful to the un-gods who no longer cared for him that the boy was not there to see him weep.

III

THE BODY OF THE MESSENGER FLOATED DOWN THE CAVE'S RIVER, buoyed by his tunic and cloak.

Breaca was not a singer; Mona's laws, which were the laws of gods and ancestors, did not permit her to sing the lay of the dead, but she could speak it, and did so. Only as she reached the part where she should have said aloud the name of the dead man did she realize that she did not know it. The current carried him beyond reach of the firelight and she heard his tunic snag and then tear on the rocks.

His ghost had already crossed the greater river to reach the lands beyond life, following a call that only he could hear. There had been a time when Breaca saw none but the ghosts of her own family and then only in the heart of battle, when the walls between the worlds were thinnest. Now, she saw the spirits of every warrior slain, every legionary, every flux-stripped man. She had not yet seen the ghost of her sister, Silla, which surprised her.

Staring into the fluid blackness of the river, she struggled to find memories of the girl around whose neck she had placed the torc of Eceni leadership.

Thoughts of Bán came first, uncalled, and Silla only after him; the two curled together as children, sharing a bed in the round-house and squabbling like hound whelps over their share of the sleeping hides and of the hounds that kept them both warm. There had been less than a year of that, and then Hail had come, the great brindled war hound with the hail-marks scattered across his body and there had been no more squabbling, because Hail had been Bán's from the moment of his birth and . . .

It did not do to remember Hail. To remember his life was to remember his death and there was too much pain in that.

Too late, Breaca closed her eyes. The gates, now opened, released a flood tide of memories; of Silla sitting astride an unrideable red roan colt of their father's with Bán behind her, holding her by the waist as he pushed the mad-hearted beast to a gallop to prove to Silla her own courage; of Bán teaching Silla how to cast a rope to catch a colt, or how to hurl a spear, or simply of Bán on his own, the solemn, earnest child with the surprising smile who had out-dreamed the grandmothers and would one day grow to be a dreamer as powerful as Airmid.

Then, because a child does not remain a child, but grows to adulthood, it was impossible not to remember the desperate broken man who called himself Valerius, whom she had last seen lying on the deck of a ship from Gaul, puking his guts into the sea, begging her to give him a clean and decent death.

Very badly, Breaca did not wish to remember that. It had been better before, when she had believed her brother dead, and had sat guarding the dreamers as they had searched the many pathways of the lands beyond life to find his spirit and return it to Briga's care.

They had failed, of course, because his spirit had not been lost, but afire in the heart and mind of a man who fought for Rome. The discovery that Bán was alive, that he had been the decurion of the Thracian cavalry who had terrorized Eceni villages for ten years after the invasion, had been told only to a very few. Efnís knew, but he would not have spread the word without need. It was possible that Silla had died not knowing the truth, but believing Bán had gone before her. The thought of her now searching for him in the lands of the dead was unbearable.

Nevertheless, it must be borne, with the news of her death and all that flowed from it. With an effort, Breaca banished the past and made herself live again in the present. The wound in her arm burned with a fire of its own that scorched her. She lay prone at the river's edge and held it under the water until cold numbed the skin.

Her cheek was pressed to the wet stone. The weak light of her fire cast rippling shadows across the water that grew more dense where the body of the messenger had snagged on a rock.

Aloud, she said, 'I never asked his name. I have been too long away from human company. I begin to treat men with less care than I would a horse.'

He is cared for well enough. It is you who needs care. You asked my aid once before, will you ask it a second time now?

The ancestor-dreamer was close. Her voice came from the river and the fire smoke above it, teasingly dangerous. It had always been so, from the first moment of their meeting on a night of the dark moon in the heart of a Roman marching camp, when Airmid had called the ancestor to destroy the governor, thinking to save Caradoc. The governor had died, but Caradoc was still in Gaul. The travesty that was Valerius had come back in his place and the ancestor had considered that a fair substitute.

Airmid had been afraid of this dreamer; Airmid who feared nothing and no-one. Breaca had urged her on through the night's work, thinking only of Caradoc. Afterwards, she had made herself forget the insidious, enticing voice that had drawn her into the darkest places of herself. She remembered it now, and wished she had not.

Trapped, she felt for the wall of the cave and braced her back against it, as she might if facing armed men. 'You asked that at the cave's mouth and my answer remains the same: I did not know you when we met last. Now that I do, I will never again ask your aid. I came seeking only the protection of your cave. You gave it and I am grateful. I will leave now, and will not disturb you further.'

The ancestor's laugh was the slide of serpents on sand, more terrifying than any legions. *Where will you go, warrior? And why?*

'To Mona, where else? The elders must know that Silla has died and 'Tagos taken rulership of the Eceni, supported by Rome.'

But will you not go east? You who are first born of the royal line of the Eceni, you who should, by right of birth and lineage, wear the torc of the ancestors, given to you to have and to hold as evidence of your care for your people?

There was a trap in the question and Breaca could not see it. She would have stayed silent, but the pressing air did not allow it. She said, 'You heard the message. It is not safe to go east. Efnís was clear that I should stay and continue the war in the west; that only

40

from here was there any chance that we might drive Rome from the land. I will return to Mona with that news. Nothing has changed.'

And yet the dead have spoken. 'If you do not rouse the east, the legions will win.' The standard-bearer's ghost told you that. Do you not know the truth when you hear it?

'I would not trust the words of a Roman, even a dead one. Efnís said differently and would not lie. He cares for the Eceni as much as I do.'

Do you care for your people? I could not tell. The ancestor's outrage writhed all about. *You who left them in the hands of a milk-soft child and a man who has sold himself to Rome? The Eceni do not love you.*

That hurt, and so was probably true. Breaca said, 'I fight in the west to free the east. There are no warriors left in the east. Rome has slain every one with the will and the wit to bear a weapon.'

But they have not yet bled your people dry. A newly slain legionary sees the oncoming future more clearly than a living warrior. Shall I show you, last warrior of the Eceni, what it is for a people to bleed until there is nothing more to give?

Breaca saw too late what was coming, and that there was no escape. With her eyes closed or open, the visions were the same, falling in from the black walls of the cave, boiling up from the turbid water, dancing from the solid rock beneath her.

What she saw was not the tribe of her childhood, with or without the memories of Bán. The roundhouses were gone, taken apart for their wood to burn when nothing else could be found. In their place were small huts and those broken. The land was gaunt, the fields over-grazed, the horses starved, the gods' pool drained dry.

Amidst the mud and ruin, stick-thin men and women in cloaks and tunics of Eceni blue gathered around a pen, as at market. All had the earth-stained hands of weeders and planters. Not one was a warrior or a dreamer; none bore the marks of an elder, none stood with any pride or fire or willingness to fight.

Legionaries in full armour encircled them. Within the centre of these two rings were the children, more than twenty, wide-eyed and terrified. Each one was chained to the next by the neck and ankle. Open sores blossomed where the iron bit. The children wept tears of gold and their parents fell to their knees and scooped them into their palms as if they were corn and were grateful.

Slavery. The ancestor hissed it, deathly quiet. *When they have taken the hounds and the horses, slaughtered the cattle and the deer in the forests, when they have taken the iron that would have been weapons and the bronze that would have been beautiful, when they have melted the torc of the ancestors to make the coin to pay for war, when they have taxed every waking moment and taken the food from the mouths of infants, then they will come to buy living flesh and put a price on that which is priceless. Do you remember the dream of your long-nights, when you were given the mark you use so freely and do not understand?*

Questions within questions within a nightmare. Breaca prayed to wake and to forget, and could do neither.

Sweating, she said, 'I have never forgotten the dream of my long-nights. I pledged then to protect the lineage of my people, to save the children and the elders that their heritage and mine may continue unbroken. I abandoned the battle of the Sea River to save the children. I have fought without cease ever since that they might carry forward the songs and dreams of the ancestors, knowing who they have been and so growing into who they can be. I fight now, risking death nightly, so that my own children and those of others might live in a world without Rome. You cannot accuse me of abandoning the children.'

The ancestor laughed. *Tell them yourself.* In the vision, the mass of children parted. From their midst, a small, fine-limbed girl-child with hair the colour of ox blood and a face made old by pain stretched an arm from the slave pen, beseeching.

'Graine?' Breaca reached to touch her and smashed her knuckles on rock. The vision broke apart, becoming ash. She found herself standing with her back to the fire and the rush of the river too close to her feet. Her bad arm throbbed to the beat of her too-fast heart.

Desperately, she said, 'This cannot be a true vision. I will not believe it. Slave merchants are not permitted to trade in Britannia. The Emperor Claudius forbade it.'

Claudius is dead and made a god. Enslaved Trinovantes build his temple in Camulodunum as we speak. Nero rules in Rome and Nero is in turn ruled by those who are ruled by gold. If you do not believe me, all you have to do is remain in the west and wait. If you do nothing, what you have just seen will happen. By the mark we both share, I swear it.

'And if I go east?'

Then there is a chance that the tide may be turned. You alone are not enough; you must find the warriors in sufficient numbers to fight the legions and give them heart. You must find the iron to arm them. You must find others with courage and vision to lead them if you fall. With these three things, you may have victory. Would you see that? I could show you, my gift of a better future.

'I want nothing from you. Your visions are not safe.'

Ah, the arrogance! Still you shall have it, my gift.

The image was brief, a flash in the darkness showing the familiar pattern of a battlefield; impossible not to watch. Breaca's vision stretched to meet them as warriors she knew well came into focus. At the left wing, Ardacos roused the she-bears as he always did, they fought on foot, painted in woad and lime, and faced a cracked and broken line of legionaries.

In the centre, the Eceni forged forward to crush the enemy. She could not see who led them, only the mark of the serpent-spear above. To the right, a woman led the mounted warriors of the west in a wedge that struck at the gathered wings of Roman cavalry and pierced the enemy's flank. The ranks of the cavalry folded and collapsed and those who wished to live fled the field leaving the centre unguarded. A second wave of Eceni rode in to fill the gap.

The battle was won long before the killing ended. Slowly, unstoppably, the warriors pushed forward to join in the centre over the mounting bodies of two legions.

The moment of meeting was exquisite. At the heart of battle, a Roman standard fell and was trampled into filth. The serpent-spear blazed in victory over it.

My gift, said the ancestor. *Mark it well.*

For a long time afterwards, there was darkness, and cool rock, and the river running by. Breaca sank slowly to sitting and then to lying and trailed her injured arm in the water.

She was not a dreamer to call forth visions, but lying on the cool rock with her face turned to the river she did her best to bring alive her own daughter, that she might see her whole and beautiful and safe on Mona, and not broken in the slavers' pen of the ancestor's threat.

Straining so that the sweat beaded her brow, she built a fire that danced on the water, and a hazing of air above it. There, feature by feature, she drew the ox-blood hair and grey eyes, the fine, wine-dark brows and the careful, cautious gaze of Graine, the daughter she had barely seen since her birth. The child of two warriors so tall should never have been so fine and so slender, but Graine was everything her parents were not, and more beautiful for it. Born into Nemain's light, she was a dreamer from the fine sheen of her hair to the soles of her feet.

Breaca could not build all of her daughter, only her face, framed by the rich, dark hair, and that took more effort than she had known possible. Then, when she thought she could only make half-formed shapes in an imagined fire, she heard the sound of Graine, weeping.

The shock of it broke the vision. Where her daughter had been, a hare fled across a hillside, coursed by Stone, last son of Hail, and then Airmid was there, peering through the flames, and Airmid's voice echoed through the cave saying, 'I don't know how she's hurt, small one, you have to tell me. I can't see where you can see.'

The vision had gone before she realized that the words were of her, not for her, and that, with their touch, the burning in her arm was a little less.

She did not try to call Cunomar. Her son had barely spoken to her in the three long years since his escape from captivity in Rome. It was no secret that he had failed in battle at his father's side in Gaul and that every part of him yearned to erase that shame; that he waited daily for the elders to call him to sit the warrior tests of his long-nights so that he might prove himself the man he ached to be.

As a mother, Breaca felt for him. As a warrior, she knew that the child could not become a man until he had learned to command his own temper – and that the longer the elders deferred their call, the less likely it was that he would find the peace he needed to do so.

Lacking that final approval, Cunomar hunted the enemy with the single-minded hatred of a wounded bear and his mounting tally of kills did nothing to heal the many wounds of his soul. Waking and sleeping, resentment flowed from him, thick and clear as river fog.

From the cave dark beyond, Breaca heard the voice of her father, Eburovic. *Your son craves your love. Why do you not give it?*

Eburovic had given his life for her and she had loved him before any other man. Alive or dead, she had never heard him speak anything but the truth. She stared into the dark and could not see him, but his presence enfolded her in his care, as the ancestor's had not done. She was not alone.

She said, 'I have made kill-feathers for my son each time he has slain one of the enemy. I have given him a horse of my own breeding and with my own hands made the knife with which he kills. I loved him and was overjoyed when Luain mac Calma brought him back from Rome. He knows this, but still he leaves the roundhouse when I enter and will not come near me from the summer's start to its end. My son is a stranger who hunts with the she-bears and I do not know how to reach him.'

And so you, too, hunt alone, *neither desiring nor requesting his company?*

He was her father; she could never lie to him. He was a ghost, who had access to the many layers of truth.

Breaca said, 'I could not hunt with Cunomar. He is not safe. He has killed and lived to tell of it only because the she-bears hunt as a pack and three or more are assigned each time to his protection.'

The truth broke through the worlds so that she saw her son whether she wanted to or not. In another place and another time, Cunomar turned his head and stared at his mother with a stranger's eyes. She met his gaze and tried to imagine him weeping tears of gold, and could not.

Because she had heard Graine, and seen Cunomar, so then also she saw Cygfa, Caradoc's daughter, who was not the child of Breaca's flesh but had become the child of her soul.

As Cunomar had been, so Cygfa, too, had been captured and taken prisoner to Rome with Caradoc, their father. Exactly as Cunomar had, she had stood in the shadow of the cross and thought herself about to be hanged on it. Exactly unlike Cunomar, she had drawn in strength from the core of herself and had not succumbed to bitterness afterwards.

When Cygfa had gone out to sit her long-nights and came back a woman, ablaze with her dreaming, Breaca had been the one who spoke for her before the elders and hailed her as daughter in all ways but those of flesh, which were ever the least.

Tall as her father and as beautiful, she braided kill-feathers by the handful into her hair before battle and mounted a horse of her own breeding. Warriors crowded close to touch her blade for the luck it would give and there was no doubt that she would fight well and kill cleanly, and that if she died in conflict it would be only because Briga had need of her in the other worlds. In all the battles since her return from Rome, she had fought at the side of the Boudica, brilliantly.

From somewhere distant, the ancestor said, *You love her as a daughter. The children of your blood see it daily and mourn. Do you wonder that they cleave closer to others than to you?*

Breaca lay on cold stone at the river's edge, her mouth a desert for lack of water. She was too hot, and too cold, shuddering. Her breath was not enough to give true voice to her words. She answered, whispering, 'You twist the truth. My children know themselves equal in my eyes.'

Are you sure?

'Yes.'

She was not sure. Her whispered voice said so, and the rush of the water, and the ancestor's words, growing ever more faint.

You are Eceni. It is your blood and your right and your duty. It is not too late to keep the children from weeping. Only find a way to give back to the people the heart and courage they have lost. Find a way to call forth the warriors and to arm them, find at least one with courage to match yours and you may prevail. At the last, find the mark that is ours and seek its place in your soul. Come to know it, and you will *prevail.*

The ancestor's words etched a serpent-spear in the darkness, cast in fire, hung against a summer sky.

The snake, having two heads, watched past and future, writhing. The spear was crooked, as if broken. Its two blades pointed down and up, to earth and sky, joining the realm of the people to the realm of the gods.

Others joined it, chiselled into the living rock over and again on the walls of the cave from floor to unreachable roof. Anywhere and everywhere, the twin-headed serpent gazed equally to past and future and the crooked spear lay across, joining the gods to their people. The fire guttered and gave more light, filling the chiselled marks with molten metal so that they came alive and stood shimmering from the walls.

The light was too bright. It hurt to look at it. Believing herself dying, Breaca turned her head away. 'What of my children?'

Would you have them in the slave pens? If you would have your victory, you must lose them. Better lost now to Mona, where they are loved, than later to Rome.

The serpent-spears on the walls faded to dark. Only the single fire-cast mark hung against the sky-blue roof of the cave.

With disturbing solicitude, the ancestor said, *There is none other who can do it, else you would not be asked. If you go with all speed, then the tide of Rome may yet be turned.*

'Do you promise me that?'

I promise you nothing. Only that I will be with you, and that if you ask it, I can give you death, which you may crave, or my aid to live, which you may not.

She woke to the smell of burning.

Her cloak lay smouldering on the edge of the fire and the wound in her arm had burst open, leaking an evil-smelling pus. The pain that racked her was more than she had ever known, even at childbirth. She stared up into blackness and saw nothing and heard nothing, only the ever-running river and its echoes into silence.

After a while, she rolled onto her side and then onto her front and doused the edge of her cloak to stop the burning and then drank a little and then, gritting her teeth, pushed her bad arm into the water and let the current strip it clean.

Later, still crawling, she found the messenger's saddlebags and the wormwood and vervain and plantain and other things she could not name that Efnís had sent, in case the bearer were injured on his journey.

Airmid would have known how best to use them. Breaca did as much as she could remember, and prayed to the gods, not the ancestor-dreamer, for help in her healing.

She slept again, for a long time, and woke cooler and shaking with hunger not fever and so knew the worst of it was over. She ate from the messenger's saddlebags, thanking his shade for his foresight and the gift of food, and went slowly to tend the horses. The roan mare knew her and whickered, nuzzling her hair. She stood scratching its withers and teasing out tangles from its mane.

In a while, because she had been thinking of it and had reached a decision and needed to speak it aloud, she said, 'We will stay here in safety until I am well enough to ride and then we will go east. Alone. We may find warriors and rouse them to battle, we may find the iron to arm them, and one to lead them. If we do not turn the tide of Rome, it will not be for want of trying. But I pledge to you now, that if the legions come to take you or your young into slavery, I will kill you, or them, rather than let it happen.'

The mare knew nothing of slavery, only heard the undercurrents of passion. She turned her head and rested her chin on Breaca's shoulder and lipped at her sweat-soaked hair and for a while, in the darkness, they were company, one for the other, before the journey east began.

IV

A THREE-QUARTER MOON TIPPED THE EDGE OF THE HILL. A WREN sang for the dawn. The child Graine lay behind a square-edged boulder with her hand on the neck of a slate-blue hound called Stone. Untrue to his name, the hound did not lie still, but quivered under her touch, his gaze fixed on the steep slope of the hill at the place where the heather of the high land gave way to grass and long stretches of bracken. Hay had been cut there in summer and the grass had regrown to a finger's height, making good grazing. Graine watched where the hound watched and, as her eyes became his eyes, a triangle of smudged outlines became the shapes of three yearling hares, feeding.

The hares were young and unwary. Graine, who was also young, had listened to others' tales of hunting: 'Watch them from a distance. When you get one alone, that's the time to strike.'

Dubornos had told her that, the gaunt and watchful singer whom the gods had returned alive from Rome when her father had been left behind. Dubornos had been talking of hunting Romans but hares were not so different.

Graine lay on the damp turf, waiting. Nemain, the moon, sank lower until the hare that lived on her surface could no longer clearly be seen. The whispers of the half-light changed and became those of day. Graine would have preferred an endless night; in the darkness the grandmothers spoke to her from the lands beyond life

49

and she felt she understood the world. In daylight, she had to rely on the unreliable words of the adults around her and they were too confusing.

It was not that they lied, simply that they did not have the same view of the world as the grandmothers did, so that it was hard to know what would please them. Her mother, Breaca, was especially difficult to read and it was her mother whom Graine most wanted to please – if she were alive. That question had ruled the morning and all the time before it since the dark evening with Airmid when both of them had seen things in the river that they did not wish to see.

The grandmothers had not helped with that vision, nor explained it since. With nothing more solid than pain seen and felt, Graine had decided to behave as if her mother still lived and would return soon, counting the Roman dead and, perhaps, quietly impressed by the actions of the daughter she had left behind.

On the mountainside, watched by the hound called Stone, one of the bucks, bolder than its siblings, moved away seeking greener grass. *When you get one alone . . .* At a certain moment, when the sun showed her the shine of the hare's eye and the blue hound ceased to quiver against her side and became instead entirely still, Graine lifted her hand.

The first few strides of the chase froze the child's breath in her throat. She had seen hounds course a hare often enough but never before had *her* hound hunted down *her* chosen hare, her twisting, turning tawny pelt and flash of cream underbelly with its pulsing life and floating run and round black eyes, perfect as polished jet. For a dozen heartbeats, Graine lay still feeling herself a true hunter at last, already illuminated in the glow of her mother's pride.

This was the heart of her plan: her uncle Bán, the traitor, had been named Harehunter when he was still a boy and a friend to the tribes. It seemed to Graine that her mother grieved for her lost brother as much as she did for Caradoc who had been the fountain of her soul. If Graine could not replace her father – and the years of his absence had shown quite clearly that she could not – then she could perhaps become another hare-hunter, fit to assuage the grief of Bán's loss.

It would not change the reality of Breaca's wounding, or the confrontation with the serpent-dreamer, but it might at the very least make her smile. Graine Harehunter. It had a good ring to it. She could hear it spoken by Airmid and see how the Boudica, surrounded by the elders, would accept it and be happy.

So close. Hunter to hunted, hunted from hunter. So close.

Stone was past his prime but fit after a long summer at war. As he ran, he stretched long and flat like a hawk and the distance from hunter to hunted closed until he could strike and almost kill – but not quite.

The hare was well grown and had lived through its own summer of danger. It knew enough of the hunt to save itself from the first strike. White teeth cracked shut in the air where its chest had been but the beast was already gone. Desperate for respite, it jinked and turned on its axis so that, for the first time, it faced Graine who had risen to her feet and stood knee deep in heather. Far away as it was, the hare raised its head and looked her full in the eyes, pleading. *Her* hare, seeking her help, pleading for the freedom simply to live.

It was not at all what she had planned. Fear cracked over Graine, drowningly. Not her own fear, but the hare's, the hammering, heart-stopping terror of the hunted beast. Before she could take a breath to shout, it spun once more on its own length, ducked under the hound's neck and fled back towards her, straight as a spear, diving between her legs for sanctuary.

She would have called Stone off if she could. She did her best, screaming at him until her throat was raw, but everyone knew that when any hound of Hail's line was hunting, or at war, the only thing that would stop it was a thrown spear. Graine was only six and she had no spear to throw, and even if she had she would never have dared to harm the hound who carried the heart and soul of the legendary Hail and was all her mother had left of her life before Rome's invasion. She stood stone still in the heather and the hound coursed past her, impersonal as lightning, as deaf, and as lethal.

The hare was an arm's reach away. Time stretched as it turned and turned again, a third time and a fourth, harepin on harepin, dodging the crunching jaws for a few breaths more of a life so precious that Graine could taste its need to survive as an iron wetness on her tongue. She reached for the beast, desperate to help, and her movement was its undoing. Faltering, it missed the last turn and Stone, excelling himself, stretched that hand's length

51

longer to reach it. The hare died, squealing, with its chest cracked shut on its heart. To the last, the shining black eyes remained locked with Graine's, pleading silently for sanctuary and release.

In that moment, at six years old, standing knee deep in wet grass with the half-ghost of Nemain's moon hazy in the western sky, Graine nic Breaca mac Caradoc, heir to the royal line of the Eceni, understood with crushing certainty the true helplessness of the gods when the forces they unleash with good intent destroy those who have called on them for help. The enormity of it, the illusion of hope when there was only certain death, overwhelmed her. She sat in the grass and cried as only a child can cry, for the hare, who was Nemain's beast above all others; for her mother and father who would for ever live apart; for herself who was lost in a world of uncertain forces where Cygfa and Cunomar had returned from the dead to lay claim to parts of her mother's heart that were already too much divided, and last for the brave, big-hearted war hound who had given his all in the hunt and came to her for praise and did not understand why she did not give it but instead clung to his neck and wept.

Airmid, dreamer of Nemain, found her shortly after noon, by the stream in that part of the wood where the sun was least. Graine sat on a fallen birch log with the hound, Stone, lying to one side and the skinned body of a hare on the turf beside her. The skin was stretched out between rocks and had been partly cleaned. The head, messily severed, sat on a rock in midstream, facing west, to the ancestors. A lock of long, ox-blood hair streamed in the water around it, pegged down by other stones. A bald patch showed on the side of Graine's head as she sat hunched and weeping at the stream's edge.

The dreamer had searched since dawn for the child who was not her daughter, but had come to hold that place in her heart. Seeing her, a morning's anxiety flared nearly to anger and fell away to a deeper fear. She stood still, believing herself unseen and unheard. The hound showed no sign of having noticed, but still, without looking up, Graine leaned forward and turned the hare to face across the water towards her. 'I wanted to honour it,' she said. 'It showed me what became of mother in the cave of the ancestors.'

Airmid could run as fast as any of the warriors when she chose to. Careless of her tunic, she crossed the river's wet stones and, coming to kneel by the child, took hold of the small, shaking shoulders. A tumble of uncombed hair fell about her fingers; that part of Graine that belonged only to the child and had no echo in her parents or grandparents on either side. It had been pale as winter thatch when the child was born and for a while it had seemed as if the dreams of a lifetime had gone awry, but the deep, ox-blood red had grown through in the first year and had confirmed at least the first beginnings of hope.

Later, as the infant had become a child, the neat smallness of her had become apparent; the fine lines of her features mirrored no-one so much as her mother's brother, Bán, with whom Graine shared only the barest splash of blood.

Graine's eyes alone were recognizably her father's: the changeable grey that moved with the weather of her soul from the density of storm clouds to the almost-blue of newly forged iron. Outwardly, the child carried nothing of her mother. One needed to understand, and profoundly to love, the souls of each to see the fire blazing in the core and how it was shaped differently in the dreamer and the warrior.

There was little fire to be seen in Graine now, only hurt and a fragile pride. The birch log lay along the bank, shedding feathery strands of white bark onto the loam. Sitting a little away, Airmid brought from her belt-pouch the handful of shelled hazelnuts and withered green crab apples that she had collected at dawn, thinking to share them with her not-daughter. Now, she offered one, staring into the water beyond the hare. 'Can you tell me what the hare showed you?' she asked.

In the woods behind, a west wind teased at autumn leaves, loosening them. Graine looked up. Her grey eyes were ageless. 'When mother was fighting against the traitor Cartimandua, you prayed to Nemain for help,' she said. 'We still lost.'

It showed me what became of mother . . . Airmid breathed deep and slow and unclenched her hands. She had been with Graine when they had seen the vision of Breaca. It had come hazily through water but even at so far a remove, it had been clear the warrior was dying. Airmid had prayed and dreamed constantly in the three days since, but nothing further had been shown her. Graine, to whom the gods sent visions beyond the minds of any dreamer on Mona, chose not to share what she knew, but instead turned her mind to the lost battles of the summer.

There was nothing to be done to hurry her; a god-touched child is not to be pressed. Wiping a palm on her tunic, Airmid said evenly, 'The gods know more than we do of how things must go. We can pray, and must do so. Not everything we ask for will be given.'

'No, or the Romans would have taken ship and sailed away long since.'

'Indeed. But it has always been this way and should remain so. If every prayer were granted, we would become arrogant, and ask for too much.'

Graine thought for a while, then, 'Would that be bad?'

Airmid said, 'It could be. I think in time we would stop honouring the gods for what they gave us. Then we would truly be godless.'

'Like the men of the legions?'

'Some of them.'

'That would be bad.'

They were quiet a while. It could have been a day like any other. They ate quietly until the nuts were gone. Airmid broke one wizened apple between her palms and offered half. The smell was sharp, like new grass with a sweet, nutty base. Graine took it, unseeing. Her gaze was fixed on the hare's. Its eyes were open, opaque, like dusted water.

Graine said, 'I think . . . maybe . . . it may be that Nemain cannot help us, however much we pray? As I could not help the hare, even though I wanted to.'

And so the pegged skin and the severed head became more clear. Stifling a bigger movement, Airmid reached forward and smoothed a lock of stray hair from Graine's brow. The gods spoke in so many small, indefinable ways. The training of a dreamer was to know how to listen. Here, in the presence of a child who embodied her own dream, Airmid's whole body vibrated with listening. A magpie flew over and called once, raucous in the morning hush. More quietly, a trout flipped in the stream and landed uncleanly, splashing more than it might have done. A frog croaked, at a time of year too late for frogs.

In these ways, the god warned Airmid to pick her words with

care. Twenty years of Mona's lessons and a handful of years before that in service to the elder grandmother helped her find what to say.

Leaning forward, the dreamer took the child's two hands between her own. 'You may be right. It may be the gods can do nothing, but the hare is Nemain's beast and if it died, it did so to return to her. Death isn't a bad thing when it comes at the right time, you must remember that. And you're not a god, but another of Nemain's creatures. You could no more have stopped the hare's death than one of the skylarks could stop you from eating the apple. It's not in your power.'

'You mean the hare died because it wanted to? I don't think it did.'

'I don't think so either. I didn't say that. I said it may be that it died because its time was right. We can't know why, but perhaps if Stone, who is the best of hunters, had not caught and killed it cleanly, something worse might have happened later; an eagle might have caught it and torn it apart to feed her young, or a fox cub that had not learned to kill properly might have left it crippled to die of starvation in the winter. Or perhaps simply it was its time to return to Nemain, who cares for it. We, who are not gods, cannot know these things.'

'But Nemain can?'

Airmid took time to think. The hands she clasped had grown cold and then too hot. She turned them over, studying the bitten nails with their constant half-moon of grime. The grey eyes drew her back.

'I don't know,' she said. 'Truly, I don't. But I think we have to believe so, or there is nothing left to believe. It may not be true. It may be that the hare died because you chose to set the hound on it and there is nothing more. Would you rather believe that?'

In the long silence, the birds sat still on the branches and the frog crooned alone.

'If I believe it, will it make it so?'

'I don't think what we believe changes anything except ourselves.'

'No . . . in that case, I would rather believe that it died because it was time for it to return to Nemain. But that means . . .' Graine faltered. She was a child of six, grappling with questions that had vexed the elders since the time of the most ancient ancestors. Her frown became so complete that her brow flattened tight against the bone.

Airmid said gently, 'It means that Nemain sees a greater part of the picture and we see only that which is before our eyes. It means that if your father Caradoc is in Gaul, he is there for a reason that we do not know.'

'And the traitor brother? Why is he in Hibernia?'

'Valerius. He was Bán but he calls himself Valerius now.' Airmid stroked a small cheek that could as easily have been his. 'It doesn't help to think of him badly. I don't know why he's there. I can't reach him or see him. He has closed himself off from the gods' touch.'

Airmid had not said as much to anyone else, certainly not to Breaca. Graine shivered in the morning chill and it was not simply her skin thrumming to the sound of the god's voice. Seeing it possible to show the depth of her care without doing harm, Airmid reached forward and drew the young body in to her chest, warming her and holding her close.

The shuddering stilled in a while. Kissing the rich, unruly hair, Airmid said, 'We must learn patience, both of us. The answer will be clear in time, if we have to wait for death to see it.'

'Does death make some things more clear?'

'Death makes all things clear.'

'Then the man Sorcha brings on the ferry will know all things by noon.'

The child was exceptional, but some things are beyond even the gods. Sharply, Airmid said, 'How do you know that?'

The small face turned up. For a moment Graine looked serious, keeping the faraway gaze that she had learned from the dreamers. Then she grinned and was a child again, bright with triumph at the success of a ruse.

'He was there when I left Sorcha's cabin with Stone. I saw him ride to the water's edge and raise the signal. He rode lopsided, holding his belly, and when he tried to dismount he fell and his horse walked away from him. They only do that when a man is dying, Gwyddhien said so.'

The hairs rose on Airmid's forearms and her throat ran dry. Certain dreams of the past nights became more clear than she might have liked. Distractedly, she said, 'If Gwyddhien said so, then it must be right. Did Sorcha go to him?'

'Not yet. She was rising to feed the babe when I left. She'll be ready by now. You should go. He brings news from the east. The hare told me that.'

'And did the hare tell you what news he bore?'

The grey eyes grew wide. 'No. It showed me his brother, who is dead. Mother met him and has his message. She was sick with the wound we saw but the serpent-dreamer healed her. She is going away now and will never come back. The ancestors are with her. They cannot hold her safe any more than can the gods. But they will keep watch so that we'll know if she falls.'

'Thank you.' So much from the lips of a child. So much held alone for the length of a morning. So much to mourn and to fear and perhaps to plan.

Airmid did not force herself to smile; with Graine, such a thing would be an insult. She rose, holding the child's hand, and said, 'In that case, there is nothing to be done but to greet the messenger. Do you think he will live long enough to deliver his message?'

'He will if we are quick.'

'Can you run?'

'Of course.'

'Let's go then.'

They ran together along the stony path towards Sorcha's cabin. A single frog at the river's edge croaked an autumn song of mourning.

V

ENCASED IN A PIT, THE FIRE GAVE OFF NO SMOKE, ONLY A HAZE OF burnt air that smeared the straight lines of the surrounding beech trees so that they wavered as if reflected in water. The clouded evening sky behind took on the ripples of the ocean so that Breaca could have been in the cave again, locked in the fever-dreams of the ancestor, but was not.

Dreams might have been pleasanter than reality. She sat wrapped in her cloak with her back to a rock and wished, without hope of fulfilment, for the warmth and companionship of a hound. In the days before Rome's invasion, no hunter, warrior, trader or travelling smith would have slept under the open sky without a hound to keep the night's cold at bay.

It was a small change amidst the greater cataclysm of occupation, but it served as a marker for the life that had been lost and was yet one more feather to weight the balance of her decision, should she ever regret it: for the promised warmth of a hound on an autumn evening, Breaca of Mona, once of the Eceni, had abandoned her warriors and the island of Mona that had been her home and her safety for nearly twenty years. She had abandoned the children for whom she had never fully been a mother and the warriors for whom she had been the Boudica, bringer of victory, and, emerging from the cave of the ancestor-dreamer with the wound in her arm half healed, she had set her mare's head to the east towards the lands of the Eceni and had not once turned back.

The gods show the many possible futures . . . it is up to the living to manifest what is offered.

The ancestor-dreamer had said so on parting, speaking from the hound stone as Breaca scoured clean the last of the grasses in fulfilment of her promise, then stood on it to mount her horse.

She thought of that later, riding east on poorly trodden pathways, focusing on the smaller sacrifices that the larger ones might not overwhelm her. It was not hard to find things to mourn: the loss of Stone, who was her best war hound and the last remaining son of Hail; the loss of the dun stallion who should have covered the blue mare in the spring and the yearling filly who was their daughter and would outclass both of her parents; the loss of the many hunting knives that lay on the shelf beside her sleeping place in the great-house; the loss of the ancient blade with the feeding she-bear on its hilt that had been her father Eburovic's and his father's before him and his mother's before that, back through the years to the distant history of the Eceni.

That blade should have gone to Cunomar on his long-nights, and might do still; Ardacos knew where it was kept and would do what was right, speaking the words of the giving as if he were father to the child-made-man, not simply his mentor. Cygfa could not be present at the ceremony – only men could take part in a boy's long-nights as only the women stood vigil for the girls – but she could braid his hair for him afterwards with Airmid and Graine when he came out to join—

Breaca stopped, cursing her undisciplined mind. She had never thought herself weak. She did not wish to do so now.

Breathing tightly, she raised her head and looked beyond the fire to the place above the treetops where the half-circle of Nemain's light made silhouettes of leafless branches. When she had lain above the Roman camp, the moon had been in the last day of waning, too old to show at night. Now, it was halfway to full, and casting shadows on the landscape. Five days had been lost as she healed in the cave, each one a lifetime.

The night was less still than it had been. A damp wind billowed from the south, spreading the haze above the fire low and flat. The darkening trees bent their heads to the north and the sky beyond sparked with early stars. The roan mare shifted, snuffing the breeze, then shifted again and blew out gently through her nose.

Move!

It was not the ancestor who spoke, but the oldest part of Breaca's mind, which was wedded to the serpent-spear and to life. She rolled to her feet, shedding her cloak and sweeping it over the fire pit to hide the glow. Her slingstones were in one hand and her sling in the other and she was already within the shelter of the trees, moving silently over rain-damp leaves and pressing through undergrowth that eased forward to let her through and closed behind her afterwards, denying that she had ever been.

Go south; the wind is from the south, and it brought the scent of man to the mare.

Breaca circled south, soft as owl-flight, exchanging her sling for her knife, the better to kill in close cover. Her mare stood as if carved from granite, a thing of the night. The rising steam from the fire-warmed cloak would eventually betray to the trackers the fact that she had been in the clearing, but it would not give away her new position.

The enemy was alone and well hidden. He lay still beneath a stunted blackthorn and only the pale smudge of his hair let Breaca see him. He was not, therefore, Roman; of the invaders only the Gaulish cavalrymen were so coloured and they did not have the skills for this. He would be a Coritani scout then, a traitor from the eastern tribe, neighbours to the Eceni, who favoured Rome, and whose best scouts were paid well in gold to hunt their countrymen. Breaca had killed two of his kind in recent days and had not found them any more skilled than their Roman masters, simply more careful in open country.

She waited, watching, then pressed her knife-blade into the dirt and, with her free hand, sifted through her black-painted stones. Two had red snake-lines on the black, painted on Mona, when the serpent-dreamer was a safe and distant memory. Breaca knew them by the sharp pain they raised in her palm. She eased one from the pouch and cupped it in the belly of her sling. These two alone not only crushed the life from the enemy, but extinguished the fires of the soul. It was a fate fit for a traitor and even the godless Coritani were learning to fear it.

Presently, as the steam from her cloak became smoke, the scout rose from his hiding place and eased forward, squirming on his belly, silent as a snake. If the strategies of his tracking were fatally flawed, the quality of his movement was exquisite; a sinuous flow that disturbed neither leaves nor small branches, but sent him forward to where she had been.

Where there was one tracker who knew his craft, there may be two. It was the knowing of that stayed Breaca's hand when the tracker emerged beyond the blackthorn and the red and black slingstone could have killed him. The Boudica had not hunted alone so many winters to be caught by a warrior prepared to sacrifice himself to trap her. She watched the place the scout had rested, waiting.

'He's good, isn't he? But not as good as you and me.'

The murmur was part of the night, a sighing of soft breezes. The voice was a friend's and the last she might have expected to hear.

'Ardacos?'

She turned, slowly. The small, wizened warrior grinned at her from the base of a beech tree. Ardacos led the she-bears and was the greatest proponent of their art. He fought naked and on foot, smeared in the grey woad-stained bear's grease that gave him his power, painted with lime-clay to terrify his enemies. He was not painted now, nor did he stink of bear, but he was naked, save for a knife belt, and his body merged with the land around it as a stone might do, or a sleeping bear. Breaca saw him because he chose to let her. In all probability she had passed him in tracking the tracker and had not felt the first hint of his presence.

Surprise waxed briefly to anger and then to a stabbing anxiety. Ardacos had been sent by the elders once before to find the Boudica and bring her home. She did not wish to have to fight him for the right to continue east.

On a silent breath, she asked, 'Why are you here?'

'I am sworn to protect your son in your absence. The she-bear asked it of me and I consented, gladly. Where he goes, I go. Whom he hunts, I hunt, even if the quarry is his mother.'

Ardacos nodded forward and what should have been obvious became so: that the scout who tracked the Boudica was not a Coritani traitor but Cunomar, her eldest child, son of his father in so many ways – but not enough.

Cunomar had reached the edge of the clearing and was working his way forward through the beeches. Breaca felt the weight of the red-painted stone in the fall of her sling. The understanding of how close she had come to killing him left her light-headed with fear. The ancestor's voice echoed in her mind. *If you would have your victory, you must lose them . . .*

'But not like this.' She spoke aloud, not meaning to.

Ardacos shook his head. 'I am here for his protection. I would not have let you throw.'

'No?' With her eyes, she measured the distance to Ardacos. Two spear lengths separated them. They could argue for the rest of their days over whether it might have been enough.

She said, 'I don't understand. Why is Cunomar here? And why is he tracking me when he could ride in and share the fire?'

'Could he so? He thinks not. Your daughter believes you have left us and so now, for the first time, your children are united in their fear and their loss. They would bring you back, or join you in your flight. Your son believed that if he rode to your fire, you would be gone before he reached you. Was he not right?'

It was late and Breaca was tired and her mind had not yet fully recovered from a spear wound gone bad. She said, 'Cygfa believes I have left Mona? How does she know?'

Ardacos ran his tongue round the white edges of his teeth. He hissed disapproval, or despair. 'Breaca, you have two daughters and it is not Cygfa who is the dreamer, but Graine, your daughter-of-blood. She dreamed your wounding and knows that the grandmothers and the greater ancestors wished you to travel east, but not why they sent you away from us. She did not know, either, if you would be well enough to travel.'

He reached out and touched the red and swollen edges of the healing wound on the Boudica's arm. In a different tone, he said, 'I have said before that you should not hunt alone. The spear went deep.'

'But not too deep, and the one who cast it is dead. He—'

'Mother?'

Sometime in their conversation they had stopped whispering and, hearing them, Cunomar had abandoned his stalking. He stood in the centre of the clearing, staring at where he thought they might be. Like Ardacos, he had hunted naked and the newly risen moon brightened his hair and the white skin beneath. In so many ways he was the image of his father, and yet so clearly flawed.

Breaca made herself see the small fragment of Caradoc, outweighing the burning fact of the red-striped slingstone held in her hand. Standing, she smiled a welcome. 'I'm here. If you could lift my cloak from the fire pit before it burns, I might wear it yet through other nights.'

He stared at her, blankly. Unlike Ardacos, he wore both the lime and bear-grease of the she-bear warriors. As if to make the point, he had painted as much of the bear-skull on his face as was permitted a boy not yet past his long-nights. White circles ringed his eyes and narrow lines ran the lengths of his cheekbones, ending in a spike that rose up to his brow. He was a stranger, as he had been since he stepped off the boat that had brought him from Gaul. The ancestor had said so and Breaca had denied it. Here, now, she understood the many layers of the truth, and the price she had pledged to pay.

Better lost now, to Mona . . .

She said, quietly, 'Cunomar? It was a good stalking. If you'll lift my cloak . . . ?'

He stared at her a moment longer, then did so, stiffly. White smoke billowed up and was followed by a wash of air-starved flame.

'Thank you. There's wood by the upright stone behind your left foot. If you feed the flames, we can sit warm at least, while you tell me how you tracked me this far. Rome's Coritani scouts would pay in gold to know that.'

She was speaking as she would to a child and her son heard it. He crouched by the fire pit and the flames lit the unworldly skull-marks on his face. Resentment and mistrust patterned the features beneath. His gaze flickered to the sling that hung from her hand and rested there.

'Did Ardacos stop you from killing me?' So much pain in the currents beneath the words.

Your son craves your love. Why do you not give it? For love, there must first be truth, and it was a long time since Breaca had given that to Cunomar.

She was about to lose him. Knowing that, she sat on a stone and spoke for the first time as she would have done to his father. 'No,

Ardacos did not stop me from killing you, although he might have tried. I thought you might be a sacrifice, sent forward to draw me out. I waited to see who was behind you.'

'And, because I was not a Coritani tracker in t .e pay of Rome, the one waiting behind was Ardacos, protector of the Boudica's children. When father fought in the Battle of the Lame Hind, Dubornos was set to look over me. Now he cares for Graine and Ardacos must keep watch over me instead. It must be very tedious for them both.'

Breaca stared into the fire, seeking answers, and found none. 'You could ask him,' she said. 'You will have time enough to thrash it out on the journey back to Mona.'

A shadow joined them. Even in firelight Ardacos contrived to be half seen. He carried with him a bearskin wrapped in a bundle. Laying it at her feet, he said, 'I brought you this. You should not return to take the torc of your people without it.'

'How do you know I'm going back to take the torc?'

Ardacos said, 'One of Efnís' three messengers reached Mona alive. He died on the straits without crossing over but Airmid heard his message and understood then what Graine's dream had shown. You are returning to take the rule of the Eceni from 'Tagos, if he will let you have it. To even think of such a thing, you should have your father's blade, and your own.'

He unwrapped his bundle by the fire pit and two swords lay together on the flat leather of the bear hide; the feeding she-bear on the pommel of the larger overlapped slightly the serpent-spear that marked the smaller, so that the two intertwined and became one. Eburovic's she-bear blade carried the soul of her ancestors back too many generations to count. Its loss had been one of her many sources of pain, but Breaca had carried the blade that bore the serpent-spear into every battle she had ever fought and she had not dared begin to mourn it.

Reaching across the fire pit, she lifted the serpent-blade now, feeling the small thrill of death it always carried. A deep peace followed that she had not missed until its return. 'Thank you. Some things were easy to leave behind. This was not one of them.'

'And we were?' Ardacos asked it, tightly. In his own way, he was as wounded as Cunomar. He had been her lover once, after Airmid and before Caradoc, and had believed himself trusted with all things.

'No, of course not. How can you think it? But I would not ask you to hang on a Roman gibbet simply because I desired your company for—'

A twig cracked under a mis-placed foot. They were warriors, even Cunomar; before the shattered silence had closed around them, they were standing in the dark beyond the fire pit. Breaca's cloak lay once again across the fire, hiding the glow. The wool steamed and then smoked, sooner than it had done before. Three knives carved the moonlight, dimly.

The twig snapped again, then a third time and it was evident that it had not been broken by accident but deliberately, as a signal.

'Is your family now the enemy?' The voice came from the trees, not blood-family, but heart-family, amused and certain of welcome. Cygfa led her horse forward into the clearing, bright-haired and alive with the night.

'Your dreamer was left without her sworn warrior and your daughter without her mother. I said I would return both to you, or you to them. I had not realized when I promised it that you would be so hard to track. I would never have found you if Ardacos hadn't been on your trail and Cunomar before him. You really should lift your cloak from the fire. It's too good to keep burning it.'

In every way, Cygfa was Caradoc's daughter. Her half-smile was his, taking the sting from the words and adding back something different and more difficult to bear. For the space of a dozen heart-beats, the young warrior stood alone in the still moonlight and Breaca had time to pray to Briga and to Nemain that the worst had not happened. Then the beeches shook and Airmid and Graine stepped forward and the night stopped and it would have been so very much better never to have left the cave.

'Airmid—'

They had not come alone. A shape blurred at Airmid's side and then, released, sprang forward. A hound did not understand the complexities of the ancestors and their visions but Stone, last and best son of the war hound Hail, heard pain in the voice of the one he loved most and knew that he alone could heal it.

A hound, at least, could be welcomed fully without risking the destruction of the ancestor's visions. In more pain than she remembered since Caradoc's capture, Breaca knelt and opened her arms. Stone crossed the last strides of the clearing as if he were coursing game and the gathered members of her family, of blood and of spirit, watched as the Boudica buried her hands in the mane of her battle hound and a woollen cloak smoked thickly beside them.

It was Graine who lifted her mother's cloak from the fire pit. She was too small to hold it up. Singed wool swamped her, trailing on the ground. Smoke stuttered upwards from a place near her shoulder. The fire, given air, flickered to life again and the orange glow lit her face from one side, leaving the other half to the dark. Patched thus in light and shadow, her small features were set hard so that she might not weep.

'We all found you,' she said, in case it was not obvious. 'I dreamed the beech trees and Cygfa found your trail. Airmid knew when you were close and that Cunomar was already here.'

She stood squarely, a spear's length from her mother, her child's fists clenched tight across her chest. The Boudica's daughter would never shed tears in the presence of others, but the prescient dreamer who had wept for her mother's pain, a day's ride distant, and then dreamed of her in a forest might well do.

These two fought each other in the soul of a child so that tears trembled on her eyelids, forbidden to fall. Graine took a step back until she came up against Airmid, close behind, and she could slip her small hand into the dreamer's for comfort.

Hairs pricked on the back of Breaca's neck. Somewhere distant, the ancestor laughed.

. . . better lost to Mona, where they are loved . . .

The truth laid her bare, like a knife. Even half understood, it had been easy to follow the ancestor's logic: far better for all of those she loved to be safe in each other's care in the west, than to risk them in the broken lands of the east where the cost of failure was paid by children shackled in slave pens. Seeing the truth laid out so starkly, in Cunomar and then in Graine, cut away all doubt, crushingly.

Breaca rose, ready to say so, and found that Airmid was standing where Graine had been and that it was not, after all, possible to speak. She sat down again, slowly.

Airmid stood very still. The dreamer was taller than the child would ever be; age-threads in her hair sparked in the full spill of

66

light and the dreamer's thong at her brow glimmered as if sewn with the scales of living salmon. A string of silvered frog bones circled her neck, the only outward mark of her dream. Her eyes were dark tunnels in the firelight.

As if they two were alone, she said, 'Breaca, what did the ancestor show you?'

They had been together since childhood, two halves of the same soul. Even Caradoc had not split them apart. Breaca said, 'Do you not know?'

'I need you to say it.'

'I saw a land in ruin, the roundhouses destroyed for their timber, the paddocks bare of fodder, the animals dead of hunger. I saw a pen of children enslaved, weeping tears of gold, and their starving parents collecting their worth as if it were corn. Then, as the ancestor's gift, I saw a battle on a hillside. The eagle of Rome was crushed and the serpent-spear hung over. The ancestor said that if I go east and can raise the warriors and give them heart, if I can arm them, if I can find one among them with the courage and vision to lead them in battle, it may be possible to turn the tide of Rome.'

She did not say, 'I saw Graine in the slave pens.' That was private and would remain so. A vision unspoken might yet be robbed of its power.

Across the clearing, the air became sharper and the moonlight more clear. Nobody moved, or spoke. Neither vision was ambiguous; there was no room for different interpretations, only for deciding how the one might be brought to bear over the other. Stone whined and leaned against Breaca's side, pushing his muzzle under her hand. Graine came to stand beside him, leaning likewise, so that the weight of hound and child crushed against the healing spear wound. There was an odd comfort in it and Breaca chose not to move them.

Cunomar was first to move. He would not look at his mother, but fixed his knife in his belt and crouched by the fire, feeding it small slivers of wood, to make heat and light without smoke.

Airmid, too, moved closer to the flames. To Breaca, she said, quietly, 'So you thought to change the world alone. Do you not know that if you set yourself against 'Tagos now, you will die? Efnís' messenger said so.'

Breaca said, 'Efnís is wrong. He forgets that 'Tagos is a man ruled second by his pride and first by his yearning.'

'*What?*' Airmid laughed harshly. 'You would give yourself to him, to feed his longing?' The scorn of the ancestor had never been so biting.

Five days in the cave and three days riding had given Breaca time to imagine all possible confrontations with Airmid. Not once had she imagined anything so public, or so unplanned. She stood, easing herself free of the hound and the child who pressed against her. It had always been easier to face Airmid standing. She said, 'How else will Rome accept me but as his consort?'

'If they accept you, then they will also accept your children as if they were his. That is the way of Rome. A man's children need not be of his seed.'

Striving to make clear the obvious, Breaca said, 'But they won't be safe, nor will you. The children in the ancestor's vision were enslaved, their parents starving. There were no dreamers: all were dead. I would not ask that of you, nor allow you to ask it of me. The gods gave me that choice and I took it.'

'And now those of us not of the gods make our own choices, which are different.'

'No.'

'You have no power to stop us.'

'Airmid, will you listen to me? I would not take you east to crucifixion, now or ever.'

If she had shocked them before, she stunned them now. Crucifixion was not yet common in the west, as if Rome saved the ultimate sanction for some later time of need. Sane adults did not speak of it, fearing to bring that time closer.

On the fringes of the firelight, Cygfa and Ardacos made the ward against evil. Bone white and shaking, Airmid said, 'Do you think we would want to hear the same of you, knowing that you had died alone?'

Her voice did not tremble; she was a dreamer and trained better than that, but the tone dropped and grew richer and so finally, too late, it became clear that it was not, after all, anger that consumed Airmid, but grief beyond bearing, held for too long.

A cloud covered the moon. The clearing closed in, lit only by the hazed amber of the fire. Those on the margins became less than shadows. Airmid stood two paces away, close enough to touch. The heat of her skin was warmer than the distant caress of the fire. The smell of burning-herbs from her cloak mixed with the lift of sea air and horse sweat and still did not quite cover the scent of Airmid, which had never changed. She waited, not moving, and they were children again, first learning of love; they were adults, knowing the endless pain of loss; they were alone, surrounded by friends who would not disturb them. All Breaca had to do was reach out, bridge the gap between them, and the world would no longer be as it had been when she walked out of the cave and scoured clean the stone of the ancestor, in payment of a debt.

Somewhere, a horse whickered, not Breaca's mare. The hound Stone, long since forgotten, became suddenly stiff, pushing up against her hand. Breaca, guessing, said, 'Dubornos?' and found that, on a night of many errors, this once she was correct.

A lean, red-haired man stood at the edge of the clearing. At the edges of her mind, she had been waiting for him; the final piece that completed the pattern and made whole her family-in-spirit.

With Cygfa and Cunomar, Dubornos had been taken captive by the legions and held for two years in Rome. Unlike those two, his scars were of the body as much as the mind. The fingers of one hand had been broken and the strings of both wrists were weak where the fetters had crushed them so that, in place of the shield and long-sword he could no longer wield, he fought now with a long knife and sling.

Tall, gaunt and melancholy, he had given his life since childhood to the rigours and training of a singer, but war had made him also a warrior and he had long since set himself as guardian over the Boudica's children. It was inconceivable that Graine could have travelled from Mona without his knowing, or following.

He stepped away from the tree against which he had been leaning and it was clear that his presence was not a surprise to the others. He would have been set to hold the horses and would not have left them now without good cause. Cygfa said, 'Is it the legions?'

'Who else? The Coritani scouts lost your trail yesterday and they never had Breaca's, but Rome has a tracker of the Ordovices and she is of a different stamp.'

Cygfa was of the Ordovices. Her mother had ruled them before she, too, was taken prisoner by Rome. White-eyed, she said, 'No warrior of the Ordovices would take coin from Rome. No gold could buy them.'

'No. They know that. They have not offered gold, but have taken her children captive and threaten to kill one at each old moon if she does not find the Boudica for them. Already one is dead. Two are living. She would not see them hanged.'

Always the children. One could ask of the gods why they allow such things to happen, but to do so would lose time and would bring no more answers than had already been given. Breaca said, 'Have you spoken to her?'

'No. I listened at their camp at dawn this morning. She spoke over-loudly to the Coritani scouts. I believe she knew I was there.'

Ardacos said, 'How much of Rome does she bring?'

'Four centuries of the Twentieth plus eighteen Coritani hunters and' – he bowed to Cygfa – 'one warrior of the Ordovices who is worth twenty of them.'

'How far—' Breaca began and then, on a wash of bile and a flood of battle-scald, 'They're here.'

A low wind soughed softly down a valley, except that there were no valleys here and the legions had never understood that a guise which worked well in one part of the land would not necessarily do so in another. That sound, heard in woodland, was only ever the horn call of one Roman century to another.

There was such solace in battle. Almost, in that frozen moment, Airmid was forgotten. Breaca reached for her war hound and found Stone ready at her side. The hair stood erect on his spine and his body trembled with the need to fight. Her blade lay on the ground where Ardacos had left it. She reached for it and found that Airmid had already lifted it, and was holding it forward, hilt first.

Airmid said, 'They have come for you, only you, with three centuries of men. If you wish to die cleanly, this may be the night. If you wish your children to live, you will not fight, but will guide them to safety. You cannot do both.'

Breaca shook her head. 'I can't take you west. They will be guarding all the routes to Mona.'

'Of course. So you must take us east, at least for now.' Airmid smiled wryly. 'I did not ask for this, or make it happen, I swear it.'

'I know. I will not lose you like this.' All her life, Breaca had trained to think clearly in the crisis of war when others could not. It was her gift, and she cherished it, even now, when the certainties of the ancestor's clarity were crumbling and could not be made whole. To Dubornos, she said, 'Your horses, are they far?'

'We can reach them in time.'

'Good. I have the messenger's mount. It will make a diversion. And if we put my cloak on it, which is marked with the serpent-spear, perhaps the woman of the Ordovices can prove that she led them to the Boudica. Ardacos?'

The small warrior was already running. 'I'll take it, and Graine's pony. Give my horse to Graine. He's better than hers.'

He would have gone alone, and if he had died they would not have known how or when. Breaca said, 'Cygfa. Go with him. Fight as do the she-bear.'

The she-bear abjured the honour of warriors, attacking from behind if needful – and they would kill those of their own who were too injured to run rather than let them be captured living by the legions. It was better that way.

Cygfa, too, was already moving. She grinned, fleetingly. 'Thank you. I will see him live through to morning. You do the same for the others.'

Cygfa was gone and those left were gathering up their mounts; three adults, a child and Cunomar, who was neither and who wanted more than anything to fight as the she-bear. Their horses were used to battle and all but Graine could mount them moving. Over the churning of hooves, Cygfa's voice came to them through the trees. 'Where do we meet?'

A part of her had already planned for this. Breaca called, 'At the place where the land of the Cornovii meets the land of the Coritani, at the joining of the four rivers. Ardacos knows it. Pray that he lives to show you.'

GRAINE LAY AWAKE, WITH HER HEAD ON A HOUND'S FLANK, watching the greased smoke of burning bodies rise uncertainly on a westerly wind.

They were Roman bodies, not those of her friends, and the souls of dead men writhed in the smoke, not knowing how to return to their gods. It was hard not to pity them, however dangerous they might have been while alive. Graine wished for dark and the quiet whispers of the grandmothers, that she might ask for the enemy dead to be escorted home. It was a good thing to wish for, and took her mind away from the uncertainty of the coming days and the horror of the flight from the clearing.

It was important not to think about the ride away from the enemy, or she might never find the courage to ride again. Graine was not a warrior and had no wish to be. Alone of her siblings, she had never ached to ride the battle mounts of her elders, and had never spent her summer days on Mona practising all the warrior's moves on horseback until she could ride anything and everything with ease. For four years, she had ridden the same pony who loved her and they had been safe together.

On Ardacos' mount, she had been overwhelmingly over-horsed. Bred and trained for war, sire to two dozen good foals, the beast was in the prime of its life and had rarely been asked to accept any rider but Ardacos, not ever to run from the scene of a battle. When

Graine had been lifted into the saddle, it had seemed not to notice that she was there. Certainly, it had ignored every attempt on her part to change its direction and, until shouted back by the Boudica, it had seemed intent on hurling itself through the forest to attack the Roman lines on its own. Called forward and urged to speed, it had raced through the trees as if across open pasture without thought for the safety of its rider. Leafless branches had lashed around it and fallen logs were taken in a single stride, arced over as by a salmon.

Graine had never experienced the horror of an uncontrolled ride. Growing amongst people who rode as soon and as easily as they walked, she had never heard anyone suggest such a thing might happen. The reality was far worse than her imagined fear of Rome. She would have screamed, but had no breath. She would have been sick, but to do so would have shaken her hold on the beast's mane and, just then, her life depended on not letting go. She might have fainted and crossed into the safety of the dream, but her mother, at last, had seen what was happening and had urged her mare alongside the racing horse.

In full flight, jumping logs and branches and ditches, the Boudica had let go of her reins and, reaching over, had lifted Graine bodily from the saddle, had prised the small fingers loose from their death-clutch on the mane and had gathered her daughter onto the relative safety of her own racing, flying, battle-crazed mount. It was the stuff of nightmares and of myth, and Graine had spent the rest of the ride too afraid and ashamed and astonished and awestruck to think how she might make it into a song.

The flight had continued through the night, and into the next day and night, going more slowly to avoid detection in the day-time, faster at night. Near dawn on the second day, they had come to the joining of four rivers and had moved a little away from it to wait for Ardacos, leaving markers to point where they had gone.

Breaca had led them into a wooded valley where one of the rivers cut deep into the earth and oak clustered densely with elm. Winter had not reached here as it had Mona. Ragged leaves hung yet from the branches; shimmering cold copper overlapped oak rust in the early light.

The wood was unused to human intrusion. Crows had clattered out of the canopy as the riders entered and made camp. They had risen a second time, raucously, shortly after the horses had been settled and a small fire laid. Breaca, Dubornos and Cunomar rolled to their feet and subsided again as quickly at the chittering of a stoat that was Ardacos' sign. He and Cygfa had appeared moments later, running in over rocks and fallen trees, sharp with the elation of battle, filthy with mud and grit and the freckled spray of enemy blood. They had not brought back Graine's pony, nor Cygfa's war-trained gelding. There had never been any chance that they would do; the she-bear always fought on foot and could outrun any horse on a day's ride. The pony had been a decoy and, by saving the Boudica's daughter, Ardacos had saved his own mount. Graine tried not to hate him for it.

The returning warriors had told their tales briefly and then settled to sleep under cover of beech furze and year-end grass. Graine was not used to sleeping by day. She had lain down with her head on Stone's flank, wrapped in her own cloak with Breaca's spare laid over. A dead elm, taken long ago by lightning, stood to the west, its leafless branches black against the paling sky. The gap it left gave light and a sight of the western horizon and, because she was watching for it, the girl had presently seen the first feather of black smoke and the greater, greasier billows that followed as the enemy burned the bodies of those Romans, and three Coritani traitors, slain by Ardacos and Cygfa.

'Graine?'

She had thought she was the only one awake. Startled, she raised her head. Her mother was sitting up by the last glow of the fire, her cloak around her shoulders, her back against an ancient, fungus-encrusted oak stump. She had been sleeping, clearly, and had woken. Her hair hung around her shoulders, part-braided. For the first time since summer – for the first time in any winter Graine had ever known – the Boudica had set aside the single black-dyed crow's feather of the vengeance-hunter and was weaving again the many braids of the warrior.

Caught under the scrutiny of her daughter's gaze, Breaca smiled, not as Airmid would have done, but warmly enough. 'Are you cold?'

'No.' They spoke softly, a murmur on the wind, not to wake the others. 'Stone keeps me warm.' It was almost true.

'But you can't sleep?'

'It's getting-up time. I can't sleep now.'

There was a short pause, full of indecision. If it had been Airmid who had awoken, Graine would have gone to her, would have curled up at her side and told her of the smoke-feather and the burning bodies and her fears for the wandering souls of the dead. Airmid, in her turn, would have sung the enemy to rest if only because Graine asked for it and then would have sung again that a six-year-old girl might sleep and dream in daytime.

Breaca was not Airmid but nor, any longer, was she the Boudica, who brought victory to her warriors and yet remained a stranger to her daughter. Over the course of two days' flight, Graine had seen more of her mother at closer quarters than at any other time in her life. Until that moment, lying by the fire, she had not known how much she had wanted that, nor how closely she had studied the changes that were happening

In the quiet, smoky morning, Graine saw her mother clearly for the first time; a woman with too much care to sleep properly, sitting by a fire, half wrapped in a cloak with part-combed hair lying in cords around her shoulders and her arms bared to the cool air so that the old scars and the new one traced their script across her skin. Her eyes were grey-green with flecks of copper and they were filled now with a turbulence that Graine had never seen in Airmid.

Not knowing what to say, Graine said nothing. Frowning, Breaca leaned forward and pulled something charred from the fire. Holding it out, she said, 'There's some hare's meat left. If you eat, it might help you sleep?'

It was the smile that made the difference more than the words. Graine had never seen her mother shy before, nor thought herself a cause of shyness. With an odd, swooping sensation in her stomach, she uncurled herself from Stone and shuffled into the shelter of her mother's outstretched arm. In its curve, in the surety of its grip, which had held her close over two days of hard riding, she was safe, who had not known how much she was afraid. She buried her face against a tunic that smelled of horses and sheep's oil and leather and clung as tightly as she had done when she was first hauled unwilling from the womb.

A while later, when the smell of charring meat lifted from the fire, mother and daughter broke apart a little and drew the hare's haunch from the embers and shared it with each other and with Stone who pushed between them to lie across their feet.

Thoughtfully, Breaca said, 'I'll shave his hair this morning, before we move on.'

'Whose hair?' Graine was leaning against her mother with her eyes shut and did not want to open them.

'Stone's. He's too good a hound to be seen as he is in the east. The Romans make slaves of hounds as they do of people, but they have no eye for what lies beneath the surface. If I cut his pelt so that it looks as if he has mange, they won't see past it and he'll be safe.'

A cool morning became suddenly colder. Graine hugged her knees to her chest. She stared into the fire and wished the grand-mothers had spoken to her in the dark. On Mona, they would have done and she would understand at least a little of what was happening. 'You're still going to go east, to reclaim the torc of your people?' she asked.

'*Our* people. They are yours as much as mine. Yes. And to raise the warriors to battle. The ancestor was clear about that. I could not, with any honour, go back to Mona.'

Too much hung on too delicate a balance and Graine saw no way to move it in the way that she wanted. She had felt the cutting pressure in the clearing when Airmid had faced her mother and the worlds lay open and all possibilities were equal. There was one thing that had not been spoken and should have been. It was in her power to do so now.

She tested it a time or two in her head and then, when the grand-mothers did not chastise her for it, said, 'Did you know that Gwyddhien was dead?'

Gwyddhien had been Airmid's lover from before Graine was born. She had led the warriors of the Silures and, in the Boudica's absence, those of Mona. She had been killed leading a late-season battle against Cartimandua's Brigantes, who fought for Rome. Afterwards, Airmid's grief had been a private thing, not spoken of. The rush to leave Mona and find the Boudica soon after had been a good way for her to lose herself in action.

There was no telling what the Boudica thought or felt. Quietly, without moving, she said, 'Yes. Cygfa told me.'

Cygfa. Not Airmid. Which meant either that her grief was too new and too raw to allow her to speak of it or, more probably, that she disdained to use so obvious a hammer to crush Breaca's intransigence.

Graine had no such qualms. She said, 'Airmid will not go back to Mona now. Without Gwyddhien to hold her, she is free to follow you.' She did not say, 'She would have followed you anyway,' because she was not sure of that, only hoped so.

'I know.' Breaca nudged the fire with her toe, shifting the sticks to make heat without smoke. 'We spoke of it last night. Airmid will not turn back to Mona and I have no power to make her. Cygfa will do as her own mind commands and she will follow me east whether I want it or not, as will Dubornos; both have said so. Cunomar might be commanded, but I think it more likely he will take it in his head to attack the legions alone to prove his worth. You are the only one I could send back. I could order Ardacos to take you back to Mona and he would do it, staying to be your protection, however much he hated me for it.'

There was an odd tone in her mother's voice. Caught between fear of leaving and terror of going on, Graine looked up. Understanding left her mute. Eventually, 'You don't want to send me back,' she said.

Breaca smiled crookedly. 'I want very badly to send you back, but I don't have the right. You are bound to Airmid as mother to daughter. Where she goes, you go. It is not for me to force you apart.'

The hollowness in Graine's midriff became a void. Swallowing, she said, 'Did Airmid tell you that?'

'No. The ancestor tried to and I didn't believe her. Then the other night, fleeing the legions, I knew it was true. When you were about to fall off Ardacos' horse and break your neck, it was Airmid who saw what was happening. Her horse wasn't fast enough to catch you, or you would have ridden these past two days with her, not with me.'

A quantity of silences made some sense, and the uncertainty in her mother's eyes. Graine found her hands wrapped tight in Stone's pelt, as they had been in the mane of Ardacos' horse. Her fear now was different, and very little of it for herself. She freed a hand and, searching, found her mother's, which was cold, and squeezed it.

There were no words that would set the world right again, or none that could be found. Presently, Graine felt herself gathered more tightly in her mother's arms, felt her mother's lips press into the top of her head and heard her own name spoken over and over, as a litany, too low truly to be heard. Warm breath filtered through her hair and the words rocked down through her skull to reach her ears from the inside.

At the very end, when the hair of her crown was warmly damp, she heard a single sentence that made sense.

'Small child of my heart, I love you; while I live, I will not let Rome kill you, I swear it.'

VII

THERE WAS SNOW IN THE LANDS OF THE ECENI, AND A HEAVINESS
to the air that smelled of old, uncleared dreams.

The thin blanket of white did nothing to cover the starved
ribs of the earth. The deeper Breaca's group moved into occupied
territory, the more the hedgerows were unkempt, ditches clogged,
field edges a harvest of weeds. Paddocks were churned to slipping
mud and yet empty; too many sheep and cattle had grazed too hard
and then died for it.

It was too much like the land of the ancestor's vision. When Breaca
said so, Dubornos said, drily, 'The people pay their taxes in the meat
of their beasts, and in corn. The land must yield twice over now: once
for those who farm it and once for those who claim its ownership.'

Ardacos said, 'And the rest of life? Where are the birds? The
foxes? The hares? Are they, too, paid in taxes?'

'Some. Rome will take fox pelts and hare's meat if there is no
beef. As to the others, would you stay in a place where the earth
itself was made slave to the legions? They have left, and will return
when the gods have restored the balance to the worlds.'

The knowledge did not make each day's travel easier. Breaca led
them, caught between the driving urgency of the ancestor's
command and the needs of her own oath, newly made on the head
of her daughter, to keep Graine safe, and as many of those who
travelled with her as may be.

She rode as she had done since the retreat from the clearing, with Graine held on the saddle in front of her. Outwardly, all was the same. Inwardly, the quality of her caring was different and those who rode with her knew it. The part of her that remained bound to the ancestor-dreamer scorned the collapse of her resolve and predicted death of the worst kind for those who travelled with her.

The rest of Breaca – the greater part – drank in the essence of her daughter as one dying of thirst drinks in cool water. *Do you wonder that the children of your blood cleave to others?* She had forgotten, if she had ever known it, what it was to be lost in the love of a child. She rode each step forward with equal weights of hope and terror balancing the two sides of her heart.

In deference to Roman laws forbidding warriors to carry any weapon longer than a skinning knife, Breaca and her party rode unarmed into the occupied territories. Their blades, and all that marked them as warriors, were left in a grave mound of the ancestors to which Airmid had led them on the evening after Ardacos and Cygfa had rejoined the group.

The mound lay low, hidden by scrub and thin plates of river mist. As they approached from the west, at dusk, the rising moon cast shadows along its length, making it larger and less welcoming than it might have been.

There was no sense of safety here. Riding close brought the hairs upright on Breaca's arms and made her mare snore steam into the frostbitten air. Stone walked stiff-legged at one side and Ardacos, cursing under his breath, held his horse tight at the other. Before them was only moonlight and shadow and a huddle of rocks and turf built around the bones of the dead; they were used to these things and should not have felt so keenly the dread of ancient wrath.

Airmid alone seemed untouched. She rode close to the mound's entrance and slid to the ground. The moon cast her in silhouette, part of the rocks and the turf. She knelt a while at the guardian stones, tracing hidden lines on their surfaces. From where she waited, Breaca could hear the cadence of a murmured half-dialogue such as she might have had with the ancestor in the cave.

'This is the place.' Airmid backed away from the mound. The pressure of the stones had softened her features, blurring them as if newly wakened from sleep. She said, 'Efnís has been here, and one other of the tribes, but not in the past three years, and no-one of Rome. The ghosts of the ancients have guarded this place against all but the strongest dreamers. If there is anywhere better to keep your blades safe from Rome, I don't know of it.'

She spoke to a gathering of silent warriors, and one child. Ardacos coughed and pushed his horse forward. It was leery of the silvered light and crabbed sideways, unwilling to face the dark.

Ardacos was not a weak man. Over twenty years, he had killed more Romans single-handed in service to the she-bear than any other living warrior. Breaca trusted him in battle as she trusted few others. It was not cowardice, then, that moved him when he said, 'This place is Nemain's as much as it is the old ones'. The god is not of the same stamp as the she-bear and I would not willingly offend either. If it would be best for my blade to be buried in some place away from here, I will do it.'

Airmid smiled. Her skin was bone white in the moonlight and quite beautiful. Her voice came from other worlds. 'The bear is as welcome here as any other, or as unwelcome. It is the danger of this place that will protect what you would leave.'

Cygfa, too, was not afraid of death. She said, 'I would not anger the ghosts of our past, any more than would Ardacos. If they resent our presence, we could give you the blades, and you could hide them.'

Airmid shook her head. 'No. If I die, then they would be lost for ever. You must each come and place your weapons where they can best lie. Then if need be, any one of us can retrieve them when the war begins.'

When the war begins . . . That much of the ancestor's visions seemed certain. Sitting on horseback in the cold night, Breaca watched the many-led Eceni flood forward to crush the legions of Rome. A legionary eagle was ground into gore and the serpent spear hung over—

'Breaca?' Airmid had a hand on her arm and Graine had turned sideways on the mare's withers and was peering up into her face. 'Can you get down? We need your blade and your father's. They must go in first. Cunomar can go in with you, to see where they are placed. It may be he will be needed to retrieve them one day. The others can follow in what order they wish.'

'You want me to go in first?' Walking unhorsed and unarmed into battle would have been easier.

Airmid raised a brow. Her smile echoed the elder grandmother's. 'I do not. The ancient ones have asked for your daughter, for which we should all be grateful.'

Breaca could forget that her daughter was a dreamer, save that the gods would not let her. As the warriors tethered the horses and retrieved their blades, Nemain edged across the sky, showing the way forward. Soft light opened what had been dark and, as had been asked, Graine led the way in. The moon made milk of her skin and dark fire of her hair. She could not ride a running horse to safety, but she walked into the mouth of the ancestors' grave as if it were her home. Breaca followed a spear's length behind, in awe of her daughter's courage.

The entrance was small, so that they must crawl in, even Graine. Inside was tall enough to allow Breaca to bend only her head and shoulders and Ardacos could almost stand upright. Around them, hand-hewn rock closed on both sides, far more tightly than the towering walls of the ancestor's cave had done. Except at the start, the stone was dry, and the marks incised in lines at shoulder height were clean-edged as if newly done. The smell was of old dust and bone and dry, crumbled turf and it tickled the nose so that, one after the other, the warriors sneezed. Graine and Airmid, who did not sneeze, led the way forward, talking to long-dead ears.

Too soon, Airmid said, 'Here. It opens into a chamber. There should be room for us all. Come forward slowly.'

They could not have done otherwise. The torches held by the dreamers were of grasses and pine resin and sheep's fat and the smoke they gave had filled the short corridor. In the chamber of the mound, they cast uneven light and made pale faces amber. Five adults and Cunomar formed two circles around Graine, looking inwards. The dead lay as dust in recesses of the walls. Their voices spat warnings of death and the fate of lost souls.

Sharply, Airmid said, 'I bring you the child of Nemain; do you not see?' The whisperings took on a new note and then stopped.

Graine stood very still. The resin and tallow torch billowed in her hand. Wavering light rippled over her hair as if ghost hands stroked it. The noise and the palpable threat diminished. Breaca breathed through strained lungs and wished for the simple dangers of battle. She heard her daughter say, 'Our warriors would leave their weapons in your care, safe until we need them to drive the men of the war eagle from the land.'

Graine spoke clearly, with adult tones. The torch in her hand flared once more and settled. Patchy shadows fluttered on the walls.

Airmid said, 'Breaca, Eburovic's blade must be hidden first. Show it now to the dark.'

Breaca drew her father's blade from the bear's pelt wrapping. It lay on her hand, bright as a fish in the torchlight. The weave patterns in the metal were seven generations old and the notch on the blade could still clearly be seen from when her great-grandfather had fought the white-headed champion of the Coritani over a boundary dispute. Newer were the welts across the metal made when her father had fought Amminios' men in the battle that had killed him. Breaca had taken the sword from his dead hand and had honed it since, but had never rasped the gouges flat.

Her father had spoken to her by the river in the ancestor's cave, but she had not seen him there. Here, with his blade and his blood in her hand, he became real for her in ways the grave-ghosts could never be.

Breaca? His voice had more body to it than it had done in the cave. *Give my blade to the stones of the past.*

He was not alone. Her ancestors stood behind him: grandfathers and grandmothers, warriors and smiths, hunters and harness-makers, all who had ever held and used the blade with honour crowded in and in until each one of them took up the space in which Eburovic stood. His many-parted voice said, *Show the blade to the dark.*

Airmid had already said that, but it had not been clear what to do. Here, close to the wall, Breaca could see at shoulder height the ledge cut into the stone wall, of a size to hold a war blade of the old style.

As if the ghosts of her lineage lifted her hands, Breaca felt her arms raised and the blade set into the ledge. It fitted, as if to a sheath, and the unstable flame of the torches brought the blade alive. Blue-black metal rippled as water in the light so that, for the first moments of its resting, the feeding she-bear cast in bronze on the pommel seemed to be drinking at a night-time pool.

Breaca had forgotten that she was in company. Behind her, Cunomar gasped aloud. Ardacos, who was older, and had better control of himself, spoke through clenched teeth the first of the hidden names of his god, then, 'I did not know your father was one of us.'

Eburovic was gone, or had become part of the blade and the un-light that now concealed it. Breaca stared at the place it had been and could see neither her father nor the weapon. If she had not placed it herself, she would believe the wall to be of solid stone.

Distantly, she heard herself say, 'Nor did he. The bear was his dream, not his god. But he would have been honoured to hear that you think so.'

An arm brushed Breaca's sleeve. Graine's hand fitted into hers, Graine's voice, full of tides and the echoing ocean said, 'It is safe. The ghosts of the many dead will keep it so until such time as the people have need of it. This is the blade that will raise the tribes and bind them together against those who would crush them. Do not forget it, nor let others do so.'

'I won't.'

It was not enough, but it was as much as Breaca could say. The world was full of fire and shadows and a wren had just died, singing with her daughter's voice. She felt Airmid's hand on her shoulder and, as if through a storm, heard Airmid's calm direction lead the others to place their own blades, and then fold the mail shirts, stolen from Roman cavalry, and hide them in the recesses of the dead. Last was a Roman officer's cloak, taken from a dead man's body and used seven times by Ardacos as a disguise to deceive the enemy.

Cunomar alone had no blade and no armour. With no obvious role to play, he stood in the centre of the mound, watching and listening. Afterwards, when they had hidden the remaining weapons, thanked the ancestors and ridden away, the memory that settled on Breaca was the sense of her son at her left shoulder and the naked hunger with which he had watched her hide his grand-father's blade. He had not spoken, but then he had not needed to; her lineage was his and the ghosts of their joint past knew both of them equally.

What was not clear, and could not be asked, was whether Cunomar had heard Eburovic's voice as the blade had slid home to its hiding place. *If my grandchild ever wields it, know that the death of the Eceni will follow. I trust you to see it does not happen.*

They rode on without blades, at night, slowly, in land that had not been free for nearly fifteen years.

By day, they camped without fires and with two of the four warriors awake on watch. Twice, they moved further into woodland, to avoid Roman patrols; not because the legions might see them, but because the officers' mounts, more wary than the men, might have scented their horses, or Stone.

Soon after they left the ancestors' grave, Breaca gave the leadership of the group to Dubornos, who had travelled in the east most recently. After three nights, he gave it to Airmid, who slept alone on a river bank and then, on waking, lit a fire and piled wet leaves on it until a column of smoke as wide as a man rose thickly white to the sky.

At dusk on the same day, a thinner, darker column, drifting to the south, showed on the easterly horizon.

Airmid said, 'We are expected. Efnís will do what he can.'

Two nights later, guided by smoke, instinct and uncertain dreams, they rode along the bank of a river and followed a track that turned east of north into dense, unmanaged forest. Neither Eceni nor the legions had been here, except perhaps on certain trails which were wider than might be made by deer or bear.

The night was clear and the sky unclouded. The pattern of stars that made the Hare had crested the horizon when they heard the voice of a single man singing the lay of lost souls with a pain that made the loss sound new and raw. Ahead was firelight and a ring of silent, seated figures. Their presence filtered through the trees, like so many hunting hounds, lying in wait.

Because Airmid had brought them this far, it was possible for Breaca to believe that those waiting were not Romans, armed and ready, but the sense of danger was no less. Through his messenger, Efnís had said that the Eceni were weak and that, lacking a leader, they no longer had the will to resist the many terrors of occupation. He had predicted betrayal and death for the Boudica and all who rode with her, should she ever come east. Only the ancestors, already safely dead, had suggested otherwise, and offered a way forward. They had not said what might happen if their path were not open.

Breaca slid from her horse and found Stone waiting. He leaned into her side, shoving his nose in her hand, as he did at those times when danger pressed most closely. She cupped his muzzle in her palm and thumbed his lips, asking for patience and silence. Around her, the others dismounted, except Graine, who sat alone on the roan mare, waiting to be lifted down.

They were her friends, her companions. Two had been her lovers and might be so again. In pride, driven by the visions of ghosts, she had led them this far into danger. Every war-honed instinct said that there was still time to turn round and lead them back.

Dubornos was closest to her. He had stood in the shadow of his own crucifix in Rome. Five years had not healed the scars of his imprisonment.

She said, 'Dubornos—'

'No.' He smiled. She could not see him, there was not enough light for that, but she could hear the lift of it in his voice. A smile from Dubornos was a rare thing indeed. He reached out in the dark and touched her arm.

'Don't think it. We are here because we choose to be and because the gods will it. You are the guide, nothing more.' His other hand lifted towards her. 'We brought you this. There are those gathered here who will not want to accept you. It may help sway them.'

Breaca's fingers fumbled for his and met warm metal. Feeling further, she found that what he offered was a torc: not the relic of her lineage that marked the royal line of her people, but a newer one, made by her father as a gift to Caradoc in the winter of his shipwreck. For five years, it had lain near her bed in the round-house on Mona. She had never taken it with her on the lone hunts in the occupied lands.

It was simpler than that made by the ancestors but the lines were fluidly perfect and he had mixed other metals with a good red gold so that, in torchlight, it matched exactly the colour of Breaca's hair. She knew the feel of it intimately and held it now, warm with the heat of Dubornos' body.

The gaunt singer was close enough now for Breaca to see the whites of his eyes. In all their adult lives, he had never lied to her. She knew of no man with more integrity. He smiled for a second time and she could have wept for the pain in it, and the promise.

Even so, there was still time to turn back.

'Efnís sings for you.' Ardacos spoke from behind her. He was not of Nemain, nor did he dream. With Gwyddhien dead, he could have been Warrior of Mona and led all the warriors of the west, adding his mark to those carved on the roof beams of the great-house, not living as nursemaid to the Boudica's children in a land under thrall to Rome.

As Dubornos had done, he reached for her. The feather he gave her was silver, wrought from unsullied metal. Gunovic had made it, in the year before he died. It marked fifty kills, or five hundred, Breaca had forgotten which and it had never mattered; only children and the newly made warriors counted the crow's feathers that marked their kills. Yet the Eceni, starved of war and its honour, might need such things.

Ardacos said, 'Weave this into your hair and go. They know nothing, only that Efnís has promised them a future. You are all he has to offer.' He gripped her arm above the elbow and clasped her, as close as he came now to an embrace. His touch alone warmed her.

Even so, there was still time.

Ardacos had been her lover once, replacing Airmid, for whom there could be no replacement. Airmid was there now, as she had always been, as she must always be, or life would be unsupportable. She was speaking, saying the same as the others, differently. 'Breaca, don't think of turning back. We have seen what Rome has done to the land we grew up in. We can only imagine what has been done to the people. There is not one of us could live with any honour if we turn back now.'

Even so.

'Mother?' Graine was still mounted on the roan mare. If they hanged her, she would take half a day to die. 'We can't go back now. It's snowing harder than it was. The Roman patrols will see our tracks as soon as it's light.'

She was a child and had never tracked another, nor been tracked, but she had grown on Mona, listening to the best hunters the west had ever seen, and she knew the realities of danger in winter as well as any adult. She spoke the plain truth and changed the nature of the choices.

So.

In the clearing, the singing grew softer. In other worlds and other times, a girl-child with ox-blood hair wept tears of gold while, on a battlefield, the serpent-spear presided over Rome's destruction.

Breaca reached up and lifted her daughter, child of her soul, from the saddle. The five who made the other parts of her heart watched her from the darkness.

With too much formality, because she could not, at that moment, speak otherwise, Breaca said, 'If the dreamers and singers of Mona will join the song to Briga, the children of the royal blood will come to meet their people.'

The deer track led forward into a clearing. Torches made an outer ring, giving off white pine smoke. Above and around hung the unshed autumn leaves of oak and elm; a thousand fillets of bronze caught the torchlight and reflected it back, warmer.

The leaves outnumbered many times those who waited within the trees. Standing with her mother, beyond the wheel of light, Graine could more easily count those within it. They were less than a tenth of the number who had filled the great-house on Mona when the war host of the west had last gathered and a great many of them were old. White hair predominated and the coughing of the winter-touched elderly wheezed over the singer's lay.

Efnís stood in the shadows beyond the circle, still singing. His voice spanned them, a wreath of woven sound. Airmid and Dubornos cut through the trees to join him. Beginning quietly, their voices joined his, rising to Nemain with the resinous smoke. As three, the interweaving melody came closer to what it might have been sung by many throats. Gaining power, it grew to a climax and stopped, suddenly. The silence after was a space that asked to be filled.

It was too late, then, to realize how poorly prepared they were for such a moment. Graine panicked, uselessly, as she felt her mother leave her side. On Mona, addressing the warriors and dreamers of the great-house, the Boudica would have worn a cloak and tunic that had hung since their making over a smouldering fire and knew neither damp nor mould nor insects. In the half-day before, she would have woven the nine-layered warrior's braids into her hair with the gold-banded kill-feathers to honour the ancestors. Her blade would have hung at her belt and her knife would have balanced it and the serpent-spear would have come alive on the hilts of both.

Here, she was at the end of a half-month spent travelling with twice that long hunting alone in the mountains beforehand. Her cloak was creased and stained from travel. Her tunic was edged in drying mud and her boots were sodden with snow-melt. She lacked her blade and her sling hung in its place at her belt. Her knife-handle was of plain wood with no adornment. Her hair bore a single braid and the silver crow's feather was dulled where Ardacos had polished it with the tail of his cloak.

This was the reality; it was not what was seen.

Breaca stepped into the light of the resin torches and a drawn breath sighed around the fullness of the clearing as the gathered warriors, dreamers and elders of the Eceni nation saw their greatest hope, and their deepest fear, made real for the first time in twenty years.

For them, the Boudica was a thing of flame and burnished metals. The red-gold torc was a living serpent about her neck. Her hair was the deep, fired bronze of a fox in winter. Her eyes were copper-green, alight with battles fought and won.

She could have stood like that, Graine thought, for ever. The Eceni elders hovered on the cusp of change, lodged at that meeting of many ways where all paths forward are possible but only one can be taken. Each of them, from oldest to youngest, felt it.

Efnís broke the spell. A single step forward brought him out of the shadows. Like Breaca, he had done what he could to dress for the occasion although his cloak was noticeably faded and the rolled bark of his dreamer's thong was fresh, still damp from the tree. Rome forbade the wearing of the dreamer's thong, as it did the warrior's blade; simply to have made one was to risk the death.

Graine had met Efnís once before on Mona and had liked him. She wanted to ask who had died that had made him sing the lay of lost souls and could not because he was already speaking.

'Breaca, greetings. The high council of the Eceni bids you welcome.'

He gave the salute, neatly. Airmid and Dubornos, coming forward to join him, did the same. It may not have been arranged beforehand, but it had the desired effect. Hesitantly, others around the circle followed. One arm rose after another, stems of winter grass rising in a sluggard breeze, until all three hundred were standing, these old men and women who had survived the purges, the hangings, the betrayals by kin and paid spies, who had gathered the shreds of their courage to meet in secret knowing that their death could be measured in days if they were found.

It was the right thing to do, done with the wrong feeling. Graine shivered and wished the grandmothers would come and tell her what to do to make it right. As if she had spoken aloud, Breaca turned and smiled at her directly, not the private half-smile of the clearing, but a public affirmation. Kneeling, she crooked her finger, calling her daughter into the circle—

—which was madness. Graine, too, had been travelling for half a month and it showed. She was not the Boudica to command the wildfire in the company of strangers. She had neither torc nor silver feather to weave in her hair. The brooch at her shoulder was a plain one in the shape of the wren, which had been Macha's but had been worn so long that the shape of it was unclear. Her hair was not combed and she had never worn a dreamer's brow band. None of this had mattered while she was anonymous in the shadows. It mattered a great deal in the lifetime it took for her to walk from the safe anonymity of the forest into the circle of her mother's arms under the stare of three hundred falsely saluting elders.

The grandmothers may not have spoken, but her mother, it seemed, had miraculously divined what to do. It is difficult to stand on one's dignity in the presence of a child and unmannerly to do so in front of a mother who kneels and ruffles her daughter's hair. As the grass had risen under the breeze, so did the breeze, uncertainly, lay it flat. In ones and twos and greater numbers the elders of the Eceni ceased to salute and sat down again.

Breaca kissed Graine on the brow and, taking her hand, walked to the folded horse hides that formed a seat at the western edge of the circle. Picking one up by the corner, she dragged the pile forward, not quite to the centre, but almost.

To her daughter, with a mother's intimate humour, she said, 'Can you sit on the hides like an elder, do you think?'

Of course. For her mother at that moment, Graine could have

flown to the heights of the sky and sung like a wren. As she had practised with Airmid many times in the small stone hut on Mona, she spread her arms a little so that her cloak fell straight back between her shoulders and, folding her legs beneath her, sat neatly on the hides.

Praying to Airmid more than to Nemain, Graine of the Eceni raised her head to face squarely a gathering of her people's dreamers. Three hundred old men and women looked back. At least half of them were weeping. Breaca stood behind Graine, a hand on each of her daughter's shoulders. When she spoke, it seemed she addressed every one alone.

'This is the first and only daughter of my blood, Graine nic Breaca mac Caradoc. If you are ever to stand and salute, it should be to her. She is the future, the one for whom we have fought these past fourteen years in the west and for whom we will fight now in the east. She was born into war as we were not. We have done what we can to raise her true to her birthright, living daily in the sight of the gods, knowing also that your children have not had that luxury. We come now to join you, to raise her in the land that is her own and to ensure that for her children and yours, that birthright is no longer a luxury. It is for this reason that, with your help, we will fight and defeat Rome.'

The Boudica, speaking thus to the warriors of the west, would not have needed to seek pledges of courage and honour from her listeners. They would have been standing by now, clamouring to be first to give their spear-oaths in the old way, throwing their lives, their souls, their freedom to her cause.

On Mona, there was courage enough and more to spare. Here, manifestly, there was not.

Knowing it, Breaca did not leave a space which might not have been filled. Instead, she signalled behind her, calling forward Cunomar and then Cygfa until they sat in a row before her, a woman and her three children; the Boudica, bringer of victory, and every part of the royal line of the Eceni.

Silence greeted them, and no salutes.

Graine leaned back against her mother, feeling less certain than she had done. In two years, since their return from Gaul, her brother and sister had never sat next to her like this, claiming to be family. Sorcha's children had been her family, and Airmid. She glanced sideways into the night beyond the torches. Stone was there, held by Ardacos. She mouthed a request and had it answered and the great hound stalked forward to her side and she felt whole again.

Breaca stood, facing the gathering. In the lack of words was the heart of her message. *I have brought my family amongst you. I take the same risks that you have taken. You can trust me.*

They were not witless, these old men and women, and they took pride in what was left of their dignity. A sigh rustled through them, barely shifting the air. Graine saw them look away from her mother and turn their attention on one of their own number.

Inevitably, they had already chosen a speaker. She rose, a grey-haired stick of a woman, tall and ascetic, starved by the impositions of life or her own will so that her skin clung to her bones and the joints on her fingers stood out like windgalls on a horse. Her cloak was Mona's grey, ragged from the attentions of rodents and rot. She carried a raven skull in her right hand with the white beak pointing forward as a sixth finger and a single black wing hung at her breast. Of everything she wore, the skull and the wing were the only things that looked truly clean.

'You are well fed, Breaca of the Eceni, and your beautiful children with you.'

She did not smile, but nor did the words sound to Graine as harsh as they might have seemed. Her voice was smoother than a raven's. 'If you had come sooner, when we still had warriors with the will to fight, or were able openly to carry our spears and blades and had not been driven to hiding them beyond reach in places of which even our families know nothing; if you had come with the ten thousand spears of Mona riding behind you to uphold your claim, or sufficient dreamers to breathe heart into the broken-hearted, we would have welcomed you gladly.'

She looked around her peers. Nobody rose to stem the flow of her rhetoric, nor turn aside its obvious course. Tilting her head as a raven does, listening, she continued, 'But you did not come earlier and although you have brought your family, and although we have heard of the deeds of the daughter of Caradoc as she fights alongside the Boudica, it is too little and too late. We are broken and we are not so easily mended.'

The raven beak rose on an outstretched arm and opened wide so that the sound of her voice came from the gaping space between them. It was no longer smooth. Whoever had taught her on Mona could be proud of their pupil.

'Go home, Breaca, once-ruler of the Eceni. We have another ruler now and his power comes from an emperor in Rome who would make of himself a god. There is no place for you here. You will do better to stay in the west and fight. We will honour you and your family. Your dreamer can teach your children the ways of the dreaming to carry down the generations. Ours are lost and there is no redemption.'

The breath caught in Graine's throat and she felt Cunomar shift beside her and then make himself be still. From their earliest childhood they had known that the safeguarding of the children had been the core of their mother's dream. Such a thing is private, not something to be spoken aloud by a stranger in the company of strangers.

If Breaca was shaken, she did not show it. She said, 'And yet you have all come to a gathering within reach of the legions, who might have remained by your house fires in safety.'

The woman lowered the skull pointer. Her voice was no longer the raven's. 'Whatever has befallen us, you are still of our royal line and we are not totally lacking in courage. We do not wish to show you dishonour, but instead to show you who we are, that you may go back whence you came and fight on. We are the example of how it will be under Roman rule. We may be lost but the west need not be, and while Mona stands, there is still hope.'

The woman sat as quickly as she had risen. On Mona, it would have been hard to keep the rest still and silent. In the forest of the east, nobody took to their feet to challenge what she had said.

In the stretching silence, Breaca looked around at the margins of the circle. Because she was closest, Graine could feel the first stirrings of tension that ran through her mother. The outward appearance of calm took more effort than it had done and for one so used to watching, the small signs were there: the whitening of the knuckles on the hand hidden by her cloak and the way she rubbed her thumb across the tips of her fingers once, testing their feel. Breaca was waiting for something and it had not yet happened. When it did, she was expecting to fight.

None of this showed, except perhaps in her voice as she asked, 'Is this the decision of you all?'

She was the Boudica, leader of armies; she could put a sting in a simple question that shamed the best and the least of them.

'No.'

A grizzled man of middle age bearing a beaver pelt across his shoulders rose to his feet. He was broad as a smith but stood unbalanced, as if one hip pained him. 'It was the decision of us all before you came but it need not be now you are here and we have seen who and what you are.' He looked around. 'We may have been broken, but it is not impossible that we mend. If the gods send us the means to do so, how will we face our children and our children's children if we do not take what has been offered? The royal line of the Eceni stretches unbroken back to the ancestors. Would we few be the ones to break it now? I take back the word I gave to Lanis of the Crows. Speaking for myself and those of my people whose trust I carry, I say that the Boudica should stay and we should re-arm, that we should unearth our blades and pull our spears from the thatch and make shields that will withstand the stabbing swords of the legions and we should fight, or be proud to die doing so.'

He had been a warrior once, his whole bearing showed it. Graine wanted to hug him. She smiled instead and was glad when he saw her and smiled back. He was respected by the others. It showed in the numbers nodding. Another rose, a woman, younger than the first. 'The northerner is right,' she said. 'The royal line is the creation of the gods. It is not for us to break it now.'

Like fire in autumn grass, agreement crept outward. Here and there, dampening it, was dissent. In places, pools of men and women argued fiercely against the Boudica's return. Almost all of these bore scars and, deeper, the dullness of constant pain that said they had lost to Rome those who mattered most, and feared to lose more.

The gathering took on the animation Graine was used to, gaining volume and stridency as measured arguments gave way to unplanned hope, or drowned in fear. One by one, dreamers and warriors rose to support one or other of the first two speakers. They were not used, any longer, to the courtesies of a council. As the night deepened and those waiting to speak became more tired and less patient, order and discipline collapsed. Men and women stood in clusters and shouted at Breaca and each other, or simply shouted, trying to be heard.

At the height of the tumult, Graine saw a lean, red-headed man, balding in front with a scar across the bridge of his nose, as of a sword cut taken in battle, jump onto a fallen log near the edge of the circle. His voice had once crested the tumult of war and did so again.

'You cannot stay! You *must* not. You will take three days dying when the legions get word that the Boudica is here, and when they come to take you, they will not rest with only your deaths. They will walk through us like wolves through unguarded sheep and our children will bleed their lives out on our thresholds. It was madness even to come this far. How did you ever think you could stay?'

His last words fell into quiet. Even in this place, he had over-stepped the mark. He stood swaying on the fallen log, his resentment bright around him, and looked to either side for support, which he was not given. Even those who had argued with him stared at the ground and did not speak.

The Boudica had remained standing throughout, outwardly listening with care to the arguments on both sides. Graine, watching with growing fear, saw that by far the greater part of her mother's attention was directed past the circle to the forest. The waiting made Breaca's hand rigid at her side in the place where her blade should have been, but was not.

She was drawing breath to speak when, from the night beyond the torches, a new voice said, 'She could stay as my wife. Rome need never know who she is.'

The void into which this fell stank suddenly of bowel-wrenching terror.

The man who stepped between two sputtering torches was not as tall as Luain mac Calma, but taller than most. His hair was like straw in colour and texture and had been cut in the Roman fashion so that it barely reached his shoulders.

When she could look past that, and the naked hunger in his eyes, Graine saw that his right arm stopped at the elbow and that the sleeves of his tunic were especially long to cover it. Thus, sickeningly, she knew who he was: 'Tagos, who called himself

Prasutagos to carry more weight with the governor, the damaged warrior who had treated Silla as a brood mare, getting child after sickly child on her until she died leaving no living children; the self-styled 'king of the Eceni' who had thrown in his lot with the Emperor Claudius and then Nero. If Efnís' messenger was right, this was a man who would see them all dead in the worst possible ways.

Belatedly, Graine thought to glance up at her mother. Breaca stood quite still. The tensions of earlier were gone. The waiting was over. She seemed, if anything, to be gathering herself in the way other warriors did before battle but she had never needed to do.

'Do you come with Rome's legions behind you?' she asked, quietly.

'No.'

'Tagos frowned, sharply. All his movements were too fast, too sharp. He did not take the time to think or to ask the gods before he acted. Graine was ashamed for him that it was so.

He said, 'I am sorry that you would think it of me. I come with an answer to conflict. I have listened to the elders of our people in their discord. They could argue through the night and three nights after and be no closer to a resolution. Half of them want you here to keep the royal line unbroken, half are afraid that the arrival of the Boudica will draw down the vengeance of Rome on them and their kin. Whichever side prevails, the other half will hate them. The Eceni nation, already broken, will be further split. We cannot afford such a rift and I would not wish to rule over a people so divided. I offer a way for you and your family to live in safety under the eyes of the governor without his knowing who you are. And I bring you this . . .'

All eyes were on him. With the skill of a trained singer, he drew out from under his maimed arm a torc of age-worn gold, woven in the old style of many-threaded wires. It looked a small thing compared to the red-gold worn by the Boudica but in a gathering of dreamers, it drew their attention as a haunch of bloody meat would draw a pack of hounds.

On the side nearest Graine, away from Prasutagos, Breaca's hand clenched and unclenched, once. 'You would offer me the torc of my mother?' Her voice was rough, like rock. Stone turned his head at the sound of it, rigidly.

'No. I offer it to the one who can be seen to bear it and not die as a result.'

The man who had eaten and drunk as a guest of Rome walked forward. Cygfa stood nearest him. She flinched at his approach but did not back away. When he raised his arms over her head and dropped them behind her neck, her hand moved to her belt-knife. When he drew the circle of gold forward so that the two open ends lay in a pool of warm light on her collarbones, she relaxed and her arm fell to her side, forgotten. It was said no-one could wear the torc of the Eceni and feel themselves anything but royal. Cygfa was no more immune than Silla had been, however foreign her breeding. She smiled, and was dazzling.

'Tagos stepped back. To Breaca, he said, 'If you took the torc, and with it the leadership, the new governor would ask questions that we do not wish anyone to answer. Under Roman law, your daughters become mine on the day that you become my wife. I offer the torc, therefore, to Cygfa, who is your daughter in name, to hold until Graine, who is of the blood, comes of age. If we have daughters, they will come after her in line of inheritance. On my death, rule will pass to whichever of them is best able to hold it.'

'And until then?' They could have been alone, just Breaca and 'Tagos. They spoke as if they had known each other lifetimes and never lived apart.

'Until then, I rule as Rome would have me rule, with Breaca of the Eceni as my wife. They will accept you as Silla's replacement. Women are of little account in their eyes and they would not be so discourteous as to question a king's choice of woman.'

'How long before a member of your household betrays us?'

'Tagos shrugged. 'I would say never but if I am wrong, I will die with you. The governor will not be inclined to leniency if he believes himself to have been betrayed. Those who have prospered under my rule would become destitute with my death. Those who hate me will put their hope in you, and your survival will be their deepest concern.' He smiled. 'A man would have to hate us both very deeply, and have no care for his people, to choose such a course of action, and whereas there are many who hate me and some who will fear your presence, I cannot think of a single one who would willingly draw on the Eceni such bloodshed. While we both live, we are safe. This is our guarantee to each other.'

He waited. They all waited. Graine watched the sudden relaxation of her mother's hand. Neither her face nor her bearing had changed, but the battle for which Breaca had been girding herself was over, and she had not lost.

VIII

'DID YOU THINK SHE WOULD MAKE THEM SEND YOU HOME?'
'Tagos, sister's son to Sinochos, closed but did not bar the door to his bedchamber. It was not a large room and a scattering of stoneware lamps made the dark spaces darker and did little to light the rest. They had been lit before 'Tagos – *Prasutagos*, she really must remember that – had opened the door and ushered Breaca in. This fact alone meant that there were servants who had known he was going to the gathering and that he would be back before dawn and would wish his cold, damp hut within a hut lit for his guest.

He called the hut a palace, after the Roman fashion, and found pride in it, not shame. True to the ancestor's vision, there was no roundhouse in Prasutagos' fiefdom, although this one had not been broken apart for firewood, but for political gain. As did the Romans, each family lived separately in the steading that was the centre of the 'King's' power. Already, others were settling into the rooms on either side. Breaca heard 'Gaius' and 'Titus', 'Tagos' two bodyguards who had taken on Roman names, and had introduced themselves, grinning. She did not hear her children, nor Airmid.

'Lanis,' asked 'Tagos a second time. His colour was high. He was not accustomed to being ignored. 'Did you think she would send you back to Mona with your honour intact and your dignity undented?'

He had changed so much. Her abiding memory of him was of a reckless, eager youth, running at her heels like a sapling hound, desperate in his enthusiasm and yet lacking the courage to act. Later, she remembered him lying wounded after the battle against Amminios nursing an arm broken beyond mending, but her father had died in the same battle and she had taken little notice of 'Tagos. She had held him while Airmid had cut away the dead portion of his arm but he had been delirious and she thought he would not remember it. Later still, he had ruined his honour trying to fight in a battle for which he was not fit. Good warriors had died in his defence. Breaca remembered their names and their families and, standing within the pooled pallor of his lamps, she saw reflected in his eyes the moment when the memory showed on her face.

He was about to ask his question a third time, and was not happy about having to do so. His temper had never been certain even before he lost his arm. After it, he had become prone to sudden violence. She had not forgotten that about him. To fight here and now would help no-one.

She said, 'It was always possible Lanis might have sent us home. She was trained by Airmid and has travelled to Mona since and she carries herself before the gods with as much integrity as any dreamer I have known. Her passion, her driving care, is for the welfare of the people. If she thought the danger of my being here outweighed the good, she would have seen to it that the gathering sent us back, whatever you and I decided.'

He had believed that. She had seen the panic in his face. Now, feigning calm, he asked, 'And would you have gone?'

'Of course. If I am here, it is with the aid of the dreamers or not at all.'

That much was true. Her only lie was that, walking into the circle, she had doubted the outcome. She had not believed she would be turned away; too much had been sacrificed by others to see her this far. She had seen the understanding of that in Lanis' eyes before the dreamer had risen to speak, and the pity that followed. Neither of them expected the path forward to be easy but it was unthinkable to turn aside. The challenge now was to learn to live in this travesty of a half-Roman village, with this man, among the remnants of her people. Nothing was impossible.

'Would you like wine?'

'Tagos hovered at her side. The beaker in his hand was glazed a deep red. He placed it with precision on the lid of an oak chest that it might sit level and not tip while he poured the wine one-handed. Everything about the act was almost, but not quite, Roman, like the setting in which he stood.

The wall behind him was plastered but the image painted on it in Eceni blue was of a running mare that had been old long before Rome became a city. Beneath it, on the lid of the chest, a constellation of silver coins winked with the brilliance of fresh casting.

Breaca lifted one and read the word: *Ecen*. Others in the same pile showed the head of boy-emperor Nero in profile, a portly youth with an excess of chins.

'Not the most beautiful of men, but by far the most powerful. It pays to be his friend. He grants great wealth to those in his favour, as his uncle did before him.'

'Tagos stood just behind her. The smell of the wine on his breath mixed with the other smells of him: the faint sourness of milk and cheese that had been turning her stomach since the door-flap closed.

Sifting the coins through her fingers, she said, 'Does it pay the people that you have Roman wealth? Can their children grind silver to make bread when the winter corn runs scarce? I hear the legions claim all the produce of the fields for their own and the people starve for lack of what they themselves have grown.'

'Tagos' mind was on other things. Breaca saw him pull up short and force himself to think. He said, 'The people may not eat silver, but it can be used to buy corn when we need it.'

'Eceni corn, grown in Eceni fields, bought back at a higher price than they paid for it.' She was angry, when she had promised herself she would not be. She played with the silver and made herself calm.

'Tagos said, 'Of course, the governor must be seen to make a profit. He must pay his army and his staff and still send money back to the emperor. As must we. See . . .' With his one hand, he swept the chiming silver from the chest and opened the lid. Beneath, lambent in the torchlight, was a fortune in unused, undulled coins. The chest was only half full but none the less, if one

101

counted one's wealth in silver, Prasutagos was an exceedingly wealthy man.

Breaca rinsed her hands in coins, watching the faces fall. The name of her people did not appear on these, nor the running mare. Claudius was there and Tiberius and the mad Gaius. Once, she saw Augustus. All of Rome was there, forming the riches of the Eceni.

'You take the gift of Roman coin?' she asked.

The man to whom she was now bound stared at her a long moment, forgetting the wine and the bed in the corner. In that look, she thought she saw the beginnings of the real 'Tagos, who was neither the diplomat nor the over-eager youth, but the one-armed man who had fought and lost too many battles and was not prepared to lose one more.

His nostrils pinched and the skin blotched on his face. Almost silently, he said, 'Not a gift. Never that. Seneca does not give gifts. I have accepted a *loan* of ten million sesterces on which I pay one tenth per annum interest. From the rest, I pay taxes and bribes, buy grain in winter and grazing rights in summer, buy gifts for the governor and his wife that they might believe themselves flattered by royalty. I set up trading routes by sea and land and am permitted to tax those who bring us the wine and olives and figs that allow us to appear more Roman.'

On the word, a wall-lamp guttered and went out. It had been filled with sheep's fat, made liquid with other oils. Lacking Efnís' pine resins, the smoke that rose from the wick was black and stank of late-season rams.

The gods pass comment in many ways. 'Tagos stopped and stared and then, defensively, 'I do this because these are *my* people, in *my* care and I would not see them reduced to the abject servitude of the Trinovantes. Rome respects two things: force of arms, and wealth. If we do not have the first – which manifestly we do not, and never will have, whatever you may think – then we must have the second or become less than cattle.' He paused a moment, thinking, then turned on his heel. 'If you are to stay here, there are things you must understand. Watch and learn.'

He walked past her, slamming open three other chests that stood against the wall opposite the bed. Trinkets that had sat atop them fell to the floor and broke or scattered: a small green bowl with a gilded rim, a horse made by a child in rough clay, a long-handled comb with an angular pattern painted in blue on the handle.

Ignoring them, he said, 'Nero is a child, he has no more control of Rome than I do. But two men rule through him and of those, Seneca is the one who has wealth to spare. He uses it to create greater riches. This' – he hurled the first of the chests on its side – 'was once full. And this. And this.'

Out of eight chests, three lay on their sides, empty. 'Tagos stood at the very edge of the lamplight, shaking as if in battle. His empty sleeve had come unpinned and he pushed it back over the stump of his arm. The flesh was purpled where Airmid had sewn it over the stump of the bone. Above, the skin was the colour of any man's arm, but pale for lack of sunlight.

He said, 'Breaca, we were not all able to run west and become heroes. Every night for fourteen years I have dreamed that Amminios' man did not strike my arm, or that I moved away, or that I raised my blade to block his and so was left whole to fight with you at the invasion battle. I have dreamed that we defeated Rome together, or that I was with you when you led the children and the warriors of Mona west to continue the fight. In my dream, we stand together and Rome is pushed back into the Ocean to be swallowed for ever and not return. Then I wake, and I am not whole and the legions have not drowned and my people are dying of hunger, of disease, of the punishment inflicted by the legions who will inflict reprisals on us for the damage done them by tribes they cannot reach in the west.'

She should pity him, and could not. She said, 'You are saying that you trade now as a Roman, and that I should not despise you for it.'

'Yes! In Briga's name, yes! The children must *eat*, Breaca. This is the reality and you cannot change it. You think you can ride in and raise your standard and the warriors will gather at your call and, come spring, you can lead them in glorious defeat of Rome. It is not like that, never will be. Live here one winter and you will see why there are no warriors left who could gather to your standard, why all of the people, men and women, are broken: they are too hungry because five-tenths of their corn has been paid in tax and they have lived for days drinking snow-melt so that they might feed the children. Your children will not die this winter because I have taken coin from Seneca and I use it to feed those whose lives depend on my protection. This is my battle and my way to fight it. You will learn it also. If you would teach Graine to lead as befits her blood, this is what you will teach her. There will be no army, Breaca, the Eceni do not have the heart for it. Do you understand that?'

'No. But I understand that you believe it.' Breaca rose. She looked at each of the three overturned chests. Not a single coin lay in the bottom of any. She became aware, suddenly, that she had not eaten since daybreak and that her stomach had long since turned in on itself, grinding. 'What will happen when Seneca calls in his loan and you are unable to repay it?' she asked.

'I am not unable to repay it. I have made more than there was here in trade and taxes of my own. It's not all here and it's in Eceni coin but silver is silver and he won't argue.' He grinned, thinly. 'But if, by chance, I were to become impoverished and be unable to pay, then, naturally, he is entitled to take goods to the full amount; gold, corn, horses, hounds . . .'

'Slaves?' Cold curled in her chest. *Shall I show you, Breaca of the Eceni, what it is for a people to bleed until there is nothing more to give?*

Misreading her concern, 'Tagos said, 'Of course, slaves. But not members of the royal household. They are careful of that. Those whose claim to royalty relies on the thinnest of blood ties and officially sanctioned incest are strangely respecting of those whose claim is genuine and goes back through uncounted generations. Whatever happens, they will not take you or your children. Even Cygfa who is yours in name only is safe. They will take whomsoever else they feel will fetch a price at market.'

'You would allow this?'

'I have no power to stop them, Breaca. I am a king because they choose to call me such. If they wish to name another in my place, I cannot stop them.'

'And if we cease to be royalty, then our family is no longer safe.'

'Exactly so.'

It was hard, then, to set aside the vision of a slave pen. Graine's tears were not of gold, but blood, and they made of her face a battlefield.

A bed lay along one wall, covered in dyed sheep skins and, underneath, a whole horse hide. Breaca sat on the edge of it and stared at the backs of her hands until she could see them clearly through the image of her daughter.

'Tagos smiled, a little sadly. 'The Romans don't want war in the east,' he said. 'Your battles in the west have achieved that much. To keep peace, they will not provoke us. To keep our lives, we will not provoke them. It is not something one dreams of, but it is enough.'

He offered her this as if it were a gift, his accolade for what she had been. The strength of it, or the power of the wine, pushed him past the invisible shield that surrounded her. Coming close, he ran his fingers down the length of her arm. Her control of her body was less than that of her mind. The skin of her forearm rose in gooseflesh behind him.

He leaned down and kissed her brow. 'I do think you should have some wine.' He poured and set the beaker on the floor beside her. She ignored it.

With his fingers stroking the back of her neck, he said, 'You have not asked how your family will sleep.'

'I don't have to.'

The torches were guttering. One by one their oil failed and they sent spider-threads of smoke to the ceiling. Breaca closed her eyes. It was nearly dawn and the spear wound in her arm ached and she was as tired as if she had been fighting all day, and she wanted water, or ale, not wine.

'Tagos' thumb circled over and over on her neck. There was a reasonable chance she was going to be sick, which would be too humiliating. Reality weighed on her after the days of living by the ancestor's words and he was right, it was not in any way as she had imagined. To ride into battle was far, far easier.

There were things yet to be said, boundaries to be set so that they might both know them.

'We have an agreement,' she said, wearily. 'We should be clear of the terms. You have stated yours: I will be your wife in all things and will support you in your rule of the Eceni. My terms are equally certain. If my children, or Airmid, or any of those sworn to me is harmed, if either of the women is touched against her will, you will lose me and your hope of rule over the Eceni. Our people may not be prepared to fight, but they are not the sheep you make them out to be and they do not have to accept your rule. The royal line has always been a link between people and the gods. You break that link at your peril.'

'Obviously.' 'Tagos did not like to be patronized. His hand left her neck. She breathed deeply.

'Is that all?' he asked.

'No. One other thing. We will have no children.'

'What?' His control broke at last. 'You have sworn before the elder council—'

'—to be your wife in all things. I am fully aware of what I have said and what it means. I have not, however, sworn that I was capable of bearing children. I am not, or so Airmid believes. To know the detail, you would have to ask her but I understand that Graine's birth caused scarring that cannot be mended.'

He stared at her, only half hearing. He was breathing too fast and the pits of his eyes were wide. 'And is that all?'

'It is.'

'Good.' With that word, they reached the moment she had accepted as the best possible option in a cave on the side of a mountain. It was neither as good nor as appalling as she had expected.

He stood in the last light of the torches and she watched him begin to remove his tunic one-handed. He had a lifetime of practice and was as deft as any whole man. The stump of his arm, revealed, was a mess of scar tissue. He stood very still, awaiting comment. He was not lacking courage; his eyes remained on hers in the silence. She had seen worse on a hundred battlefields and said nothing. Nodding, he shed the undertunic and the belt that held it.

He was so close to what he wanted. He sat on the edge of the bed and his hand moved unbidden to her waist. He kissed her hand and then her arm and then her neck. His voice, muffled by the pulse of her throat, said, 'I may not have children, but I have my life and I will keep it. Know now that if I am harmed, if I die, if your dreamers, in fact, do not work their hardest to keep me in health and long life, those of my men who have taken Roman names will see to it that the ones you care for most suffer hardest in the retribution that will fall. Are we clear on that, my *wife*?'

He used the Roman, *uxor*, there being no equivalent in any language of any tribe. Twenty years of waiting sank into the word.

'Quite clear.'

'Excellent. In that case, we should celebrate, you and I. If you won't drink wine, there are other ways to seal a bargain. It has been a long time since Caradoc was taken. You must hunger almost as much as I do.'

He was naked and required her to be also. He was not such a child and did his best to be attentive. She lay in the lamp-fouled darkness and thought of Caradoc first, then Airmid and Graine, Cygfa and Cunomar and last, inevitably, because she was home, of Bán.

II

SPRING AD 58

IX

'BELLOS? BELLOS, WAKE UP.'

The boy lay still, with his white face crushed into black peat and both arms thrown out, embracing the earth. Valerius knelt at his side and struggled to clear his mind of the night's dream.

It took longer than it should have done. The dream clung tightly so that, even as he felt the fluttering pulse and lifted the boy's slack lids, the greater part of Valerius still rode the red mare's foal in the heart of battle. As Airmid had predicted, the dream-colt was black with a shield and slanting spear in white splashed across its forehead. Grown to adulthood, it carried its rider with all the passion of the Crow-horse, that had been lost to the legions.

For a man whose life had been given to battle, it was a dream to revel in, bittersweet with the urgency of action and the knife-edge of hope that lingered long after waking. Airmid had always been the most careful of dreamers; if only half of her promise came true and the foal grew to be the barest shadow of the Crow-horse, Valerius believed his life would be the richer for it.

That hope seemed less certain now. Pulled unwilling from the clamour and noise of dream battles, Valerius had staggered out into the mild night and across the foaling paddock behind the smithy to find another kind of carnage, less readily resolved.

There, beneath an oak tree, in a mess of wounded turf, the red mare that had been mac Calma's gift lay stretched flat, shuddering. There was no foal at her side, nor any sign of one emerging, but the honey-salt smell of birth waters was all about, and the mare groaned the deep belly-groan of a mother who has given everything to push out her infant and has failed in the trying.

All this Valerius understood as he crossed the paddock. Coming closer, he had found Bellos lying near her hind feet and the black stain of peat on the white blond of his hair showed where one hoof had caught him squarely and hard behind the left temple.

It was dark and Valerius had brought no flame. He had already lifted the boy's head and pinched his cheek and spoken his name twice before he noticed the dribble of blood coming from his nose and the other, finer, thread at his ear.

He froze and his mind froze with him.

'Bellos?'

Valerius smoothed the hair from the boy's lifeless face, tucking it in behind his ears in a way he would never have dared do if he were awake. Six years in each other's company had not broken the barrier of formality that had been raised in the first days of their meeting when Valerius had still lived for the legions and Bellos had been the boy whore bought, not out of pity, or love, or even to use, but in the hope that he might keep one of the more persistent ghosts at bay.

The understanding that he had won his freedom for who he was not had damaged Bellos' pride even in their first days together in Gaul as he had clung to Valerius for safety in the face of the legions and the malign power of the ocean. His growth to adulthood, so clear this last winter, had sharpened, not lessened, the hurt.

For his part, Valerius had never known what to say and so had said nothing. In half a decade, they had not spoken of love, or its lack. Only the red cavalry mare, with her clear care for the boy and none at all for the man, had come to embody the wall between them and opened the wounds again.

The red cavalry mare, who was dying.

She stank of fear and defeat and the iron-blood of a battlefield death. Her breath came in great heaving gasps that shook the earth around her, and perhaps the whole land, from one ocean coast to the next, so that all of Hibernia and Mona beyond would know that the horse for whom the Elder, Luain mac Calma, had paid a year's wages in gold to a duplicarius of the Batavian cavalry, had twisted her womb at the start of birthing, and would be dead by dawn, taking her unborn foal with her.

It was twenty years since Valerius had last seen a twist. His life had been simpler then, so that the most upsetting moment of his young life was when his mother, Macha, had taken her wedge-pointed lump hammer to the head of a foaling mare, striking between the eyes to free her from life and pain together. Even as the mare had slipped into death, Macha had sliced open the heaving belly and released her foal, dragging it into daylight, sluggish but living, to feed and thrive on another mare. The filly born that day had grown to be dam to the Boudica's grey battle mare, and the boy who grew to be Valerius had come to accept that his mother had been right.

The adult Valerius had used his own hammer on horses and on men, releasing each from life that had become intolerable. There would be no effort in doing so again now and, knowing the mare, he did not believe her soul would wait for him as others did in the lands of the dead, seeking vengeance for a life cut short without cause.

Bellos, though, would certainly do so. His care for the mare had grown through the dark months of winter, the quiet romance of two strangers marooned without their consent on a foreign land. He had some facility for healing; given time and tuition, he might grow to that as a profession. In all probability, he had believed his friend would recognize him and would still her struggles as he lay in the peat behind her, striving to draw out her foal. For a boy raised in a brothel, he had a long way to go in learning the nature of pain and of love and how the first can override the second.

Valerius moved his hand down and checked again the erratic patter of life at Bellos' throat. In the clouded mess of his thinking, another fact became clear to him.

'If I kill her now, what will you live for, child? Would you return to life only for me? I don't think so.'

The understanding of that hurt more than he had imagined. Smoothing the same errant strand of hair, Valerius said, 'Bellos, if you're listening, I'll do what I can to keep your mare alive. If she dies, it will not be for want of trying.'

With the decision made, Valerius worked efficiently. If he were to attempt the impossible, Bellos had to be made safe first. The boy weighed more than it seemed from the slightness of his build, but it was easy enough to carry him into the single room of the smith's bothy and lay him in bed with warmed stones around, wrapped in wool. He could not drink of his own will, but could be made to swallow mashed infusions of comfrey and plantain, boiled and cooled and kept in a stone jug for women too spent to eat after childbirth.

The mare had not moved when Valerius returned; she lay shuddering as she had since he first found her. Bellos could not hear him with waking ears, but there was no harm in talking to him as if he might listen from some other place. Conscious of a presence looking over his shoulder, Valerius said, 'Watch now, and learn. We may save both of them yet.'

It was not easy work. He should have had two others to help, to turn the mare one way as he turned the womb the other. He considered walking down to the steading to wake one of the quiet, stolid women who knew as much of birthing as he had ever done. For Bellos, he would have sacrificed his pride, but the walk down and the waking and the walk back would have taken until morning and he did not believe the mare would live to see the dawn. Alone, then, Valerius fought and sweated and cursed and it was no different from being in battle, except that the mare was not actively trying to kill him, but only groaning in her turn, and straining to give birth to a foal which had no clear passage to freedom.

'Please . . . turn with me now . . . just . . . turn.'

The mare heaved and kicked, striking backwards with both feet. The crush of her haunches drove Valerius' face into the sodden peat. His arm burned and chilled and burned again and an old wound at his shoulder screamed fresh pain. He braced his elbows against the earth and pushed with outstretched fingers and, finally, magically, the foal hovered on the brink of turning, then fell sluggishly over, opening the neck of the womb.

'Thank you . . . thank you. Wait now, it's not over yet. Let me think. Just give me time to think.'

He lay flat on the peat, heaving in air as the mare had done. He was weeping for no better reason than relief and an end to exertion. He wanted Bellos to know what he had achieved and what was yet to be done but could find no way to tell him. The boy had not returned miraculously to life, but equally, when Valerius ran up to the bothy to check, he had not yet left it.

Returning, Valerius lay down once again. He patted the mare gently on the rump and spoke as he would have done to a birthing woman, with only the barest of lies. 'That's the worst of it over. Let me feel how the foal's set and we'll bring him out and you can rest.'

The foal: the white on black phantom that had stormed into his dreams one day in autumn and had come to inhabit them to the exclusion of everything else. Luain mac Calma, elder dreamer of Mona, had sown the seed with casual ease and it was hard not to believe the act deliberate. *Airmid believes it will be a colt, black and white with a shield and a spear on its forehead.*

Valerius had denied him, saying, *That dream is long dead.* At the time, he had believed it. The truth had become apparent only later that night, and then other nights and then all nights and into the days so that he had to fight to keep his mind clear for the forging or the healing or the leatherwork or the simple making of meals for himself and a Belgic ex-slave-boy who had fallen in love with an aged cavalry mare and did not give more than a passing thought to the foal that she carried.

Bellos' dreams were not Valerius' dreams and the man had not explained to the boy the nature of the first true dream of his childhood in which he had ridden a black horse with a shield and spear in white on its forehead in a battle that defined the fate of his sister. Equally, they had not discussed the return of the dream with Luain mac Calma's gift of the mare and the hopes that arose from it, too deeply hidden for Valerius to name.

Until now, when the foal, so long crushed in the womb, stretched a foot to Valerius' searching hand and then, as if to prove itself alive, reached its muzzle forward and sucked on his finger.

It had been so long since he had been alone with a foaling mare, he had forgotten what it was to have new life at his fingertips, seeking to set itself on the earth. The foal nudged and nuzzled again and, with that small plea, that promise and prayer of later life, Valerius, who had thought himself immune to love, felt it again, with all the astonishing, annihilating force of the past.

As they had done in his youth, the doors to his heart fell open, so that the cold night became sharper, and the colours of the dark more dense. Weeping, he reached forward again, no longer tired, and Bellos was only a small reason for bringing the foal to safety.

There had never been any chance that the birth would be easy, but he had not imagined it impossible.

Through the darkness and into dawn, Valerius fought as he had only rarely fought before, for life instead of death. He could not have named the point when retreat became inevitable, nor the far later moment when he accepted it and stopped trying to proceed. The mare was spent and lay as if dead, with only the rise and fall of her breathing to show otherwise. The foal had long since stopped nursing at his fingers. He had felt its heart, once, in trying to draw forward a leg, but even that, it seemed, had faded.

Valerius sat back on his heels and tried to think. The mare was black down one side with peat, and lay quite still; to shudder required more effort than she could muster. The foal, if not dead, was close to it. In the recesses of his mind, Valerius heard his mother speak the invocation to Briga that precedes a death and watched as she lay on her side with a blade in one hand of a sharpness that could slice through rawhide, and cut the leg of a dead foal away from its body, and then the head and perhaps another leg, allowing the now-dead beast to be drawn out in small parts and the mare to live.

Valerius had foaled mares on his own for twenty years and had never yet needed to cut up the foal to bring it out. With his mind held carefully blank and his heart closed, he walked the short distance to the forge and back again and the knife that he held was as sharp as his mother's had ever been.

Later, when the foal had been given in pieces to the crows, he returned with warmed water and some herbs and set about bringing the red mare back to life. Such a thing was not beyond him and the vengeful gods, who could give a man a reason to love and then remove it, did not see fit to include the mare in their retribution.

Near noon, with the mare dried and sitting upright, with oat straw packed along her flanks to hold her square, Valerius returned to the bothy and built up the fire until the room was as warm as it ever was and set about preparing a broth that an unconscious boy could swallow.

At no time did he allow himself to think of the crow-given carcass, which had been a colt, nor of the prophecy, spoken correctly, that it would be black and white with a shield and a spear on its forehead.

Airmid had always been the most careful of dreamers. She had never promised that the foal she so accurately described would be born alive.

The mare thrived on warm mashes and attention through day and night. She came to recognize Valerius, and welcome his ministrations. On the second day after her failed birthing, she rose to her feet and, free of the burden of the foal, walked across the paddock and out through the open gate to the bothy's door. Bellos still lay unconscious inside, but there was a change to his colour afterwards.

Thereafter, the mare ate the good hay that Valerius bought for her and drank the warmed water with the finger's dip of honey and infusions of burdock and valerian. Given the freedom of the holding, she spent her time standing at the door to the bothy, blocking the sunlight and upsetting the hens that scratched dust baths on the threshold.

Bellos did not thrive. Three days after the foaling, when the boy showed no more signs of waking than he had done on the first night, Valerius admitted his own limits and walked down to the small coastal settlement that he had very carefully not made his home. There, he found the extent to which the strange, dark smith on the hill, with his strange, blond boy, had become a valued thread in the fabric of life.

Valerius had implied once that the Hibernians were all large and uncouth and that Bellos was not safe in their company. As with all falsehoods, the phantom of truth lay at its heart, but it was not the men or women of the settlement who wished ill on the boy. Any threat, if it existed at all, came from the seafarers who used the sheltered bay and clear springs as a port for clean water and bought meat and ale and were not always reliably sober, or safe.

Those with whom Valerius traded were not all tall and red-headed and none were uncouth. They had not come near his forge, nor offered help without its being asked, but still word had passed amongst them of the mare's bad foaling and the kick to Bellos' head. Their only question had been whether the smith had the skills to heal the boy and, if not, how long it might be before he must go for help, and where he might choose to seek it.

Opinion had been divided, but the weight of the betting said that he would go to Mona, to the lean dreamer who had brought the mare, rather than the Hibernian elders who held court around the hill of Tara. There was a deal of satisfaction amongst those who mattered most when the former view was found to be correct.

They were not direct people and Valerius' conversation drifted, as courtesy demanded, to the welfare of those whom he had helped or healed or armed and clothed, and in the course of this it became apparent that there was a cart he might have that was newly covered with hides to keep the boy dry and that a newly gelded carthorse was fit and good for the journey and that there were hard-rinded goat's cheeses already packed in the oat straw that would both keep the boy warm and feed the horse, and that a quantity of dried fish and mutton and fresh eggs and pitchers of water had been packed elsewhere, because it had been found early that the smith, contrary to all appearances, drank neither the wine of the Latins nor the more wholesome ale of the tribes.

Last, because they really did value him and wished to see him return, a wiry, dark-haired girl gave him a small pot sealed with wax, with a bee inscribed on the flat surface. Honey was not common on the wild coast of Hibernia and what little was found was kept for healing, being worth rather more than its equivalent weight in gold.

Touched beyond telling, Valerius gave care of his forge to the same wiry, dark-haired girl who had shown some facility for both metalwork and healing. He gave his good riding horse to her father, who had recently re-covered his cart with the hides of three cattle. He gave his supplies of dried leaves, tree barks and roots to the midwife and free use of his bothy to whomsoever amongst them might find need of it.

Mounted on the cart and moving, with Bellos packed in straw as tightly as the eggs and pitchers behind, Valerius promised to return with all speed to those who had become his people. In the moment of speaking, he believed it.

Bellos continued to sleep. Through four days of rutted travel, Valerius came to understand the limits of the amiable bay cob who drew his cart. The red mare, originally tied to the cart's tail, followed the command of Valerius' voice and, after a while, proved that she did not need to be tethered. Twice she led the way across spring-full streams when the gelding balked at the torrents. The cart proved sturdier than it looked and the wheels more strongly bound.

Valerius passed through hills heading north, and then at a certain way-stone, remembered from past journeys, turned due east towards the sea. The track here lacked the strong curved surface of a Roman road, but it was solid and wide enough for two carts. White stones marked the waysides so that, as evening fell and the light waned, it might have been possible to push on through the night to the port.

Valerius had planned to do exactly that, but the scent of salt sea air met the sharper acid of the peat bogs and he remembered, with nauseating certainty, exactly how much he hated ocean travel. Without giving the matter much thought, he turned the bay cob to the side and pushed it out beyond the track to a flat, hard patch of ground where the burned-out embers of others' fires and a small stack of firewood neatly cut said that the land and its people were hospitable.

The hides covering the cart could, at need, be stretched out beyond the tailgate. Supported on new-cut staves, they offered a measure of shelter from the persistent Hibernian rain. Valerius hobbled and watered the two horses, then lit a fire for the night just beyond the overhang of the hides.

It was far easier than it had been to lift Bellos down from the cart; no broth, however nourishing, can keep weight on a growing youth. Laid out straight on woollen cloaks, with straw padding beneath, he could easily have been newly dead after a long illness.

His hair was no longer the bright white-blond of the Belgae, but lankly dark, so that it hung about his face like wet straw. His limbs were thin sticks with folds of skin and angry bruises at elbows, hips and shoulders where his own weight had pressed on the shrinking flesh and made it bleed. In the last two days, the broth had come through as a thin, rancid scour that leaked from his guts as thinly as urine and scalded any skin left unsalved.

Valerius had never cared for an infant; the dead slave-boy, Iccius, had been his own age when he had nursed him through the insults of beatings and gelding and the use of men. Bellos was older than that, but his incapacity was greater than Iccius' had been, except at its worst, and it lasted far longer.

Valerius found himself nursemaid, who had never considered fatherhood. Before he ate, or made his own bed for the night, he stripped the boy in stages and washed him clean with water warmed from the fire, then clothed him again with padding built around the sore points and an ointment of goose grease and haws and a flavouring of honey smoothed all down his thighs to keep the diarrhoea from destroying his skin.

All the way through, he talked to the boy as if he were listening, sending his voice out into the night.

'Goose grease because it's lighter than pork fat, but binds well to the skin. The haws are for suppleness and to keep the lice away. Honey for healing, but then you know that. I saw you give it to Finbar's ewe when she had a hard lambing. The bay cob went well today. I think they gelded him the night you were kicked and broke him to harness the day after. He'd be better as a riding horse. If your mare was of a strength to pull the cart, I'd let him out and put her in the shafts. Be glad she's not. She would never forgive either of us for the shame. As you may not, when you come out of this and find out how you've been.'

At a certain point, when the cob and the red mare had both shifted in the hobbles, Valerius laid aside the goose grease and lifted his sword. It was not the Roman cavalry blade with which he had fought for nearly fifteen years, nor the long-sword of his ancestors, but something in between, fashioned to fit his own hand and his own weight and used in practice daily, privately, as a man might who keeps an oath which has no meaning save in its own fulfilment. He continued to speak in the language of the Belgae, coarsening it to the south and west, until it sounded more Gaulish and less Germanic. His voice echoed off the damp, resonant hides of the shelter and it was impossible to say exactly whence it came.

'Of course, when we get you to Mona and the healers there know nothing more than goose grease and honey, it may be that you will not recover at all and I will have wasted the best part of a month on a journey with no reason. Luain mac Calma, doubtless, will pretend that he can dream his way to your soul and return it intact. If he is still alive, of course, which he might not be if he continues to— What *exactly* are you doing here? And don't turn round; you would lose your nose, which might make the explaining harder.'

This last was in Hibernian, spoken with quiet certainty and far less emotion than his earlier slander of the dreamers.

Luain mac Calma, dressed in plain wool with no marks of rank or of dream, did exactly as he was told. Without moving any part of himself, he said evenly, 'I came to find you, to warn you that there are Roman traders in the port and that you might not wish to meet them. One or two are ex-auxiliaries recently come from Gaul, where you are somewhat notorious amongst your erstwhile comrades-in-arms.'

'And you, naturally, just happen to be in the port at the time I might want to have use of a ship?'

Valerius' blade pressed forward, bridging the small space to mac Calma's neck, so that it pricked the skin and a thin string of blood seeped into the wool of his tunic.

'I'm a dreamer. I am, in fact, the elder dreamer of Mona. Would you like me to lie and agree that I am here by chance?'

'I would never ask any man to lie.' Valerius did not lift his blade away. 'But equally, I prefer not to ask any question more than once. Perhaps I did not make myself clear. What is your concern with my welfare, and that of the boy?'

'Bellos is dying. You were right in your assessment of me. I do, indeed, believe that I can heal him and, no, I will not limit myself to the use of goose grease and honeyed water.'

'Why do you care?'

'Because you do.'

The blade eased forward. The string of blood became a stream. Valerius said, 'One more time, dreamer. Your life's end is a leaning of weight away. Why are you here? What is it about me that you wish to entrap? And if you mention my parentage, you will die. I have killed more men than you have and in far harder circumstances than these.'

'I know. I have watched you do it in the fire.' With slow, deliberate precision, Luain mac Calma, elder dreamer of Mona, turned to his left, so that the sword's tip scored a circle about his neck. When it reached the edges of the great vessels at his throat, such that to turn further would have cut into them, he stopped. The skin of his face was weathered with hours at sea in strong sun. His eyes took on the yellowed flare of the firelight, as a wildcat's might.

With no hint of irony, or of fear, he said, 'You are Macha's son. To the best of my knowledge, you have never questioned that side of your lineage, nor should you – to even think it would dishonour your mother's memory and, in any case, there are plenty of men and women still alive who were present at your birth and can attest to your origins. Until Airmid grew into her strength, Macha was the most powerful dreamer Mona – or Hibernia – had ever known. Had she chosen to stay in either land, she would have been an elder within five years. She chose instead to bear her son and her daughter in the lands of the Eceni, who were her people. Her daughter is dead – and in any case, Silla did not inherit from her mother any of her powers. Her son still lives. His people and hers have need of him.'

'No.'

'No?' Mac Calma allowed his eyes to widen, in anger, or maybe scorn. 'You deny the need? Or you turn down the request before you have heard its terms?'

'I don't need to hear its terms; you asked me once before. I will not come east to lead the spears of the Eceni in my mother's name.'

'I am not asking you to do that.'

'Then what are you asking?'

'That in exchange for the healing of Bellos – which will have to take place on Mona if it is to happen at all – I have your services, as a son to his father, for the time that it takes for him to recover.'

Luan mac Calma mentioned parentage for the second time and did not die although the possibility remained real for a long and delicate moment.

At the end of it, the blade in Valerius' hand angled a little back, so that the tip no longer drew blood. Thoughtfully, warily, with a world of things unspoken, he asked, 'Who defines the duration of a healing?'

Luain mac Calma did not smile, but the effort he made to prevent it was obvious. 'I do. But I will not be over-greedy. The day Bellos can stand and lift his own sword and match you two strokes without dropping it, I will agree that he is healed and you are no longer bound to me.'

'And if he dies before that happens?'

'If he dies, then of course you are free.'

X

WINTER WAS NOT OVERLY HARSH IN THE FIRST YEAR OF THE Boudica's return to the Eceni but snow blocked the trading routes for four months and then the smaller tracks, until the steadings were isolated one from the other and she had seen, as 'Tagos had said she would, why it was that her people lacked the heart for battle.

The elderly had died first, taken in the early months by cold or disease or starvation or a mix of all three. Eight were lost of those who had attended the covert gathering in the clearing; eight who had supported the Boudica's return and were eight less to aid in the gathering of warriors, and in giving them heart.

For a while, that had seemed important, as if their loss might tip the balance of a strategy yet to be formed. Then the children had begun to perish, which was unheard of in the years before the invasion, and the middle-aged had followed, who should have been strong enough to survive any cold.

It was too close to the ancestor's vision. Rome had taken in taxes that which might sustain the tribes, leaving the land gaunt, over-hunted and over-grazed. The people were skeletally thin and if the children had wept tears of corn, their parents would have eaten them with gratitude. Each death made more urgent the need to raise an army and throw off the parasite of Rome. Each death lessened the heart of the people and undermined their willingness to fight.

By spring, as the snows began to clear, and the urgency and the impossibility matched each other equally, Breaca set aside the ceaseless circling of her mind and took her son and her hound and her spear and went hunting; it was the best and most concrete thing she could do.

'Here!'

The body lay beneath a hand's length of melting snow, blanketed as if under night-time hides with only the point of one elevated elbow sticking up to throw slanting shadows across the white. Stone found it and ploughed into the drift, baying. The noise soaked into the landscape and was gone.

'Cunomar! Over here!'

Breaca dropped her game bag and turned off the track into the untested depths at the side. She sank up to her knees and the butt end of her hunting spear made a staff as she gouged a way forward. Encouraged, the big blue hound fell silent and began to bite the snow, hurling all of himself at it in a delirium of released frustration. His winter had been no less hard than hers, his joy at being outside no less expansive.

The drift was rotten at its core; the spring warmth was eating at its base even as Stone broke through the crust. He clawed out ragged clots of slush and hurled them backwards, making rain in the full sun.

Breaca leaned on her spear and let him play, watching the gradual uncovering of a man who might simply have been asleep, but that the rats and the crows had found him before the last blizzard so that his eyes were gone, and parts of his cheek laid open to the cold. He was well clothed; neither his cloak nor his tunic had been taken from him at a time when cold was the biggest killer and those who died were routinely stripped before their bodies were given to the gods. Nor had he been slain for his wealth; an arm-band in yellow Siluran gold lay frozen at an angle just above his elbow.

Stone whined and nudged the man's face. Breaca laid a hand on the hound's shoulder and eased him back. 'Leave him. He's past our help. This one was beyond help before he died.'

'Who's beyond— Oh . . .'

Cunomar had forged his own way through the drift. He arrived at her shoulder, breathing hard. The steam he made wreathed the air about them, blurring the crispness of the day. He had grown over winter so that the crown of his head reached beyond her shoulder and it was harder than it used to be to see his eyes.

He made to push past his mother and thought better of it, asking instead, 'May I look?'

'Of course.'

He knelt, touching the armband and the ravaged face and Breaca watched her son take in and consider the facts in ways he would not have done before. Of all her family, six months in Eceni lands had changed Cunomar most. He had grown in more than height since coming east; in his soul, he was calmer than the fretting youth who had followed his mother from coast to opposite coast, complaining all the way.

The ravages of winter had been part of it; no-one could watch the half-starved deaths of the cold and the sick and not be touched, but friendship had moulded him most and the pity was that no-one had seen the need sooner. On Mona, Cunomar had been the Boudica's son who had been taken prisoner to Rome, who had stood in the shadow of his own crucifix, and had yet come back alive. He had found himself the subject of songs and of wide-eyed observation, but boys his own age went out to sit their long-nights and came back as men and none of them, before or after, called him friend.

The Eceni knew nothing of the Boudica's son, save that he was an outsider, so it had come as no surprise when he had bonded with another the same. Eneit was a wiry, dark-haired youth, son to Lanis, the raven-dreamer who had so deftly steered the elders' gathering to bring the Boudica back to her people. Eneit was old for his years – Lanis did not tolerate childishness in those around her – but he was unfailingly cheerful and harboured no grudges and Cunomar's bad temper had bounced off him again and again until, of itself, it had begun to blunt.

Through the grim tedium of winter, Cunomar's mellowing had been a spark of hope for which Breaca daily gave thanks. He was not yet his father, nor even Ardacos, whom he worshipped, but he carried enough of both, and some things only of himself, so that Breaca could see who he might become if the gods granted him time to grow.

He showed the essence of it now, as he leaned forward to study the mess of crushed snow and the corpse within it. After a while, he laid a hand to the face. Flesh moved waxily under his fingers and the head lolled. He sat back on his heels and said, 'Not winter-dead.'

It was a masterpiece of understatement. Ardacos could not have done better. Breaca smiled and felt the cold skin crease her face. 'No,' she said, 'not winter-dead. And not slain for his weapons or wealth.'

The stranger had not died unarmed. His knife lay beside him and his spear a little way beyond. He may have used them in his own defence but not successfully. At his death, the blades of both had been broken cleanly across and, lest it be thought unfortunate mischance, the two halves of each had been laid carefully apart, with the tips reversed so that they pointed in towards the hilt.

Breaca lifted the knife pieces, fitting each back to its mate to make them whole again. It was ten years since the Romans had visited their vengeance on Eceni villages, destroying the warriors' blades to seal their mastery of the tribe, but the dreamers had been breaking the weapons of convicted traitors for generations before the legions landed. Iron was only the first thing broken. Death, in all cases, followed slowly and the spirit cracked open long before death gave release. Treachery was never taken lightly among the tribes.

This man had died quickly, which would not have happened in the days before Rome, but the reason for his death could not have been more clear.

'A traitor.' Cunomar fitted together the two parts of the spear blade as Breaca had the knife. 'Who was he?'

'One we should have watched from the beginning, I think.'

Breaca cupped her hand under the ravaged head and lifted it. The left half of the face was gone, with the marks of small teeth chiselled on the cheekbones. The sockets of both eyes had been picked clean and tufts of reddish hair torn away from the back half of the scalp, at the place where hair ended and baldness began. What was left of his flesh hung loosely on bone, smearing the features to a caricature of the over-heated warrior who had jumped onto a log at the elders' gathering and screamed over the chaos, casting the Boudica back whence she came.

She did not know his name, but it was impossible to forget his face, and a warrior so ardent in his convictions would not readily set them aside.

In the forest, at the elder council, she had asked, *How long before a member of your household betrays us?* and 'Tagos, relaxed, had answered, *I would say never but if I am wrong, I will die with you.* And Breaca had taken him at his word, which was foolish.

'I have spent winter worrying how to raise an army, while this' – she opened her hand and the head fell back, loosely – 'has spent it planning how to betray us to Rome. They broke his neck, which was kind. I wonder why.'

'Who did?' Cunomar nudged the lax head with his toe. ''Tagos couldn't have killed him. It takes two hands to break a man's neck and he has only one.'

'No.' In a clutter of unanswered questions, some things had been obvious from the first. Breaca said, 'He sent Gaius and Titus out hunting when the snow first began to melt. They came back with nothing. I thought then that they looked too pleased.'

'That was four days ago.'

'I know. So if our ardent traitor reached Camulodunum with his news and was on his way back, then we are as good as dead.'

Breaca rinsed her hands in the snow. Sharp fragments of ice bit at her fingers, savage as rats. Stone, seeing her distracted, came to push at her thigh and was welcomed. She stared south, to where white met unblemished blue, and felt the pulse rise in her throat. Battle was easy and a part of her yearned for it. The greater part urged caution, and waiting, and the gathering of warriors, and needed time that might not be given.

'Can the legions march over snow this thick, do you suppose?'

'If you listen to 'Tagos, they can do anything.' Cunomar had crouched and was cutting a lock of hair from the man's head. Burned on the night fires, with the right words sung by Airmid, it would mark him for ever a traitor in the lands beyond life. 'That can't be true, but I think that to arrest the Boudica, they would dig a path through the snow from the shores of the ocean to the far edges of the world. Even in this weather, it can't be more than four days' march from Camulodunum to here. We'd have seen them by now if they were coming.'

'Maybe.'

The silence settled whitely about them. Stone whined and dug without purpose at the drift, feeling the ache of danger and not knowing the cause. The wind blew from the west, sifting snow thinly across the dead traitor.

Breaca said, 'If they're coming, there's nothing we can do, but meet them and hope to die cleanly. If they are not, then we have time to find out if this man had others sworn to his cause and if they may yet be halted.'

Fine snow had almost re-covered the corpse. With blunted fingers, she sprang the armband away from the elbow, then unhooked the broken knife from the belt. 'I'll remake the knife. It's time I opened the smithy again. His family can have the armband. If they thought to follow his lead, it might give them cause to reconsider.'

'And 'Tagos?' Cunomar watched her, smiling faintly. Cold carved ten years into his features. 'He ordered him killed and didn't tell us.'

'I know.' That thought had been growing since Breaca had first understood what Stone had uncovered. Standing, she said, ' 'Tagos will certainly have cause to reconsider.'

'I don't know if he got through. Gaius and Titus believe not, but it was dark and snowing and they did not take the time to question him fully.'

'And you chose not to tell me.' Breaca was coldly angry, each word an accusation. She stood in the doorway to 'Tagos' inner chamber, making the most of the light. After the crisp dazzle of the snow, the lamplit gloom was more dank than she could bear.

'Tagos kept away from her, in the farthest corner. Through the entirety of winter, he had not seen the measure of her anger, nor learned to fear it.

'What would you have done? Gone back for your swords and launched an attack on Camulodunum with three warriors, a singer and a boy who has not yet learned that courage is not all about loud words and unchecked action? I thought you best protected from the knowledge. There was no need for both of us to live in fear.' He took refuge in righteous indignation, which was not new. Livid patches flared widely beneath his eyes, shadows of a deeper dread.

Breaca pressed her palm to the doorpost, crushing the flesh to white. The post was solid and would not give and the resistance afforded her some release so that she could think through to the things that mattered.

She said, 'You gave your oath in front of Lanis' council that there was not a single Eceni who so hated the people that they would betray us. This man stood less than a spear's length to your left as you swore it. He spoke just before you did. He saw you, he heard you, he knew you. I fail to believe that you didn't know him equally.'

'Then you believe me a liar.'

'I am waiting to hear that you are not.'

'Gods, Breaca . . .' 'Tagos' voice cracked and he swung round, towards the coffers on the far wall. Breaca stepped forward, blocking his way. The wine, which had been his target, lay behind her, inaccessible. He hissed through his teeth and turned back again. His left hand gripped hard around the stump of his lost arm.

Facts fell out of him, trimmed short by fear and the need to prove his own honour.

'The dead man's name was Setanos. He was a warrior of the northern Eceni, wounded at the battle of the Salmon Trap, that Dubornos led. He lost friends and family in the battle – we all did and did not turn traitor for it – but he lost the mother of his children afterwards when the legions visited their reprisals on the villages and he was away, still caught in the retreat from the battle. She was with child again and so could not fight and he was not there to die with her or to save her, as his honour required. He hates himself and so hates Rome, but he hates Dubornos more and you through him. He has waited ten years for the chance to visit vengeance on you both. I knew none of this when I spoke at the gathering, I swear it.'

'But you found out and chose not to tell me.'

'Tagos spun round, his eyes over-bright in the lamplight. 'I made a mistake. I took action to rectify it and, no, I did not find it necessary to tell you. Would you have done differently?' His eyes glanced to her and away again, unable to sustain a meeting.

He did not want her pity; winter had taught her that, but even through the ebb tide of her rage, she pitied him and could not change it. He was a sapling hound and did not know how to be otherwise in her presence. Leaning back on a wall where her features were less visible, she sought calm and found it in the memory of the dead man's face.

'Was Setanos alone in his hatred?' she asked.

'No. They were four in all: a cousin who was half-sister to the woman who died and two brothers who lost their village to the Romans at the time of the reprisals.'

'Where are the others now?'

'Tagos snorted. 'Dead, of course. I may be stupid but I am not suicidal. You may believe that a slow death at Roman hands will seal your place in the winter songs – your son certainly does – but I would prefer to hear mine sung with living ears. Gaius and Titus killed the other three as they killed this one. He was the last. The bodies will be found when the snow thaws. If we're lucky, the wolves and carrion birds will have stripped them to bone and none need know how they died.'

Breaca said, 'Their families will know. Four warriors went out with a common purpose and none came home. Those who remain behind will have been waiting for something like this.'

'And that's what will stop them from sending anyone else.' 'Tagos grinned, thinly. 'It's a lesson well learned from Rome: gold and gifts may buy promises, but the stench of death buys fear, which lasts longer. We have to pray that it weighs against the passion that calls for revenge.'

He believed it, or wanted her to think that he did. Breaca found that she needed to breathe fresher air. Outside, Graine had found Stone and was playing with him. Cunomar was nearby with Eneit, practising their mock battles with an energy that sent their voices high over the raucous reunion of child and hound. If she wanted to build an army, she had two at least with the heart for it; they only need be armed and taught how to fight without dying.

She said, 'If you find it useful, you may pray that fear outweighs the need for vengeance in the hearts of our people. I am going to build a forge to make the spears to arm those warriors I can find, in the fervent hope that it does not.'

'And if the legions come?'

'If the legions come, those of us who can will fight them and die, as we always would.'

*

The legions did not come. Over the days of waiting, Breaca built her new forge as her father had done, of stone and with sods of turf as a roof that could be kept damp through the dry days of summer. She had planned it through winter; collecting the stones and the work of building took less than five days, each spent with one eye on the building and one to the south where Cygfa and Ardacos, Cunomar and Dubornos kept watch, with a signal fire to be lit with white smoke if they saw the legions marching up the trackway.

There was no white smoke. The snow melted from the trackway and still the only incomers were a pair of salt and iron traders from the south-west who asked gold in payment when once they had wanted corn and hounds and worked metal. Gold could not be eaten; the chests of the Eceni king were still full of it while his granaries were empty.

Breaca paid for iron with 'Tagos' gold and promised him a profit on it. At the forge, Cunomar and Eneit gathered wood for the fires and she promised them spears in payment. Lanis took her to a place a day's ride away where ash and yew had been set to grow straight, with poles on either side, so that their boughs would make spear hafts. Lanis asked no payment, only that the legions be driven from the land quickly.

Half a month after Stone dug from the snow the body of the traitor, Breaca slipped a leather apron over her head and tied it at the sides as part of the small, private ritual that her father had taught her that culminated in lighting the furnace of her forge. A small fire blossomed, fed by chips of apple wood and pine cones, dry straw and the tail hairs of a brood mare heavy in foal.

Aired by new, stiff-jointed bellows, the fire grew to eat twigs and then whole logs. In time, it took charcoal and burned at its heart the colour of the noon sun. The iron that Breaca laid in the centre grew waxen and white and, with some work, took on the shape of a spear-head.

Over the rest of that month, the smells of scalding metal and burning leather, of charcoal and smoke, of sweat and blood and spit replaced the damp, earthen smells of stone and turf. The pile of raw iron at the back of the Boudica's forge became, increasingly, a pile of spear-heads, awaiting their hafts and their warriors.

'Can you hear them sing?'

'What?'

'The spears. Can you hear them sing?' Breaca asked it of Graine one afternoon in the height of spring, as they sat alone together in the forge.

This once, the fires were cool; of Breaca's two projects, neither needed heat and Graine's carving had never done so. They had discovered early that the Boudica's daughter, although she would never be a warrior, had a facility for carving onto the spear-hafts shapes and designs that were called from the wood and her own dreaming. She had gone with Lanis into the forest to cut the straight-formed boughs and, later, when she had been given a knife to shape one to fit the neck of a blade, she had instead carved the shape of a running hare along the length, with spirals and small circles that wove with the knots and contours of the wood so that, when the two were fitted together, the match with the dream-lines on the metal had been perfect.

Mother and daughter had worked together daily after that. From spears, they had begun work on the short, single-edged skinning knives that were the only other weapons permitted under Roman law. Breaca had made the blades and Graine had carved in wax and wood shapes of dream marks to be cast in copper or bronze for the pommel of each. In the last two days, they had begun work together on a larger project: the creation in gold of an armband for 'Tagos, that he might appear more clearly a king when the spring's round of tribal delegations met the governor at Camulodunum.

Graine sat on the beaten earth of the floor carving a serpent-spear while Breaca stood at her workbench on the back wall and drew fine wire finer, so that it might be twisted into a rope after the fashion of the ancestors.

She had asked her question quietly, in a long period of silence, and Graine stopped to think of the answer. The serpent-spear lay part-finished in her hands. It was the third she had carved and each one was subtly different, as if, each time, she learned more of how it should truly be, but had not yet reached perfection. Stone lay at her side, hunting in his dreams, so that his toes twitched and his ears flagged sideways. Outside, a redbreast flew onto the rim of a leather bucket and dipped for water and flew away again. She heard the high twin notes of its call, and the crows and the bark of a hound in the steading, not quite out of earshot.

Behind that was not silence, although she would not have noticed if her mother had not drawn her attention to it. Sitting still, she put her mind into listening and, perhaps because of that, saw the slight thickening of the air that she had come to recognize, so that when she looked into the back of the forge and saw the old woman sitting there, who had not walked in through the door, she was not surprised.

That was not good. Hoping the world might change, she said, 'I don't think I hear the spears as you do. I've watched you beating out the blades and each one has its own rhythm and you are a part of it. A warrior would hear it, who was matched to the blade, but what I hear in the wood is different.' And then, because her mother had looked up and was smiling and had not said anything of the old woman sitting on the pile of hides by the workbench, she said, 'The elder grandmother is here.'

'Is she?' Breaca leaned back, letting her own weight draw the gold wire of the king-band-in-making. She was no longer smiling. 'Is there a reason?'

There was always a reason. Once before, Graine had been a conduit for a message from the grandmothers to Breaca, and it had not been welcome. Then, the ancestors had sent back from Gaul not her father, as they had been asked to, but the traitor brother who called himself Valerius.

Graine did not want to be party to a second betrayal. She glanced fleetingly at the grandmother and away again, as Airmid had taught her. Seen like that, the old woman was as real as Breaca, an ancient, wrinkled relic of the past leaning back into the corner of the forge, dressed in her finery as if for council with a fox skin draped down her back like a cloak, weighted at the edges with nuggets of gold and eagle feathers, and a pair of crow's wings lancing forward across her sagging breasts to meet in the dip of her chestbone.

In life, the grandmother had been the bane and the boon of Breaca's life, and Airmid's before her in the years when each had served as the old woman's eyes and limbs in the infirmity of her old age. In death, the grandmother had ushered the Boudica-to-be through her long-nights, and then come to her since, in moments of need, to guide the way. More recently, she had guided her to the ancestor-dreamer and the slaying of a Roman governor which had gone so badly wrong afterwards. Since then, the grandmother had appeared more to Graine than to Breaca. This was the first time she had shown herself in the company of them both.

Graine glanced at her askance. The grandmother grinned. Loudly, she said, *Tell your mother that she should stop wasting her time making blades for a war host that does not yet exist.*

Graine stared at the floor. 'Why can you not tell her?' She did not ask it aloud. Breaca was watching her, studiously avoiding the far corner.

In her mind, the grandmother laughed. *Your mother chooses not to hear me. She has closed herself off from us and thinks herself stronger for it. Tell her to make a set of spears after the manner of the Caledonii and to take them to Camulodunum as a gift for the governor. It will impress him more than an arm-band that confers no powers on the one who wears it.*

Breaca let go of the gold wire. It sprang into a coil and fell to the floor. With exaggerated care, she laid her pliers on the bench.

Speaking directly to Graine, she said, 'Rome knows nothing of the power of a king-band. They see gold and recognize good workmanship and neither Tonomaris of the Coritani nor Berikos of the Atrebates will have anything like it. Thus 'Tagos will be set apart when we go to meet the governor at Camulodunum next month and may be given added trading rights. If that helps us to feed the starving next winter, I will do it. The war host will exist in time. I spent last summer finding those who could be trusted to join me. This summer we will train them to fight. It is not something that can be done fast. Tell that to the grandmother.'

'She can hear,' said Graine, and then, a little desperately, 'You could see her if you looked.'

'No.' Breaca would not look. Stiffly, she took a small rake and riddled the ash from the furnace. As if it had been Graine's idea, she said, 'Why should I make the heron-spears? They have not been used since the time of the ancestors. I only know of them from Ardacos. Even if it were wise, the blades must be made of unalloyed silver. I may not have enough.'

You have plenty. It's in your work chest. Make three, said the grandmother, nodding. *Box them in yew and blue wool and take them as your gift.*

'Why?'

Because I ask it and I have never yet let you down, however much you think so. You will know what to do when it matters.

The old woman's laugh was the call of a crow, and then she was a crow, and then nothing but a thickening in the warped air above the furnace and the fine cry of a redbreast in the beech trees outside.

Graine breathed out, heavily, and saw that the serpent-spear on her lap was spoiled and she would have to start again. Breaca was standing at the forge with a rake in one hand and the beginnings of a spear-head in the other. As her voice had been, her face was shorn of all humour and warmth. Graine stared at the floor and found her mouth too dry to swallow. There were aspects of her mother she had never seen and she did not want to find them now.

'You don't have to make the spears,' she said. 'But I know how to carve the hafts if you want to.'

Breaca's attention came back from a long way distant. There was a moment when Graine thought she had judged wrongly, and that she had just damned herself for ever as a mouthpiece of the ancestors.

The horror of that must have shown on her face; Breaca frowned at her and then simply frowned and then stared out of the door and blew air hard through her cheeks and when she looked again at her daughter, it was with the sharp, dry humour that held all of her family safe at its centre. 'Did the grandmother tell you how the hafts are made?' she asked.

Giddy with relief, Graine said, 'Maybe. I didn't dream it, but I know that I know. Do you want to make them?'

'No. I want to make a spear for Cunomar, and then one for Eneit, and then I want to take those two out to the forest and teach them how to hear the songs so that they can sit their spear-trials with some chance of success. But that doesn't mean we can't do both. We don't have to sleep, after all, or eat, or do anything except work metal for the next half-month. We'll need Airmid's help; this is too dangerous for you to do alone. The heron-spears of the Caledonii are as much a work of dreaming as they are of the forge.'

They were, and it was an old dreaming, older even than the elder

135

grandmother and the ancestor-dreamer who came to help with it. They worked together for the next half-month. At the end of it, there lay on the workbench a king-band by which 'Tagos might impress the governor in Camulodunum, three silver-bladed heron-spears, packed in wool in a box of yew as a gift for the same governor, and two others, for Cunomar and Eneit, that were just as much an act of dreaming, but held it differently, without such a tangible promise of death.

XI

THERE WAS NO BREEZE IN THE CLEARING. THE STRAW SACK HUNG at the height of a warrior's heart, quite still. Thirty paces away lay a spear, product of Breaca's forging and Graine's dreaming, with help from Airmid. The blade was the length of 'Tagos' right foot from heel to central toe; the longest Roman law allowed. The haft was of pale ash, polished to a matt smoothness so that it came soft to the hand, and a bulb of knot-grown blackberry wood made a balancing weight at the end. It was a weapon with which any youth might be glad to take the warrior's tests of the long-nights.

Breaca picked it up from the forest floor and held it out, balanced on both palms. 'Eneit, this is yours, made for your height. As the elder, you should throw first. When the dreamers name the dates for your long-nights, you and Cunomar will be sent out separately. The gods and your dream will send you home again, but if you both return together, you will take the spear-trials in order of age. You should be prepared to go first.'

Eneit stroked his palm along the wood with the shyness of new knowing. In so many ways, Lanis' son was Cunomar's opposite; his oak-dark hair grew no more than a hand's breadth long so that it would have been impossible for him to weave the warrior's braids at the temples even were it legal to do so. His wide, open face was already brown from the weak spring sun, so that his eyes, his hair and his skin were all of a colour, with only the shades of them different.

Eneit's parentage was the only blight on his life and he bore it, as everything else, with a quiet fortitude. Lanis was not a woman to cross without serious forethought; she had forbidden from the outset her son's acts of rebellion against the enemy, particularly his efforts to learn from Cunomar the warrior skills that would make him a man. Because it was the enemy's rule first and his mother's second, Eneit had no difficulty flouting it; his doubts were rooted elsewhere.

Still absorbed in his spear, he said, 'You know I have never thrown anything such as this.'

Any other boy might have been ashamed of his lack; Eneit told the truth and did not expect censure. Breaca said, 'I know. How could you? There was no smith to sing the soul into the blades at their making, no dreamers to fashion the haft and no-one to teach you the ways of the warrior. But you have the mind for this; just remember that it's a test of heart, not of strength or skill. Anyone can throw a stick in a straight line, that's not the point. Take it. I'll show you.'

The blade of Eneit's spear was not the elongated wedge of Breaca's normal making, but a flattened leaf shape, curved from tip to hilt. The wood of the haft was straight and smooth and the balance clean. Airmid had sung over it and Graine had made the pattern that wove as salmon scales down to the blade. No-one living could hold it and not be touched.

Eneit, who was the son of a dreamer, swung his new gift to his shoulder and gasped, a soft indrawing of breath, as if caught unawares by a lover's touch, so that days of struggle at the furnace and the turning lathe were made worthwhile.

He glanced shyly at Breaca. 'Thank you.'

It was easy to see why Cunomar cared for this boy; the morning became warmer in his presence.

Breaca smiled. 'You are more than welcome. Not everyone is touched by the soul of the spear on first meeting. But that's not the test. You must not only feel it, you must quiet your mind until your soul sings with it, as one. And then you must let it go. Do you know how to hold for a throw?'

He made a good attempt and she helped him to find the place of effortless standing. He naturally used his left hand and so his left foot was fore and his right arm slack. She had him test the balance point of the spear, finding the one spot where, held at shoulder height, the butt and the head matched each other and it felt weightless.

'Good.' Breaca stepped back. 'Now we wait. You need time to quiet the noise of your thinking so you can hear the soul-song of the spear. Cunomar and I will go for a walk through the forest and come back. Then we will walk away again, and again until you no longer know that we are there. When the time is right, I will tell you to throw. You are aiming for the straw sack but you must not try to cast towards it, simply let it become the end point of your thoughts. If your mind is clear and your soul is at one with the spear's, it will seem to fly of its own accord and will strike true. You don't have to make anything happen. Just still the voice of your mind.'

Eneit grinned at her. 'Just?' He was Lanis' only son. He had lived all his life watching his mother work to still the voice of her mind.

Breaca clasped him lightly on the shoulder. 'It takes practice and we have plenty of time. If it doesn't happen today, there is always tomorrow and tomorrow and tomorrow. Don't try to do anything, don't try to get it right, just open to the song of the spear.'

On Mona, as Warrior, she had taught hundreds their spear-trials. Each had come fit and well-trained and had single-handedly hunted and slain boar or deer with a spear before ever they came to her. Each had believed the spear-trial the easiest of the warrior's tests and each had learned, slowly, over months, that it was the hardest.

Eneit had never made a kill in the hunt, nor wanted to. He had never held a spear, but he had a quiet mind and understood the many pathways of distraction. Breaca did not walk far into the forest with Cunomar and never out of sight. As the sun rose slowly and the shadow of the target sack became shorter, she watched the stillness settle on the older boy's face and the half-smile linger on his lips. He did not tense, or test the wind or plan the arc of the throw, but simply watched the swaying mass and listened for the song of the spear.

Breaca watched with admiration and faint regret; if she had been given a hundred like him on Mona, the war against Rome might already be won.

When his face was most still and his left arm most relaxed, she positioned herself a spear's length behind him and said, softly, 'Throw!'

The spear arced in the windless air, a foot high and a foot to the left. It passed the sack by an arm's length and skidded on the grass of the forest floor. Eneit's face lost the peace of lightly focused rapture. 'I missed.'

Breaca said, 'Eneit, that was the best first throw I have ever seen and I taught the warriors for ten years on Mona. Anyone can throw at twenty paces with accuracy. Not everyone can hold themselves still for a thousand heartbeats before they do it, nor let the song of the spear free with such grace. It was beautiful, truly. If we practise like this every day for a month, you will be able to hold still for a morning and cast at forty paces.'

Eneit's brown eyes grew wide as pebbles. 'Do I have to do that in the spear-trial?'

'If we follow the rites of the ancestors exactly, the cast is at fifty paces and there are crow feathers hanging from the neck of the spear to catch the air and twist the path of its flight. The elders are unlikely to make you wait for a morning but in the world of battle, the Romans might easily do so.'

Breaca spoke for Cunomar as much as for Eneit. Her son had watched the trial with a growing sense of disquiet, as if it were both meaningless and unnecessarily difficult. A winter in Eneit's company may have mellowed his temper, but his patience wore thin as quickly as ever, and he still lived and breathed for the right to sit his long-nights and the spear-trials that were part of the ceremony.

She said, 'If you were waiting in ambush and the enemy were delayed in coming, you must keep your mind clear and ready, through rain and insects, gales and the close or distant deaths of your shield mates until they reach you. This is why the tests are set as they are; we wouldn't ask of you anything that would not be asked in battle.'

'Father won the spear-trials of three different tribes. Did he have to wait half a morning for each?'

Cunomar had retrieved the thrown spear and brought it back. He stood close by, turning it over in his hands, seeking the soul that Eneit had so readily found.

Breaca said, 'In the spear-trials, as in battle, each time you throw is the first time and the last. Your father was different because he requested the right to sit the tests with three tribes. Most of us are happy to pass them once.'

'But in the winter tales, Dubornos says that you were never called on to sit the spear-trials. Is that true?'

'It is. I had already killed, as had Cygfa; the warrior-trials were not required of us.'

She knew the mistake as the words passed her lips and regretted it. Cunomar's pride, always a fragile thing, cracked on the rock of his half-sister's fame.

His lips set in a thin hard line that had nothing of his father about it. 'I have killed,' he said. 'Ardacos keeps the tally so that I may wear the kill-feathers one day, when such a thing is no longer "illegal".' He spat the word, as an insult to all who had allowed Rome to set and keep the laws.

He was her son; if he was arrogant, or ignorant, she had helped to make him so. Knowing it, Breaca said, 'You have not killed with a spear. The ancestors' rites do not allow kills with a knife or a sword-blade to exempt the child-become-adult from the warrior's trials.'

As did all of the she-bears, Cunomar hunted with his knife; it was part of their courage, to reach close enough to the enemy to kill with a short blade. It was also the reason the boy had survived this long; in the heat of battle, he was always shielded, left and right, by others sworn to the bear and those he killed were distracted. To fight with a spear, one against one, would have killed him. No mother could say that, only let the silence read it and wait.

Cunomar did not listen to silence. He said, 'So, then, let us see if the ancestors find me as acceptable as Eneit.' He picked up the second spear, made for his height and his arm. The haft was of dark yew and the butt-weight of burred hazel. The marks of the she-bear ran the length of the blade. Very carefully, staring straight through his mother, he paced an additional ten paces back from Eneit's stance.

'I have killed boar with a spear before,' he said, 'Ardacos taught me. It wouldn't be fair to Eneit if I threw from as close as he did.'

'Cunomar, it's not about—' Eneit stopped. He had lived through the winter as the foil for his friend's anger; he knew as well as anyone the futility of reason when pride was in the way. He pursed his lips and shrugged and said, 'Think of the wild geese we watched yesterday and the way they flew. It helped me to quiet the voice in my head and hear the soul-song of the spear.'

He was wise beyond his years and cared deeply for Cunomar. Once, a long time ago, in another context, the elder grandmother had said, 'It is the care of others that makes a man.' If anyone could achieve that, Eneit could. Breaca prayed for them both.

Cunomar had already set his feet for the throw and found the balance point of the spear. Every bone-hard angle of his body said that he wanted no help from his mother. Nodding for Eneit to follow her, Breaca backed out of the clearing, leaving her son to seek the quiet at the centre of his soul.

He was no less rigid a thousand heartbeats later when she returned. His face was set hard, the lines of his nostrils white with tension. His eyes were narrowed as if the sun pierced the mind behind them. When Eneit trod on a dried leaf, crinkling it under-foot, Cunomar twitched as if stung by a wasp.

There was no point in waiting further. As she had for Eneit, Breaca stood a spear's length behind and said, 'Throw,' and knew before she spoke that it was too soon, or too late, or that the time would never have been right.

Cunomar threw as if his life depended on it. The spear hurtled forward, in a long, flat line, screaming a little in the wind of its own flight, as a sword may, if swung fast. The tip tilted slightly up so that from the first it was clear that it was not going to hit the straw, but it flew straight and hard and glanced off the rawhide rope by which the straw sack was suspended, so that the target spun dizzily on its own axis.

'Yes!' Jubilant, Cunomar punched the air. 'I aimed for the rope, truly I did, mother. The sack was too easy, but the rope was a warrior's—'

He stopped. Breaca was the smith and she could hear the death-song of her spears as they died; long before her son had turned, her face was schooled into something close to approval and warmth.

Eneit was less practised in hiding the river that ran beneath the surface of his being. Looking at him, Breaca's son met a barely suppressed horror where there should have been congratulation and joy, and his own face fell.

'Eneit, it's all right. I've practised with the spear for years. I can teach you as well as mother can. If we try every day for a month we'll teach you how.'

Numbly, Eneit said, 'It's broken.'

'Is it? That's good. I thought it only touched as it flew past. But we can get more rope. We'll need another anyway if we're both going to try. Pick up your spear and we'll both try again.'

'No. Cunomar. You can't try again. Your spear is broken.'

Eneit was the son of a dreamer. He had been raised in a land in which dreaming was forbidden on pain of crucifixion, but still he knew the pathways of the dream and the inner core of the ancestors' teachings in ways most youths of his age did not. 'The spear is your soul,' he said gently. 'We need to take the pieces and heal them, else your own heart will break.'

A year – half a year – before, faced with this, Cunomar would have turned his own pain into anger, guilt into recrimination, disappointment and damaged pride into the acid, biting sarcasm that drove others from his company.

Breaca watched the first waves of that rise in him; he stared past Eneit to his mother and the blame was hard in his eyes, all of it hers. 'Cunomar—'

There was no need to say anything more. Of his own accord, her son had lowered his gaze. He stared a while at the forest floor, frowning. When he looked up, for the first time the man who might one day hear the soul-song of his spear shone clearly through the child who never could. He lifted the two parts of the broken blade and held them out. 'Can it be mended?' he asked.

Thank you! Breaca said it silently to the soul of her son, to the listening mind of the ancestor-dreamer, to Nemain, to Briga, to whomsoever watched and listened and understood the magnitude of what had happened.

Aloud she said, 'Of course. It may take me two days, but I can remake the blade. I'll make it stronger next time, so that it can break open a rock.'

He nodded, still unsure of his ground. Where Graine or Cygfa might have lost themselves in the broken blade and its meaning, Cunomar's attention had already passed on to the promised goal.

'What will we do while we wait?' he asked. 'If we're to sit our long-nights by midsummer, we can't waste the time now.'

He was her son. What she had made, she could not change, only help him to build on the foundations he was given.

Nodding, Breaca said, 'You are of the she-bear. You could teach Eneit the ways of tracking. And you could continue to practise with the wooden blades. Keep in the forest and be sure you're not watched. Lanis will have your hides if she finds you and she is a better tracker than most Romans. If you can keep clear of her, you'll be safe.'

The crack of striking blades splintered back and forth across the clearing, rousing the roosting ravens. The power of the impact shivered up Cunomar's arm, numbing it. He dropped his guard, dragging a breath pointedly through his teeth.

'Eneit, wake up. You need to raise your blade higher and hold it directly across the line of the cut. If I had a real blade, you'd be dead.'

'Not if I had a real one too.' Eneit grinned blithely. 'Then I'd have blocked you – here – and you'd have been off-balance and I'd have come in like this—' He thrust forward and flicked the tip of his blade deftly upward under the rib cage. Cunomar doubled over, choking.

Eneit stepped back out of range, his brown eyes alight. 'See? That's a kill.'

He stood with his hands on his hips, grinning. Two days had passed since the ill-fated spear-cast and they were young. If the shadows of fate worried Eneit, he kept it well hidden. In the heart of the forest, facing his friend, he balanced evenly on his feet, his eyes bright with the promise of victory.

Cunomar drew his first full breath since the strike. On the second, he stood up and let his hands fall from his belly.

Eneit blazed a smile. 'Good. I thought you really were dead there. Come on. We've hardly started. That's one kill each and mine was a real one; yours was only pretend. I challenge you to the best of five strikes – real fighting this time, not half-baked training.' He raised his wooden blade in salute.

It was a good offer. Three days ago, Cunomar might have accepted but the first lessons of the spear-cast were growing within him, showing that place within himself where rash foolishness took the place of true courage. It was a fine line, and not always certain, but he felt it now. He shook his head. 'No, we should stop. It's past dawn; someone will hear us.'

'You mean, my mother will hear us and you're afraid of her.'

'Eneit, any sane man would be afraid of your mother. *Ardacos* is afraid of your mother and he faced down a she-bear defending her cubs. You and I are not yet bear-dancers and even when we are, I think we will tread carefully in the presence of the raven-dreamer who gave you birth.'

Cunomar stooped and slid his wooden sword into an oiled cloth roll at the side of the clearing. He had spent half the winter carving it and was proud of the result. For length and balance, it mirrored his mother's serpent-blade but for the blank space at the hilt which would be filled when he had sat his long-nights and found his dream. Eneit's blade, which had been made first, as a gift, was slimmer and had a crack already along one edge of the blade. It, too, awaited a mark on the pommel.

Encit was not ready for the morning to end. 'Did you ever hear of Sinochos, the warrior who was Dubornos' father?' he asked.

'How could I not? He fought with mother at the invasion battle, and then won honour a second time at the battle of the Salmon Trap when the Eceni defeated a whole century of Romans and two wings of their Gaulish cavalry. I could sing the songs of his battles in my sleep. I probably do.'

'Not that I'd noticed.' Eneit found a green twig and chewed on it, cleaning his teeth with the frayed ends. 'Did you hear how he died?'

'Sinochos? I didn't know he was dead.' The wrapped blades lay snug in a pit at the side of the clearing. Cunomar crouched and began to back-fill the hole with the sand that made the forest floor and the black, friable loam that topped it.

Eneit chose his words with care. 'It was after the battle of the Salmon Trap. Sinochos and his honour guard came home and found that the Romans were breaking everyone's swords to stop them from being warriors. Sinochos saw the beginnings of slavery and swore not to live under it. He took his three best warriors with him and hid the blades that had been in their families for seven generations. Then he went back to the village and fought the Romans with his bare hands. He killed three before they hanged him.'

Cunomar rocked back on his heels, staring. 'Sinochos hid the blade of his ancestors before the Romans could break it?' he asked.

'Yes.'

'And you are telling me that you know where it is?'

'Yes.'

There was a pause. Cunomar felt the colour wash up from his throat. Ardacos always said he showed passion too readily to the world. In Eneit's presence, he did not care. Eneit was the one person in the world who knew all of his heart and his longings; which was, of course, why he had said what he had said.

More than anything else, more than passing the spear-test, or learning to lie immobile for a morning's ambush, Cunomar dreamed of wielding the sword of his ancestors in battle – and could not, because the ghost of his grandfather had made himself visible in the grave mound where the blades were hidden and had forbidden it.

Hanging between them were the words that did not need to be spoken. *I offer you a blade with a history that has not been cursed by the ghost of your grandfather. With that as your prize, you could sit your long-nights when the dreamers give the word and come home a true warrior.*

The birds roused for a second time as Cunomar whooped and threw a handful of damp loam at his friend. 'Eneit nic Lanis, you call yourself my friend and yet you have waited seven months to tell me this? Are you *so* tired of life?'

'No.' Eneit's slow, wide smile spread across his face. 'But I didn't find out how much it mattered to you until the snow was too deep for us to go looking for them. I promise you, this is one place where we don't want anyone to follow our tracks.'

He was grave and there was an unaccustomed wariness in his eyes. Seeing it, Cunomar said, 'Are the swords in a grave mound of the ancestors? Made of stone, with grass over, so that it looks like a long hill?'

Eneit's grin died. 'How do you know that?'

'I've been in one like it.' With his foot Cunomar swept dried leaves and some muddied ones over the place where the wooden blades were concealed. Cygfa or Dubornos could probably find them, Ardacos or the Boudica certainly, but no Roman would know where to look. He squinted at the sun, weighing fear against passion, and finding the balance wholly uneven. Ardacos had always said that the mark of a true she-bear was the ability to seize the gift of the gods as it was given, not mourn its passing afterwards when it had been missed.

Slowly, feeling the moment grow within him, he said, 'The snow's gone; no-one will track us now that way. We'll go as she-bears and if we meet anyone else on the way, we'll stop and come back. We must treat this as war. If the Romans find us with weapons, 'Tagos won't be able to stop them from hanging us.'

'I know.' Eneit laughed. 'And if my mother finds us first, they'll be lucky to have anything to hang.' He spat on his palm and held it out. 'We'll go as she-bears and that way no-one but Ardacos, and maybe Cygfa, could find us. I know the way so I'll have to lead. You follow my tracks. Close your eyes and sing the lay of the fallen warrior. When it's done, I'll be gone. I bet you a new sword belt that you can't touch me before we reach the grave mound.'

Eneit had learned well. He left no trail that an untrained eye could have followed and the one he did leave was so faint that Cunomar was grateful for the intermittent markers, the newly broken twigs and scuffles of stones and, once, a dead branch planted in the earth, that had been deliberately placed to point the way.

Hunter and hunted left the forest and moved out across the open fen. Eneit knew this land from birth. He was at home in the flatness, where only the early flowering gorse broke the straight line of the horizon, and solid ground gave way to marsh with no warning so that a man could drown if not wary.

Cunomar lay flat behind a clump of reeds on the edge of still water and watched for signs of movement. A stone's throw away, a band of mares nursed their foals, grazing. A skein of ducks made an arrowhead against the almost-white sky. A hawk skimmed low over the marsh and twisted sideways for a kill. Feathers plumed upwards where it had been and it rose a while later carrying a pigeon.

If he had not been watching that, Cunomar would not have seen the smooth, rolling movement that was a body sliding over flat ground and into a dip. The land was not, apparently, as flat as he had thought. With a small flame of satisfaction leaping in his chest, he studied the ways he might approach the dip without attracting attention – and could see none. Ardacos' teaching for these circumstances was clear; when there is no way to move without being seen, everything must move to cover the one thing that matters.

Cunomar carried a handful of pebbles in a pouch at his belt for exactly this reason. Squirming down behind the clump of grass to gain room, he drew his arm back and flung a round river stone in a high arc, aiming for a bay roan mare whose foal was the newest and most vulnerable of the band grazing nearby. He counted to five before the stone landed, hitting her squarely on the flank, and another two before all eight mares were at a full gallop, spread out across the fen with their foals at their sides. The drumming of hooves roused roosting birds from the sedge and sent them spiralling for the sky.

The movement had come from his right. He ran left, therefore, and doubled back on himself like a hare, diving into the shallow dip in the ground in which Eneit lay, looking out towards the horses. He landed just short of it, but struck with his fist as if armed, and on the aching end of a breath shouted, 'I have you!'

The strike that caught him came from behind. A stick hammered hard and squarely under the ribs, bruising his kidneys and knocking the wind from him for the second time in one morning. His vision blurred, shading to deepest red with orange flares at the centre. For a moment, he thought he might be sick. Floating over his head, he heard a joyous, joyful voice say, 'I don't think so, bear-man. I have *you*.'

He rolled over, choking. Eneit, naked and grinning, stood near his ankles, a length of knotted gorse root in his hand. Eneit's tunic, stuffed with pulled reeds, lay in front of him, a clod of overturned mud near the neck for a head, the roots artistically tangled to simulate Eneit's hair.

'I'm distraught,' said his friend solemnly. 'I had no idea you thought my hair looked like a handful of marsh grass.'

The words spread out in the air and their meaning drifted down piecemeal to Cunomar who, frowning, fitted them back together. Slowly, still gasping for breath, he began to laugh. It was a long time since he had laughed and meant it. A tight, unpractised bark of amusement grew, achingly, to something uncontrolled that hurt with each breath, that rolled out across the fen, louder than the steadying horses, lower-pitched than the fluting cries of the birds, and left him, in the end, lying flat on his back, helpless as a kitten, giggling weakly while Eneit looked on, feigning quizzical bemusement.

The sky was no longer the pale grey it had been, but showed the first shimmer of blue. The circling birds had begun to settle, but for a duet of jackdaws that flew over, cawing. The turf beneath Cunomar's back was warm and springy and ripe with the scents of sand and sedge and standing water. His chest ached and his kidneys were bruised but there was a warmth spreading out in his belly that he had not felt since early childhood and possibly not even then. It dawned on him slowly that, for the first time he could remember, he was genuinely happy. It was a sensation to savour, not to destroy. Quite consciously, he chose not to examine the causes of it.

The world grew calmer and more mellow. Taking a deep breath, Cunomar levered himself up onto one elbow. Eneit, dressed again, sat on the top of the bank, an elbow propped on one knee. He had stopped grinning some time ago and simply watched. His wide, open face was intelligent in ways he often took pains to conceal.

Cunomar sat up. 'Thank you,' he said.

Eneit shrugged. 'You don't have to say that. I couldn't have done it if you hadn't taught me.'

'I didn't teach you to make me laugh.'

'No. But then I didn't make you laugh. You did that all by yourself.' The youth drew a stalk of old grass, examined the end and then chewed on it, neatly stripping the core of fresh green and leaving a hollow husk. 'It was good to see, though. It's been a long time coming.'

'Yes.'

They were an arm's reach apart, and a little more. Neither moved to bridge the gap. They sat in a silence that had more weight to it than before while the morning settled and tranquillity spread over the broad fen. A spear's throw away, the mares dropped their heads and their foals nursed, then drifted away to play with their peers. When he had watched them for too long and his mind would not settle, Cunomar looked up and found that the air above him had cleared until all he could see was a hawk making lazy circles in the blue.

Needing to talk and not knowing what to say, he asked, 'Would you want that as your dream if it came to you in your long-nights?'

'What?' Eneit's voice was distant, as if returning from far away.

'The hawk. Would you want it as your dream on your long-nights?'

'Why? So I can carve it on the pommel of a cracked wooden sword?'

Eneit was not grinning. His eyes were lazily lidded and, for once, impossible to read. When Cunomar did not respond, he rolled over and propped himself up on his elbows.

Not once through the whole winter had he questioned Cunomar's obsession with the warrior's rites and the passage to adulthood. Now, he said quietly, 'Your mother has taught me to hear the soul-song of a spear and you have taught me to wield a blade like a man and I have found a new life through both of these. If the time comes – when it comes – I will kill as many Romans as I can before they kill me, knowing that, in the end, they *will* kill me because however much I still the voice in my head, however hard I train with my wooden blade in the forest before dawn, I will never become as practised in true battle as they. Why, then, do I need a dream, Cunomar mac Caradoc, son of the Boudica? Will it bring me closer to what I want?'

The weave of the morning changed, became too raw, too serious where before had been geniality and simple friendship. In Cunomar's world of black and white certainties, too many things were newly uncertain. He stared at his hands and the hawk and back again, not at Eneit. An image of a broken spear-blade fixed in his mind and Eneit's voice telling him that his heart would break if the weapon were not mended. He wanted to say that his mother could mend anything but the words would not come.

Presently, when the press of the silence grew too great and he needed to hear the sound of his own voice, he asked, 'Why are we going to the mound of the ancestors if not to help find your dream?'

Eneit breathed out slowly and audibly through his nose. After a space, he said, 'To find yours, of course. Or, at the least, to find Sinochos' sword for you so that when the dreamers name your time and you spend three nights alone and come back to take your spear-trials, your mother has a blade to give you when you pass them.'

His voice lost its harshness and discovered instead the god-moved lilt that he got from his mother, the dreamer. More gently, he said, 'You forget, I haven't lived on Mona. I've never seen some-one come home with the rising sun at their backs and the new dream alive in their eyes. I have never seen a warrior school, or stood on the heights above a battle and witnessed acts of heroism that will last in the songs a thousand years. I live in a different world and the things I want are different. We all dream. You and I just have to know that where our dreams take us is not the same. Come on . . .' He pushed himself upright and kicked Cunomar accurately on the sole of one foot. 'Get up. You owe me a sword belt. The mound's in the next dip. If you're fit to walk, we'll find you a blade with a history to be proud of and see if it pushes the dreamers into naming a date for your long-nights.'

The ancestors' grave was half the size of the one in which the Boudica and her warriors had hidden their weapons. It was roundly flat, half submerged in the sand, and grass had gained hold in the cracks between the rocks so that even from close by, it was hard to pick it out from the surrounding turf. The entrance was a once-square hole low down one side, rounded at the corners and rubbed almost circular by weather and the passage of many people.

There was no question now of simply looking and leaving. Eneit led the way and Cunomar followed. The opening did not lead directly to a passage as the one in the other mound had done, but rather opened over emptiness so that anyone seeking entrance had to lower himself down and then, trusting, let go and fall the last distance to the ground below.

The drop was not as far as Cunomar had feared it might be, less than a spear's length from his dangling legs to the floor. He landed unsteadily on stone in the half-dark and the cold, in a place where shadows made the space seem larger and the draught of their land-ing raised for a while the old dust of the ancient dead.

The dead here were no more welcoming than they had been before. Cunomar felt the ghosts' impatience as a fluttering in his abdomen. Belatedly, he remembered Eneit's fear. Lanis' son stood directly under the gap in the roof, wide-eyed and with an unsteady tilt to his smile.

'Have you been here before?' Cunomar asked.

'No.' Eneit moved a step away from the light, waving an arm out in front of himself to feel for the walls. 'Until you came there was no reason to look for a blade. I wouldn't have known how to pick it up, never mind use it.' He took another two steps and stopped, barely visible in the dark. 'There's a wall here.' Then, after a pause, 'And the roof comes down low.'

'If there is a blade, it will be hidden off the floor, in cracks where the stone makes a lip, so anyone bringing in torches won't see it.'

Cunomar spoke into silence. He could have been alone. After a while, Eneit, strained, said, 'How do you know that?'

'My mother and the warriors hid their blades in a mound like this. I went with them, to watch.'

'Did you feel as if they hated you?'

'Yes. But they loved my sister.'

Cunomar found himself wishing for Graine's company. She was at home in the grey places between the worlds in ways he himself was not. His outstretched fingers brushed against stone.

'There's a wall here too. You go right, I'll go left, we'll meet in the middle and cross over, that way we'll have each felt all of the wall. Feel in front of you at shoulder height for cracks that stretch sideways and are long enough to take a blade.'

Following his own advice, he stepped sideways, slowly, sweeping his fingertips across the stone in front of him. The clamour in his abdomen became a grinding ache. The skin of his neck and arms prickled. Greasy sweat gathered along his brow and slid down to his cheeks. He took a third step and felt something substantial flutter past.

A wounded man groaned the name of Briga. Cunomar said, 'Your mother should come here. The shades of the battle-dead have not all left for the other world. Lanis is of Briga. She has the raven as her mark. She could help them find their way across the river.' His voice bounced off the walls and came back to him, hoarsely rasping.

Eneit's sounded no better. 'She comes here often. She came before the gathering when she spoke against your mother, and came out knowing how to speak so that the gathering would vote for the Boudica to stay.'

'She has a courage beyond any warrior's.'

'I know. All the dreamers do. Has it really taken you this long to discover that?'

They spoke to keep the silence at bay, all the while shuffling side-ways, feeling the walls. Space and time stretched, immeasurably. From the far side of the blackness came a bump and a brief, bitten curse, called back at once.

Thickly, Eneit said, 'Cunomar, I think we should leave.' He sounded close to weeping, which was unheard of. Even in the face of his mother's temper, Eneit never wept.

Cunomar said, 'Stay where you are. I'll come round to you.'

He stopped looking for the cracks in the stones and concentrated simply on stepping sideways, one pace at a time. In the beginning, he swept his hand ahead of him, but a second flittering shadow brushing his fingertips made him draw his arm back and hold it tight to his side. The space of the mound was less than the span of Airmid's hut on Mona and had seen, he thought, fewer dangers. He had heard the story of Lythas, the traitor of the Brigantes who had tried to lure the Boudica to Cartimandua's encampment, and of what had been done to him by the dreamers. The horror had been exaggerated, certainly, but Cunomar had never felt the same about Airmid's stone hut after he had heard it.

In this smaller, older, less congenial place, each step forward required the whole of his will and each brought him closer to the brink of panic. Through all Ardacos' lessons of stalking, even on the journey east when they had been within a stone's throw of the legionaries, his heart had never raced as fast as it did now, nor beat as hard. His body shook with the hammering in his chest and sweat washed his face, running in tracks to his shoulders. He felt as if he were walking through water along the bottom of a lake and that great fish swam near, hunting him, or that he squirmed on his belly in fog and darkness and snakes swarmed over his naked skin. He felt thumbs press on the globes of his eyes, crushing them, and beasts with the hands of men and the jaws of bears cracked his long bones and ate the marrow and his feet were rooted to the floor preventing any escape.

'Cunomar?' A toneless whisper.

'Yes?'

'Where are you?'

'Here.'

'You're going the wrong way.'

'No. I'm coming left.'

'Then you've stopped. You should have reached me by now. It's not a big place.'

Darkness swallowed him. The fish and the snakes and the bears sucked at his soul. In blind panic Cunomar stared into the dark and, for the first time in his life, prayed to Nemain for help and deliverance. Unexpectedly, astoundingly, magnificently, Graine gazed back at him from the echoing blackness. Her wide, solemn eyes scanned his face, seeking an explanation, and found it. Smiling her shy smile, she said, *Get away from the wall. Seek the light. You are of Belin, who is the sun. He will care for you.*

Cunomar took half a step back. Light drew him like a beacon. Reluctantly, the horrors loosed their hold. 'Eneit—'

'What?'

'Step back. Don't touch the wall. Come back to me and the light.'

They met in the centre, speechless. Eneit's skin was a sickly grey and his breathing ragged, as if he had run too far, too fast. Cunomar looked at his own hand and saw it shake worse than Claudius' had done, who had palsy and could never control it. He looked up at the gap in the ceiling a spear's length over his head and knew that if he panicked now, he would never get out. Bracing his feet wide, he looped his fingers together.

'Step on my hands as if you were mounting a horse,' he said. 'You'll be able to reach the edges of the rock and pull yourself up.'

'What will you do?'

'I'm taller. I'll jump.'

He had tried to make his voice sound as his mother's did before battle. If he did not exactly succeed, still Eneit did as he was asked without stopping to question it. The older youth's feet slithered up through the hole into the light. After the briefest pause, his head reappeared at the gap. 'I'm safe. Are you sure you can jump that far?'

'No, but I can try. If I fail, you can go back home and get a rope.'

'And leave you alone in there? Do you want to go mad or are you already there?'

'Neither. That's why I'm not going to fail.' Cunomar heard the shadow of his father in his own voice and the small part of him that was not terrified knew a brief moment of ecstasy.

With a prayer to Belin as his sister had ordered him, Cunomar, son of two warriors, jumped and felt his fingers grip on rounded rock and Eneit's fingers close on his wrist. The wriggle to the surface cost him skin on his shins and thighs but he had never before been so glad to see the light.

Afterwards, lying in the sun on firm grass, free of nightmares, Cunomar looked for the hawk and could not see it. Thoughtfully, he said, 'I am beginning to understand why we need to hear the soul-song of the spear. It was the sound of my own voice that was driving me mad. If I could have stayed there in silence, I would have been safe.'

'Safer maybe. That's what the dreamers know and we must learn. We have time. The elders won't call our long-nights until midsummer.'

'If they call them at all.'

There was no hurry to return to the steading. They lay still, each lost in his own recovery. In a while, Eneit said, 'I think we went in with the wrong intent and they sensed it. I wasn't honest, I'm sorry. I was trying to find you a gift you would value.'

'I know that.'

'I wanted you to think well of me.'

Cunomar rolled over. 'I think well of you, Eneit.'

'But you know me a coward. I fled from the grave mound before you got your blade.'

'No. I know you to be honest and steady and sure and possessed of extraordinary courage. You knew what it would be like and you still went in. I wouldn't go in there again if it were the only place in the world where I might find myself a blade. You have the courage of a dreamer. I couldn't begin to match it.'

Cunomar braced his chin on one palm, raising his head so that he could look Eneit clearly in the eye. He felt a safety and a certainty of himself and of the world that was new to him, and welcome beyond all expressing. Questions had been asked that probed the core of who he was and he found himself happy with the answers. Between himself and Eneit, everything and nothing had changed and they could still be friends. In absolute honesty, he said, 'If we were in battle, there is no-one I would want more at my shield side. Before Cygfa or Braint or Ardacos, even before my mother, I would want you. In Belin's name, I swear this is true.'

It was the best he could give, the best he had ever given. It was, it seemed, more than had been expected. They were an arm's reach apart. Cunomar reached out and offered his hand in the warrior's clasp. Eneit took it; his hand was slimy with old sweat but steady. They held tight a long time. Eneit loosed first. His smile was widely lazy, if a little crooked. 'Thank you.'

'You don't have to say that.'

'No. But I mean it.' He rolled to his feet and stretched, clicking the joints in his back. 'I don't think we should tell my mother where we've been.'

Cunomar rose, grinning. 'Do I look as if I want my skin flayed from my body? I wouldn't think of it. But I think we should talk to Graine when we get back.'

There was no time to talk to Graine. They returned to a steading that buzzed like a swarming hive. Eight Roman cavalrymen stood beside their horses just inside the gates, staring ahead as if those around them did not exist. One, less well schooled than his comrades, turned his head to stare at Cunomar. Distaste and a pained superiority flashed from man to boy. For the second time in a day, the Boudica's son felt his heart falter and learned what it was to cross the boundaries of his own courage.

Ardacos met him as he walked past the last of the sentries. The warrior bridled in the presence of the enemy and anyone with half an eye could see that he ached for his sword.

Speaking rapidly, in the dialect of Mona, he said, 'Get yourself cleaned and be ready to leave for Camulodunum. There's to be a meeting of the client kings at the colony to bless the new temple, and 'Tagos has business after with the governor. You are required to attend him. The governor wishes to meet the "King's" new family.'

Ardacos spat, which was probably treason. Before the morning, Cunomar would have crowed at the sight of it. Now, he had other preoccupations. He said, 'I am not of 'Tagos' family. Why do I have to go?'

'Because, in the eyes of Rome, you are his son, which is all that matters. You leave after noon.'

The world beyond Eneit and a dead man's sword came slowly back into focus. It was not the safe land they had left in the morning. Cunomar caught Ardacos' arm. 'Wait – mother is going to Camulodunum? Are you mad? She can't go. She'll be recognized. What if one of the Romans has served in the west and fought against her when she led the warriors of Mona?'

'Then we'll have to hope that the circumstances have dulled his memory. She has no choice. The invitation expressly requests the presence of the king and his new wife. It may have been written as a request, but the governor of Britannia is not a man to be denied. If she refused to go the cavalry would bind her and throw her on horseback, or try to.'

'But—'

'Airmid says the best way to hide is to be seen most clearly. That's why your mother sent the gift-knives to the governor when she did. People see what they think they are seeing and the governor is no different. We have put out word that she is a metal-smith of the northern Eceni and she carries a gift that will, when he opens it, take all of his attention.'

'We have to hope so, or we will all die with her.' Cunomar found himself less afraid of that than he had been. He wanted to share with Ardacos the finds of the morning but the she-bear warrior was not in the mood to hear stories of ghosts and weapons. He was closed in on himself, as if pained. On the sudden cold gust of intuition, Cunomar said, 'You're coming with us, surely?'

'No. The invitation was extended to the family only. Neither your friend nor I can go.' Ardacos' gaze slid sideways to Eneit. 'Your mother thinks she knows where you've been. I'd have a good story of hunting an injured deer deep in the forest, if I were you, and make sure there's no holes in it. You'll have the next ten days to keep it right without Cunomar to spoil it.'

Cunomar felt a wrench that caught at his breathing. 'Are you serious? Eneit can't come? Why not? He's my honour guard; I need him.' He had never said that before, not openly.

Ardacos grimaced. His eyes held pity and sorrow and a depth of concern that they had never shown on Mona. He forced a smile that touched neither of them and faded fast. 'I'm sorry, no. 'Tagos has forbidden Airmid to go on the grounds she might try to curse the governor. I can't see he'll let a dreamer's son who's just spent the morning in a grave mound go in her stead.'

Ardacos clapped Eneit on the shoulder. 'Look on the bright side. If Cunomar and all his family are hanged for treason, you can have Sinochos' blade all to yourself.'

XII

FROST SPARKED ON THE LIME-WASHED WALLS AND RED ROOF TILES of the hospital at Camulodunum. Almost alone of the buildings in the veterans' colony, which had once been the fortress of the XXth legion, it was unchanged. Theophilus of Athens, physician and mender of souls, stood with his hand on the latch and breathed in the cold air. Here, the new day was still; the clouds of his last exhalation hung around his head. Elsewhere, men, women and children were stirring, as they did in every city, town and village throughout the empire; fires were being kindled, buckets filled, chickens fed, livestock moved to new pastures.

The walls that had once hemmed the fortress had been gone for a decade. Without them, Theophilus could see the full sweep of the horizon and the thin blue threads of rising smoke that marked the waking of a thousand homes. As he did every morning, he offered a prayer to the vast, impersonal universe, that the day should not see too many of their occupants brought to him sick or injured. He did not do so for himself; his life was medicine and he enjoyed the challenge, but he had never been one to ignore the human cost of those things that gave his life meaning.

The air was like good wine, heady and refreshing at once. He breathed in one final time then pushed open the door and entered the warmer, moribund air of the hospital.

The ward reserved for Roman citizens was larger than the ward for the tribes and less crowded. Working through his two apprentices, Theophilus discharged two victims of food poisoning, a half-Parthian, half-Gaulish wine trader with a monstrous hangover who had claimed, endlessly and at length, that his great-grandfather had served in the cavalry under Tiberius in the Pannonian war and been awarded hereditary citizenship and thus the wine trader should be admitted to the citizens' hospital. The man was lying, but had won on the grounds that it was the best way to shut him up. He left in poor humour, cursing physicians throughout the empire as witless, unprincipled scum.

Lastly, the apprentices discharged Publius Servillius, an ex-legionary of the IXth who had been gored in the thigh by a bull two days previously. The wound had bled a great deal at the time of the injury but, in doing so, had cleansed itself and was draining well without undue infection.

Theophilus gave instructions for the man's care and orders that he return daily for his dressings to be changed and left the ward before his clerk had finished the delicate negotiations concerning payment for Servillius' treatment. The cost would be substantial, certainly. Theophilus' rapid and effective binding of the wound had saved the man's life and they both knew it. As importantly, the man had sired several children on native girls who, until now, had been unable to pay for their care when they came to childbirth too thin and too young.

Theophilus' clerk was a young man of the Trinovantes with a head for numbers that surprised the physician and astonished his own kin. His ability to deal civilly with the men who routinely raped his mother, aunts and sisters was less good, but he was learning, slowly, that there was other and safer retribution than ramming an eating knife in the guts of those responsible and that, in Theophilus, he had the ideal means to achieve it.

The physician, in leaving, heard mention of the sum of one thousand sesterces, more than a legionary's pay for the year. He heard, also, the beginnings of Servillius' attempt to browbeat the clerk into a reduction. He signalled to the closer of his apprentices, a rotund, red-haired youth who could grind a goose-grease ointment to perfection but had yet to learn the causes for which one might use it.

'Remind young Gaius that he may have forgotten to add the cost of bandaging to the bill and perhaps he might like to recalculate the sum. I would suggest an additional three hundred sesterces might be appropriate. Remind him also that if he forgets to book veteran Servillius in for the changes to his dressings, our patient may yet lose his leg to gangrene, possibly even his life, and that would be a grave misfortune to fall on the head of a clerk.'

The physician smiled coolly, as befitted a man of learning. The rotund apprentice, less restrained, allowed himself a momentary grin of undiluted wickedness, cleared it and crossed the room to deliver his message with a commendably straight face. A moment later, Theophilus heard the man whose life and limb depended on the physician's continued good favour agree a schedule of payment that would ensure the health and long life of this year's crop of infants and their mothers and pay for the physician's lodgings and those of his staff for the remainder of the year. It was a better start to the morning than he had imagined.

The non-citizens' ward was small and lacked windows. It was not yet obscenely overcrowded but then the quarries had not yet opened and building work on the temple to which they supplied their flint and sand had not yet begun for the day; the minor abrasions and broken fingers and greater, life-wrecking calamities had therefore not yet started to flow in. With luck, they might not do. The numbers injured had been fewer since spring when work on the roof itself had begun, having reached a peak in midwinter when the oaf of an Alexandrian overseer had considered it constructive to take men with no experience of stonework and set them to building the columns that would support the roof.

The crush injuries – those sustained by falling masonry, or by men falling onto masonry – had begun as the columns reached half-height and increased as they neared completion. When Theophilus had sent a complaint to the governor, he had been reminded that he had complained in the spring that able-bodied men had been taken away from the sowing, and in the autumn that they had been taken away from the harvest, and that if he were going to complain in winter also, then when, exactly, did he think the temple to the God Claudius might be built?

Over dinner at his villa three days later, in more congenial circumstances, Theophilus had been informed that the emperor required that the temple be built in time for the twentieth anniversary of the invasion and that if Theophilus wanted to make a direct representation to Nero himself explaining why it was madness to build of stone in a place where no stone had ever been used; and where skilled labourers brought in from the continent died of cold or disease or simply took the next ship home to wine and warmth; and where the natives were penniless and were yet expected to pay for the construction of a temple to honour the man who had defeated them, he was more than welcome but he might like to write his will first.

Theophilus, not being noticeably tired of life, did not make any such representation to the emperor. Instead, when spring opened the shipping lanes, he sent to Athens for texts on building and read them at night and in the spare hours of the day that he might make suggestions to improve safety on the construction site. It was not required of him as a physician, but he had long ago been taught that an injury averted was a life preserved and he considered it his moral duty to do his best for his patients.

In the smaller, more crowded ward he found evidence of three patients for whom he had done his best and failed. Two had died in the night and one, a child of eight with coughing sickness, would be dead by noon. For the protection of the others, it would have been good to transfer the child to a separate room, but none was available. Theophilus had him moved to the far end of the ward, to the bed of one of the two women who had died before him, and turned his attention to the combination of injury, malnutrition and disease that afflicted the rest of his charges.

As had always been the case, a suite of small private rooms facing into the inner courtyard was reserved for officers and their families. Few of them appreciated being woken in the early morning and so, saving emergencies, these rooms were routinely left until last. Washed and dressed in a fresh, clean tunic, the physician moved along in reverse order, starting at the southern end and moving north up the corridor, saving the best for last.

The frost had melted by the time he reached the door at the north end of the corridor; a film of drying moisture shined the tiles on the roof. The door to the room had been repainted many times since the days when four legions and their auxiliary cavalry had all made this place their home. On each occasion, in an act of uncharacteristic superstition, he had asked that the eye of Horus be repainted in blue on the lime-washed white. In his mind, it had always been Corvus' room and was so still. Of all the army's officers Theophilus had met, some of whom he had liked, the dark, scarred cavalry prefect was the one who seemed to him least Roman and most Greek; the greatest accolade the physician could bestow. That the prefect was back in Camulodunum made the days brighter. That he was injured, and there as a patient, dulled them only a little.

A brazier burned in the room and someone had thrown cedar chips on it recently. The smell lightened the corridor as one approached the room. With something of his earlier cheer, the physician pushed open the door.

'Good morning.'

The man who had been left under absolute instructions not to leave his bed stood by the window looking into the inner court-yard. He stood carefully, bearing the weight of his left leg on a stick. A linen bandage bound over the left side of his head looked unnaturally pale against the black hair and olive skin. His smile was as drily intelligent as it had always been. He turned a little away from the window as the door closed.

'How is your headache?' Theophilus asked.

'Better than it was.'

'You said that yesterday.' The physician's long fingers probed his patient's skull. 'But not gone?'

'Not quite. And, before you ask, my leg is healing well. I looked under the bandage this morning. Your rosewater and honey are working well. There has been no poison in the wound for three days now and it hardly throbs at all overnight. I think it may be time to dispense with the poppy.'

'You mean you have already stopped taking it?'

Corvus, prefect of the cavalry wing, the Ala Quinta Gallorum, currently assigned to the XXth legion in the west, had the good grace to look guilty. 'I didn't drink last night's dose.'

Theophilus sighed theatrically. 'Remind me to have Nerus whipped for failing to see that a patient was treated as prescribed. If you want to be a physician, you should tell me. You can have my job with pleasure and I'll go home to Athens.' The bandage came away and the head wound was, indeed, clean and healing. Theophilus considered the air and decided to replace it with one of

163

lighter linen weave. Moving to the leg bandage he said, 'And how is your other project?'

They had not spoken of it in over a year. It was a mark of their mutual respect that, after a moment, Corvus answered, 'Valerius? I don't know. He was taken to Hibernia after the others returned to Mona but I have no idea what happened to him afterwards. Segoventos refuses to talk to me and no-one I have sent has been able to find him.'

'Hibernia is not a small island.'

'It's big enough for a man who wishes himself dead to achieve it with nobody any the wiser.'

'Do you think he's dead?'

'No. But I think he is living as if he is. Can we talk of something else?'

'If you like. Or you can sit down and display your famed stoicism while I clean the wound on your ankle?'

Corvus sat on the bed. Theophilus probed with care at the healing spear wound in the man's calf. The blade had penetrated just above the ankle, sliding between the tendon and the bone. A finger's breadth either side, and the prefect would have lost the use of his foot. As it was, he would ride again as ably as ever, if he would never walk as well as he once had.

The wound was a month old and close to healing. Theophilus applied himself to a newer, smaller dressing and listened for sounds of distress in the other's breathing. When it seemed the pain of his intervention was less, he said, 'I understand there is to be a demonstration of Caesar's justice in the theatre after tomorrow's ceremonies?'

'So I heard. The governor wishes to demonstrate to his favourite client kings that the law falls equally hard on those who have attained Roman citizenship as on those who have not.'

'So a man will die to prove to a group of high-born traitors that they made the right choice.'

'Not the kings – they know exactly who they need and who needs them. The people still to be convinced are those who plan rebellion in their forest groves and think we know nothing of it. So two men will die; one of ours and one of theirs, to make it even-handed. Marcellus who led the second cohort of the Ninth at the invasion will be hanged for the murder of his stockman, although he claims the man was trying to kill him and it was self-defence—'

'It may well have been.'

'It probably was. He had just ordered the ploughing of a site that has been sacred for as long as the Trinovantes can remember. I'd have tried to kill him too. But he shouldn't have struck the man down in broad daylight with three of the governor's household and any number of tribesmen as witnesses.'

'And the other? The brother of the man he tried to kill, perhaps?'

'No, he's already dead; Longinus Sdapeze had to kill him to stop him running amok amongst the remaining garrison – we can't afford a riot now. I don't know who the second man will be. I suspect the governor may not yet know. They'll pick some poor bastard at random and make up a charge. If one of the client kings wears a knife half a thumb's length too long, he'll live long enough to regret it.'

Theophilus finished binding the dressing and stood back to observe his patient. 'Or they could choose you simply for looking disreputable. As your doctor, I would suggest that if you're intent on going to listen to small men make speeches of no significance, you should wear something warm that doesn't look as if you've fought a battle in it. We are supposed to be a province at peace.'

'Thank you. One day someone will tell the warriors of the west and we can all go home.' Corvus stood, smiling sourly, and flexed his ankle, testing. His face showed no obvious pain at the result. Leaning ostentatiously on his stick, he said, 'In view of which I should make the most of my time in Camulodunum's version of peace before I return to the western kind. With your permission, I would like to go to the baths and then to find a dresser who will make me a set of clothes fit to greet a delegation of royalty on behalf of my legate and my men. Do I take it I may go?'

'Of course. I only kept you here because I wanted to talk to you. And if you don't need the stick, throw it away. I hate to see a man pander to his doctor when he doesn't really need to.'

They hid very little from each other and there was much that did not need to be said. Some things, however, should be explicit. As he was leaving, Theophilus turned. 'You know the Eceni are coming?'

'Of course. Prasutagos is the model client to which all other kings aspire; friend to two emperors and every governor since Plautius. But Valerius won't be with him. Wherever else he is in the world, that man does not live in the care of his people. It doesn't matter if the others recognize me; we're allies now. We can afford to share the entertainments of a trial and judgement and take dinner afterwards and recall old times in friendship.'

XIII

'CAN YOU STAND, DO YOU THINK?'

'You asked me that yesterday.' Bellos, blond child of the Belgae, had grown dark through a winter without the sun on his hair. His skin, always fine, had become translucent, so that the vessels beneath showed blue against white, and the whole was coated with a fine sheen of sweat that never seemed to dry. He lay on a mat of rolled and woven straw on the turf between the small stone hut and the stream that ran to the west of it, shielded from sight of the great-house and the war-weary warriors of Mona.

The seclusion was not solely for the boy. Julius Valerius had spent fifteen years of his life fighting the warriors of Mona. He had slain their shield-mates and their soul-friends on the battlefield in fair combat and hanged them off it in circumstances that were fair only by the standards of an invading nation. He had taken captive those who were wounded and given them neither Briga's clean death nor healing, but nursed them alive to the legions' inquisitors and laid their bodies afterwards on the high peaks with dream marks and items of clothing for recognition so that, even when flesh and features had been burned, torn and flayed beyond all knowing, their kin might still find them and know how they died.

If Valerius regretted anything, he did so in the quiet corners of his heart where the fire of his mind shed no light. He had not come to Mona by choice and he did not stay by choice. He did not, either, make any effort to heal the running sore that was his presence among those who continued the fight against Rome. Luain mac Calma was Elder of elders; throughout the free tribes, his word was law and his word had ensured Valerius' continued safety. Without it, the once-Eceni would have died over days for his betrayal of his people, and the boy Bellos with him, so much had been made plain.

Given this, they could never have lived in the great-house with the other warriors; mac Calma would not so have insulted his people and, in any case, in the early days Bellos had hovered on the cusp of death and had needed solitude and the peace that only solitary living could afford. The small stone hut at the stream's edge had been made ready for them at mac Calma's request and if the neophyte dreamers who swept it and laid the fire and scattered rushes on the floor had done so with their eyes averted and making the sign to Nemain as they left, Valerius had chosen not to comment.

He had been naïve then, and sick from the sea crossing, and that part of his mind not obsessed with Bellos' welfare had been concerned with care of the red mare and the stocky bay cob, which had been turned out in a small paddock for watching, in case they brought hidden disease to the gods' island.

Midwinter had come and gone and Bellos had opened his eyes and accepted food and water before the day when a girl-child had come across Valerius as he relieved himself in a pit and had cursed him with living in a dreamer's house. Enquiring at last of mac Calma, he had found that the stone hut in which he lived had been Airmid's and that the dried plants and roots and pastes that had been used in Bellos' healing had been hers.

It was too late to move then and there was no point: the winter storms had sealed Mona from both the mainland and Hibernia, and snow had cut the great-house from the hut so that they and the warriors might as well have lived on different islands. The red mare had been released from her quarantine paddock and had taken to standing against the wall with her head inside the door gazing in at Bellos, who had gazed back. Long before he could speak, he had smiled for the mare, and then for Valerius.

Thus Valerius had spent his winter and the first months of spring in the hut of the woman he had last seen on a ship in the middle of the Hibernian sea; a woman who dreamed with Nemain so deeply that she had built her home beside water, which was known to drive lesser mortals to madness; a woman whose mark of the frog was carved in the small, dark corners of the hut where Valerius did not find them until spring when he stripped the reed thatch from the roof and re-set it afresh. What worried him more than any of these things was that, in the hut of a dreamer, within sound of running water, and beneath the many changing cycles of the moon, he had not dreamed.

He chose not to consider that, immersing himself instead in other work. Helpfully, Luain mac Calma had departed on the first ship to set sail after the equinoctial gales and he had left Valerius with instructions enough to fill his days. Through the growing warmth of spring, he nursed Bellos through the first days of slurring speech to a coherence that the boy had not shown before his injury. With speech had come strength and with strength should come, so Valerius reasoned, the ability to rise. If he could stand, he could hold a sword. That was all.

The day Bellos can stand and lift his own sword and match you two strokes without dropping it, I will agree that he is healed and you are no longer bound to me.

Through the dark of winter and nights spent awake listening to the distant howl of the she-bear singers in the great-house, Valerius had built in his mind the moment when Bellos could stand and hold a blade and match two strokes against him. Or even one stroke. One would be enough.

He knelt at the side of the straw mat. The sun was still weak and the shadows it cast were not fully black. Bellos lay with his head on a slight upward slope at mac Calma's insistence, to keep the blood from filling the crack in his skull. Valerius dipped a hank of raw wool in a pitcher of water and wiped the boy's face clear of sweat. Eyes the colour of cornflowers blinked up at him. Bellos smiled, faintly. 'What happens if I don't try to stand?'

Valerius sat back on his heels. 'If you can't even try, then I build up the fire and boil the water for the wormwood infusion.'

The wide eyes widened further. 'Again? I thought we'd finished that.'

'No. According to mac Calma's instructions, it needs to be taken for the first nine days of each new moon until you can stand. Yesterday was the old moon. Today it's new.'

'And if I try to stand?'

'If you can raise more than a hand's breadth off the floor, then we don't need the wormwood, we can go on to the vervain and hare's foot.' He grinned encouragingly. 'It only tastes of hounds' urine, not like the rotted dung of a badger in season spiked with putrid shellfish, as the wormwood does.'

'Thank you so much.' Bellos' eyes drifted closed. His strength had its limits and talking sapped it. Presently, without opening them, he said, 'You know, I have an urge to pass water onto real grass, not into a jug held by another man. Do you suppose we could set that as a reasonable target? I know it's not the same as matching you with a blade, but it's a good place to start.'

It was a very good place to start. They had nine days of wormwood infusions and were on the last sliver of the old moon by the time Bellos, kneeling, passed water on his own onto good honest turf.

Valerius held his shoulder to stop him from falling forward, but only lightly. As milestones go, it was a great one only to these two, but to them it was greater than a victory against a legion. Later that night, with Bellos propped up on a sack of dried mosses, they burned the last of mac Calma's dried wormwood in celebration.

'You should have become a dreamer, Julius Valerius, not a killer of men.'

Bellos said it one evening in mid-spring, speaking from the cool of his day-seat. He could sit now for half-days at a time, and could hold himself up to pass motions and water. His skin was stronger with greater colour so that his vessels no longer made patterns across his temples, nor throbbed as he spoke. His arms had gained strength before his legs and Valerius had set him exercises for both, giving him strands of rawhide to plait into ropes as work for his fingers and a boar's bladder filled with straw as somewhat less profitable labour for his feet.

When he had proved he could lift the bladder between his ankles and hold it steady for a count of twenty, Valerius took it away to fill it with the coarse-grained sand from the edge of the strait, near to where the ferry left and landed on its thrice-daily trips to the mainland. He had just returned, juggling the bladder and a length of seaweed that, smoke-dried and powdered, might help the red mare to overcome her bouts of colic, when Bellos delivered his judgement. Valerius threw him the bladder, saying nothing.

It was a difficult throw. Bellos caught it, sagging a little under the new weight. He balanced it on the ends of his feet without looking; all his attention was on his companion. 'I'm serious,' he said. 'Dreamers are healers and you have the gift. My mother could heal almost as you do, before the slavers took her, and my father's grandfather, but I have met few others.'

Valerius absorbed himself in his rinsing of the seaweed. Without looking up, he said mildly, 'Perhaps they were not there to be met in the slums of Gesoriacum. I can't imagine a healer would choose to spend time in Fortunatus' whorehouse.'

It was a mark of how far they had come that Bellos would talk now of his family in the few years before his capture and that Valerius could make a joke of the filthy, louse-infested tavern from which he had bought the equally filthy Belgic urchin who had been offered him as an afternoon's entertainment.

Bellos grinned and twisted his plaited rope into a halter. His hands moved with an easy fluidity as if they had always made rope of leather and given it a beauty that was lost to most.

After a while, he said idly, 'My father always said I would make a good potter. It was his trade and he expected his sons to follow him. If you had stayed with your people, would you have become a smith, do you think, or a healer?'

'I was going to be a warrior. My sister was to be the dreamer, or she thought she was.'

'But you didn't agree?'

Valerius looked up. They did not often speak of his sister. His eyes showed the danger of it, the proximity to places not even Bellos could go. He said, 'She killed an armed warrior with a single thrust of a hunting spear when she was twelve. She woke from sleep and had no shield nor time to plan her actions. No, I didn't ever think she would be anything but a warrior.'

'So then you were proved right.'

'Yes.'

'And was it because of that, you, too, took to the sword?'

Valerius lifted his dripping seaweed from the river and sat back on his heels. His face was clear and his smile bland. Only his eyes were more hooded than they had been, as if there were things behind they might prefer to hide. 'No,' he said. 'I did that because Rome paid me to. When I was a slave, nobody came to buy me from Amminios' household. Signing up with the auxiliary was the only alternative left.'

Bellos recognized the warnings and chose to ignore them. He had come this far before and backed away. Knowing exactly what he did, he said, 'Corvus would have bought you, I think.'

The hooded eyes became quite blank. The smile was an automatic one, distantly polite. 'Possibly, but I did not wish to be bought by Corvus.'

'Why not, when you loved him?'

His last words fell into silence. Valerius' speed and lightness of foot had surprised Bellos from the first moments in the whorehouse. Now, in the spring sun on Mona, the boy found himself abruptly alone. He forgot, sometimes, the depth of pain in the other man, and the oceans of anger that kept it submerged. He shook his head at himself and the watching gods and looked around for the wren that had taken to visiting. It came almost to his hand daily whenever he was on his own. Being entirely alone now, and likely to be so for some time, he whistled and reached for an oat bannock he had saved and scattered pieces of it out on the streamside.

Nothing more was said until two days later when Valerius emerged from the back of the hut with two rolled goat hides. He laid them out one across the other on the turf in front of Bellos, who surveyed them with evident curiosity. 'What's in there? Crutches?

'No. I think we can bypass those.' Valerius took one end of a hide and rolled it out. Metal clashed on metal as two blades skidded free on the grass.

Bellos' face changed in much the same way it did when he was asked to drink wormwood. 'What are they?'

'Practice blades. What do they look like?' Valerius grinned. 'Your father said you could make a good potter. Myself, I think you would have made a warrior had you been given the chance. Luain mac Calma will be back by the next moon's end. He said if you could match me two strokes, standing, we would be free to go back to Hibernia. I thought it would be good if we could show him something more than simply two strokes.'

'You would make a warrior of me?' Bellos laughed, weakly. The wren, which had been feeding on a rock, flittered away, crying alarm. 'Julius, you can't be serious!'

'Why not?'

'Because I'm terrified of fighting. I sat behind you on your horse while you killed Romans in Gesoriacum and I have never been so scared in my life. If Fortunatus had stepped like Neptune from the seas and offered to take me back to the tavern and beat me daily for the rest of my life, I'd have thanked him for it.'

'Really? Not afterwards, you wouldn't. The man was obscene. In any case, terror is the right place to start. If you walk onto a battlefield and don't have your heart stuck in your throat, you'll be dead before you have time to realize your mistake.'

Bellos shook his head. 'I've watched you fight, Julius. I had my arms round your waist. I could feel each and every crash of your heartbeat. You were desperate. You were murderously angry. Near the end, at the sea's edge, you were anxious about the ship, not knowing where it might take us. Never, at any moment, were you afraid.'

The sun warmed them both equally, but Valerius' skin was, briefly, the darker. He shrugged. 'Sometimes anger covers fear. When there's no choice, it's useful. Here – take this and we'll work with you seated until the full moon. After it, we'll see if we can get you standing.'

'I'm not a warrior. You can't make me into one.' Bellos sat on his three-legged stool, panting, and ran a shaking hand through sweat-darkened hair. A gash ran the length of his forearm and his shoulders were dark with old bruises, some of them green at the margins. 'Why can't we practise with wooden staves as children do? Did mac Calma say it had to be a real sword?'

'He did, actually. In any case, children don't practise with staves if they want to live beyond their first battle. Warriors who practise with wood are the second rank to die in any conflict, after those who think they are too big to be afraid. Wood doesn't teach the reflexes necessary to face iron.'

'But I'm not going to face iron, except yours, and you want me to win so we can go home. You're not going to try to kill me. This is pointless.' Bellos hurled his blade at the ground. It hit a rock, ringing. 'I can match you two strokes sitting. That's enough. All we need now is for me to be standing and for you not to be— Julius? Are you listening? I said, I need to be standing and then we can . . .'

He trailed into silence. Speaking to empty air was becoming too much of a habit, particularly when that air was filled by a living man, the entirety of whose attention was given elsewhere. Bellos stared out along the line of Valerius' fixation and saw, on the track beyond the great-house, a delegation of dreamers walking with funereal slowness around a hand-carried bier. Nothing could be seen of the body lying thereon but the colour of the hair, which was the copper red of a winter fox. Leading the dreamers was a man who was not Luain mac Calma, but who carried himself with the same authority.

In a voice wiped clean of emotion, Valerius breathed a name – 'Efnís' – and was gone.

It was not yet the full moon, but the day was young and warm. Abandoned for a man of greater interest, Bellos set himself to complete alone the last of mac Calma's requirements.

He was lying near the stream when Valerius returned, with his head uphill, as the healer mac Calma had dictated. As mac Calma had emphatically not dictated, his head lay on one edge of the wren's rock; gelling blood made a dark mess of his hair and leaked a little onto the earth below.

'Bellos—'

'I know. Don't shout at me. I have a headache.' Bellos opened both eyes, too wide and too suddenly. 'Was it your sister on the bier?'

'What? No, it was a dreamer who tried to infiltrate the fortress of the Twentieth legion. The inquisitors had her for three days. The legate ordered what was left of her body to be dumped within sight of the ferry. What have you—'

'And is the dreamer, Efnís, once again your friend?'

'No. He loathes me. Without mac Calma's protection, he would do to us what Rome has just done to the dead dreamer. You know that. Is Efnís the reason you—'

'No. I just wanted to see what the world looked like from standing. It's been so long, I've forgotten.' Bellos' grin was a shadow of the morning's easy cheer. 'Or, if you want to wallow in guilt, we could say it's all your fault because you wanted me to stand and fight. So if we're both equally to blame, we don't need to argue about it. Could you move me out of the sun sometime soon, do you think? It's too strong and it's hurting my eyes. I can't see you properly.'

His head rocked sideways and it became apparent that he was weeping; slow, thin tears had already coursed their tracks on his cheeks. His gaze, clearly meant for Valerius, was directed a half turn too far, so that he stared instead at the blank side wall of Airmid's hut.

'Oh, gods, Bellos . . .' Valerius knelt. He passed a hand in front of the over-bright gaze. When nothing happened, he moved his head so that he looked the boy straight in the eyes. 'Bellos? Can you see me?'

The world grew cold in the small hiatus where there should have been an answer. Valerius felt the small rush of nausea that used to come whenever Corvus had been wounded. 'Oh, gods,' he said again. 'Bellos, I'm so sorry.'

'Don't.' A pale hand fumbled for his and, finding it, gripped gently, as if Valerius, and not the boy, were injured. 'Just get me inside and give me the wormwood or whatever other unspeakable concoction your Hibernian healer left behind and all will be well.' Bellos' grin was more certain this time. 'I've had all afternoon to think about this. Luain mac Calma talks to the gods as the rest of us talk to our horses. They tell him everything that happens or might happen in the world. He must have expected it. He'll have left something that will work.'

Luain mac Calma may have conversed daily with the gods, but they did not see all futures, nor tell him all of those they saw. Amongst the many wax-plugged bottles and beakers of his pharmacy, nothing had properties that could restore sight to the suddenly blinded.

Valerius knew that, but he searched anyway, because it was expected of him and it gave hope, which was necessary. On exactly that basis, he poured out a half-measure of dried and ground goose grass which was good only for an inflammation of the eyes, not true blindness, and mixed it with dock roots and gall to make it taste bad to hide the vervain and poppy which would buy an untroubled sleep.

He succeeded only in part; Bellos drank as he was asked to, but in the waiting time before sleep, while Valerius laid clods of wet wool on his hair to leach out the blood, he said, thinly, 'If mac Calma left nothing, then there is nothing we can do, is there?' Then, when Valerius gave no answer, 'Perhaps you could put in more poppy next time? I could bear life as a boy who has poor use of his legs. I am not at all sure I want to live it as a man who is both crippled and blind.'

They were in a dreamer's hut, where, more than anywhere, words have power. With his left hand, Valerius made the sign to ward against evil. 'Don't say that. You fell and hit your head and it's bleeding within the bone as well as outside. When the bleeding stops, you will see again.'

'And the pain in my head will be less? I hope so. You should have put in more poppy anyway. There wasn't enough to draw a veil over this.'

Bellos was wrong: the poppy was sufficient to buy him dreamless sleep; and he was right: in the morning, the pain in his head was no less and he was still blind.

'We need mac Calma.'

Valerius said it, because Bellos would not. He had carried the boy to the midden to relieve himself and fed him and washed him and their life was as it had been in the first days, except that this time Bellos' mind was alive and active and, when not crushed by the pounding ache within it, he could think and speak clearly. Now, he said, 'We may as well need snow in summer. Unless I have lost more time than I know of, our god-favoured dreamer isn't due back until the end of next month.'

'Perhaps not, but we can summon him, or, rather, Efnís can. He is Elder of Mona in mac Calma's absence – there must always be one so designated on the island, to hold the dream of the ancestors. There are ways for one dreamer to speak to another if the need is strong enough.'

Bellos stared dry-eyed at the place he believed Valerius to be. 'Efnís won't call mac Calma for you.'

'No. But he may call him for you. I can ask. At worst he can only say no.'

XIV

'N o.'

'Efnís, Bellos is not your enemy. He is as much a victim of Rome as any man or woman of the tribes. He was sold into slavery when he was six years old. He was sold again nightly in a brothel in Gaul for the next four years. He was kicked in the head trying to foal the red mare because he didn't want to wake me and he fell because he was trying to fulfil Luain mac Calma's ludicrous requirements so that we could leave your precious island and go back to Hibernia. If he isn't healed, we may never leave. Is that what you want?'

Valerius stood at the entrance to the great-house, as close as he had ever been to the heart of Mona's dreaming. Oak uprights as wide as his arm and twice his height stood as door posts on either side. The carvings on them made his head spin as they had done once in his childhood. To avoid them, he looked straight ahead, towards the fire trenches and weapons, the warriors and dreamers within.

Eight warriors stood around him in a part-circle and the waves of hate were as tangible as any he had felt on a battlefield in a burning village. Some of them were not much older than Bellos. It was possible that Valerius had, indeed, burned their homes and hanged their families.

Efnís stood in the centre. He had been a quiet lad in his youth, thoughtful and open-hearted, and the boy Bán had cared for him and cherished his presence. He had not imagined him ruthless, but then, he had not imagined it of himself and had become so, for a time.

The man who faced him was more than ruthless; Efnís embodied a power that gave life to the door carvings simply by his presence. The gods of his people walked with him and through him and they were not inclined to pity. His eyes looked through Valerius as if they had never met except in battle.

'No,' he said again. 'Luain mac Calma is not yours to whistle to heel like a hound. If the boy dies, it is your loss, not ours.'

Valerius caught the fraying edge of his anger and held it. When one has no power, temper is a luxury not to be indulged. He said, 'The loss would be also mac Calma's. If Bellos dies, I am free to go and our year together will be less than half over. I doubt very much if he would have subjected you to our presence through the winter had he not wished me to remain beyond spring.'

'Nevertheless, I will not summon him. If the gods wish the boy dead, he will die. If not, he will live. If he is blind, he is still alive and that will suffice.'

If he is blind . . . Valerius had not mentioned Bellos' blindness to the dreamer. Efnís could only have known from some other source.

Valerius' anger did rise then, whitely, so that he felt the pressure on his cheekbones and behind his eyes. He stared at the warriors surrounding him and they matched him, hate for hate. Not caring to conceal the challenge, he said, 'Did you make this happen, any of you?'

Three warriors stepped forward, hounds straining at the leash. The death of the red-haired woman clung to them, demanding vengeance in kind. Valerius felt the pull of battle as a rising tide in his blood. For Bellos' sake, he fought it. 'Efnís, did you make him blind?'

The dreamer shook his head. 'No. But mac Calma said that if the boy fell it might happen. He has fallen and you are here asking our help when you have not approached the great-house in six months. Why else would that be so?'

'Did mac Calma leave instruction for what I should do if such a thing came about?'

'No.'

Valerius opened his mouth and shut it again. There was a change in Efnís, a barely perceptible softening of his voice. He had not said, 'I'm sorry' – he could not do so in such company – but the words had been there for one desperate to hear them.

Dry-mouthed, fearing to believe, Valerius said, 'Then, without help from the Elder, what would you do in my place?'

The ghost of a smile crossed Efnís' features. 'I would dream, what else? It is my training. And my birthright. I would find a place of god-given power and I would use everything I could find there to help me.' His gaze slid past Valerius towards the hut that lay down near the river: the dreamer's hut which had, for nearly twenty years, contained and moulded Airmid's god-given power.

Valerius caught himself at the last minute so that he did not turn to look. The movement became instead a jerky sweep of his cleaner hand through his hair. He did it without thought and did not know how much of the boy Bán he had been showed in that move. He said, 'Let me be clear. In my place, you would dream to mac Calma to call him back?'

Efnís leaned one shoulder against the gate post and the forefinger of his left hand traced again and again the shape of a running horse that was carved at the level of his heart. This time his smile was open for everyone to see, and it was not kind. 'No,' he said. 'I am more arrogant than that. If I needed help, I would dream to ask the gods for a healing. But if mac Calma had not taught me how to do that, then yes, I might dream to the Elder of Mona himself and ask for his help. It would be almost as good.'

I would dream. It is my birthright.

The words danced in the flames of a birchwood fire. Familiar faces resolved and dissolved beside them, casting shadows in the smoke. Efnís smiled intermittent encouragement from the heart-fire but would not speak. Theophilus, physician to the legions, shook his head and laughed at the fantasies of barbarian minds; Xenophon of Cos, physician to emperors, did not laugh but neither did he offer advice. Longinus Sdapeze smiled a greeting, a cavalry officer with not the slightest hint of dreaming about him, and later, with old barriers burned to ashes, Corvus appeared and sat for a while, watching the long trail of the dead who had followed him.

The ghosts of Valerius' past did not arm themselves with anger as they had once done. Eceni and Trinovante, Roman and Gaul, they came and went, dispassionately, nodding curtly to the man who had slain them, but not hurling curses or promising an eternity of retribution. It might have been easier if they had done; none of them was a dreamer, none of them knew how to summon a dreamer, or if they did, they were not prepared to share their secret.

If you had stayed with your people, would you have become a smith, do you think, or a healer?

My sister was to be the dreamer. I was going to be a warrior.

It is my birthright.

And mine also.

He believed it, because he wanted to. Through the cold and sweating night, Julius Valerius, who had been born Bán of the Eceni, son of a dreamer – son of *two* dreamers – and childhood friend to several others, drew on every memory of his youth while he held or burned or drank or prayed over every god-touched item in Airmid's hut in an increasingly desperate effort to call any of those, living or dead, who might help him to reach the gods or, as a close second best, Luain mac Calma.

He failed.

'You're trying too hard.'

'What?'

'You're trying too hard.' Bellos spoke sleepily from beyond the smoke. He sounded amused but there was no telling how long he had waited, lying awake, until he was sure he could sound so. 'I know nothing about dreaming but all night I have listened to you shouting down the dream-paths of the poppy and I don't think the gods are brought closer by shouting. The apprentice who brought the oat bannocks says that the gods speak only into silence.'

Valerius felt the motion of his mind crash into rock. He stared across the fire at the boy. 'What apprentice?'

'There's a girl of the Caledonii who has come twice now. Her people have not suffered under Rome and so she doesn't hate us as much as the rest and it seems she has an affection for bedridden boys with blond hair and blue ey— Don't be like that. I'm not a whore any more. She brought me oat bannocks and a hound whelp that wanted to play, that's all.'

'Really? How very disappointing for both of you.' Valerius' head swam. Facts collided and fell out at random. He said, 'Let me get this straight. You spoke about dreaming, with a dreamer of Mona, who did not try to peel your skin from your back? Was this before or after you had the poppy?' The certainties of his winter faltered and then disintegrated as his stomach, his mouth and his flooding saliva registered the single most important fact. 'You have been hoarding *oat bannocks* and you didn't tell me?'

'I'm not hoarding them. Yes, I spoke to a dreamer. It was before I fell and I hadn't taken any poppy. We talked of the whelp, and she said that when hounds sleep and dream by the fire, they are visiting the lands of the gods. She didn't offer to show me how to follow them. And I'm sorry I didn't tell you about the bannocks. I was saving them for a celebration when I'd stood and matched you two strokes.' His voice faltered only a little and recovered its humour as he fumbled in his pocket, then: 'Here – catch.'

It was not a bad throw for a blind youth, and not a bad catch for a man who had sat awake through the night. The bannock became only mildly singed in the heart of the fire and possibly the better for it.

Valerius said, 'Are there any more?' and then, when Bellos nodded and held up a single finger, 'Put it next to the fire to warm it. I think there's some honey left somewhere,' and so, for a moment, the world was no bigger than a meal remembered with joy from childhood, washed down with stream water and eaten in the first light of the morning sun.

Presently, thinking, Valerius said, 'I don't understand why Macha didn't come through the fire with the other ghosts. For ten years, she haunted every sleeping dream and too much of the days. Why, when I need her, does she stay away?'

'Because you need her, perhaps? It does not seem to me that your mother's haunting was designed to help you in your times of need.'

'No. But she didn't kill me, or drive others to kill me, and there were times when she could have done.'

Valerius lay on his stomach, his head pillowed on his forearm, staring into the fire. 'If the bannock-girl would help you, I could go to Hibernia to find mac Calma.'

'If you will give me two days to learn, I can find where everything is in the hut and I won't need anyone's help. I can move to the midden and back and there is food enough for a month unless you've eaten it all in the night while I was asleep.'

It was a poor attempt at humour. Valerius ignored it. 'No. I can't leave you alone. What if you were to fall again?'

'I might go deaf as well?' Bellos rolled onto his side and pushed himself to sitting. Staring at where he thought Valerius sat, he said, very quietly, 'You have to leave me, Julius. I would rather manage here alone in hope than wait with you through the spring for mac Calma to come back, praying daily to your gods and mine to hear his voice. I don't think I have the strength for that.'

Bellos had more strength than either of them had realized, in body as well as in mind. Valerius stayed for a day and guided him through continual practice, at the end of which the youth could prepare a meal without cutting his fingers and had demonstrated that he could find a jug and drag himself to the stream to fill it.

Towards dusk, the bannock-girl appeared with a jointed hare and Valerius walked off to check on the horses, leaving Bellos to speak to her. Returning, he found Bellos with more colour to his cheeks than at any time since he had fallen, and a smile that was not so clearly forced. A pot simmered on the fire and the smell of stewed hare meat and wild garlic filled the still air by the stream.

They ate together after dark when there was nothing else to practise or to clear or to clean. Bellos said, 'I told her you'd be gone with the dawn and that, whether you found mac Calma or not, you'd be back by the full moon. I think she'll help while you're gone. She won't be in trouble for it. Efnís knows that she comes here.'

'I thought he might.' Valerius had spent his walk considering the timeliness of the girl's appearances. 'I'd wager that mac Calma told them both to act as they did before he left. Very little he does seems to rely on chance.'

'I was right, then? You will leave with the dawn?'

'I will, unless I can call mac Calma tonight in the dream. It's

183

worth trying. You never know; the hare is Nemain's beast and Airmid was always of Nemain. Perhaps having eaten the god's beast in the god's domain, I will find that I can live true to my birthright.'

Bellos stared at him. For the first time since his fall, his eyes focused close to where Valerius sat. He asked, 'Does that matter to you now?'

'Only as a tool. I am tired of being another man's toy. If I could heal you on my own, I would do, you know that. Because I can't, I must call on mac Calma's aid. If I could call the gods on my own, to ask their help in healing, I would be free of all men.'

Bellos laid down his bowl and stretched out like a hound near the fire. 'And would it be good to be free of all men?'

'It would be little short of perfect.'

As an officer of the auxiliary cavalry, Julius Valerius had passed many nights without sleep in situations far less clement than a fire-lit hut on a stream's edge, with his belly filled and the scents of garlic, woodsmoke and hare's meat warming his senses.

Perhaps because of that, he did not, as he had intended, remain awake to seek the gods' help in the fire, but slept and, in sleeping, dreamed, disjointedly and unpleasantly, of his mother and mac Calma walking, sleeping, lying together as lovers in the ancient, sacred places of Hibernia in the year before his birth.

Rome had been a distant enemy then, and all conflicts small, although they had not seemed so. Valerius' mother had been young, and not angry. She had felt the presence of the boy-child growing in her womb and had loved him. She had lain alone under a white full moon and named the child Bán, meaning white in the language of Hibernia, for the colour of it. Pressing her hands together over his heartbeat and hers, she said, 'You will be Nemain's, and will grow in her care. I will see to it.'

Luain mac Calma had come to her later, with news of conflict growing in Gaul and the death of the dreamers at the hands of Rome. Macha had always known that he must leave, but Valerius, who had once been Bán, felt in the womb and in his dreaming self the pain of their parting, the emptiness of promises not made because they would be hollow.

The loss was too sharp to be borne. Breaking free from his

mother, Valerius watched from afar as she bought a good mare from the Hibernian breeding herds and a hound that had taken deer in full flight and journeyed east, to the village of her birth where her sister had a two-year-old girl-child by a man named Eburovic.

Macha was clearly pregnant when she arrived. Eburovic did not love her, nor she him, but they had known one another from childhood and there was a great affection between them. His fathering of her child was to be a temporary thing, until Luain mac Calma came back from Gaul. Neither the gods nor the dreamers told them it would be close to fourteen years before the Elder's return.

The dream of Macha wavered as she came closer to birth. Breaca was there, a fox-haired girl-child learning to walk with Graine, her mother, but it was Eburovic, big and blunt and kind-hearted, with nothing of the dreamer about him at all, who, smiling, filled the last, thinly woven moments.

Valerius woke, too sharply, and lay with his eyes open gazing at the shuddering light on the back wall of the hut. The fire burned behind him, warming the small of his back. He stared at stone and saw the face of Luain mac Calma, wet from the shipwreck with his black hair hanging in sea-ropes to his shoulders.

The man smiled, sadly. 'Eburovic raised you. It was the gods' will, not mine, but he did it well, however much I might regret it. Still, you are my son, not his. You can run, but you cannot deny who made you. I offer you now your birthright. Will you take it?'

Often before, Valerius had thought himself awake and found it not true. In Rome, he had watched Dubornos attempt to prove himself dreaming by passing his hand through a wall and had noted it as a dreamer's technique, simple in its concept and likely to succeed. Now, he sat up and, very deliberately, put the heel of one hand against the embers of the fire, holding it there until the pain crushed his breathing and layers of reddened skin peeled away.

The pain drove both the voice and the image of mac Calma from his head, but the dream still held him, as tightly formed as any memory, and as real. Cursing softly, he found his cloak and stepped quietly past the sleeping Bellos into the night.

The night was still and warm, lit by an amber half-moon. Owls called in the woods beyond the dreamers' great-house. Closer by, the stream whispered in foreign tongues. The small beasts of the night shuffled and blundered in old leaves and new spring grass. At the foot of the hill, the bay gelding whickered a quiet greeting.

The route Valerius took was not planned. He needed only to prove himself firmly awake and he could return to bed, to sleep one last night in a hut that he had begun to consider his own. He crossed the stream in bare feet, letting the chilled water swill at his ankles, then turned left, through the trees towards the horse fields, searching as he did so the vent in the hem of his cloak where he hid the grain for the horses.

The hawthorn hedge bounding the paddocks was served by a gap, the width of a man, but not a horse. Valerius had fitted his shoulder through and was reaching for the gelding when a voice behind him said, 'When you were dreaming, which gods did you petition, yours or mine?'

He was still dreaming, then; the fire had been an illusion, as much as the water of the stream and the coarse grass beneath his feet. In this dream, he had some control of his own actions, which was pleasant. He pushed on through the hedge and met the gelding, warming his hands on a muzzle that was nothing more than a product of his mind. The beast seemed as solid as he did in life, but then dreams always seem so from the inside. It is only on waking that one can see the gaps that make them unreal.

Mac Calma's voice said, 'Valerius, answer me. It matters.'

The voice was entirely compelling. Unwillingly, Valerius said, 'I have no gods. I served Mithras once, but do so no longer. I abandoned him when I was banished from the legions. The gods of the tribes abandoned me long ago and take their vengeance where they can. I called on none of them by name, only made my need known.'

'So. And it surprises you, therefore, that none came? Have you learned so little in your life?'

'You sound like my mother. Her ghost despises me also. Are you dead, then, that you can sound so?'

'Hardly. I don't despise you. It is you who hates me. Have you found the key to Bellos' healing?'

In dreaming there is an honesty that waking may lack. Valerius said, 'No. But I have found that I no longer wish to depend on you to make it happen. It occurs to me that you have never told me why

186

you brought me here. If it was to learn healing, you have never tried to teach it, or dreaming, but then I have never asked to learn. I remember, once, the grandmothers saying that a dreamer must ask to be given the dream. Last night, I asked it of the nameless gods. Tonight, I ask it of you.'

'Thank you.' The hedge shivered and Luain mac Calma stood in the moonlight, soothing the neck of the gelding, which was not surprised to see him.

Valerius tried to pass his hand through the horse and failed. He stared at his feet and moved his toes and they remained his toes and did not become cloven, or bird-clawed, or grow the nails of a hound. Self-loathing curdled in the pit of his stomach. Raising his head, he said bitterly, 'You woke me. Why?'

Mac Calma shook his head in mild reproof. 'To save you taking ship with the dawn to look for me. I thought I might prevent at least one journey's seasickness. Some men might be grateful.'

'You could have woken me by touch. That did not take a dream.'

'But there are things you will believe in dreaming that you will not believe waking. Do you believe now that I am your father?'

'We have spoken of this before. Eburovic raised me. That's all that matters.'

'No. You are the son of two dreamers and that matters now. You were born to be a dreamer. You were named for the white moon and the black night about it. Bán of the Eceni, you have spent the past twenty years running from your birthright. I offer it to you now, this once, this last time. Will you take it?'

'Will you heal Bellos if I do?'

'I will heal him anyway. If you come to sit your long-nights, then you must come willingly, not under coercion. You must know that you come through a gateway as dangerous as any you passed when you led your cavalry wing. You must know that the commitment is total, that any failure means death, not only of your body but of your soul, and that even I, who am Elder of Mona, cannot keep you safe from that. Knowing all of that, if you wish still to take what is yours by right, I will teach you, however those of my great-house loathe me for it. If you do not have the courage, I will heal Bellos to the best of my ability, and you will be free.'

Valerius gazed past the Elder of Mona to the moon, which had risen higher and was white. The hare had not yet come to rest on its surface and the salute Valerius made acknowledged that, as his mother had taught him.

From the corner of his eye, he saw a tension leak from mac Calma that he had not known was present. Softly, the man who claimed to be his father said, 'If you wish a day to consider you may have it. I will work on Bellos while you think.'

'Thank you. A day will not make any difference to this decision. You offer me the chance to sit my long-nights. I accept.'

'THEY ARE NOT BUILT FOR US.'
Graine spoke with the assurance of a sworn dreamer and
was not heard. Breaca knew that her daughter had spoken,
but the words merged with the meaningless sounds of morning: the
slowing breath of her mare and the creak of harness leather as she
settled to stillness on the crest of the hill; the clash of chain mail
from the auxiliary escort still riding the slope behind, and the
fainter, identical clash from the century of legionaries marching in
formation out of Camulodunum's triumphal gate onto the plain
below; the rasping cry of a single crow, far back, in the place where
there should have been forest, but instead was bare earth.

All of these Breaca registered and none made sense. From the
moment of cresting the hill, from the moment of Cunomar's first
startled oath and Cygfa's war curse, every part of her had fixed on
the two newly made oakwood crosses that stood alone on the
north-eastern corner of the city. Twice the height of a man and one
across, they were more than enough to hang the Boudica and any
one of her children.

Pale in the morning sun, they cast angular shadows across the
turf in a statement more eloquent, more shattering, than the
governor's deftly phrased invitation. *We have you, we own you.*
Your death is ours, the time of it and the manner. Do not expect
mercy from the emperor or those who serve him.

It was impossible to look elsewhere, impossible, for that moment, to think. Cunomar had said as much in a rare moment of honesty when he had first come back from Rome; that however much one tried to imagine the worst to make it bearable, however much one built the nightmares and dismantled them, the solid presence of a cross shattered the world.

Breaca had never stood in the shadow of her own execution as had her two older children. In the long, still breath at the top of Camulodunum's hill, she learned the nature and extent of their terror and her respect for them both reached new heights.

A small hand closed on Breaca's wrist. Graine said for a second time, distinctly, 'Don't look at them so. They have not yet tasted blood, but they were not made for us. A warrior of the tribes will die and one of Rome and both are already held in prison. We have not yet been betrayed.'

She was a child. All the way up the slope, she had ridden her new horse with both hands gripping the front of the saddle as an infant might, but her voice was as old, and as sure, as it had been on an afternoon in the forge when she had spoken for the elder grandmother.

Breaca nodded, lacking words. Beside her, Cunomar stirred. 'And so are we to believe that legions are marching out to do us honour, not arrest us?'

He tried so hard to appear unmoved. His voice was lightly detached, his words the casual comment of one observing the distant return of a bird to the nest, or the birth of a mid-season lamb. His face was set, held still by a thin shell of pride and an obstinate refusal to show fear in the presence of the enemy.

Only his eyes gave him away. His gaze danced from the stark shadows of the execution site to the western gate where eighty men, led by an officer on a grey horse, marched out through the vast, twice-arched triumphal gate that spanned the entrance to Camulodunum, and formed three lines across the road. They made a spectacle, and knew it; the chain links of their armour were a net of silver across the path of the sun and the heads of their spears were herons, awaiting the careless fish. Painted thunderbolts crossed on their shields, newly painted since winter, and their bronze helmets burned from night upon night of polishing.

Behind them, Rome's capital city – its only city – in the province of Britannia spread out across the wide plain that had once been Cunobelin's richest farmland and pooled in what had once been forest. It was unwalled and undefended and that alone screamed out the arrogance of Rome. In a land defeated, what need had they of the walls and dykes on which the Sun Hound had relied for his safety?

'One day, you will regret the loss of that.' Breaca spoke aloud, but not loudly. Even had she shouted, the men below would barely have heard her, but one, finally, chose to look up and his oath carried faintly on the breeze. Eighty faces flashed pale in the sun. The red-plumed officer gave an order, too distant to be clearly heard. The line tightened, visibly.

Breaca grinned. 'Graine, heart-of-life, before we left, Airmid said that the best way to hide was to be seen most clearly. If I were to hold your reins, do you think you could join us in being seen very clearly indeed? The legionaries have sighted us now; there's no point in hiding. I would not ride into their care as one defeated.'

She watched her daughter's eyes grow wide. They were green-grey in the sun and beautiful. Graine had always listened carefully to the singers' tales. She knew what Breaca planned before her brother, but she was not yet a confident rider, even on the new horse.

Swallowing her fear, she passed her reins to her mother. 'You and father came here once before,' she said. 'Before any of us were born. You did not ride in meekly then.'

They had not. With forty of her people, Breaca had charged the ranked hundreds of Cunobelin's spears in the days when both his tribe and theirs had been free.

'We are Eceni,' she said. 'We ride nowhere meekly.'

She lifted her hand in signal and Cygfa and Cunomar, trained in the battle signs of Mona, moved to either side. For the first time since leaving the steading, Cunomar smiled. He still mourned the loss of Eneit's company, but he would ride as a warrior with his mother given the chance to do so. Cygfa set up the war chant of the Ordovices and the tone of it infected them all. Breaca missed her blade more badly than she had done since leaving it in the ancestor's mound.

What she planned was madness, but she had lived through a winter of sanity and the legionaries who waited in front of the gates had already been given their orders. If death were coming, she did not want to meet it weakly, nor bring her children to the enemy shorn of their pride. Cunomar and Cygfa felt it with her; the change in their eyes was a gift in itself.

Graine was afraid and trying not to show it, which was worth more. Breaca leaned over and kissed her, winding a lock of loose hair behind the small ear. 'Child of my heart, hold the front of the saddle and trust your horse. She's the best I've ever bred. She knows how to take care of you.'

Breaca spoke to her own mare and it grew still under her, waiting. To her two older children, she said, 'Spread your arms so that they see we come without weapons.'

They did, and waited. Behind, 'Tagos saw, understood and was too late to act.

As she had so often in the west, the Boudica raised her arm high and brought it down hard.

'*Go!*'

The noise of Camulodunum faltered and fell silent leaving the morning to echo as three warriors and a child of the Eceni hurled their horses at lethal speed towards the triumphal arches that marked the magnitude of Rome's victory over their people. The wind raised their cloaks and carried away the dust of their passing. 'Tagos and the cavalry escort, caught unawares, were left hopelessly behind. They slowed and stopped, deterred by the pitch of the hill.

The Eceni were born for a ride such as this; even Graine found the joy at the end. At the last moment, as the legionaries, who had not fought in the west and had been a long time away from war, struggled to hold their line, three warriors and a child reined in to stand on sweating, heaving mounts before a junior tribune of the XXth legion and his wide-eyed men. At the final stride, seeing them stop, the officer resheathed his sword.

Breaca faced him, smiling. For nearly twenty years, the best minds on Mona had been her tutors. In faultless Latin, she said, 'Breaca of the Eceni brings greetings to the governor and asks if he will do her the honour of accepting her gifts.'

'Be welcome Breaca of the Eceni, wife to Prasutagos, king of that tribe.'

The best way to hide is to be seen most clearly. Believing it, Breaca had brought her family into the death trap that was Camulodunum at a gallop, and had not been arrested. If Graine was wrong and they were bound for crucifixion, the junior tribune detailed to meet them did not know of it. Holding fast to his dignity, he ordered his men to form ranks around Breaca, the children and the lately arrived 'Tagos. With every evidence of respect, he led them through the mud-slimed, noisome streets of Camulodunum to the forum, where they stood in line to be announced.

'Be welcome Cygfa and Graine, under Eceni law heirs to Prasutagos, and Cunomar, his son.'

A pasty-faced secretary stood to one side of a podium and read from a prepared script. Looking up, he chanced to catch Cygfa's eye and she smiled for him, bright with a hate so well concealed that only a dreamer would see it. He dithered and lost his lines. Finding them, he rattled to a close, losing the customary emphasis of the syllables.

'Quintus Veranius, by the grace of his excellency the Emperor Nero governor of Britannia, formerly consul of Rome, formerly augur, formerly first governor of Lycia and Pamphylia, bids you welcome and thanks you for your exceptional gifts.'

The secretary bowed his way back into the row of Roman officers and local magistrates who formed a line before the marbled back wall of the forum. All of them studied the incomers. None of them was so ill-mannered as to stare although the king's new armband, of woven gold with enamelled copper at the end pieces, drew their eyes and their attention, as it was meant to.

The governor of Britannia, the emperor's representative in the province, with the power of life and death over every living soul within it, stepped forward to the podium and, for a while, it was impossible to look elsewhere. Quintus Veranius' parade uniform, while sober in its colouring, was nevertheless quite easily the most costly item of clothing ever seen in the province of Britannia, the Emperor Claudius' gold-woven gown-of-entrance notwithstanding.

The governor's chased gold cuirass bore a complex interweaving of the fish-tailed goat with oak leaves and a standing vine. His shoulder cloak was so deep a brown as to be almost black and his plain-woven tunic beneath it seemed in contrast to be perfectly white, marked only by a sober border of blue and venous red.

No-one would ever be allowed to forget that the middle-aged, grey-haired man who now ruled Britannia in the name of the boy-emperor in Rome had once led his troops in person in the mountain provinces of Asia, defeating tribe after tribe on their home ground. His gaze had weighed each member of the tribal delegations as they entered the forum. Each had felt it as an uncomfortable probing, not unlike the scrutiny of a dreamer.

Only for the children had it softened and then only truly for Graine. He was said to have no children of his own; it was his only lack. He smiled at the girl now, and then at 'Tagos, who purported to be her sire, before he looked down at the wooden crates and boxes arrayed on the table in front of him.

Breaca's gift lay open before the assembly: a long case of polished yew wood lined with wool dyed in Eceni blue on which lay three finished spears, each with a single heron feather dangling from the neck. The hafts were made in the same pale russet wood as the box with a bulb of burr oak at the butt end for balance, each a subtly different colour. The blades were of silver and delicately leaf-shaped, with copper inlaid in spiral shapes in the tapering necks and the sign of the running hare etched along their lengths on both sides. The blades' edges showed the brilliance of fine honing and the tips glittered sharply. Each was exactly twice the length of those permitted to a hunter of the tribes.

The governor ran his thumb along the length of the box, testing the texture of the yew. It was said of him that his skill in war was superseded only by a winning charm in the council chamber. There was an easy warmth to his smile and humour in the creases around his eyes that might well have passed for genuine candour in the council chambers of Rome.

'I am told you are a smith.' The governor spoke in Latin, slowly, and left a pause. His voice was warmly bronze, like a bell, and it held no more threat than his written invitation had done. If he were acting, if he knew the identity of the woman to whom he spoke and was concealing it, he was exceptionally skilled.

Before the interpreter could fill the space, Breaca said in the same tongue, 'Your honour, yes. My father was a smith. He taught me his trade before he died. It has been a pleasure to recreate his work for those who can appreciate it.'

'Indeed?' Crooking one eyebrow, Veranius lifted the first spear and moved his hand along until he found the balance point. The haft sprung in his grip. The blade quivered in the dusty light so that, for those closest, the hare etched along its length seemed to run. A sigh seeped from the assembled ranks of the tribal delegations behind. Those who had ever sat a spear-trial knew what they saw. The rest understood only that they were in the presence of a beauty that transcended the world of the forum.

The governor stopped smiling. If Rome did not have its spear-trials, still, those who fought did so under the sway of their gods. Slowly and with more care than before, he rested the spear's haft across his flattened palms and spent some time examining the blade, taking care not to tarnish the sheen of the surface with finger grease.

At length, raising his head, he looked Breaca directly in the eye. Abandoning the formal language of court, he said, 'I didn't know the Eceni hunted with silver weapons?'

He was not acting, and the question held more than the words alone.

Breaca returned his gaze. 'Your honour, we don't, but the ancestors are said to have hunted bear with these blades when called upon to do so by the gods. Silver is finer than iron and holds its edge for less time. According to our most ancient lore, the blade must be made and used within the turning of one moon or it is useless and must be melted down again. A spear would be made on the instruction of a dreamer and used within the month or not at all.'

She did not say that the tradition was far older than the Eceni, that those who had hunted in this fashion were the direct ancestors of Ardacos' she-bears. Nor did she say that the month would end in five days' time.

The governor was not a stupid man. Over the course of his career, he had taken the time to study the ancestral histories of several cultures. Nodding thoughtfully, he said, 'Silver is far softer than iron. Does it not bend on hitting its target?'

'It may do. Such a spear as this must be thrown with absolute accuracy. If it hits any bone, it will bend and will not kill, leaving the hunter in mortal danger. If, on the other hand, the spear flies between the ribs and strikes the heart, or through the neck to the great vessels of the throat, the kill will be perfect and the hunter will survive. In former times, it was a test of courage. Even to own such a spear was a mark of honour. This is the first time in our history that one has been given as a gift to a warrior who is not of the tribes.'

'Thank you. I am deeply honoured. I am constantly astonished by the beauty and craftsmanship of Eceni metalwork.'

The governor returned the spear to its bed of blue wool. Tracing his fingers along the fine polish of the haft, he said, 'And of course, they would be perfect weapons for use in battle for one with the skill to throw them. If hurled at the enemy, the blades of those which did not lodge in the soft parts of a man's body would bend and could not be returned. We do the same with our javelins.'

He was a man with the charm of a diplomat and the intellect to prosper in Claudius' Rome. He threw his rock lightly into the flow of their conversation and waited for Breaca to run aground on it. Shorn of its languid humour, his gaze was an open challenge. Twenty years' training on Mona prevented Breaca from returning it in kind.

Without rancour, she said, 'Your honour, we had heard as much, but these spears are for sacred ceremony, not for battle. I would not suggest that the governor use these against the Silures when next he goes to war, but he may wish to try them some time against bear in our northern forests. If not, I would feel honoured if he would consider them worthy to take back to Rome as evidence of his governorship when it ends.'

Her own rocks were smaller but no less obvious. She felt 'Tagos twitch at her side and force himself to stillness. Quintus Veranius, by Nero's grace governor of Britannia, stared at her for a moment in naked astonishment, then threw his head back and laughed. After a pause, several members of his entourage laughed with him, though uncertainly.

The smile the governor directed at Prasutagos was genuine, possibly his first that day that was so. Reaching over the table, he clapped the king on the shoulder.

'My friend, your late wife was a delight to us all and I am sorry for her passing, but this one is a gem beyond measure and you should treasure her. A woman with a sharp mind who is not afraid to use it is an uncommon gift. My lady' – he bowed deeply to

Breaca – 'I will convene a council later tomorrow at which several officers recently in the west . . .'

He spoke, his mouth moved and there was doubtless meaning in the words, but Breaca heard nothing. The world shattered and fell to pieces in the face of the dark-haired man behind, whom the governor's bow had revealed and at once concealed; the man with the head bandage who had recently served in the west. The man who, once, had been shipwrecked on the Eceni coast and lived through a winter in a roundhouse as a guest of Macha, first of the royal line of that tribe.

Graine reached up and placed her hand in her mother's. Her small, cool fingers gripped fiercely and the pressure brought Breaca back to herself and to the meaning of the governor's considered, amused reply.

'. . . as to your second point, only his grace the emperor knows when I may be recalled from my position here. I was honoured by the deified Claudius in being allowed to hold my first governorship for the full five years and I have a liking for your country such that it would sadden me greatly to leave Britannia early. I will do my best to stay as long as the law permits.'

He smiled at Breaca, showing white, strong teeth with a slight gap in front. 'Does that answer both of your questions fully?'

'Your honour, it does, thank you.'

She could speak, which was good. The governor moved on to her left, which was not good at all, but inevitable, and to be faced with courage. Holding herself still much as Cunomar had done on the hillside, Breaca of the Eceni raised her head and looked full in the eyes the man she had known as Valerius Corvus, officer of the legions and friend to her brother.

In the strange, slow world of the forum, with its whorled marble floors and white plastered columns, Breaca was a girl again, standing outside her father's forge in the mellow sun of late spring, polishing the naked newness of her serpent-blade. The air was warm and held more promise than any now in Camulodunum. The hank of lamb's wool in her hand was greasy with lanolin and it blued the blade of a weapon that had never yet taken a life.

With the naivety of one who believes the world will never change, Breaca had laid her blade flat on her palms and offered it to the dark-haired Roman whom the gods had seen fit to throw from the sea at her feet. He had need of a blade; the elder council had met to try him and, once condemned, his death would have been the slow agony of a traitor unless he could fight in single combat against a warrior of the tribes. Caradoc respected him and had offered to fight. With courage and quiet pride, the Roman had come to ask for her sword so that he might not die unarmed. Because she did not wish Airmid to have to kill him, Breaca had offered it.

The day had been slow and peaceful and the world had not been at war. His eyes had been brown, like Bán's, and painfully honest. Afterwards, when the elder council had freed him and he had not been required to fight, he had been Bán's friend.

Now, feeling the burn of his eyes on her face, Breaca remembered that one fact most strongly: Valerius Corvus was a man of unshakeable integrity and a valued friend to her brother. Even so, if any man of the legions might know the true identity of Breaca, wife to Prasutagos, Corvus was that man.

Whatever his integrity, or his care for her brother, his duty would not allow him to keep the knowledge from his governor and there could only be one outcome of that. Graine may have been correct that the crosses by the theatre had not been built for them, but the men of Rome were ever resourceful; they could always build more.

The best way to hide is to be seen most clearly.

Only if those seeking do not know for whom it is they look. Breaca had not imagined that the gods would play such games as this.

The world became a smaller place and time ran slow. Graine's hand lay still within her mother's, warming a little, her fair child's skin unbearably soft against the old sword calluses, made new again by a spring's forging. Her hair was the rich, deep red of ox blood; it had been combed on waking to the gloss of horse hide and then furled again by the ride down the hill so that it lay in shining ropes to her shoulders. The top of her head came barely above Breaca's waist. Her neck was slim and straight and achingly long, the skin a translucent milky white, bluing a little over the veins, like flint newly picked from a river. Her whole body weighed little more than a three-month-old foal. Even to imagine it bruised was hard; to see it in vivid colour twisted and broken by a rope should have been impossible but was not. In the early tales of the first hangings in the eastern steadings had come the stark truth that a small, light-weight child does not die quickly and might easily outlive her parents to die alone long after the rest of her family has gone. Crucified, she could live a day and a night before the gods brought the quiet of death.

Not while I am alive to prevent it. The decision slid between other thoughts and did not seem unacceptable. In the early days of Rome's purges, mothers had drowned their own children in the rivers to keep them from the legionaries. The Boudica had no river, but she was a warrior; she had killed often enough to know the many ways by which a life might end. Suspended in a cold, un-natural clarity, Breaca began to plan the means by which she might most swiftly bring about the death of her daughter.

Cunomar stood on her right. He felt the change in her but was too old to hold her hand. He leaned in slightly and his shoulder brushed hers. Valerius Corvus, the man of integrity who held all their lives in his hand, saw it and smiled. Cunomar, too, should die before they could take him; he had stood once beneath his own cross and should not do so twice. It would be more difficult, but not impossible.

In her mind, Breaca began to sing the death song of Mona, that is at once a gift of life to Briga and a prayer for a swift and easy death. In place of her own name, she uttered, clearly, those of her three children.

'Tagos stepped forward to sign his will on the governor's table. Of the eight kings present, his was the last to be witnessed. Along the line, men and women shuffled, sensing an end to the tedium of rote-learned speeches and stilted Latin. As happened sometimes in the moments before battle, Breaca felt her skin grow thinner until the air around her was a river of languid, living sound that seeped into her blood. The dust-laden light of the forum became a patchwork of men's breath, and, within it, their weapons shimmered.

She had no weapons. The loss pressed on her as it had not done in the six months since she had left her blade in the care of the dead. The space at her side where her blade should have hung let in the cold as if a child had left open a door in winter. The memory of the ancestors' grave mound made dark the already dim light of the forum until the only shine came from the silver-bladed heron-spears that had been her gift to the governor. They hungered for blood and it could be a child's shed in mercy as much as an enemy's shed in battle, although neither was what they were made for. Breaca measured the distance from her place in the line to the yew-wood box lying on the table and knew that the officer Corvus watched as she did so.

Her eyes met his: always in battle she knew the one of the enemy who was most dangerous. He smiled a little, inclining his head, and lifted one shoulder in a half-shrug that conveyed at once an apology and a warrior's honour. Breaca nodded back and the air became a blood-link between them. He was a man of integrity. She did not believe he would find it necessary to crucify children, or a warrior of Cygfa's beauty.

At the table the secretary gave an order. The governor's signature was shown to the crowd. 'Tagos' will, copied onto two scrolls, was not read out. The content of a king's last behest was rightly considered a private matter, not for discussion by his peers who were also his rivals in the constant competition for the governor's approval.

A sigh stuttered the length of the room, the exhalation of diplomacy forced beyond its limits. Outwardly, all was perfect. None of the infants had disgraced themselves. Of all those attending, only the young, prettily pregnant wife of Cogidubnos, king of the Belgae on the far south coast, had asked to be excused. Everyone else had waited it out and took the time now to stretch legs that were not used to long periods of standing.

A river of slow-moving bodies separated Breaca from Corvus. A slave pressed a goblet of wine towards her.

She shook her head and smiled, motioning down to Graine. 'My daughter must relieve herself. If you will forgive me?'

Graine looked up. Her eyes were the eyes of the elder grandmother in the days before the old woman went blind. She smiled and pursed her lips and did not argue in front of strangers.

Breaca pushed on towards the door. Cygfa followed behind. She had fought too many battles with the Boudica not to feel another coming; her eyes asked questions that could not be answered but her body moved to the left and became a shield. Cunomar took the right as if born to it. For both their sakes, Breaca prayed as she had never done, that she might find at least one edged weapon before Corvus found her.

They reached the door. Armed with a valid excuse, Breaca smiled at the guards, who smiled back. The smooth flow of those leaving became briefly turbulent on the steps leading out of the forum as men and women stopped to speak to old acquaintances, so that it was harder to keep formation than it would have been in battle.

Breaca looked back and saw a dark head, marked with a bandage, reach the top of the steps and look round. Urgently, she sought escape and took it, stepping sideways into a blind-ending alleyway running between the governor's house and its neighbour that already stank of many men's urine.

Graine, released, played her necessary part, raising her tunic to squat in the dirt and it seemed that Breaca had not actually lied to the sentries; her daughter did need to come outdoors. Unbidden, the warriors who were her brother and sister set themselves at the alley's entrance; Cunomar decorated a wall not far away. Cyfga leaned idly against the opposite corner.

Privacy was impossible: others joined them, and for the same need; the alley was the first obvious gap after the steps. An elderly, white-haired Atrebatan warrior delayed his business for long enough to stare at Breaca, frowning. 'I have heard tales of the heron-spears of the Caledones,' he said, 'but never seen one. Is it true they are cursed?'

Breaca shook her head. A winter spent in Prasutagos' company had taught her a faculty for duplicity that Mona had never done. 'Only if you're a bear and their dreamers want your teeth and pelt for their winter ceremonies.'

'I see.' The Atrebatan gazed at her thoughtfully. 'Perhaps, then, the governor will use them to hunt the she-bears. I hear they are still active in the west and he will be grateful for any help he can get. I must remember to congratulate him when the opportunity presents itself. Your daughter wishes to speak to you.'

Graine had completed her mission. Standing, she slipped her hand in her mother's again, squeezing on and off in a signal that Airmid might have recognized, but Breaca did not. The child's ox-blood hair had picked up the dust of the alley. Smoothing it down so that her hand fell, as if naturally, on the nape of her daughter's neck, Breaca led her back out into the open, away from the prying eyes of a man who had once been her enemy. Berikos of the Atrebates, who had once betrayed all of Britannia to Rome, stayed behind her to add his own measure of piss to the tainted mud.

Cygfa waited near the alley's mouth. Cunomar was behind. Corvus was not in sight. The space in front of the governor's mansion was filled with milling delegates and their Roman hosts and it was impossible to pick out one bandaged head amongst the crowd. Breaca took a guess and led her daughter towards the left.

They were slowed by the crowd. Twisting her neck under her mother's hand until she could look up properly, Graine said, 'Berikos only thinks he has seen you before. He isn't sure.'

A dreamer with such power should not be made to die so young. Closing her eyes, Breaca said, 'Does he know where he thinks he has seen me?'

'No. He is old and confused and his attention is mostly with the governor and the trading rights he seeks from him. But the Roman with the bandage on his head knows.'

'He does. He was a friend to your uncle Bán long ago, before he was taken away. He knew all of us then, even your father. He offered to speak for Bán at his long-nights, but—'

'Look, he's coming now.'

Too late, Breaca looked directly at the steps to the mansion. Corvus was a stone's throw away, walking straight towards her, while managing to look as if he had no real goal. There was nowhere to go, no chance to run that would not leave a seven-year-old child to the mercy of the legionaries.

Crouching, Breaca made a show of re-settling her daughter's tunic and unpinned her cloak. The brooch that held it was newly made in bronze, an old shape, that could from some angles be a spear-head and from others a hunting owl. The iron pin was half the length of Breaca's hand; not long enough to pierce an adult heart, but enough to kill a child if used swiftly and accurately. The weight of the metal settled in Breaca's hand and the pin angled forward.

'Graine, please know that I—'

'I do know. And I love you. But we have not yet been betrayed.' Graine stood very still. Her wide eyes were the colour of clouds after rain, as Caradoc's had been, with her own haze of sea-green at the inner edges, where grey met the central black. It was not possible to look into them and think of a life ended.

A shadow crossed theirs. Still lost in the surety of her daughter's gaze, Breaca asked, in slow Eceni, 'Will the Roman with the bandaged head betray us, do you think?'

From behind and a little to her left, Corvus said in the same language, quietly, 'Not if he is not forced to.'

The green-grey eyes released her. Graine drew a shaky breath. Breaca let herself look past the pin in her hand. Cunomar lounged at the entrance to the alley, keeping watch to left and right. Cygfa was close, standing amongst the crowd, guarding her left side. Caught in the crush of her own whirlpool, Breaca said, 'What might force him?'

'An action on the part of a woman who was once a warrior which could be considered an act of aggression against Rome.'

Berikos passed them by, staring curiously. In Latin, Corvus said, 'The governor is genuinely grateful for the gift-spears. In every way, you are a credit to your father and his craft.'

'Thank you.' Breaca began in the same language and changed back to Eceni partway through. 'I will never be what my father was, but I may be good enough to teach his skills to my children. Do you still have the blade that he made for you?'

'I do. I keep it safe in honour of better times.' Corvus looked weary. Age had thinned his face and added more scars, but the core of him was the same as it had always been. Looking down, he laid a hand on Graine's head. 'Is this your daughter?'

'Yes.'

'She's exquisite. You and her father must be proud.'

It was what the governor had said, more or less, but spoken with a knowledge and an integrity that the governor's words had lacked: Corvus knew the identity of Graine's father where the governor could not have done.

The Roman officer knelt, took the spear-head brooch from Breaca's hand and repinned her daugher's cloak. Happy that it was secure, he smiled as any adult smiles to any child.

Graine was not any child; he had been watching her through the ceremony and should have known better. The cool sea-green dreamer's eyes had locked on his before he could look away. She frowned a little, and, for a moment, looked achingly like Airmid.

When her brow cleared, she said, distinctly, 'Valerius Corvus, you have been good friend to my mother's brother, the traitor whom she once loved. Because of it, I would make you a gift of my horse. She is the fastest we have ever bred. You and she will do well together.' She used the formal language of Mona's council, learned at Airmid's knee. The word she used was the one that signified a gift between battle partners, or from sister to brother.

Corvus stayed very still. A muscle beside his eye twitched. In a while, he looked up at Breaca. 'Is this so?'

'You would know better than me. You were a friend to Bán when you were with us; I am prepared to believe you were so afterwards when he fought for Rome. As to the horse,' Breaca shrugged, 'she's the best mare I've bred yet. She was my gift to Graine at year's turn, to be the beginnings of her own herd. If she chooses to give her to you, it's her right. Do you have a good battle mount?'

Corvus grimaced. 'Not any more. I had a good black colt, son of a horse called the Crow out of a Trinovantian mare. Riding him was like riding black lightning, but he was killed under me by a woman of the Silures who went on to break my skull. I have a remount to replace him; a good-hearted gelding but without the fire of the black colt. I would not ride him into any battle that I wished to ride out of alive.'

A handful of his fellow officers passed by. Corvus' knees cracked as he rose. He patted Graine on the head. His face conveyed polite interest in the child of a client king's wife. In Latin, he said, 'The governor wishes us to assemble at the new theatre. Have you seen it?'

They were not going to die. Corvus, the man of integrity, did not find that his duty demanded it.

The understanding came slowly. Relief left Breaca hollow. She breathed in the cold and the stink and the noise that was Camulodunum. Graine's shoulder pushed into her thigh as a hound's might have done, for reassurance. Corvus, prefect of the legions, who had been Bán's friend, gazed quietly into the middle distance, where a sow rooted in a sty, and waited while the governor's guest brought the fractured parts of herself together.

From the new stillness of her mind, Breaca found the right words to answer him. Formally, as he had done, she said, 'Perhaps you could guide us to our first view of the theatre? We have not yet had the pleasure.'

XVI

S EEN FROM THE HILLSIDE ABOVE, CAMULODUNUM HAD BEEN A brick-and-whitewash fungus leaking unchecked across land that had once been green. In the clutter of paved and muddied streets and pathways, painted merchants' booths and shacks, pigsties, wooden stables and loudly colour-washed villas, only the triumphal gates in the west and the theatre in the east had stood out from the rest.

Following Corvus through the mire, the noise and the smell crowded Breaca more. The city was not a quiet place. Even close to noon, the crowing cocks were barely outdone by the shrieks of children and the bawling of men; men in armour and men in chains, men ordering other men, men ordering women, men ordering mules and packhorses and bullocks. A girl screamed, but only once and not for long; Camulodunum was man's domain.

The smell was eye-watering: the ripe rottenness of too many people crammed in too small a space, with their old food and their new food and their goats and pigs and cattle and ordure and urine and death. Of all the stories told to Breaca of Rome's new city, none had mentioned that underneath the cacophony of life, Camulodunum stank of death.

The wind backed round, hurling the full ripeness of it full in her face. Breaca inhaled, regretted it, and spat.

Beside her, Cunomar grinned, sourly. 'Rome smells worse,' he

205

said. 'And it's bigger.' He was enjoying himself and it showed. The almost-confrontation with Corvus – his mother's need for him, and her trust – had left him sharper than before. As after the spear-trial, the beginnings of the man shone through the child and he walked taller because of it. Twice, Corvus drew a breath to engage him in conversation, and twice, seeing the hate in his eyes, he stopped. Instead, he fell in beside Breaca, who did not hate him.

'The theatre is ahead and to the left. The path is a little unkempt. I'm afraid the construction of the temple to Claudius has some-what taken over this part of the city.'

'So I see.'

Breaca lifted Graine to her hip, to keep clean the hem of her tunic. The path Corvus had indicated was a trail of much-trodden straw laid across a sea of mud that was one with the building site to their right. Within it, in isolated splendour, the part-finished temple to Claudius grew from the slurry like some long-dead animal drawn out by the gods, all bones and teeth and no flesh. Its ribs lay open to the sky, faced on the inside with marble. Around lay other piles of white marble slabs and squared-off roof beams, heaps of freshly quarried flints, not yet washed clean, and numbered stacks of gilded roof tiles which were under permanent guard.

Those guards excepted, there was no sign of life near the temple, no engineers, no architects, no slaves working under the whip. Abandoned for the day, it sat amongst the bones of its scaffolding, and it was as easy to imagine it shattered and the land beneath green again as it was to imagine the heights it would reach and the fire that would blaze from the gold-tiled roof when it was complete.

Corvus led them past slowly; one does not rush past the temple to a god, even when that god was not so long ago a drooling idiot whose own wife ordered his death.

Breaca held Graine close, feeling the patter of the small child-heart against her shoulder. She recognized by now the change in her daughter when Graine began to see with the eyes of the dream. Feeling it, Breaca smoothed a tangle of rich red hair from her face.

'What do you see?' she asked.

The green-grey eyes were widely vacant. 'Too many dead,' Graine said. 'They don't know how to sing home the ghosts of their dead.'

'The Romans don't?'

'Yes. And also the Trinovantes. The Romans break them as slaves and when they die, the people do not have the dreaming to sing them home.' It was said without passion. Where others would have cursed Rome, or themselves for allowing it to happen, Graine shook her head in disapproval and unforced sorrow. 'There are others too, burning. It's not a good death.'

Breaca kissed her daughter's brow. 'No. Fire is never a good death.'

The horror of the thought brushed both of them, trailing goose feathers across too-fine skin. They held each other close, submerged in the moment, and so were the last of the small group to round the north-western corner of the temple and see what had been placed there as a warning.

'*Stop.*'

Corvus said it, a man used to giving orders and having them obeyed. Breaca had already stopped, because Cygfa had come to a halt and was urgently making the signs to ward against evil. Beside her, Cunomar was shaking as Breaca had never seen him, swearing the oaths of the she-bears in a single unbroken stream that cursed Corvus, the governor and all of Rome to an endless dying on knives that cut but did not kill.

Beside them, the Roman officer Corvus stood stone-white and still. Breaca walked into him as she rounded the corner, so that the hissed curses of her two older children mixed with the Latin of his apology.

'Breaca—' He put a hand on her arm. 'You must believe me. I didn't know they were here.'

She believed him, if only because he looked so sick. It was the smell that did it, as much as the sight. Breathing through her teeth, Breaca looked past him to the paired crosses she had seen from the hilltop, and knew, with a hollow hurt in her abdomen, that Graine had been wrong, at least in part, when she said that the crosses had not yet tasted blood.

It was not human blood, and the sheep hanging from the right-hand arm of the right-hand cross had not died there, but somewhere else, where its throat had been cut and its skin flayed off so that its pink flesh showed in a way that could at first seem human. It had been gutted, to stop the gas of decay from blowing it open, but neither cleanly nor recently and streaks of greened intestines hung rotten from the open gap of its belly.

It was swaying slowly in the wind, turning on the rope so that Breaca saw late what Cygfa and Cunomar had already seen: that on either side of its chest, burned with an iron, the serpent-spear mark of the Boudica soared over the eagle of Rome.

Graine was sick.

Of all her three children, the Boudica's younger daughter had been most sheltered from the raw brutality of war. Faced with the evidence as never before, there was a small gap as she struggled to understand, and then she vomited violently and colourfully into the mud at Corvus' feet.

'I'm sorry.'

Corvus said it again, in Eceni as well as Latin. 'I don't know who did this or why and when I find out there will be a reckoning. I swear, if I had known, I would not have brought you this way. Or I would have found a way to warn you. I am truly sorry.'

He knelt, offering water from a belt-flask to Graine, who was sobbing now, and drawing the attention from those in front and behind. Her shock was real, but overdone to turn eyes away from Cunomar and Cygfa who stood together, finding their feet in a world that had suddenly become unstable.

Breaca would have gone to them, but to do so would have attracted more attention. She let Corvus tend to Graine and accepted his apologies and found it within herself to smile at the governor's secretary who brought the humble apologies of his master and his wish that her family be seated soon within the theatre where they might be sheltered from an ugliness which had no bearing on them.

Three centuries of legionaries stood in ranks around the tiered arc of the theatre and made avenues leading in towards the many entrances and staircases. Breaca and her family arrived late, the last of a few stragglers to make the journey from the forum. Ahead of her, in a sea of gossiping humanity, eight delegations, with their families, friends and retainers, made a show of being at ease in Roman company.

They could not have missed seeing the hanged sheep, symbol of cowardice and a failure to fight, but they chose not to speak of it;

instead the talk was loudly and pragmatically commercial. After the heavy dignity of the early ceremonies, the gathering at the theatre had all the subtlety of a cattle market. The contracts made and broken here were every bit as binding as those witnessed in Roman law throughout the morning session.

'Tagos was already there; this was a world in which he flourished. His lack of an arm was no impediment, easily compensated by a quick mind and the ability to strike sharp bargains. As it had been designed to, the workmanship of his king-band had won much attention and set him apart from the other client kings so that his monopoly of Roman wines and olives from Greece had not been broken.

Breaca and the now-silent Graine were conducted to his side and, as Cunomar and Cygfa joined them, he was pleased to present his family to the Iberian master mason who had designed and was building Claudius' temple, to the balding Gaulish wine merchant who was the third most senior magistrate of the city and who had funded one hundredth of the temple's building costs to date, and last and most effusively to the tall, white-haired Greek physician whom he spotted waiting by the stairs to the central tier of seating.

The physician was one of the few men held in equal regard by Rome and the tribes alike. 'Tagos was rapturous in his greeting. 'Theophilus, what a delight! I had not thought you would grace us with your presence on such an informal occasion.'

'Had you not? How could I not come to watch when one of my former patients is to die?' Theophilus did not return the smile. His clear hawk's gaze was directed exclusively at Breaca. 'This must be your new wife. I am honoured to meet her. If I may?'

He bowed, not waiting for the completion of formal introductions, and, taking Breaca's hand, laid his fingers on her wrist. She felt a probing across the surface of her thoughts, not unlike Airmid's or, more recently, Graine's, and a pull in her midriff that was exactly like the first feather-touch of birth pains and then the dry grip was gone and the physician was bowing again.

'My lady, I had intended to offer my services should you ever come near childbirth but I see that will not be necessary. My best wishes to you and your three beautiful children. They do honour to you and their father.' He nodded in turn to Graine, Cunomar and Cygfa and the colour returned, a little, to each of them without words exchanged.

If his intent was to crush the king of the Eceni, he succeeded. In one short speech, 'Tagos' hopes of a dynasty were prised open and shown empty to the world. He opened his mouth and, fish-like, shut it again. His eyes roamed the crowd around, seeking to find who, if any, amongst his rivals had been close enough to hear. Finding none, he turned away, calling Cunomar and Cygfa to follow him.

Left alone, Breaca lowered Graine to the ground where the girl could find her own feet and, catching the whisper of a thought, said, 'I met an old friend this morning with a fresh bandage on his head. Did you put it there?'

Theophilus' slow smile grew from the blankness of his stare. 'I did. If he is a true friend, you are fortunate.'

'So it would seem. Is he a friend also to your patient who is to die?' The crucifix jarred the corners of Breaca's mind. No man, Roman or otherwise, deserved such a death.

'Ex-centurion Marcellus? Alas, no. That one is a man of few friends and a great many enemies.'

'Is being friendless enough to sentence him to death?'

'It is if he has made the mistake of slaughtering an innocent man in front of witnesses. His death will be an example to show that Romans are not above the law. You will be expected to approve.'

Graine was right, then, at least in the first part. *They are not for us. A warrior of the tribes will die and one of Rome and both are already held in prison.* Breaca let the understanding show on her face.

'In that case, I am sure we will appear to approve although I would prefer it if the children did not have to bear witness. You, I am sure, will be expected to disapprove and may thus be asked to leave before us. Perhaps if there is time later, we could meet? Or you could visit us in our own lands? I have a friend who would be glad to meet you. She has some skills in childbirth but there is always more to learn.'

'There is indeed.' Theophilus' eyes lit as Airmid's would have done if the offer had been made to her. He touched a finger to the caduceus that hung from a thong at his neck. 'I would be honoured. The hospital is in the south-west of the city, two blocks down from the governor's mansion. Ask anyone for directions and when you get there find Nerus and tell him that you are there by express invitation of Theophilus of Athens and Cos. Remember that, Athens and Cos. If you say those two, he will let you in.'

Dressed in their togas, their bordered tunics, their tribal cloaks – visible statements of the wearer's affiliation to Rome, or its lack – three thousand gossiping, preening citizens of Camulodunum filled the banked benches of the theatre by the time the governor led his officers in to their reserved seats on the lowest row of the tiers. Breaca and her daughters sat at the governor's left hand, with 'Tagos on his other side.

The air in the theatre was still, hot and rank. Spring sun reached over the top of the marbled walls to cast direct light onto the sanded semicircle that separated the seats from the wooden stage opposite.

A row of tables to the left of the stage held the delegates' gifts to the governor. The sun blessed all of them, polishing already over-polished metal to blinding brilliance. A vast crater in gold bore Berikos' Atrebatan mark of the oak tree combined with the eagle of the legions. Beside it, Breaca's boxed spears seemed small and unremarkable. Further along, a pair of red and yellow enamelled brooches and a hollow gold torc displayed the heavily Romanized style of Cogidubnos' Belgic smiths. A knife scabbard in dyed leather, a belt, a set of horse harness and a newly woven cloak in moss green completed the gifts of the Belgae. At the end of the table closest to the audience, a chequered board of polished wood in two colours bore a set of blue and yellow counters set out in rows at either edge. It had not been on the table in the forum when the gifts were first presented.

From directly behind Breaca, Corvus said pensively, 'Someone's given the governor a game of Warrior's Dance. Do you suppose he knows how to play it?'

Without turning, she answered, as if to Graine, 'I expect one of his officers could teach him. It would be a useful skill for a man who would rule the tribes. If he could think with the cunning of Cunobelin, war would be a thing of the past.'

'I'll see what can be done.' Corvus was grinning, she could hear it in his voice. Then, without the humour, 'There will be some

211

unpleasantness now. It would be wise to appear unperturbed.'

The physician had offered the same warning and in the same spirit. Breaca bent down to adjust Graine's cloak and whispered, 'A man is going to be crucified. A Roman. One of those held in the prison. We will do what we can to send his soul home but we will not speak out loud and we will not complain to the governor.'

Graine nodded. From the first moment of sitting, she had stared ahead at the oak platform in front of her. Now she asked, 'Where are the doors they will bring the prisoners through?'

'I don't know. I'm not sure there are doors.' Breaca looked where her daughter looked. Finely planed oak planks made a resonant floor to the stage. Curtains in Trinovantian yellow draped the sides, hiding the wings. A multicoloured mural painted across the back wall showed scenes of pipe-playing fauns frolicking by a waterfall with androgynous nymphs, watched over by a god in the form of a grazing bull. If there were doors, the gaudy curves and splashes of the painting obscured their lines. 'Are you sure there are doors?'

Graine frowned. 'I think so. I dreamed something like this but it may not be here.'

Alert, Breaca asked, 'What happened in your dream?'

'Someone died. We wanted to stop it but couldn't. Cunomar was unhappy.'

Cunomar had spent the winter 'unhappy' and the effect on others had not been good. He sat now beside 'Tagos on the governor's right. Breaca looked across and her son looked back and he raised his hand in greeting. She wished for his sake that Eneit could be there to take away the sourness of sitting next to 'Tagos. She smiled back encouragement and saw it accepted at face value, with good grace.

To Graine, Breaca said, 'Cunomar hates injustice; it's his greatest strength. Why don't you go to him now and tell him what you dreamed and remind him that we are guests here and mustn't interfere with the governor's justice. Can you do that?'

Graine frowned. 'Does the governor speak Eceni?'

'I don't think so, but you must assume that he does. Say nothing impolite. We *are* his guests.'

For a solemn, watchful child, Graine could be playful when it served her own will or that of the gods. Cheerfully, she scampered off and clambered onto her brother's knee, tugging at his ear and whispering loudly in Latin that she had a secret only for him. Surprised, he embraced her and tipped his head so that, lowering her voice, she could breathe into his ear. Those who overheard would have caught enough of the subsequent story to know that she had given her chestnut mare that had been a gift from her mother to a nice man who had once known their uncle, but any coherence was lost after that in a welter of excited, incomprehensible child-speak that only one reared on Mona could possibly have understood and only then if standing improperly close to both.

At the end of it, Graine drew back and, grinning, kissed her brother on the nose. Cunomar blushed and ducked his head away, then relented and kissed her back. Two dozen watching adults, almost all of them parents, remembered childhood and its easy freedoms and wished for themselves and their children the same liberation.

Graine scrambled down from her brother's knee. On the way back to her mother, she patted her stepfather's leg as she passed and smiled dazzlingly for the strange, grey-haired Roman who ruled her land.

The governor turned to his left. 'A quite exquisite child. Truly, you are blessed, my lady.'

Breaca said, 'Thank you. Our gods have not deserted us while the children can laugh.'

A horn sounded from somewhere nearby. Drums answered it. And a sudden change in the stage proved Graine right in at least the first part of her dream. A door opened, cutting in half the largest of the dancing fauns on the stage-wall mural.

A detachment of retired veterans, glorious in their old parade uniforms, marched onto the stage, turned about, drew their weapons in synchrony and, striking up and out, made an avenue of raised short swords. The tips clashed like cymbals as they came together, a counterpoint to the resonance of the stage. Through this avenue of violent brilliance, marching in slow time as if to a funeral, two of the governor's personal guard escorted a prisoner, marked as different only by the chains on his wrists. In an act of calculated defiance, or of solidarity, the man was dressed in identical parade uniform to the veterans.

The effect was dramatic. Every step forward showed the prisoner as a man of courage who had served his god and his emperor with exceptional valour and who was now prepared to martyr himself for the sake of his governor. Ex-centurion Marcellus may not have had many friends, but there were plenty of men at whose side he had fought who resented his use as a political tool and did not wish to see him abandoned in extremis.

The Trinovantes in the audience had fewer scruples. Whatever their affection for Rome and its institutions, Marcellus had been universally loathed. A slow, low chatter spread around the arc of the theatre, approving the man's status as prisoner, disapproving the sentiment of the veterans. Someone stamped a foot and the rhythm became, slowly, that of the Trinovante death song, an intricate patter of long and short beats that is learned from the cradle or not at all. Others took it up and the beat spread round the arc, a muted roll so that it might have come from drummers at the river, but that the rock of it rang through the benches as bodies moved to its sway.

The sound rose to a peak and then stopped, suddenly, and no-one could have said who had given the order. It was not an act of overt hostility; it could have been argued that they did the man great honour, but it had not felt honourable. Fear rippled belatedly round the theatre as those who had most to lose by the onset of reprisals realized what they had done and began to speak, too loudly and too late, to cover it. Presently, that, too, faded away.

Everything waited. If there had been birds perched on the high walls of the theatre, they would have held their breaths and stilled their flight and waited.

An order was given in Latin. The two junior officers of the guard brought their prisoner forward to the front edge of the stage. All three men saluted.

The governor stood to return their greeting. Nothing overt in his bearing changed but, in the silence that awaited his speech, three thousand men and women of the tribes, the waiting veterans and a dozen visiting officers were reminded that he had led two legions in a summer's long campaign and that he knew exactly what it was to be a soldier in the field.

His voice had commanded armies in the chaos of war and the acoustics in the theatre were the best that his empire's engineers could achieve, unmatched on any battlefield. When he spoke, it seemed to those on the furthest tiers as much as the front benches that he barely raised his voice and yet spoke directly to them.

'Marcellus, veteran of the legions, formerly centurion of the second cohort, the Ninth legion, recipient of three crowns for bravery in combat, you are accused of the murder of Rithicos, harness maker and tenant farmer on your land. Three witnesses have attested to this, two of them citizens, one a trusted tribesman. Your guilt is not in doubt. Sentence has been passed. You will die today, in the sight of those whom you have wronged. It is your right to speak before sentence is carried out. Do you wish to do so?'

'No. But I would show you who it is that you sentence so.'

The stage was Marcellus' alone. For his last performance, his former comrades-in-arms gave him all the space he could need to enact his own drama. The ranks who had made his entrance avenue laid their naked blades in crossed pairs on the stage. From Breaca's seat low down in the first rank of benches, they made a lake of sun-washed iron and it was hard to see beyond the brightness of it. From higher up the tiers they would be more symbolic, an array of battle weapons, made decorative for the purposes of peace.

Marcellus did not wait for silence to settle but simply, and without drama, bent at the waist, placed his palms on the floor and shrugged so that his mail shirt inverted and slid over his head; an armoured skin, shed in shining links.

The chime of iron striking iron rang on the resonant stage as the former centurion knelt and set the shirt straight as he might have done after a day's campaign. Beneath, he wore a simple woollen tunic belted at the waist. This, too, he removed, folding it and laying it on the floor atop the mail. No-one moved to stop him.

The prisoner stood again and it seemed that he had spent a great deal of his life walking in sun without his tunic. He was no longer fit; his belly hung over his belt half the size of a pregnant woman, but he had not always been so. The scars on his chest were many and varied; through his years of service, he had met, and failed to avoid, sword and spear and arrow-head. The mark of the bull in the centre of his breastbone was old, the brand dulled with age. Its presence explained, perhaps, the leeway he had been given so far in his display.

Raising his arms, Marcellus began to turn a slow circle so that those with experience of battle – the governor, his officers, the warriors amongst the tribes – could see that he bore no scars on his back. He had never retreated or, in retreat, had never encountered those who could catch him. He would have preferred, doubtless, that they believed the former.

His circle was almost complete. The men on the stage with him had seen the long line beneath his left armpit and were remembering the day it was new, recalling the battles they had fought with Marcellus at their head. Only one of the officers of the guard saw the danger and he too late to act. His shout served only to highlight the climax of the prisoner's drama.

In the closing step of the circle, Marcellus flung himself down and sideways, stretching out flat to reach the line of crossed short swords lying forgotten on the stage. His open hand connected with the grip of the nearest, swinging it back in a practised move that brought him upright again, slightly breathless but armed in the company of fifteen men, only three of whom had the presence of mind to stoop and pick up their own weapons.

If the silence before had been polite, it was charged now with the slamming power of a lightning strike. Three thousand men and women each held their breath. Tribal warriors who had fought in battle reached for blades they were not permitted to carry and let their hands fall empty and useless at their sides. Breaca heard Corvus stand and begin to work his way between the seats and down the aisle. Two other officers of the legions did the same; these men were chosen for their ability to balance politics with war and to act appropriately. They could be trusted to contain this situation now.

Marcellus watched them come. Raising the blade, he saluted each one by name.

'Valerius Corvus: I will never forget your charge against the hill fort of the Durotriges. The god saw it on the day and will hear of it again from me. Cornelius Pulcher: I have heard of your actions against the warriors of the west. You will prevail in time, I am sure.' His sneer said otherwise. It fell away as he turned to face the last of the officers, an ageing, white-haired centurion of the IXth legion who looked easily old enough to have been pensioned as a veteran himself. To him, Marcellus bowed. 'Rutilius Albinus, first father under the god. I will give him your greetings as I give you my honour, my oath and my life.'

Albinus, at least, saw what was coming. With a report like a thunder clap, he sheathed his own sword and raised his arm in salute at exactly the moment Marcellus reversed his grip on the hilt of his stolen blade and, without error or hesitation, thrust it home in his own chest, a hand's breadth to the left of the bull god's brand. With his last conscious movement, he tipped forward, so that he could have been said to have fallen on his sword and could go to his god with honour.

He was dead before the first of the officers on the stage reached him. They were slow, rendered sluggish by their own fear. Under some governors they would have replaced Marcellus on the cross for allowing a prisoner to escape his own execution. The legions did not look favourably on men who failed in their duty.

The first of them knelt, his fingers laid flat against the great vessels of the prisoner's neck, seeking signs of life that he would never find. Thinking himself useful, he pulled the blade from the lifeless chest and thereby released the ocean of blood waiting within. The oak stage soaked it up, hungrily. At the sight, the massed voice of the audience was released, creating its own sea of astonished sound.

The governor was not one who visited unnecessary death on his men. A brief move of his head caught the attention of the ageing centurion of the IXth. 'Albinus? Your man, I believe. Please see to his removal. The veterans may wish to claim his body. They may do so.'

With practised alacrity, the old men on the stage formed an honour guard and removed the body of the man they had respected but not liked.

In death, Marcellus' memory was transformed from a battle-hungry officer and drunken abuser of men to a hero who spoke his mind when all around him were silent. For now, he was simply a body who was leaking blood and ranker fluids across the governor's new stage. The veterans made a litter of two shields and carried him away, doing what they could to minimize the mess. A servant in tribal dress returned shortly afterwards with sifted sand and poured it over, soaking up the worst of the excess. On the ground below, two others drew across a long rake and smoothed away the splashed debris from the deeper, paler sand that filled the semicircle between the front row of seats and the stage.

Breaca watched Corvus return to his seat. His face was closed to her but his eyes held a warning: *There is more. Don't relax yet.* She lifted Graine onto her knee and said quietly, 'I think there's a break now. Do you need to go out?'

The girl shook her head. Breaca bent to kiss her and said, more softly, 'Is this what you dreamed of that made Cunomar angry?'

'Not yet, but it was here, in this place.' She faltered. 'It may not have been today.'

'Then we will watch and see. If anything bad begins to happen, will you let me know as soon as you see it?'

'I'll try.'

If Graine did not need to go out, a great many of the adults who had drunk wine in the morning did. There was a shuffling and a changing of seats and men and women passed each other on the long stairs that led down the back of the theatre from the upper ranks of benches. Breaca held Graine and talked lightly of nothing to Cygfa while 'Tagos regaled the governor with his best tale of the boar hunt by which he and Dubornos had together celebrated their ascension to adulthood.

The governor, who had almost certainly heard the tale before, or others like it, evinced total absorption and only one watching him as closely as Breaca did could have seen the signal to the officers on the margins of the theatre that ordered the start of the next phase of the afternoon's demonstration.

The ranks of benches were full again and settling. A horn called for quiet. The governor rose and stepped into the central area of freshly raked sand, as visible from the top tiers as any man on the stage. He had shed his cloak, leaving it on the seat when he rose so that his armour took the full glare of the afternoon sun and lit his face to a silvered gold. A dreamer, doing such a thing, would have known how to use the impact to bring the people closer to the gods. The governor of Britannia, being Roman, blinked firmly and set his face at a different angle to the glare.

'Warriors of the Trinovantes, of the Eceni, the Atrebates, the Belgae . . .'

The entire crowd gasped. He was not speaking Latin, that was the first surprise. In less than a year, he had learned a passable version of the Trinovante dialect that was familiar throughout the south-east, and he had called them warriors; that was the greater shock.

His smile encompassed them all. 'Today we have seen that Roman justice is impartial, that it is the righteous arm of the distant emperor brought close. It protects the weak and restrains the over-strong, allowing all to prosper equally without fear of death or injury.

'And yet, for justice to work, the emperor's laws must be scrupulously kept. We can be lenient in allowing any people to continue their ancient rites and ceremonies in peace. Our gods have no quarrel with your gods; in the heavens, all gods live together in mutual respect. Our laws have no quarrel with your laws save in the instance where the one overrides the other.'

He said it smoothly, so that only a churl could choose to take it as an insult: *We own you; our laws have precedence over yours and the world is a better place because of it.*

Holding her own mind still, that her eyes might not betray her, Breaca felt Graine slip off her knee.

The governor was not watching the movement of children. His gaze roamed over those whose lives had changed most and who still resented it: men amongst the Trinovantes who had been called to fund the temple to the Emperor Claudius and had been required, on occasion, to help with its building; warriors among the Cantiaci and the Coritani and the Catuvellauni who had fought against the legions and might take up arms again if they had a good enough reason; the Eceni, who had rebelled once, and might yet do so again.

Speaking most to them, he said, 'Thus it is that when one is found flagrantly to be flouting the most basic of our laws – laws passed for the protection of all – then we must act with expedition and no compromise, as we did with ex-centurion Marcellus.'

A signal was given. The drums marked the arrival of a new prisoner. A door opened on the stage. The governor said, 'Such a one has been found. He was captured in possession of a weapon of length and size forbidden under the law and, when challenged, he attacked our men, killing two and injuring one other so that he will never fight again. For either of these alone, he must die. For both together, he must face the harshest of penalties.'

His timing was perfect and must have been practised. His last words reached the top tiers as those sitting in them caught their first sight of the tribesman who had disregarded Roman law and been caught doing so. The prisoner could not walk unaided. Two fresh officers of the guard, older and more experienced than those who had gone before, manhandled him through the faun's door onto the stage and held him upright, naked and bloody, in full view of the benches opposite. In the first shock of seeing him, all that anyone could have said was that he had resisted arrest, or been gratuitously beaten, or both.

One of the officers grabbed a handful of hair and forced the prisoner's head up and it could be seen that his nose was broken, one eye was swollen to a pulped mess of ruddy purple, a sword cut ran the length of one forearm and a broken finger stuck out at a painful angle. The way his left arm clamped to his side suggested a second wound there, or bleeding inside. His breathing was ragged and he showed no sign that he knew where he was.

Breaca counted all these things first; the blink-fast assessment of the warrior in the field that seeks to find if the injured can fight on. This one would never fight again without urgent treatment and Rome did not waste the time of its field physicians on condemned prisoners. The best that could be said, then, was that, even nailed to wood, his death would not last beyond sundown.

A small, voiceless part of her celebrated his two kills and sought a dreamer who could, equally silently, begin the song of soul-parting for one about to die in battle. Graine was her only dreamer and she was no longer sitting on her lap or on the bench next to her.

Dragging her eyes away from the stage, Breaca searched for her daughter and found her sitting instead on Cunomar's knee, her small hands clamped fiercely on his wrists, her face next to his, speaking intently, quietly, in a constant stream of instruction. To a stranger, possibly even to their stepfather, it was a continuation of the whispered secrets of earlier. To Breaca, shockingly, Graine was the only thing keeping Cunomar from attempted murder and a fate identical to that awaiting the youth on the stage, because it was a youth, not an older man, but a lad with short, wiry hair, sticky with his own and others' blood; with brown skin that darkened too fast under the sun; with a fine scar running the length of his left arm from elbow to wrist, where Cunomar had landed a lucky sword cut before his soul-friend had learned properly how to defend himself.

'*Eneit!*'

The name broke from her, uncalled. The youth's head turned stiffly and with difficulty; his hair was still held by the guard. He stared at Breaca with his one good eye and slowly, fuzzily, an understanding of where he was dawned on him. He opened his mouth and closed it again on the impossibility of speech. His eyes travelled along the benches seeking Cunomar and finding him. His smile was a private thing and carried all possible messages from apology to the joy of the warrior who has made his first kill in battle. Over them all was love and an abiding sorrow.

Without question, he was Eneit.

XVII

REACA ROSE IN HER CHAIR. CYGFA WRAPPED COOL FINGERS round her wrist and held her back. From behind, Corvus said, in quiet, forceful Eceni. 'No. Think. There is nothing you can do.' From her right, the governor turned her way and said, 'Do you know him?'

'Your honour, this is Eneit nic Lanis. He is Eceni, the son of a friend.'

They had the beginnings of friendship, she had felt it. His eyes reflected the same, and a moment's indecision, then he said, 'I'm sorry. Justice does not know the bounds of friendship. Marcellus, too, had those who cared for him. The youth must die; that is not in question.'

He had been a diplomat before and after he had been a general. In that last sentence was an opening. He had not said, 'He must be crucified,' when it had clearly been planned.

From Cunomar's lap, in the language of Mona, Graine said, 'This is my dream. His death can be yours or theirs. You must decide.' She said it, lightly, in exactly the tone she had told her brother of the gift she had made of a horse to a nice man. The threading imperatives of a dreamer carried in other ways, beyond the words.

From Breaca's other side, Cygfa said, 'The governor has just pretended a respect for our laws. Offer him the spear-challenge of the she-bears. You have the spears ready and waiting. The grand-mother did not ask you to make them without a good reason. This may be it.'

Trust, Airmid had said as she was told of the elder grand-mother's instruction, *trust the gods and yourself. You will know what is right when it is right. I cannot guide you beyond that.*

Cold washed Breaca, and a sharpening of the senses that came with the breath of the gods. Airmid's voice echoed from the distant past of their shared youth, long since forgotten: *We dreamed her son. He was killed by one of the tribes and one of the legions, and those who could have stopped it looked on and did nothing.* She got up and moved out into the open space between the chairs and the stage.

'Tagos had never been to Mona and had only the barest under-standing of its dialects. The governor leaned over to ask him a question and he was not able to answer it. From the raked sand in front of the benches, in full view of the entire theatre, Breaca spoke for him.

'My daughters have suggested that, since we have seen Rome's justice once today, perhaps for balance this man should submit to the justice of the tribes. This event is unprecedented but there are parallels within our laws. The spear-challenge of the she-bears is similar to the trial set to our youths who would be warriors, but with important differences. In the warrior-test, the youth must throw at a target of straw. In the challenge of the she-bears, the target is a living warrior. It is a test of courage equally for those who throw and the one chosen to die. I believe it would be suitable here.'

Like the governor, Breaca was used to addressing thousands in far less clement circumstances. Her words carried to the upper benches as the governor's had earlier done but that here was the sense that she was addressing the man alone and the others were eavesdropping on a private conversation in a way that breached the bounds of decency. Throughout the theatre, adults shuffled and coughed. Younger children asked a whispered question, loudly.

After a pause in which a number of possibilities were considered and discarded, the governor asked the same question. 'Tell me the nature of the spear-challenge?'

'It is a test of courage undertaken on the eve of battle. Three spears are dedicated to Briga, who rules the outcome of war. Two are cast together by warriors on opposing sides of the conflict. The one which strikes most closely to the heart of the one-to-die is deemed to have made the kill, and the warrior who threw it is permitted to throw the final spear.'

A greyed eyebrow rose a fraction. 'At a dead warrior? I had not thought the tribes would stoop to empty symbolism when your lives are bent most surely to practicality and function.'

'No. In the original form of the test, the third spear is cast at the warrior who failed the throw, the one who did not make the kill. Thus, in starting, both know that they risk death and must throw their best, not knowing the accuracy of the other. The gods hold it in their hands to change the flight of a spear, or for the condemned warrior to stumble or fall so that a spear thrown truly may yet miss.'

'He is not tied?'

'No. He, or she, must stand upright and embrace the coming spears. Thus is a warrior's courage tested, and a chance given to honour the gods.'

The governor was staring at her with an intensity he had given to nothing else that day. Breaca said, 'It is a way of deciding the outcome of a battle with minimal loss of life. The tribe of the one warrior left alive is considered to have won.'

Softly, the governor said, 'My lady, your people and mine are no longer at war.'

'We are not. The battles have long since been fought and their outcome is in no doubt. There is no precedence for this in our rites, but I believe we could throw for honour and in celebration of the gods, yours and mine. The third spear could be thrown symbolically into the body of the prisoner as you proposed. It must take some part in a death, else Briga will be dishonoured.'

'I see. Of course, we should not dishonour so formidable a god.' He was nodding, his gaze fixed on hers. 'It is fortunate, perhaps, that we have three spears to hand. Would they be similar to those used in this trial?'

'Identical. This is the second use for the heron-spears of the Caledonii.'

'And is that a coincidence?'

They were no longer speaking for the crowd. Breaca said, 'Your honour, under the eyes of the gods there are no coincidences, but I swear in the name of everything we both hold sacred that I had no idea that the spears I fashioned as a gift for you would be used against a member of my tribe today. Had my daughter not mentioned it, I would not have remembered that the spear-challenge existed. It is a thing we speak of in our histories but do not practise. It was carried out in the times of the ancestors and then only rarely; no-one living has attempted it that I know of, nor back in time for over three generations. If the governor would honour us by accepting it, he would be recreating one of our most ancient ceremonies.'

She raised her voice only a little for this last sentence, but the theatre was well made; her words echoed out to the back walls and round again. Men and women of the tribes who had been born into freedom remembered the shadows of the grandmothers' tales. Few, if any, would know the deeper details of a ceremony carried out by a distant northern tribe, although the more astute, knowing the ways of the she-bears, could imagine it.

The governor of Britannia was one of the most astute men of his generation. He said, 'Was it ever the case that the rulers of the tribes took part in this trial? Or was it their chosen champions?'

'It could be either. That decision was taken by the dreamers and the gods. All three of those taking part were chosen by lottery.'

'So the one to die was not necessarily either a prisoner or a law breaker?'

'Not always. It was a position of honour as much as the other two. The one who died first did so taking the messages of both tribes to the gods. By his integrity were the lives of the other two measured.'

Breaca was talking automatically, not choosing her words. Her attention had shifted almost entirely to Cunomar, who had ceased to struggle against Graine and was sitting upright in his seat, his fair skin bone-white in the afternoon shadow, his eyes large and black.

In a dry, taut voice she knew intimately but had never heard before from her son, he said, 'If it must be so, let me be the one to throw for the Eceni.'

He had cast his spear not hearing its soul-song and did not understand the lack. Eneit did. The warning on his face worked past the bruising and the cuts. Cunomar chose not to see it and

Breaca could not explain in public. Her son's eyes drained her, the shine of his soul and the desperate courage it had taken to make this request in this place amongst these people, and the conviction that he would succeed. Her heart broke open on his certainty, on his pride and ignorance and the cost to them all of his certain failure. Caught in a tidal wave of pain, he had not thought through to its end the fate of a warrior who failed this trial.

The governor was waiting, his face a model of restrained curiosity. Cunomar had spoken in Eceni, which he must understand, at least in part. Breaca could not change to another language without arousing undue suspicion.

Cunomar felt her decision before it came. With a desperate courage, he abandoned the last of his pride and begged. 'Mother, please? It is his life and mine.'

No battle had ever been harder. Holding her son's gaze, knowing what it cost him, Breaca said, 'No.'

'Mother! It's *Eneit*. You can't let these godless, bull-worshipping sons of—'

'Tagos stopped him, physically. In the eyes of Rome if nowhere else, the king of the Eceni was the boy's father and responsible for his conduct. He clamped his one hand over Cunomar's mouth, harder and more fiercely than Graine had done, and with less love.

'Your honour? If I may make a suggestion?' The voice from the benches caught the attention of all but Cunomar's immediate family. Valerius Corvus, prefect of the auxiliaries, squeezed past his fellows and stepped down onto the raked sand from where he saluted the governor, crisply. The bandage on his head showed cream in the sun, the one on his leg was in shade and grey.

He said, 'Your honour, as I understand it, in the days of the ancestors, the dreamers of the she-bear would have named those who should take part in such a trial. No dreamers are permitted to practise their craft, but we must uphold the honour of Rome and the emperor and it behoves us to do our best in this. The heron-spears of the Caledonii are not balanced as are the spears of the legions. Their flight and cast length is different and the feathers hung from the neck make them exquisitely sensitive to any gust of wind. As you know, I spent a winter and a spring in this land before the invasion and I have thus had some experience in the use of Eceni war spears, which are similar. Thus I would offer my services in this, as one fit to uphold Roman honour.'

All the way through his speech, Breaca had warned Corvus with her eyes. He had acknowledged the warning and chosen to ignore it.

The governor placed his palms together and tapped the peak of his fingertips to his lips. If he had been a warrior, one would have imagined he asked advice of Briga and was given it.

Presently, he said, 'Thank you for your offer and the arguments surrounding it. I accept the first part, which is that this trial is an honourable one and should certainly take place. I agree also that it is not without its dangers, both told and untold. I do not accept your second premise. You are injured and, as such, are not fit to represent Rome.'

If he had been slapped on the face, Corvus could not have looked more shocked. 'Your honour—'

'No. With respect, prefect, you are like the boy; ardent and willing but blind to your own defects. He is too young and too unskilled. He has not yet shed blood in battle and his affection for the prisoner is too apparent. You have age and skill enough for any task, I would never suggest otherwise, but you are less than a month from wounds that nearly killed you. You bear the evidence yet in your dressings, and for those who know you it shows more clearly in your walk and the way you hold your head when you believe yourself alone and unwatched.' Unexpectedly, he turned to address someone on the bench behind. 'Theophilus? In your opinion, is the prefect fit to take on a role equivalent to combat in battle?'

The physician jerked his head from a study of Eneit. 'Absolutely not.'

'Thank you.' The governor stood and was a younger man, scenting battle and eager. To Breaca, he said, 'Your gods are not my gods but they lived on this land long before we came and will do so long after we are all dust and ashes. We will honour them with our best endeavour. I believe myself to be capable of that. Do I take it that you will represent the Eceni, from whom the prisoner comes? You may be assured that in this place and this time you have my full permission to take up and cast a blade of a length forbidden to the tribes.'

'Thank you. Yes, I will represent my people.'

Her words carried throughout the theatre. By the end of the day, they would have spread to those Trinovantes not present, and by the end of the month to the tribes beyond. If Breaca had ever wanted to stake her place as a warrior without saying aloud the name of the Boudica, she had just done so.

Only give them heart, and you may prevail. She offered a prayer to the god that this might be so, and safely.

A smaller ripple moved the ranks of benches beside the governor. Cygfa had wanted to throw for the Eceni but had not been able to say so. Cunomar struggled against his father and was held silent. His eyes screamed unending anguish at his mother. Of her children, only Graine, with her shy smile, approved.

From the back of the stage, Eneit, forgotten, said, hoarsely, 'Thank you.'

There was room enough in the semicircle between benches and stage for the governor to pace back thirty paces away from one end and mark a line in the sand with the heel of his boot. Fresh guards, summoned at a nod, cleared the audience from the ranks of benches on the eastern side of the theatre lest one of the three spears, chancing to fly high or a little to one side, should taste the blood of an onlooker.

Eneit was unbound and escorted to his stance by the officers of the guard. Breaca followed, holding back until they had left him. She was not a dreamer and her memory of the rites was not perfect. She wanted to ask the details of Airmid who was half a day's fast ride away, or Graine, who had to stay with Cunomar and was equally inaccessible.

Trust the gods and yourself. You will know what is right. She could and did pray, and felt the touch of the god's breath on her neck. Holding the three names of Briga in her head, she watched the guards walk back out of earshot. Each of them made the Roman sign that was the ward against evil as he left. She was glad of that.

Eneit could stand unaided, which had been her first question. His one good eye was alight and lively. He attempted a smile and held it against obvious pain. Using his body as a shield so that none of the onlookers, from Rome or the tribes, could see, Breaca sketched her own sign of the serpent-spear on his forehead, on the centre of his breastbone and in the space below his navel. She made the signs slowly, with obvious ceremony, giving him time to empty of words.

On the first of the three, he said, 'I went back to the ancestors' mound. It was a mistake. I was seen by a tracker of the Coritani who reported it. The legionaries took Sinochos' blade and broke it. I'm sorry.'

'Don't be. Blades can be mended. It is you who cannot, for which we are all more than sorry. If there were a way to free you, we would take it, I swear.' Breaca made the second sign.

'I know. And my mother knows. She always told me that the day I held an edged weapon would be the day I died. I had always thought it would be in battle.'

'It was. You killed two of theirs. You go to the gods with one more dead than the cost of your life. There are many who die in battle who could not say the same. The spear-challenge of the she-bears is only for proven warriors, did you know that?'

His good eye sparked, joyfully. 'I had hoped it was. Do I carry a message to the gods?'

'Ask them to look over us when the final battles come. We will need their help more than ever.'

The third sign was complete. She had done all she could. On an impulse, and nothing to do with any rites she had witnessed, Breaca held the boy's shoulders and, very gently, mindful of his bruises, kissed him on the brow. His body shuddered under her touch, but not with pain.

Thickly, Eneit said, 'Tell my mother I'm sorry to have hurt her, but not sorry to have killed the enemy in battle. Tell Cunomar . . .' He faltered, losing the words.

'I will tell him you love him. He knows it already. You will know how he feels for you.' She had not seen the depth of their care for each other and should have done. The failure scoured her.

Eneit smiled. 'I do. Thank you. Tell him from me that he must find the courage to live on from today, that I will be watching from the lands beyond life and will wait to greet him from a place where a year passes in a heartbeat.'

'In the place of no time, a heartbeat lasts also eternity.'

'I know. Don't tell him that. He has no patience. Remind him of the meaning of my name and say that he should give it to his son when he has one.'

Eneit's name was the word for spirit and it filled him. He was neither weeping, nor plunged in self-pity. She had seen warriors ride into battle with less courage. Breaca said so, backing away, and the wide, lazy blaze of his smile lit the highest stands.

She walked back the thirty paces slowly, giving him time to savour the sun and the lingering moments of life beyond grief and loss. He had not seemed in pain as she left and the shaking had stopped. He had, she thought, already begun to see Briga circling with her ravens. There was no better sight for one entering battle.

Breaca's gift to the governor had been retrieved from the table by the stage and laid out so that the spear-blades rested on the edge of the box and the butt ends of the hafts lay wedged in sand. The undyed heron feathers dangled loose and twisted in the breeze. The different colours of the butt ends distinguished them.

The governor had already picked the palest, most gold of the three. He stood beside it, stripped of his cloak and the gilded cuirass. Another man might have looked plain; he did not. He said, 'Have you ever thrown a spear of this design?'

'No. It is not permitted to lift one except under the guidance of a dreamer. They have only a single throw and then are broken. I made them; I did not test them. I would not put you at so great a disadvantage.'

'I apologize. I had not intended an insult.'

'None is taken. The wind is from the south-west but it has been caught by the arc of the theatre and is turbulent in the middle of the space. As Corvus said, the large blades and trailing feathers make the spears sensitive to the air. They are the hardest to throw of any weapon. You need to hear the soul-song of the spear to make a true cast.'

'I am in your debt.' He dipped his head towards the spears. 'Shall we?'

They lifted their spears. The sun was low and at their backs, stretching their shadows across the sand. The guards had been dismissed and stood at the back of the stage with a shield to carry the body. They were alone, but for Eneit, thirty paces away. Breaca said, 'Someone neutral who is not of our tribes should give the order to throw. Might I suggest Theophilus of Athens?'

'A man known to have affection for both sides? Yes, a good choice.'

The governor signalled. After a moment's confusion, the physician joined them. He was not displeased to have a part to play. A faint flush warmed his high cheeks and the flanks of his nose. Taking care not to be seen to smile, he said, 'Is there a sign for which I should watch?'

Breaca said, 'Yes, but only you will know it. I cannot.'

'Of course. You must have no advantage.' He was a man used to listening to the world, if not to the gods, and it did not trouble him to know that the lives of others hung on his observations. 'Raise your spears then, and make ready. I will tell you when to throw.'

Breaca had picked the darkest of the three spears, blessed by Nemain, god of night who guided both Graine and Airmid. She raised it to shoulder height and turned to face Eneit. The governor copied her. Silence enclosed them. In a world where time passed in a heartbeat and was eternity, they waited.

The crowd could have filed out and been replaced by cattle or crows and Breaca would not have known it. Her world was Eneit and the wind and the change in length of a single, crisp linear shadow that was the heron-spear, with its dangling feather. The muscles of her throwing arm burned. The pain lived outside her and was not important. Eneit shrank until he was only a caged and beating heart. He swayed and she swayed with him. A raven settled on each of his shoulders and she knew she was not seeing the world as others saw it. She slowed and stilled and only the beat of her heart shivered the tip of the spear. Its song settled about her, rich with moonlight and the joys and pains of motherhood and the beckoning whisper of the ancestor-dreamer and the gods as they—

'*Throw!*'

The word struck Breaca's soul as a hammer an anvil, releasing the pain of the song. Her arm moved of its own intent. The spear thrummed and flew with a will apart. She watched its flight as if time had stretched and the air become thick as blood, slowing it. The circling wind in the centre of the orchestra teased the blade, drawing it down; she had aimed high expecting it.

The tip settled on a line for Eneit's heart. Relief drenched her prematurely. Sweat greased her palms, which had been dry. On the edge of her existence the crowd sighed. The second spear caught up with hers and they flew together, converging on a single space. She blinked and both spears became one, became two, became his and hers and hers and his and one or other struck skin and she did not know whose. The elongated blade slid cleanly between ribs that barely shifted as Eneit, in a final act of outstanding courage, drew in and held his last breath. The spear-song ended, exuberant, and all grief and joy were hers.

She felt the punch to his heart as her own and saw the third of Briga's ravens descend. Eneit jerked back and a little to his right. The second spear, which had aimed truly for the centre of his chest, hit a rib, glancing sideways before it sank into flesh. By will alone, the boy held himself upright one last moment and fell back heavily onto sand. A single member of the audience shouted approval and was hushed.

The heat of waiting sucked the air from her lungs. Flushed and breathless, the governor said, 'He's dead. I have never thrown more truly in my life, but I could not say which spear is the more central. Theophilus, as our adjudicator and our physician, will you tell us which of the two spears made the kill?'

'I'll try. You should come with me. Waiting here won't make the answer any different.'

Eneit lay on his back, his eyes open to the vacant sun. The spears stood upright, their hafts trembling a little on the closing beats of a twice-pierced heart. The blades were a hand's breadth apart in the boy's chest and at differing heights. The paler of the two sat in the rib space above the darker.

Theophilus, unwilling to kneel and reduce the dignity of his office, leaned over and studied them a while. Presently, he said, 'I feel like an augur staring at the cut surface of a liver on which nothing is written. The boy's heart is the size of a man's fist across and a little longer from apex to base. It lies in the chest slightly to the left side and the top is behind the nipple. I would need to open the chest and examine the body in greater detail to be certain, but I am as sure as I can be that each of these spears has hit the heart and that either one alone would have killed him. If this were a Greek contest, the prize would be equally split between the two contenders. That may not be so in the rites of the dreamers.'

Most emphatically, it was not. Still soul-struck, Breaca felt the blood flood from her head and return, sluggishly.

The governor, who was still studying the spears, said, 'Not bad, I think, for two warriors, long out of practice.' He stood and extended his hand to take Breaca's. 'My lady, in the rites of your ancestors, which of our tribes would have been said to win the battle?' He did not ask, *And which of us, as the loser, would have died?*

Breaca had no idea, and no way to find out. One spear must kill and the other fall into dead flesh, one warrior win, the other forfeit not only the contest, but life; the gods did not allow it otherwise.

A decade's training on Mona furnished her with the words the governor wanted. Knowing it untrue, she said, 'I think it possible the battle would have been won equally by both. It would have been a sign from the gods that the two tribes were to be allies.'

Quintus Veranius smiled as a youth might smile, having asked a favour and had it granted. 'Then the third spear should be lodged by us both together. Perhaps, if we are careful, we might not damage the blade and I can have at least one whole representation of your craft to hang on my walls as a reminder of this day?'

Theophilus brought the third spear. Under his direction, they each held the haft and slid it together with extravagant care into the left side of the boy's chest then drew it out again, leaving only a smear of new blood across the skin as evidence. The governor took possession of his new prize and had his cloak brought so that he could clean the blade before nesting it in the raw wool within the gift-box.

Breaca felt a shadow cross hers and turned. Corvus was walking over the sand towards her. He saluted, crisply. In Latin, he said, 'Congratulations, my lady. I have rarely seen so sweet a throw. If you will allow me, it would be my pleasure to escort you back to the stands.'

More quietly, in the language of Mona, which he should not have known, he said, 'Your son Cunomar has gone. Cygfa asked for permission to follow. I would have given it, but Graine said not. I am thus revealed as a man who takes orders from a seven-year-old girl-child. My only consolation is that Cygfa heeds her also. I think you should talk to them both. If, as Graine believes, your son intends to sit his long-nights and is caught, he will suffer the same fate as this boy would have done. The crosses are still empty. They thirst for blood as deeply as does the third of your spears.'

III
MID-WINTER AD 58−AUTUMN AD 59

XVIII

THROUGH ALL THE YEARS OF CHILDHOOD DREAMS AND THE many more of adult desperation, Julius Valerius, who had once been Bán, brother to Breaca of the Eceni, had never imagined that he would pass his long-nights in a dreaming chamber in the heart of a stone-built mound in the wild lands of Hibernia in the company of a hound whose sheer size would terrify him, nor that he would pass the time in deeper terror at his own impending failure.

The hound had been there from the start. Valerius had brushed against it as he crawled in through the lightless tunnel into the chamber and it had risen, grumbling, and pressed its nose to his face so that he had known it was as big as Hail, if not bigger, and that it resented his intrusion. Then, he had not known how small the chamber was, only that the tunnel had finally opened out so that he could rise from his elbows and knees and he was grateful for that.

Stretching his fingertips to touch the stone, he had found he could touch both walls and press his head to the roof without ever standing fully upright; thus a mound which, from the outside, had looked large enough to house half the elders of Mona was reduced on the inside to a space barely big enough for a war hound and a man to stand together.

The hound had not wished them to stand together. The grumble

237

had risen to a snarl, increasing in threat until Valerius sat on the earthen floor and pressed his back to the stone wall and drew his knees to his chest. He had been an officer in the emperor's cavalry, had led armies into war and burned villages to the ground, and a single hound reduced him to the smallest space he could occupy.

He would have laughed at the absurdity of it, but the beast was too close. Instead, he had spoken to it in Eceni as if it were Hail and it had calmed a little, circling and then stretching out along the far side of the chamber so that the wash of its breath had flavoured the air, sending currents round the close curves of the walls to warm the back of Valerius' neck.

In its own way, the presence of the hound helped to balance the claustrophobia of the chamber. The smallness of it left him mute at the same time as he marvelled at the means by which the ancestors had taken a mass of stone that would have built the outer wall of the emperor's palace and shaped it instead into a perfect beehive to protect the sanctity of the chamber at its heart.

Lacking any other distractions, the man who had once been an engineer to the legions explored by touch the place that might well become his coffin and the last repository of his soul. Square-edged stones pressed into his back, as sharp as the day they had first been cut. The stone pavings of the floor met with joins so finely matched that he could not pass a fingernail between them. Only a shallow dip, worn exactly where he sat, gave testament to the hundreds – the thousands – who had sat through their long-nights in exactly this place in the generations since the ancestors of the ancestors first built the mound.

Each of those who sat before had, presumably, known exactly what it was the gods and dreamers required of them. Valerius sat in ignorance, increasingly afraid of his own fear and his own lack of knowledge. He had expected instruction and had been given none and there was no way, any longer, to ask for it.

Mac Calma had sent him in and it was the memory of mac Calma's voice that filled the breathless air. *When you were dreaming, which gods did you petition, yours or mine?*

'I have no gods.'

Valerius had said it first in the paddocks behind the dreamer's hut on Mona. He said it again, quietly, now, to the hound and the waiting dark and did not know whether the silence that rolled back was a good sign or bad. At the very least, he believed that what he said was true: Mithras had spoken to him once in a cave in Britannia, and the gods of the Eceni had shown themselves in Rome by their actions, but none had touched his life in the five years since he had first set foot on Hibernia and he had no reason to think they would do so now. He had not noticed the moment when he had become free of the gods, but he had believed it a good one; his life was more peaceful in their absence. He had no wish to see them return, except that, without their direct intervention, the rite of the long-nights was doomed to failure and Valerius to an ending more final than death.

Mac Calma had been clear about the risk of that: *You must know . . . any failure means death, not only of your body but of your soul, and that even I, who am Elder of Mona, cannot keep you safe from that.*

Valerius did not want to be kept safe by any man. Life was not safe and could not be made so. To believe otherwise was a child's delusion and Valerius had abandoned his childhood when he abandoned his old name and his mother's gods; he had no intention of being seduced back to any of those, however great the threat.

Every child knew of someone who had failed in the rites of manhood, but never personally. Rumour spread from generation to generation with details of the many routes to death. Some chose badly in the place to sit and were slain by bear or lightning or sudden floods. Some met with dream-makers, living warriors who came against them to test their skill, always with orders to kill if the boy-who-would-be-man did not respond with a warrior's speed. Some simply walked out into the night and never came back. The dreamers scoured the pathways of the dream time for their lost souls. Only rarely did they find them. Too late, it occurred to Valerius that, very badly, he did not want to lose his soul.

Knowing that, the only clear alternative was to face the dark and all it held and he did not wish to do that either.

He had a lifetime's practice in ignoring those things he most wished not to see; in this, if nothing else, he was expert. Alone with a sleeping hound, with a world's weight of stone all around him and lacking all delusion, Julius Valerius, once-Eceni, once an officer in the armies of Rome, son of two dreamers and killer of many more, sat with his knees hugged to his chest and chose not to consider what it might mean to lose his soul.

Some time later, unthinking, he stretched his legs flat and leaned his back against a differently angled stone in the wall. Mac Calma's last words skittered through the gap thus opened in his discipline.

You will know when it is time. I cannot help you.

The Elder's voice had been distant, even then, at the start. The tunnel leading into the chamber had beckoned and Valerius had crawled along it, welcoming the dark after the too-bright fire and the scorch of mac Calma's scrutiny.

He had borne that same searching gaze for nine months of the Elder's company and had come to fear it and the questions it presaged. Naively, accepting the offer of his birthright, Valerius had expected to be trained in the ways of the dreamers. Instead, with Bellos left in Efnís' care, becoming more able in body if not yet in sight, Valerius had found himself talking back through the convolutions of his own past with Luain mac Calma guiding the path. Through nine months of nights, he had revisited the false peace of the smith's bothy in Hibernia, marched with Caradoc through Rome, trained with Corvus – and loved and been loved by him – in Camulodunum, in Germany, in Gaul.

Drained of adult love, he had walked back through time to childhood; had nursed Hail to life, helped at the birth of a dun filly, ridden his father's battle horse and the red Thessalian cavalry mare in the homelands of the Eceni and once, gloriously, defeated Amminios, brother to Caradoc, in a game of Warrior's Dance with a slave boy's life as the prize.

Like running water, the questions had worn at him, probing the cracks in his self-possession until, three nights out of four, he had retired to bed swearing that he would leave and return to Hibernia alone. Each morning, he had awakened and continued, as they had both known he would, as he did now, in the hound-warmed dark with no-one to push him or hold him when he wept.

Only mac Calma's voice came at him through the silence, an echo of reality made real again in stone.

I offer you your birthright.

It was what his soul had craved through all his adult life and there was no point in denying it.

That single promise had sustained Valerius through the ghastly crossing from Mona to Hibernia and had kept him silent, at least temporarily, when word reached them near midsummer of the long-drawn death of the governor of Britannia. Rumour said that the dreamers had killed him as they had killed his predecessor, Scapula, in revenge for a boy's death.

Asked, mac Calma had smiled and said, 'That wasn't us. The ancestor-dreamer killed Scapula at Airmid's request but your sister slew this one alone, with a little help from the she-bears of the Caledonii and their unique understanding with the gods.'

His sister, Breaca, whose name was not, and never had been, mentioned.

Valerius' mind slewed away from that and mac Calma did not drag him back again although it was the closest the Elder ever came to discussing the ways of gods and dreamers and the means by which one might talk to the other; that and the single cryptic sentence, given as Valerius was already closing himself off from the world.

You will know when it is time.

There was no time; the ancestors' dreaming chamber was too dark for that. Lacking light, Valerius had lost all sense of time. Lacking time, he had lost himself, a soul trapped in its own company with his past too much alive around him; nine months of talking had made it so.

Fighting a rising panic, he tried to take refuge in the present, discovering too late that there was no longer anything to hold him but the slow, safe breath of a hound and the endless echo of mac Calma's voice speaking riddles for which he had no answers.

You will know when it is time.

Time to do what?

I offer you your birthright . . .

And I accept. Only tell me what I must do.

I cannot help you.

Who else if not you?

Valerius would have wept, had there been any point. Even in the despair of adult dreaming, he had never imagined failure of this magnitude. The boy who was Bán had dreamed of his long-nights, safe in the care of his mother, who would not let him fail. Now, he was failing and could do nothing about it.

You will know.

He knew nothing, and had no means to find out. In despair, he turned sideways and lay down, squirming until his back was safe in the curve of the hound and the weight of its breath guarded his neck. Lying like that, as he had lain in childhood, Julius Valerius closed his eyes and sought the freedom of sleep.

Which gods did you petition?
'I have no gods.'

His own voice woke him, too loud for the dark. Mac Calma's question drifted ahead, as if recently asked.

The vengeful gods laughed and made Bellos blind again, slaying a foal as their own blood-price. Mithras walked on fire and water and the blood of a slain bull filled the ancestors' chamber and washed away with the tide.

'You have too many gods. You can't keep them all. Which do you choose?'

The voice was his own, brought outside himself. It came out of the dry air and the drier stone and tapped at his bones.

Half a dozen answers crowded for space. If he had been in company – if it were mac Calma, or Theophilus, or Corvus who asked such a question – Valerius would have picked the response that kept them safely distant. In their absence, he stared at the dark and waited for the clamour inside to die away. He did not intend to play games with a mind shaken loose of itself. Too much of his life had been given to ghosts and half-dreams forged in pain and isolation. He craved a long-nights that was real, or none at all.

When there was silence, and Valerius was sure of himself, he said, clearly, 'Go away.'

The dark fell silent. Time moved on and he was given his wish; the air did not speak again. The waiting lay on him like a mountain.

Light-headed, he rolled over and sat up. The hound roused with him, slowly. They had shared sleep together and the beast's size and presence were no longer a threat. It was free to leave, where Valerius was not. That it chose to stay was a gift and accepted as such. It stood and stretched in the cramped space and turned and came to lie with its chin on his thigh, as Hail had lain in the joy-filled days of their youth.

This hound was bigger than Hail, close to the size he had

imagined Hail to be when the skewed scales of childhood had made all hounds vast and Hail greatest of them all. Its hair was long and coarse as Hail's had been and, in the dark, Valerius was free to imagine the patternings of white on brindle that had given his first hound, the best of all hounds, its name. He buried his face in the wild ruff of its mane. The smell smothered him; hound and woodsmoke and hunted hare and family and home and all things lost.

The man he had been would have walked away from that rather than remember it. The man he had become, product of the dark and the gods and the unknowing, walked willingly into the mire of his past and begged it to drown out the voice of Luain mac Calma.

It worked, for a while, possibly for days – he had no means to measure the passage of time – but it could not last for ever. Luain mac Calma reached out to him from the recent past, blocking any further escape. His voice was more solid than it had been, as if he spoke from the bedrock of the chamber.

Any failure means death, not only of your body but of your soul.
Failure.

The blackness stank of it, and would not be made clear.

Faced with no other choice, Julius Valerius, who had once been Bán of the Eceni, pushed the hound's head from his thigh, drew his knees for a second time to his chest and began at last to consider exactly what it might mean to lose his soul.

The process was not pretty, or dignified. To imagine the loss of his soul, he first had to discover it, to map its margins, its contours and textures and the many ways in which he had not lived by its calling. He had believed himself honest in his own dishonesties; possessed of an integrity which, if warped by the standards of his family, tribe and friends, was nevertheless true to itself. Every action he had ever taken had been tested against the too-sharp weapon of his own judgement and the fabric of his life had been woven around it.

With an honesty that stripped to the bare bones every hidden feeling, Valerius set about testing the truth of that. Far more than mac Calma had asked for, he stepped back to the earliest memory of his life and walked forward through the months and years, cataloguing for himself and the absent gods every failure of integrity, every self-lie, every instance of mortal weakness.

If he were to guess, another day and part of a night might have passed in the slow unpicking of his life's failings. The hound left once and came back, smelling of fresh blood and, less strongly, of urine. It did not bring any meat for Valerius, but it was doubtful if he could have eaten by then; he was too immersed in the dismantling of himself.

He expected the ghosts to come, hissing their anger and sucking at his sanity for vengeance as they had done when their deaths were fresh. Perversely, their absence left him hollow; there had been comfort in the discomfort of their rage. He did not ask for the gods' help and they, unpetitioned, did not answer. Every step was taken alone, without assistance, and by their absence Valerius came finally, unwillingly, to recognize their presence in all that had gone before; whether he liked it or not, every part of his life had been shaped within the protective arms of the unnamed gods.

Even now. Even here. He passed through the last memory and came to rest in the present and he was not alone. The gods of his past were all around: Briga and Mithras, Nemain and Jupiter and Manannan of the waves who made him sick but did not kill him. The chamber was crowded by their presences, watching, waiting for him to act. The hound felt them and whined, stretching a warm tongue to his wrist as comfort for them both.

Aloud, Valerius said, 'What do you want of me?'

The gods gave no answer. Their silence crushed him. Their waiting drove him, ultimately, to act.

Over hours, over days, Valerius attempted every feat of dreaming he had ever imagined – and failed in each one. He built images in the dark and they melted. He spoke tales that mac Calma had told him and their heroes did not come alive. He named the thousand ghosts of his dead and they walked past and past until all that was left was the memory of their shadows. He viewed and reviewed and discarded every particle of his life, scouring the passageways of his soul until the winds whistled through and he was emptied of all thought and all feeling. The gods watched and waited and offered nothing.

You're trying too hard. Bellos spoke from the safest part of his past.

Valerius said, 'I know. I don't know how to do anything different.'

The hound came to sit in front of him. In his memory, its eyes

244

were amber. He chose to think of them so. He held its great head between both of his hands and said, 'Friend, I'm sorry. You have guarded the wrong man against dangers that did not come from the outside. I wish you luck with the others who come after me.'

He did not end out of self-pity, or bitterness, but only because there was nothing else he could do. Pressing the flat of both palms to the floor, Valerius pushed himself upright against protesting joints and muscles that burned from too long cramped tight. The roof of the chamber rubbed the top of his head. Stretching out both hands, he touched his palms to the stone on either side. The hound pressed its chin against his thigh. If life had been different, it would have been good to have ridden with it into battle.

He bowed a little to the waiting dark. 'I have failed. I apologize. Perhaps I would always have done so. I thank you for keeping me from the understanding of this long enough to live the life that I have done. With all its failings, with the deaths and the loss and the pain, it has been the fullest and best it could have been, for which I offer my deepest thanks.'

He expected no answer and was given none. He felt his way round the walls and came to the tunnel that the ancestors had built. Crawling in, full of hope, he had felt the place a womb and had imagined himself emerging, reborn into light, a man at peace with his gods and heir to the legacy of Mona's dreamers. For that hubris alone, he deserved whatever was coming. Crawling out towards fresh air past the spiralled carvings of the past, he tried to remember the many ways in which those who had abandoned their long-nights had died. In this, too, he failed.

Valerius emerged into a night of no moon and few stars and it seemed to him bright.

Expecting death, or the slow beginnings of it, he scrambled with what dignity he could over the guard stone at the tunnel's entrance. On the way in, the light of mac Calma's fire had flooded the carvings on the surface of the boulder, sinking shadows into the spheres and circles etched by the ancestors. Now, there was nothing but warm winter wind and the silvered greys of a land that believed itself black.

The hound did not follow him out. He thought to call it and decided not; it was safer for it not to be caught up in whatever was coming. Putting his hands to his mouth, he sent his voice away from the dream mound.

'Hello?'

He felt foolish, more so when he was not answered. His flesh crawled and his hungry guts cramped but no-one came; no waiting dreamers, no knives, no ropes to bind him down as they flayed the skin from his chest and opened his living belly to the crows. The turves had been relaid over the circle of mac Calma's fire. If Valerius had not sat before it for a night, awaiting the dawn to enter the chamber, he would not know where it had been.

The gods and the hound had abandoned him, but Valerius did not believe Luain mac Calma would leave before the end. Unwilling to be seen to search, he sat down on the guard stone to wait. After the intensity of the ancestors' chamber, there was a welcome peace in not thinking.

Presently, when still no-one had come to kill him, he remembered the place where the wood was stored. Searching through a cavity in the dry southern side of the hill, he found tinder and a fire pot packed with old, dying embers. He was an officer in the auxiliary cavalry, or had been; he had built fires with less than this and been warmed by them.

Instinct drew him away from the hill, towards a swath of old oaks with a river winding through the centre. He had been a long time without water. In the dream place, it had not seemed important. In the presence of an unending stream of cold, clear water, thirst consumed him. He lay down and sank his face into it and drank for an eternity that stretched as long as the time he had spent in the ancestors' mound.

The cold steadied him and gave him purpose. He laid out the wood at a place where the river bent back on itself so that water surrounded three sides. His fire burned with small flames. By its light, he lay on the bank and slid his hands into the water and dribbled spit onto the surface to lure winter fish. They were few, but he was possessed of a patience that would have astonished those he had led, amongst whom the shortness of his temper had been legendary. At the blackest part of the night that comes before dawn, he caught a small trout and roasted it. The smell alone was of the gods; the taste consumed him.

Afterwards, he sat by the fire to wait. If he had been concerned for his own safety, he would have kept the river behind him as protection. Safety was the least of his concerns and so he faced east, to where the late-rising moon lifted over the horizon, and kept the water ahead and on either side with his back exposed to whoever might come.

It did not seem possible that any night would ever again seem dark. The sliver of Nemain's moon was as bright as the noon sun. Unable to look at the god directly, Valerius watched her reflection slide over the river. Water was her domain. As a child, he had believed that proximity to water drove men mad and women madder. Now, he welcomed the calm that it gave.

The water was alive; small fish kissed the surface, larger ripples backed off stones and wove into each other, the moon broke and scattered so that the whole surface of the water became boiling silver, oddly inviting. When the shine stretched from one bank to the other, Valerius stood and shed his clothes and stepped down and out to immerse himself to the neck and beyond in water so cold that it burned.

As the ancestors' chamber had scoured his mind, so did Nemain's river scour his skin. He lay back with only his nose above the surface, and then not even that. His hair was longer than it had ever been and it floated behind like weed, both buoying his head and teasing it under. His skin grew to like the cold, so that the water and the smooth rocks of the river bed caressed him rather than chafing and he revelled in the feel of it, who had slept five years alone and forgotten what it was to be touched with care. He spread his arms and his legs against the current and slowly, between one breath and the next, the river became a lover, moving him with a passion as great as any he had felt for Corvus or Longinus or the unfulfilled, unacknowledged longing for Caradoc.

He fought it at first; the river did not just belong to Nemain, it *was* Nemain, daughter to Briga, watcher of all life, birth-bringer, holder of cycles. All his life, he had imagined this god as Airmid, so that often in his dreams the two were one. Valerius had never knowingly wanted Airmid, or any woman, could not imagine ever doing so, but the river touched him elsewhere than the flesh, and his mind was too tired to resist the pull of a god and he gave himself over to it, remembering only to breathe when the surface came to meet him.

Afterwards, he wondered why he had done that; drowning was by no means the worst way to die. Shivering, he drew himself onto the bank, cold and spent, empty in ways the dream hill had not left him. He dressed and made the fire bigger and the flames were no longer too bright to watch, nor the eastern horizon where the first fire of the sun poured molten gold on the earth.

The moon still dallied in the west, a ghosted sickle outshone by the greater light of the sun. Valerius turned to face it and sat a while, unthinking.

In the past, ghosts and gods alike had spoken to him in voices too loud to be ignored. Here, on the banks of the river that was for ever sacred to the daughter of Briga, Valerius found for the first time what it was to hear the whisper of a god, to sense a knowing that passed beyond words as Nemain came to rest in the core of his being.

She did not offer a vision of future glory, or an end to all grief; he would not have believed either of these, nor asked for them. Instead, through the slow setting of the moon, he discovered within himself the totality of all joy and all pain and the place of his soul as the balance between. It was as great a gift as he had ever been given and there seemed no possibility that it could be taken away.

Presently, when the whispering ceased and all that was left was the feather-touch of moonlight and a passing memory of water, he stood and extinguished his fire, dismantling it and covering the ash so that no trace was left of his passing.

He was kneeling, scattering dead leaves over the cut-lines of the turf when, from somewhere behind his left shoulder, Luain mac Calma asked, 'Where are you going?'

It was not unexpected, only later than it might have been. Still kneeling, Valerius answered, 'I was going to Mona, to find Bellos and discuss with him his future as one blind in the land of the sighted. With the right training, I believe he may still make a good healer. After that, as soon as the seas are open to shipping, I thought I might cross the water, to Britannia. I met Mithras there once, in a cave. If I am to live, I must make my peace with him.'

'And are you going to live?'

'I have no idea.'

The morning air was sharp with frost; the first furrings of it etched the oak leaves behind mac Calma, so that his hair seemed a deeper black. His face was caught partway between the sun and the moon, not quite lit by either. He wore his dreamer's thong of rolled birch bark at his brow for the first time in nine months and the blade at his belt was curved back at the tip to make a flaying knife.

Valerius was unarmed, and had been so since they reached Hibernia. Standing, he felt more naked than he had done when he walked into the river. His skin cringed against the rub of his tunic. Nemain had not promised long life, or the absence of pain. The awareness of that hung about him, sharply.

He ran his tongue round the edge of his teeth. 'What *is* the penalty for a man who abandons his long-nights?'

Mac Calma balanced his knife on his palm. 'Death, of course. Those who do not cut their own throats or give themselves to Nemain's water are dealt a swift death by the one standing watch. There's no need for further retribution. Failure itself is enough.'

'Indeed.' So mac Calma had, after all, been present through it all. Valerius regretted not having searched for him more thoroughly. He said, 'I have no blade of my own with which to cut my throat.'

'I know. And the river did not take you, although you gave yourself fully to the god. What does that tell you?'

'That the man who claims to be my father chooses to watch without making his presence known.' Valerius spat as they did in the legions, with much noise and a profusion of phlegm. 'We should do what needs to be done. I don't think there's anything left to say that hasn't been said in the last nine months. If you give me the blade, I'll do it myself, to save you the blood taint.'

'Will you fall on the blade as do the Romans? Do you so badly want to die?'

'I don't want to die at all. I rather think I have just been shown how to live and would welcome the chance to do so. But if there is no choice, I would rather die cleanly, by my own hand, than by the false care of another man.'

'Valerius, you always have choice.'

Mac Calma was the Elder of Mona; he could put more meaning into one sentence than others could speak in a day, and did so. A god and a world waited while the many layers of meaning span out into being.

Valerius sat on the turf where his fire had been. The last warmth kept the frost from his feet. He looked for the moon and found the last insubstantial edge of her on the western horizon. Her presence warmed his soul. Mithras had never done that, even in the cave.

He frowned and stared at his fingers and then at the grass. A number of things became clear, and unclear.

After a while, still sitting, he said, 'Breaca's long-nights did not end like this.'

Luain mac Calma shed his cloak, folded it and sat on the pad. Gooseflesh stood on the bare skin of his arms. Resting his chin on the heel of his upturned hand, he said, 'Your sister was a child who had to learn what she might become as an adult and a warrior. She had to experience in the depths of her soul the reality of life and death. You were made adult before your time and there is nothing anyone, god or dreamer, could teach you of living and dying. Where others sit their long-nights to pass from childhood to adulthood, you had to pass backwards, to unlearn what you have been in order to find what else you might yet become. Have you done so?'

Nine months of questioning were thus glibly excused. Valerius considered what he was, what he had been and what he might become. The ancestors' chamber had loosened the anchors of his past, and Nemain had given the surety of her presence through death and beyond. Neither of these offered a solid foundation on which to build a living future. One memory tugged at him. 'Was the hound real? The one that shared the dark?'

'Did it seem real to you?'

'I thought so at the time.' The memory of a tongue on his wrist was as real, or unreal, as it had been in the chamber. Valerius said, 'Is the hound then my dream as the hare is Airmid's? The elder grandmother called me horse-dreamer.'

'And hare-hunter, as I remember. Which has never stopped you hunting deer, or boar.'

'Or men. Indeed. I didn't know one could choose.'

'Few can. You are one of those few.'

'Thank you.'

More than any dreaming, Valerius badly wanted the hound to be real, to have it run from the chamber and walk at his side, to hunt with it and ride with it and remember all that was lost. Disappointment led full circle to first hope and first loss.

I offer you your birthright.

As a child that asks for the hare who lives on the moon, Valerius said, 'You asked me if I had found what I might yet become. There was a time when I wanted more than anything to be a warrior but I have been that and my soul was not whole there. If I were given the choice anew, I would become a dreamer. Do I have that choice?'

'What?' Mac Calma barked a laugh. He pushed one hand through his hair, disturbing the careful placement of his dreamer's thong, then set it straight and pinched the end of his nose.

After a while he said, a little desperately, 'You've been a dreamer since you were seven years old. You made Hail live by your dreaming. You called the red Thessalian cavalry mare across an ocean in storm by the power of your need. You saw Amminios and named the nature of his treachery in a waking vision long before any of us saw anything but the son of a warrior. Do you really not know what you are?'

The hare on the moon came close but would not be caught. Too dazzled to think, Valerius said, 'But I don't know how I do it. I don't know how *you* do it.'

'But you wish to learn?'

Valerius was weeping and did not care. Nemain held him and made him whole. 'Gods, yes, I do. Yes. Before all other things, whatever the cost, I want to learn to be as you are.'

Mac Calma smiled and was ten years younger. He stood and swung his cloak over both shoulders. 'Good. Very good. In that case, I think I can teach you. You should make your peace with Bellos and Mithras as you planned. I'll wait for you on Mona.' He turned towards the river and then turned back again.

'I think if you put your mind to calling the hound from the chamber, you may find that it will come.'

X I X

SACRED TO THE MEMORY OF QVINTVS VERANIVS,
FOVRTH GOVERNOR OF BRITANNIA,
FIRST GOVERNOR OF LYCIA AND PAMPHYLIA . . .

A YEAR, EXACTLY, FROM THE DAY HE CAST A SILVER-BLADED heron-spear into the heart of a young Eceni warrior, a monument to the late governor of Britannia was unveiled just outside the steading of his friend and loyal ally, Prasutagos, king of the Eceni.

Like its twin, which was set into the wall of the theatre in Camulodunum, the stone was of grey marble, tinged almost to silver and polished to mirror brilliance. Unlike its twin, this one stood alone, set to one side of the trackway just as it left the steading. The height of a man and half that width across, it had been positioned by the Iberian mason who had fashioned and delivered it so that the rising sun might cast clean shadows across it and onto the track. Carved on its surface, square and boldly cut, was the written history of a life.

. . . RESOVNDING VICTORY OVER THE MOVNTAIN TRIBES
CREATING PEACE FROM DISORDER.
AVGVR AND CONSVL IN THE YEAR . . .

Mist rolled over the stone and past it, heavy as water. The unveiling ceremony had been delayed for a day in the hope that the weather might clear. Instead, the gods had thickened the air further, sending waves of swirling fog to cloak and conceal so that Breaca, standing in front and a little to one side, was locked in a land apart, sharing it only with the physician, Theophilus, on her left, and on her right Decianus Catus, the emperor's thin, bored, arrogant and supremely dangerous procurator of taxes.

They were the best and the worst that Rome could offer. Theophilus had spent the spring and early summer after the spear-challenge ministering to the dying governor, but by late summer had been free to accept Breaca's offer and had spent the better part of three months thereafter in Eceni lands exchanging lore and healing with Airmid. Another half-year and she could have named him a dreamer and none would have argued.

The procurator, by contrast, was vermin: a leech on the life veins of the tribes. *If you do not rouse the east,* a ghost had said, *Rome will bleed your people dry.* Breaca had spent the past winter turning out spear-heads and knife-blades, and the summer before that in the quiet, careful quest for those warriors who could be trusted with her life and her plans for a future of war, but she had not yet raised an army. Lacking that, the procurator was the one who would do his best to bleed dry the Eceni and all of the eastern tribes.

He was also, in the continued absence of the governor to the western wars, the most powerful of the emperor's men in the province of Britannia. Until Breaca had raised warriors in sufficient numbers to face the legions, there was nothing to do but offer him guest rights and let 'Tagos negotiate such reductions in tax as might be wrenched from a man who valued everything in finger's weights of gold.

'Tagos had done his best. Behind, waiting in the mist, were the eighty mercenary veterans of the procurator's personal retinue. They stood guard now over his wagons, within which, bound and double-sealed with wax and molten lead, were the bags of coins given by 'Tagos from his money chests to be sent to the emperor's treasury, less a judicious percentage for the procurator.

The wagons did not contain the significant quantity of hides that had been requested and nor had the procurator taken into account the worth of the three breeding stallions in the mist-bound paddocks behind the steading, or the breeding herds of mares that ran with each. He had not, either, ventured out as far as Breaca's forge or the newly built hut behind it that harboured a store of raw iron and the bundles of blades that had been made over winter.

For these things, and the respite they offered, Breaca gave thanks.

The mist closed in more tightly. Black-carved letters lifted from the surface of the slab and snaked out across the day.

... SENATOR AND VALVED ADVISER TO THE EMPEROR CLAVDIVS,
MAY THE GODS FOR EVER HOLD HIM ...

If the gods held the governor now, they had taken their time in doing so. His dying had been drawn out over four months and was in every way as unpleasant as that of Scapula, the governor slain by the ancestor-dreamer at Airmid's request.

The beginning had been slowly insidious; from the last day of the old moon after Eneit's death, Breaca had lain nightly awake, listening to the winds of the gods whistle south to Camulodunum to take what was theirs from the one who had failed the ancestors' trial. They did not take Breaca's soul, nor rack her body with pain as they did the governor's, and by that fact alone she confirmed that her spear had slain Eneit, and the Roman general's had not.

Thus was one of her two questions answered – which of us killed Eneit? The second question – where is Cunomar? – was answered later, near midsummer. As the governor came closer to death, Ardacos had returned from a hunting trip with news that a corn-haired youth of the Eceni had been seen to travel north to the mountains of the Caledonii.

Soon after that, Cunomar himself had begun to haunt Breaca's dreams, stalking naked through untouched forest, painted in the spiralling white lime and woad of the she-bears.

Her son had been taller and broader in the shoulder than she remembered him. He carried a spear identical to the one she had thrown, but that the feathers bound to the haft had come from a cormorant, not a heron, and the blade was not of silver, but of iron, with signs etched along it that she had never seen.

It was a good spear, balanced well for his arm, and he was beginning to learn how to match his soul to its. In the dream, she watched him track a wounded male bear that had already torn the limbs from two others who had tried to stalk it. When, on the second night, he killed it, Cunomar cut the bear's heart from its chest and held it high in both hands, speaking directly to Breaca with an earnestness that made it essential to hear what he said.

She could not hear him. For three nights in succession, she returned to the same place and time and watched the same kill. Three times, the dream of her son held up the still-beating he-bear's heart and spoke to her and three times she strained every sense and still could not hear the message it mattered so much to him to give.

Nor could Cunomar hear his mother. There had been no word left when he ran from the theatre, no chance to speak and set right all that was wrong. Wherever he lived – or died – it mattered that he know Breaca had killed Eneit cleanly, that the governor's spear had fallen into flesh already dead, that Eneit had died with the heart of a warrior, that he had sent his love and his name to Cunomar as his last gift.

Nightly, she struggled to say each of these aloud in the dream, so that he might hear and be healed of his hate, but the soul-song of the spear came out of her mouth and she could not make the words have any meaning. Nightly, the dream that was Cunomar looked through his mother to a space beyond, and Breaca woke, always, with the taint of that gaze clouding the day, and the void of need that was in it.

By late summer, the dreams were different and Cunomar no longer walked in them. The world had moved on and other lives mattered more than a youth who sought manhood. The governor died as the moon turned from old to new, four months after the spear-challenge and three after the start of his illness. He had known what was coming and had planned for it, but still the emperor and his senate in Rome had not considered it urgent to send a new governor to their northernmost province. The legions of Britannia had once again been left leaderless and the warriors of the west had taken advantage of it, launching waves of attack on the frontier forts.

News of slaughtered legionaries had filtered eastwards and the cohorts stationed around Camulodunum became nervous and took to patrolling the trackways with a fervour that made even trading difficult. Thus Breaca had spent the months leading to full summer trying to find ways for her people to tend to the fields without every adult being held at swordpoint for possession of a hoe and every child beaten for lifting a stone to the side of a paddock.

The ancestor-dreamer had stalked her dreams with images of children starved and enslaved, and Breaca had been perversely glad when the new governor had arrived in the late autumn to restore a semblance of order.

Suetonius Paulinus, fifth governor of Britannia, brought fresh men and officers and the legions had imposed a kind of peace so that the harvest had been brought in without bloodshed and the late-season cattle markets held without the quartermaster at Camulodunum's commandeering the best bullocks for his men.

With the governor had come Decianus Catus, the emperor's procurator of taxes, and then, in the spring, the Iberian mason and his slabs of marble, and the old governor became a man recorded in stone, set in earth and swirling mist.

To the last line, it was a worthy memorial. Breaca read it without interest, and then stopped, and read the last line again.

FIRST MAN NOT OF THE TRIBES TO VNDERTAKE
THE SPEAR TEST OF THE CALEDONII.
BY MY OWN HAND, I CAST IT TRVE.

'He knew.'

'Tagos paced the length of the roasting pit that contained the bullock that had been killed too early, especially to feed the procurator and his mercenaries. The procurator had gone, taking his wagonload of gold and a gift of wine from the king of the Eceni.

Breaca watched the darkening space that was the retreating wagon and knew that the god-sent mist was lifting. Around her were only Eceni, and Theophilus, who was a friend, and 'Tagos, who was unnerved and let it show.

' "By my own hand I cast it true." ' He came to the end of the fire pit and turned, abruptly. 'That wasn't on the stone at Camulodunum. The old governor wrote this for us. He knew why he died and he wants the world to know with him. If he wrote of this to the emperor, his successor will crucify us in sight of his monument, so that we, too, will know why we die.'

Breaca sat on a log at the edge of the fire pit. 'Of course he knew.

256

There was never any doubt. He sent word to Airmid asking her to help him die cleanly at the end.'

The request had been in part of the note sent with the old governor's final letter to 'Tagos, addressed to *Breaca of the Eceni* and sealed with the elephant mark of Britannia that made it a capital offence for anyone other than the one addressed to open it.

'Tagos had tried to find what the note said, and failed. Now, he stared openly. 'Did she give it? Did Airmid make easier the death of a Roman governor?'

'Yes. Theophilus knows.'

The physician nodded in agreement. Some time after the ceremony, he had swapped his good cloak for one heavier and older, much patched, that smelled of beech smoke and pork fat. He held a jug of ale in one hand and warmed the other in the smoke of the fire pit.

At the sound of his name, he raised his jug in salute. 'He does indeed know, and is grateful. Xenophon, who was physician to Claudius, knew the skills of these things, but they were not passed to me.'

'Tagos coughed. A muscle twitched in his cheek. 'I see.'

'I'm not sure that you do.' Theophilus came to sit on the log Breaca had brought forward. 'That inscription was not only a warning for you. The governor was genuinely proud of his spear throw. He was convinced until his dying breath that his spear had killed Eneit, not yours, and that the gods were punishing him for success, not failure.'

Breaca said, 'The gods punish no-one. It is men who do that. The gods take what is their due and was given freely as a personal offering. I did try to tell him.'

'I know. And he believed you did your best to warn him and that you threw as well as you were able – which is exactly why you are not currently dying by slow degrees within sight of an over-polished mass of marble. He could not give orders to his successor to leave you alone, but he could honour you and make it clear that he did not hold you responsible for his death. He has done exactly that.'

The fog had thinned almost to nothing. Breaca could see the full round of the stockade now, and the square, small houses within it. Beads of mist ran like sweat down the oak stanchions of the gateposts and children began to emerge from between them, drawn by the smell of roasting meat. Graine was there, and a half-dozen others of her age who followed her as if she already led them.

They were safe; neither starved nor enslaved. 'Tagos' fears remained unrealized. The procurator's wagon and the century of ex-legionaries he paid to guard it were gone beyond sight and would not be back for a half-year. Neither they nor the marble slab explained the small knot of nausea that had taken root in Breaca's belly, or the ache along the scar on her palm that was the gods' warning of danger.

She took a stave and broke open the clay crust on the fire pit. The air became damp with the smell of roast beef. Reaching in with her knife, she said to Theophilus, 'So what is it about the last governor's death that we have not read in his stone, but that brings you north in the cold of spring for its unveiling?'

'Did you know he consistently refused trading rights to the slavers?'

Breaca stared at him through the rising heat of the fire. The knot in her belly swelled to a hammer-fist. In broad daylight the voice of the ancestor-dreamer resounded. *Shall I show you, warrior, what it is for a people to bleed until there is nothing more to give?*

Graine was a spear's throw away. She was not weeping tears of gold or of corn.

Reaching down, Breaca cut a long thigh muscle from the bullock in the pit. The meat came away in her hand, greasily friable. She said, 'No man of honour would grant trading rights to slavers,' and then, because it must be said aloud, 'Are we to understand that the new governor is not a man of honour?'

Theophilus leaned in to the heat of the fire. He said, 'Suetonius Paulinus is a general. He has led legions in the worst parts of the empire. He has been ordered to subdue the tribes of western Britannia, or die in the attempt. Under such orders, would any of us be men of honour? Thank you. I thought you were going to feed it to the hounds before me.'

'They come next.' Absently, Breaca tossed a flake of roast hide to Stone, who was closest, and others to the grey bitch and her whelps who waited beyond. 'We should be plain. You are saying that the new governor has granted trading rights to slavers?'

Theophilus said, 'Yes, although the actual administration will be given to the procurator, the sucking leech who has just driven south with a wagonload of your gold. If that man has pity, it is well hidden. If I were you, I would do everything necessary to safeguard my children.'

He said it to Breaca but his eyes, and hers, were on the king of the Eceni, who had listened to his news and had not been surprised.

'Tagos flushed and made a show of settling the torc he wore at his neck, laying the kill-feather flat against his collarbone. 'Graine won't be harmed,' he said, eventually. 'He has promised it. The old governor said she could be sent to Rome to be taught the ways of the emperor's palace, as befits the child of a king. I have said the Eceni would not allow it, but that she is being taught here. The procurator has sworn she will not be touched.'

'*The Procurator has sworn?*'

The morning was suddenly thin and brittle, like ice on a puddle. Very quietly, Breaca said, 'If you tell me you have agreed with that vermin, or with the governor, or with anyone else, a quota of slaves from Eceni lands, I will kill you.'

'Tagos swallowed on nothing. 'I have not agreed any quota,' he said. 'None has been asked.'

'But they will come to trade here, in the Eceni territories? They will buy Eceni children from Eceni parents? Or will they simply take them by force or carry them away if they are left unattended?'

Shall I show you what it is for a people to bleed . . .?

'I don't think even the procurator would allow—'

'Of course he would.' Theophilus' voice cut in the way Airmid's could, at need. 'The procurator's life depends on making a profit from Britannia and tax on trade is his biggest source of income. Slave traders make more profit than all the rest added together. The first group landed at the full moon tide. They're Latins, men of the country around Rome who have not gained full Roman citizenship. They think themselves almost Roman and robbed of their true rights and are bitter about it and doubly dangerous. Eight of them have crossed the ocean with a group of Gaulish harness makers coming north for your spring horse fair. If the Eceni were in my care, I would watch these men and take whatever steps were necessary to ensure they made no profit from the flesh and blood of my people.'

XX

THE SPRING HORSE FAIR WAS AS CROWDED AS A BATTLEFIELD, AND as noisy. The forest around made a wall that sent the sound in again, with only the wide path of the trackway in the south-east to break the circle.

A second circle of gathered firewood lay within the ring of trees and a third of the tents and single-draped hides of the traders made a patchwork in the growing dawn. These, too, sent the hollering of traders inwards and upwards, so that the crows took umbrage and deserted the forest and even the redbreasts, who would have sat around the fires for crumbs, departed.

Within these three rings were gathered traders in their many hundreds, if not the thousands there had once been and that the site was built to hold. The Eceni had travelled in ones or twos from each steading across the territories to sell the produce of a winter's work; the Gauls and Batavians and Iberians and Mauritanians and Latins and Romans had travelled up in their hired wagons from the sea ports on the great river with the sole aim of taking as much as they could in exchange for as little as possible of their ocean-travelled goods.

This fact was understood between them; it fired the passion of the trading. Always, the first days were spent in setting impossible targets and the next two in whittling down what was offered to what was expected and reaching ever closer to what might be accepted.

The site of the horse fair was less than half a morning's ride from 'Tagos' steading, but Breaca had arrived late, when all the trading positions were set. Leading her pack horses through the crowd, she made two circuits of the wide, open clearing before she found an opening that suited her needs. There she laid out the bay horse hide that set off her metalwork to best effect and set about unwrapping the goods she had spent all winter creating.

'Have you seen the slavers yet: the ones Theophilus told you of ?'

Graine asked it, throwing herself down on the damp grass behind the horse hide. She was picking daisies and buttercups and weaving them into a torc for Stone, who lay close to her side. Through the winter, with Cunomar gone, Breaca had sharpened the hound's training so that, more than ever, he had become Graine's protector. Her daughter had grown recently, becoming more young woman than precocious child, but the hound still stood almost to her shoulder, so that she could reach over him and lean her weight on his back. Like that, they had explored the beginnings of the fair together.

It had been interesting to watch: Stone had been taught that any-one not introduced by Graine as a friend was a possible enemy and there were a lot of those at the fair. However foreign the gathered traders might have been, however strange their language or dress, every man and woman among them recognized the sight of a hound trained to attack. Steadily, while stalls were set out and the first frantic bargains begun, Graine had traversed the chaos in a halo of emptiness, knots of bartering adults split apart by her progress re-forming after she passed.

She had walked straight to her mother's stall, which was touch-ing, but not ideal; Breaca did not want traders to stay away from her stock of knives and spear-heads, and even bearing his own king-torc of buttercups, Stone did not inspire anyone to approach.

Breaca sat down and ruffled his neck. To Graine, she said, 'I think the men sitting round the fire behind you are the slavers – that's why I'm here – but it might be good if you stayed with Ardacos. He has charge of the roasting pits. You could help him there.'

Graine frowned at the split stem of a daisy. 'Or I could leave Stone with Ardacos and come back to you?' She tilted her head, like a thrush on a snail, in a way that her mother had come to recognize.

'Is there a reason you should be here with me? Have you dreamed something I should know of?'

'No, only that I want to see how you trade. You learned from Eburovic and Macha when you were my age. One day, if we clear Rome from the land, I'll need to know.'

'And I've never taught you. I'm sorry. I forget sometimes what it is to be a mother.' Breaca laid out a row of seven elm-hilted skinning knives with their blades curved back at the tip. The sun pushed through the morning mist and the first watery light made mirrors of the metal so that she saw herself seven times over, too serious, too protective, too concerned to make things right. Her father had been all these things, but carefully, so that the child who became the Boudica had been given room to grow.

Moving her head, so that the mirrors became dull iron again, Breaca said, 'Stone should stay close to one of us; he'll pine else. Sit behind the hide and keep him close. If you see me doing something you don't understand, ask me about it afterwards, not while the trade is happening.'

'Thank you.' Graine settled cheerfully on the turf a little way back from the stall. She drew a handful of grubby amulets carved in amber from her belt-pouch and began to polish one on the hem of her tunic. They were northern work, from the Caledonii or even further towards the roof of the world; neatly carved stags with men's faces beneath the horns, or horses that would stand if you put them on their feet, or owls that would guard against the dark chills of night. Airmid must have given them to her, or Ardacos; either of those would have seen that the child needed to learn and that her mother might not have brought anything to teach her.

'If you wanted to trade those,' Breaca offered, 'we could lay them out on the hide.'

It was what was expected of her and she had played her part. Graine grinned a little ruefully, as if she might have lost a bet, but won her wish instead, and arranged her pieces out beside the knives.

'Did Airmid say I wouldn't let you stay?' asked Breaca.

'No. Ardacos did. He bet me that I'd be back at his roasting pits before the trading started.'

'What did you win?'

Graine grinned and, briefly, was the image of the elder grand-mother. 'A morning's trading with you?' she said.

Their trading together lasted more than just a morning. For three days, Breaca of the Eceni, metal smith and spear maker, taught her daughter how to calculate the worth of a thing at first seeing, how to bargain in foreign languages with the brown-skinned men and women from Iberia and Gaul who brought their enamel and bars of raw iron, with bitter-eyed Latins who brought finely fashioned gold and tanned leather dyed in colours never seen in Britannia, with the northern Belgae and Germanic tribesmen who brought horses that were not as good as the ones the Eceni already rode but whose hounds were good and who wanted silver mirrors, or the elm-hilted knives with the sign of the hare on the blade, in return.

Graine was an exceptional trader. The discovery of that surprised them both. Like finding a new shield-mate in battle, Breaca felt a door closing that had been open and a sense of sudden safety she had forgotten she lacked.

She had forgotten, also, how beautiful her daughter was; in the isolation of the steading, it was easy to see her as yet another grow-ing child, gangly with youth and always in need of a newer, longer tunic. The traders, coming on Graine unprepared, were as taken with the freshness of her features and the ocean of her eyes as with the spears and brooches and replenished supply of amber amulets on her mother's bench.

Very quickly, Graine learned who could be won with a smile and a sideways glance at her mother that asked permission to make the trade on her own, for the first time. Each first time, the man or woman, however foreign, however different the language, knelt at the bench and made extravagant offers for a stag carved in amber, or, later, for a spear-head or a horn-handled knife. As long as Stone kept his distance, each without fail knowingly struck a poor bargain for the sake of having made Graine smile and went away glad to have done so.

By the end of three days, Breaca's bench was empty of goods and the space behind, guarded by Stone, was littered with sacks of salt and malted barley, with ingots of beeswax and raw iron and tanned leather and tiny slabs of Belgic enamel in blue and red and yellow, with harness and bronze harness mounts and silvered mirrors that would make good gifts for the exiled Eceni dreamers, if they ever returned from Mona. At the sleeping place, guarded by Airmid, were three new hounds and a matched pair of bay yearling colts, at least one of which had the potential to sire good battle horses.

Graine, for her part, had two new belts with bronze buckles, a necklace of raw amber strung on elk hide that was worth more than her entire supply of amulets, a skinning knife she didn't need and a dark brindled hound bitch so close to birthing that the whelps could be seen kicking against the side of her flank.

Better than any trade, Breaca had the measure of the eight silent, watchful men who sat around the lone fire nearby.

The Latin slavers Theophilus had warned of were striking in their complacency. Of the eight, three bore short swords in the size and style of the legions and two of those wore mail shirts that might turn a thrown spear at the end of its flight.

The rest were unarmed and unshielded and if they had ventured west of the high mountains with so little protection, they would have died, one at a time, between sunset and moonrise, before it was fully dark. In the flat lands of the east, where retaliation for the death of any man under Rome's patronage would destroy whole families, they were as safe as the legions could make them.

The slavers built their own fire as the last day of the fair grew quiet, and cooked their own food. Elsewhere, as the sun touched the western horizon, the roasting pits were opened. The mingled riches of hare and pig and deer spread out slowly in the still air so that knots of chattering men and women fell silent from west to east as food took over from tales of the days' bargains.

Breaca's stall was set on the easternmost margins where a drifting breeze kept the scent away. She sat with her back to the slavers and watched others work their way towards Ardacos' fires. A slim man branded up the full length of both forearms with the lizard marks of a Coritani warrior hung back and scratched the top of his head more than even lice might have made necessary. After a while, when no-one paid him attention, he wandered to the forest edge and stood to urinate against a tree. A while after that, he stepped behind the tree and did not return.

With his departure, the eight slavers at the ill-fed fire found it necessary to finish their meal in haste. The tallest, who bore a brooch in the shape of a leaping salmon on his tunic, wiped his hands on the grass and tipped out a bag of gold to count it.

Breaca turned her back on him and reached for three bridles with iron bits that lay nearby. She handed them to Graine and, not over-loudly but clearly enough to be heard at the neighbouring fire, said, 'Could you take these to Airmid? She'll need them to tether the new filly away from the colts.'

There was no new filly. Graine opened her mouth to say so and shut it again. Her eyes grew a little wide with the effort of not looking over her shoulder at the slavers. 'Should I take Stone?' she asked. 'Or will you need him?'

Breaca grinned. For a few last moments, she was trading again with her daughter, speaking secretly in open hearing, and the feeling was as good as battle. 'Take him with you,' she said. 'I think I may have help waiting for me in the forest.'

She was not sure of that, but the songs of the spears on her selling-hide had gained a new, almost-familiar tone as the daylight died and there was a tug in her soul that was not only the promise of action.

Graine picked up the bridles, trailing the reins so the leather darkened in the evening dew. She paused a moment, chewing her lip. 'You're right, there is help,' she said. 'He's been here for four days, but he told me not to tell you. He gave me the amulets. I think he carved them himself.'

Always, Breaca's children defeated her. She should have been glad. She was glad, only that it was lost beneath a welter of other things, less benign. She picked a small jar of honey and threw it lightly to Graine.

'Then keep this for him, as a gift from me. You can eat it together if he decides to come home with us afterwards.'

Dusk ate the sky from east to west. Breaca waited, watching the slavers, who, in turn, watched the place where the lizard-branded Coritani warrior had left the clearing. At a certain point, when the eight shapes round the fire became darker than the shadows cast by the flames, she rose and moved outwards, away from the sources of light.

The song of the spears followed her away from both the traders and the woman of the northern Eceni who had taken all eighteen of Breaca's hare-marked spear-heads in exchange for a pair of good knives and a red fawn bitch with coarse hair and a soft blackness round her eyes. That trade had been for show and Graine had not taken part, although the bitch was a good one and would match well with Stone.

The spear-heads were of a length for hunting but the woman knew how to hear the songs of their souls and she had others who would train with her to hear them also. Quietly, without alerting those who watched, the Boudica was equipping the first ranks of her war host.

On the outskirts of the fairground, where war was prosecuted in stealth by men who measured the values of others' lives in gold, Breaca moved through ranks of coppiced hazels where the under-growth had been trained upwards to make withies for baskets and sheep pens. The leaf litter beneath her feet was damp from the afternoon's rain and she made no noise.

The spear-song that had been with her all afternoon threaded through the halls of her mind, becoming louder with every step. She moved deeper into the trees, following it as a hound follows a scent until that single song alone rose over the many others as a single pure, unsullied note and she could trace it back to its source.

The spear and the one who bore it were waiting, hidden, in the darkest part of the forest. Breaca came as close as she dared then set her back against the hollowed stump of a long-dead hazel. The moon had risen, but not enough yet to cast light into the wood. She saw what she saw by starlight and that was hazy.

Breaca could have spoken first, and chose not to; too much was at stake and too much unknown. It was enough simply to let her-self be seen for what she was: alone and not heavily armed. She dared not risk more.

After a moment, from her right, Cunomar said softly, 'How did you know it was me? Did Graine tell you?' His voice had deepened in the thirteen long months of his absence. It was resonant now, possessed of a certainty that mirrored his father. He sounded curious, not petulant, drily amused, not defensive.

'No. Your sister keeps her secrets well. I heard the song of your new spear and recognized it from a dream I had in the early spring when I saw you kill the wounded he-bear. It was well done.' Breaca used the formal courtesy she would don in council, facing a warrior she did not fully know.

Her son tilted his head to look at her more directly. His fair hair was grey under the stars and the unrisen moon. He asked, 'Have you become a dreamer since I left?'

'Not at all, although I wondered if you had done so. Sometimes the most powerful of dreamers can send their dreams to others. If it matters enough.'

This last was a question. More hung on it than either would have openly expressed. To Graine, Breaca could speak of her care and her desperate fear and how the one wove into the other, but not yet to Cunomar, perhaps not ever.

His new spear sang while he considered his answer. The sound carried with it the scent of moss and high mountains and falling water and the iron-gall of bear blood. More faintly, men spoke invocations to the gods of rock and forest in the tongue of the Caledonii. Cunomar was one of them.

In the forest of the Eceni, Breaca's son studied his hands for a moment, then lifted his head and looked his mother directly in the eye for the first time she could remember. He was not naked as he had been in her dreams, but she could read him as if he were and did so, feeling a hope she barely dared name. He was no taller than his father had been, but broader than Caradoc, even at the height of the battle season. He wore a sleeveless tunic and a mass of white scars showed along the curves of both shoulders, as if a bear had mauled him, except that they were too evenly spaced to have been made by a bear. Lines of blue dots traced on either side confirmed it; the dreamers of the Caledonii marked their bear dancers thus, cutting into the flesh with hot knives and laying horse hair along the wound to raise the scar.

Cunomar bore her scrutiny quietly for a while, then said, 'At the time of the hunt, it mattered more than anything to show you what I had done. I didn't know that I sent you the dream, but I prayed to Nemain and the horned god of the forest that you saw what I had done. If the gods carried the vision to you, it was in answer to my soul's prayer with three days of fasting to give it strength. I don't know if I could do it again. Certainly, the elders of the Caledonii did not teach me their dream ways in the year I stayed with them, only how to become a man.'

Only. She ached to embrace him and it could not come from her. Stepping away from the hazel, she loosed the knife from her belt and held it out. 'I have this for you, and a hound bitch bred by Efnís' sister which will match Stone in the hunt.'

The knife lay on her palm, dull in the dark. In daylight, a dozen different traders had tried to bargain for it. The blade was plain, single-edged, of the greatest length allowed with a slight curve at the back edge so that it could kill or skin a body with equal ease. The hilt was not ornately tooled, but cast in bronze in the shape of a hunting bear, rounded along the back so that the hand slid over it easily and the head made the pommel. Inset at the place where the bear's heart would be, on the left only, was a piece of obsidian carved in the shape of a spear-blade. At certain angles of the fire-light, it shone red, as a wound freshly made.

The stars did not light it so, but silvered it, softly. Cunomar stepped for the first time away from the tree in whose shelter he had been standing. Cautiously, almost reverently, he lifted the knife out of her hand.

'You made this for me after the dream of my hunt?'

'Yes.'

'Gods . . .' As a child, he had never appreciated beauty for its own sake, only for what it could give him. He breathed now as reverently as Eneit had done when he first heard the soul-song of the spear. To hear the song of a knife was much harder.

Cunomar heard it. With the care of one guarding the sacred, he knelt and laid the blade on the leaf litter. Less carefully, he rose and threw his arms around his mother.

He had grown in height and breadth, but so much more in other ways. His grip was solid and knew where he ended and she began, respecting them both. Breaca felt a warmth on her neck that she thought was his breath and then realized wasn't.

He had not wept for Eneit as he did for her now.

Clouds had smeared over the stars by the time they stood apart. Speaking was hard. Breaca said, 'There is too much to say and we can't talk now. Do you know why I'm here?'

'Of course.' He grinned; a year with the Caledonii had not dimmed his delight in his own achievements, nor should it have done. He said, 'I've been here three days. The slavers are due to

268

meet one of Berikos' men – a lame warrior of the Coritani who fought against you before the Romans came. He has the marks of the fire lizard burned on his arms as proof that he has both killed and taken wounds in war. He raps a knife against the hazel stump as a sign he is here. The noise it makes carries further than you'd think and there's always one of the Latins listening. When they hear it, the big one with the leaping fish as his shoulder brooch comes to meet him.'

'The Coritani lizard-man left the clearing before it became dark. If he hasn't been here, it's because he is waiting for someone.'

'You, perhaps? Did he know you were watching him?'

'Possibly.' Breaca spun on one heel, listening to a forest at night. Distantly, men in mail moved heavily between the trees. A faint light glowed that was more than the fires and less than the moon. She asked, 'Do the two slavers with mail stay close to the fish-leaper?'

Cunomar had heard what she heard. He knelt and retrieved the bear-hilted knife. 'Only one of them comes this far,' he said. 'The other waits nearer the fair, to keep away passers-by.'

'In case they discover that the Coritani have taken to selling human lives for gold and a fish-badged Latin buys them.' Breaca drew her own knife. 'They're on their way. Bringing torches, no less, which should blind them to anything beyond their reach. Good. We should move . . .'

They stepped back and back and the space around them was black compared to the fire of the resin torches the slavers brought with them and any noise they made was lost in the clatter of men not trained to stalk in a forest at night.

The Latin trader came first, with his mail-clad ex-legionary bodyguard. The jewelled fish on his tunic leaped bright under the flame. The lizard-marked Coritani warrior was slower to arrive and came without light, treading silently; he had been a hunter once, of men as well as animals. He spoke Latin with a Gaulish accent and was answered in kind with passwords that both sides knew. If he was aware he was being watched, he hid it well.

Both men were used to dealing and gave no concessions; the trading passed smoothly, as if they were, indeed, exchanging a war-trained colt for a wagon of hides. Breaca listened less to the detail than the tone. It was not a new venture, nor a first meeting, simply the latest in a series of tightly made bargains.

Beside her, Cunomar knelt on one knee with one hand on his spear, his whole attention focused on the meeting. He shivered all over, lightly, in the way Stone did in the hunt, transfixed by a hare. She had seen the same in Ardacos before battle when the she-bear filled him most. She wanted very badly for him to see Cunomar now.

The bargain was struck: a dozen youths nearing adult age were to be delivered to the sea port just south of Camulodunum in exchange for the payment of thirty flagons of good wine, marked with the emperor's stamp, three pitchers of olives and an unspecified amount of gold that changed hands on the spot, as surety. The lizard-man counted the coins and tied them in his belt-pouch. They chimed gently against his thigh.

At a signal from the fish-badged Latin, the men parted. The slaver and his bodyguard took their torches and threaded back along the paths to their fire. The lizard-marked Coritani waited with his back to the hazel stump. He had been a good warrior in his day, the lizard marks said so; he must know he was being watched. He glanced around, warily, but without fear.

Breaca felt a tap on her shoulder. So quietly that his voice came into her mind as had the spear-song, Cunomar said, 'We can't kill the Latins, their deaths would bring down reprisals on everyone at the fair, but Rome will not care if a lizard-warrior of the Coritani dies to a bear in the forest.'

'Or if he falls into the river and drowns?' Breaca had thought the same. A prickle of almost-danger thrilled her skin. The Coritani warrior could feel it as well as she. He had drawn his knife and was stepping back into the deeper forest, keeping trees at his back for safety.

Breaca said, 'There may be more of them waiting. He would be a fool to have come alone.'

Cunomar flashed her a shattering smile. The moon had risen enough to fire the gold of his hair. His eyes were amber and alive with the night. He said, 'I don't think he's a fool. At least three other warriors wait beyond the margins of the trees. But we are the Boudica and her son, who is the bear. For us, four men are as nothing.' His voice was rich and deep and full of promise. 'Will you hunt with me, Boudica, bringer of victory?'

*

For five years in the mountains of the west, Breaca had hunted alone at either end of the battle season.

She had done so out of choice when there were others who could have accompanied her and shared the risk and the elation of each kill. At different times and in different ways, Ardacos and Cygfa, Gwyddhien and Braint had all offered to join her on the crossing to the mainland and she had turned them down with platitudes, never saying that she cherished each year the months of solitude, the freedom of self-reliance after the necessary dependencies of battle.

Through the years, she had thought that she could have shared the experience only with Caradoc, and the loss of that had been yet another layer in her grief for the greater loss, wearing thin over the years until it became simply another part of her soul.

On the night she hunted the Coritani lizard-warriors in the company of Cunomar, her son, Breaca learned for the first time what it might have been to hunt with his father. The joy of it matched the pain, and both were outmatched by the pure, fluent beauty of the hunting.

The enemy were five; the fire-marked Coritani slave seller and the two men and two women of his honour guard. All were lizard-marked for kills and wounds in battle, and they were not as nothing.

Starlight and the cloud-veiled moon made the forest a place of shifting greys and blacks. The first of the enemy, who had taken gold from the slave traders, backed away from the meeting place knife-handed, showing a flash of iron where sense would have kept him still.

Knife-song joined the spear-songs in the whisperings of a forest at night. Cunomar tapped two fingers across his own forearm and angled his head west. They were on Eceni territory, in Eceni hunting lands; he knew the forest as Breaca did, and the Coritani lizard-fighters did not. Breaca nodded and made her own signal, pressing the heel of her hand towards the earth.

They separated, mother and son, folding into a forest that welcomed them, and when they met again they were between the Coritani slave seller and the four warriors of his honour guard.

They did not kill him then; the honour of the hunt demanded that he be last. Breaca lifted a stone the size of her fist and sent it rolling to her left. Leaf litter and small branches creaked in its path. The slave seller froze and twisted and pushed himself into the bole of a beech tree and the whipping undergrowth around it. Ahead, two of his honour guard separated, and were no longer acting as shields, one for the other.

There was no room to use her sling and no need yet for a knife. Breaca broke the neck of the one who took her path, stepping out of the dark to cup a chin and force it sharply up and back and to the side; so much easier to kill an enemy than it had once seemed to kill Graine, even in mercy. Only as she lowered the body did she find that it was a woman, and was sorry.

Cunomar joined her. He had shed his jerkin. The night made armour of his bear-scars, that ran in long crosswise ribs from shoulders to waist. His knife was blackly wet. The song of it had deepened to the one she had known in the forge, where it would stay now, until broken.

He knelt, and on the body of a woman whom Rome had turned to slaver cut marks that could make it seem as if she were a bear-kill. The night became loud with the stench of fresh blood and a stomach laid open.

The wood held its breath, so that even the hunting weasels became briefly still. Ahead, a deer barked in darkness and another behind. No deer barked at night. They were known now: hunters and hunted; two against three.

Cunomar rose, and stood at his mother's shoulder. He no longer grinned for her; his face was closed, a still mask of focused intent. They were beyond speech, or the arm-tap signals of the she-bears; for the duration of that hunt, the Boudica and her son became one, two blades of a single weapon. His eyes were her eyes, her thoughts his, from the shame of killing a woman of the tribes to pride in the perfection of the kill. His almost-death was almost hers.

Passing along the edge of a tiny clearing lined with mossed stones and plates of moonlit fungus, Breaca scented blood and heard the grunting exhalation of one fatally struck. Only the prescience of a thousand such hunts made her turn away from the flash of iron that might have been Cunomar's death, or his kill, so that she stepped instead into the path of the warrior who would have slain her and was able to duck and sidestep and make her own strike. His blade carved a scallop from her shoulder, near the scars of the old-festered spear wound. Her blade caught him messily on the cheek, glancing into his eye.

He was good. A lesser man would have screamed and given way to the pain and so lost his life. This one switched his blade to his left hand and circled her, even as the blood flooded the right side of his face.

Aloud, because it no longer mattered to be silent, Breaca said, 'If such as we fought together and not apart, Rome would have been banished long since.'

He laughed at her, breathlessly. 'They are too many . . . Rome will win and we their allies . . . better that than slain foe.'

The stones of the clearing hid a small spring. She drove him towards it, using the advantage of two eyes against one. When he stepped on the edge of it and lost his balance, she killed him, stepping in past his knife hand to thrust into his chest. He died choking on blood and the noise no longer mattered.

Cunomar was backed against a tree with cuts across his chest. On a path running away from the clearing, he faced two, openly: the first of the slave sellers with the lizard brands laced up the full length of his forearms and another, older and less marked, who wore his hair raised high in a knot at the back with hawk feathers dangling from it.

The older was the wiser. Hearing Breaca's kill, he turned to put his back to his shield-mate, so that those two, also, became welded to one.

Breaca stepped back into the night. The height of the moon showed her son braced against the fine bark of an elm with his knife held cleanly in front, as focused in the face of death as he had been in the first moments of the hunt. The elders of the Caledonii had schooled him well, but they had not hunted for five years amongst the enemy as the Boudica had done, where to live took more than the facing of death without fear.

To live now, to enable her son to live, required silence, and unyielding nerve and a lifetime's understanding of men.

Any man knows when eyes are on him. A warrior awaiting attack knows it soonest and most reliably. Breaca did not, then, watch the elder of the two warriors, the one with the strong nose and the high cheeks and the red hawk's feathers in his bound-up hair, but exclusively and intently his companion, who faced Cunomar's knife and could not shift his attention without risking death.

A hawthorn thicket scratched her back. Above, damp branches dripped the aftermath of rain. Undergrowth gave way before her and the forest's floor yielded beneath each measure of her feet as, slowly, so slowly, Breaca came up alongside the two back-joined Coritani warriors.

An eternity passed amid the rising scents of a damp woodland and then only branches separated her from them. They were two heads, two pale ears with hair bound up behind them, two necks left vulnerable because no warrior of the tribes wore a helmet or neck armour when hunting.

Moss sprang underfoot. A leaf stroked her cheek. The Coritani slave seller who would trade her children for Roman gold felt the weight of her attention.

Harshly, he said, 'Watch to your right!' and the warrior of the red hawk did so, and swore, violently. The Boudica was less than an arm's reach away, a blood-splashed face framed by branches, when he had thought that same dense woodland was his protection.

He was fast, but she had come at his right, and a little behind, which is hardest to strike for a right-handed man unless he can reverse his blade in time. He tried, and in the trying lost the chance to drop and roll, which might have saved him. Still, he ducked sideways and so the strike which was aimed at his chest caught him instead across the abdomen, messily. Dying, he could still attack and did so, catching her across the calf before she reversed her knife and struck his temple with the hilt and then laid open his throat to the backbone.

The lizard-branded slave seller died more swiftly, caught between the Boudica and her son. Breaca caught the man's knife arm from behind and Cunomar struck at his chest and then his throat so that the body she held became rigid and then lax and she could lower it to the ground.

She took a breath and then another and chose not to watch the swift departure of souls, but instead to watch Cunomar, who took one deep breath and then sank to his knees and was sick.

'I'm sorry.'

'Don't be. It's worse to feel nothing.' She held his shoulders and waited while another wave of nausea rocked him. He was shaking, as he had been before, from the exertion and the intent and the nearness of death. From the first kill to the last had been less time than it took to drink a beaker of ale, and had felt a lifetime. She said, 'You have been in battle before, but never as a warrior. Do you know the difference now?'

'Gods, yes.' He knelt on all fours and spat, taking a handful of leaves to wipe his mouth. 'I thought the bear-kill was hardest, but it's not like killing a warrior, alone and . . . unprotected. The she-bears spent so long protecting me when we fought in the west. I didn't know . . .'

He rocked back on his heels. He was filthy; leaf litter smeared his face and blood ran freely from the cuts on his chest. He looked down at himself, in shock.

Breaca said, 'They'll hurt later. A lot. Airmid has a salve that will help keep them from festering, but very little helps the pain.' She let go of his shoulders and sat down away from the bodies of the two Coritani warriors. 'I'm sure the she-bears have salves the same.'

Cunomar picked more leaf litter and cleaned the blood from his chest. 'Are you sending me back?'

'No, of course not. You are a man now. I have no power to send you anywhere, and I would not wish you to leave now when you have barely returned. But still, you should consider it. The steading is no different from when you left. I have not yet raised a war host, only begun the arming of those who might join me one day. We may yet all die to Rome, or find ourselves taken by these . . .' She nudged the dead slave seller with her toe. 'The gods have let us meet, you and I, for which I am more grateful than I can say. I would welcome each day your light in my life, but you've tasted true freedom and grown through it; are you certain you want to live again under the yoke of Rome?'

Cunomar had stopped shaking. He sat back against the tree that had been his protection earlier. Lacing his hands behind his head, he looked up at the stars. 'The elders of the Caledonii have made me a bear-warrior. If I wish, I can go back to them, I can dance with the she-bear in the autumn and perhaps become one of their warrior-dreamers. I can fight their small battles against small tribes, and the Belgic seafarers who land on their coast and take their women. Or I could come home and live among the Eceni, and starve when they starve and fight with the Boudica when the time comes to fight.' He unhooked his hands and wiped another smear of blood from his chest. 'What did Eneit say before he died?'

'That he loved you, which you knew, and that he would wait for you in the lands beyond life. That you were to find the courage to live on from that day – which you have done. And he said to remember his name, which means "spirit", and to give it to your first-born son.'

He was silent a while. The bodies of the slain warriors cooled and the blood ceased to leak from their death wounds. Cunomar reached forward and stripped the hawk feathers from the high-tied hair of the older man.

'We should make the bear-marks on their bodies and give them to the river,' he said, absently, and then, standing, 'If I am to have a son, and to name him Eneit, I would have him born and live among the Eceni, with Eceni blood in his veins.' He was smiling at Breaca, shyly, in a way that took her heart and twisted it apart. He held so much of his father, and was so uniquely himself. 'If I wanted to come home, would you have me?'

Before, he had been the one to make the first move. Now, Breaca pushed herself to standing, and found that the cut in her leg had stiffened and made her lame. He met her partway and they embraced this time as adults, as warriors who have staked their lives on each other's skill, as mother to her first-born son, with all that entails, as the Boudica to the son of Caradoc, who had left a child and come home more than she had ever hoped he could be.

His welcoming arms enfolded her. She pressed her head to his shoulders and smelled his skin, as she had when he was first born and never since. She looked into his eyes, which were level with hers and waited calmly, as the bear-dreamers of the Caledonii had taught him.

'My world would be broken without you,' she said, and meant it and then, because tonight all things were possible, 'If we had five hundred like you, we could rekindle the heart of the Eceni. Even fifty would be a beginning. Will you journey with me through the summer and see if we can raise enough to make your honour guard?'

XXI

T HE HOUND FROM THE ANCESTORS' MOUND ACCOMPANIED
Valerius on the boat over from Hibernia to Mona and the
ferry journey from Mona to the mainland, watching as he
retched bile and the last of his old meal onto the deck. It travelled
with him as he trekked along the high mountain paths south and a
little east and only abandoned him again as he passed the vast,
sprawling fortress of the XXth legion and reached the foot of the
track that led up to Mithras' cave. He missed its company, but
the beast seemed so clearly bound to Nemain that he could not
expect it to follow him into another god's demesne.

Of necessity, his progress up to the cave was excruciatingly slow.
The followers of the bull-slayer did not deal kindly with those who
profaned their places of worship and Valerius was no longer an
injured officer, ranked as Lion before the god, trekking up with his
Father's permission to sanctify his soul before battle. The route up
had never been easy, but this time each step must be tested before
it was taken, each yard forward checked for guards or trackers or
youthful initiates, who might choose to spend a night out on the
mountain, eager to prove their worth in the capture of an apostate.

At each step, Valerius sought to keep open the god-space that
Nemain had made in his soul. She had not asked him to abandon
his service to Mithras – he could not imagine her doing so – but,
having laid bare his self in her presence, it seemed impossible now

277

that he could serve also the soldiers' god of the legions whose worship was offered only to the best, to the sharpest, to those most dedicated to Rome and empire.

Valerius came on the god's place in the greyness of dawn and at first did not see what it had become. On his last and only visit, on the eve of Caradoc's defeat, the entrance to Mithras' cave had been an unmarked cleft in a rock face at the side of a waterfall, easily missed but for the offerings of honey and corn and small pieces of gold placed with care on finger-wide ledges around the opening.

Now, four years on, a Father who wished to leave his mark most visibly had ordered white lime painted in a band a foot wide around the opening so that the black scar of the cave's mouth shouted down into the valley and anyone, given to the god or not, would know where he resided.

Valerius would not have done this, nor, he thought, would the grey-robed tribune who had been the Father of the order in his time. That man had cared more for the old way of things and would not have needed to scream his presence to the world. Valerius wondered if the new governor were branded for the bull-slayer: the act had the mark of a man who fed on self-publicity and the adulation of others as Suetonius Paulinus was said to do.

On this morning, of all mornings, the effect was not quite as had been intended. The wind had risen and was playing with the water-fall so that the white-painted mouth was blurred by the whiter spray and Valerius saw the full horror only when he stood directly before it.

It was crushingly ugly. Brash offerings had been left, to match the paint. A gold chain hung from a peg driven into the rock; a flagon of wine lay unbroken, its wax seal stamped with Claudius' mark to demonstrate the age and worth of the vintage; a single ocean pearl threaded on gold wire dangled from the hazel that drooped over the waterfall, a drop of shining milk in the wet. Only the last of these added to the sanctity of the place. Valerius felt an ache in his back teeth that was the first whisper of the god's discomfort.

He did not want to enter the presence of one he had served tainted with the gloss of false offerings. Leaving his pack, he tracked back one hundred paces and waited, watching. When he was certain that neither men nor animals had tracked his climb up, he stripped and eased his way gingerly down over wet rocks to the pool at the foot of the waterfall.

Water thundered around him, spray-bright and savage. A decade's service in the west had not dimmed his awe at the sheer, mind-numbing power of a river falling over a cliff. Like a child, he spread his arms and let the water sting his face and chest, flaying him awake. The brand at his sternum tingled lightly but no more; the time was long gone when the pain of it reminded him of his duty.

More alert, he stepped off the last rock into the water. The cold did not steal his breath as it had in the river outside the dreamers' chamber; he could think this time, and not lose himself. Grateful for that, he ducked his head under and let the raw current sweep the rest of his skin clean.

With cleanliness came a fresh awareness. He had not been welcome on Mona and the pain of that stayed with him. It did not leave now, but he was alive in spite of it, free to drink in the sharp air and the crystalline water, the piercing sky and the cry of the yearling buzzard that hunted early, ragged from winter and too hungry to wait until full light. That pain touched him, but pleasantly. Valerius found he could see forward to a time when it would be assuaged by food and rest and the play of high winds. That surprised him; he had not known that Nemain's soul-opening would allow him to see forward, even for an impatient bird. He rediscovered her presence as a gift and bathed himself in it as he bathed in the water.

Later, dry and clothed, he gathered the gold and the wine from the cave's mouth and cast them into the river. It was no longer his duty, but he wished Mithras no ill and this was a service he was uniquely placed to offer. Any land-sourced water was sacred to Nemain, but she had always been the gateway to the other gods; she could devour such things without harm as the bull-slayer could not. The ache in his teeth died away as the pool took the last dazzling chain. He left the pearl. It had been hung in the hazel with different intent by one who understood the gods' love of beauty.

There was nothing left, then, to keep Valerius from entering the cave. Holding his mind open, he lit one of the tallow candles he had brought and squeezed in through the white-painted mouth, stealing himself for the belly-crawl in darkness through an ever narrowing tunnel that would bring him into the presence of the god.

That much had not changed. As he had before, he reached the bend in the tunnel where the floor sloped steeply and the only way forward was with his arms outstretched in front and his body bent into the rock. For long moments, it seemed impossible to go either forward or back and he had to crush the urge to panic. When he reached it, the opening out into the cave came as a blessed relief that was as much memory as reality.

He was not the man he had been; his appreciation of this place was greater than before. The ancestor-dreamers of the Hibernians had built of stone the dreaming chamber in which Valerius had passed his long-nights and had made it lightless. Here, the gods, without the help of any dreamers, had built a vaulting cavern within a mountain so high that it scraped the clouds and they had set within it a lake and a lacing of water that, when touched by a candle's flame, had been the most heartbreakingly beautiful thing Valerius had ever seen.

The shock of it had brought him to Mithras before. He hoped it would do so again. By feel, he lit the second of his three candles and set it on the rock, then shut his eyes and waited a moment before looking out to where the lake had been, and the dripping jewels of water that had quivered from the ceiling like the gold-wrought tears of the god.

Just too late, the ache in his teeth returned, sharply, but he was too full of expectation to make sense of it.

He should have known; a man who will paint white the mouth of a cave will put his stamp also on that which is most sacred within it. Iron ringed the lake; a barrier of staves of the kind the legions might place on the margins of their night camps except that these rods were of iron, not wood, and they had been fired and drawn and hand-beaten and stamped at the ends with the mark of the raven, exactly as it was branded on Valerius' chest, and whereas the legionaries could place their staves with a single stamp into the ground, here, men with chisels and mortar had worked for days to root them into the rock that was the cave's floor.

It was sacrilege, perpetrated in the name of the god, and Valerius' every sense screamed at the sight of it. He turned and found at the back of the cave an altar of marble and the small part of him that could think tried to imagine how it had been brought in through the tunnel. The rest of him studied the carvings around it and the wrought gold and the painted icons and saw them, too, as sacrilege.

In disgust, he said, 'Do they not know you?'

They think they do. Are you any different?

Valerius turned back to the water far more slowly than he had turned away. Nemain had not appeared to him in a vision, nor spoken aloud so that her voice rolled off the water-jewelled rock, shaking him where he stood.

Mithras did both. The god was not kneeling in fire as he had before. He had no bull, alive or dead, at his feet, but the hound that was shown with him always in the carvings and the friezes of the cellars beneath each Roman fortress stood at his heel, its head level with his thigh. In the images, it was small and lop-eared; a smooth-haired southern sight-hound, from the hot deserts of Mithras' birth.

In the cave of the god in the mountains of Britannia, the hound was tall with prick ears and a harsh, broken coat and the spatterings of white stood out on its mane so that it could have stood recently in snow. It was the hound of the ancestors' dreaming chamber, that had departed at the foot of the god's mountain, and it was Hail, who was dead and had been given to Briga. It should not have come also in the company of any foreign god, much less one so closely entwined with the legions.

Valerius opened his mouth and closed it again. Nemain watched and offered no help.

Amused, Mithras said, *I ask you again. Do you know me, Julius Valerius, smith of Hibernia?*

Valerius found his voice, which surprised him. 'I do not presume so much. I never have.'

And yet you clear the false offerings from the mouth of my cave and feel grief at the entrapment of my lake.

'I would not see you in pain.'

So then you understand that much. I will ask differently. Do you know me, Bán of the Eceni?

'No.'

Valerius spoke without thinking, from the twisting place in his chest where old pain was still rooted. Four years before, that would

281

have been enough. Today, now, from the openness into which Nemain had drawn him, he said, 'As Julius Valerius, decurion of the cavalry and servant of the emperor, I could have come to know you. As Bán, I can only be given to Nemain.'

But you are not Bán. You do not answer to that name, nor think of yourself so in your dreams. I ask you again: as Valerius, whom do you serve?

One does not speak twice without due thought in the presence of a god. Valerius stood in the centre of the cavern and watched the light of his candle bleed through the gaps between the iron staves. Once, it would have been light enough to set fire to the lake and bring the place alive, but no longer. The god stood on mute water while channels of withered flame barely touched his feet. Valerius let his mind stretch out to meet them, and reached for an answer.

For three years on Hibernia, he had lived only as Valerius, and had believed himself godless. Now, knowing differently, he had not found who he might be, except that he was not yet Bán of the Eceni, nor was he any longer Julius Valerius, citizen of Rome and decurion of the Thracian cavalry.

At the feet of the bull-god, the hound dipped its head and drank of the firelight. Here, in this place, its pelt was clotted at the neck where the death wound had bled out. It snuffed the air and pricked its ears and trotted forward, leaping the iron staves as if they were sticks laid flat on the ground. Reaching Valerius, it nudged its nose into his lax hand and, as he had in the ancestors' chamber, he felt the warmth and wetness of it as if it were real.

In the presence of the gods, nothing happens by accident. Valerius knelt as Mithras had once knelt and ruffled the dream-hound's ears. Looking out over the water, he said, 'Is this my hound, or yours?'

If you are given to me, what is mine is yours.

If . . . The word spanned the air between man and god, vibrantly, opening doors that Valerius had long believed closed.

If . . . The god walked forward along avenues of fire. His face was that of a youth, his eyes eternally old. His hair was the colour of the morning sun and in his smile he held the beauty, and the savage power, of every dawn there had ever been. No man could meet him without love, nor fail to know regret at his departing.

Valerius, who had served him for fifteen years without such a meeting and so without love, felt himself crushed beneath a mountain's weight of loss.

In anguish, he said, 'I cannot be what I was. I cannot go back.'

Would you wish to?

'No. I have been given my birthright. Who I am now is the truth.' Desperate, Valerius searched for Nemain and found her and nothing changed but that his soul came into balance and his confusion was not unheard. She did not force a choice, as Mithras had not. Even so, he could see no way that a man could serve two such disparate gods and hold himself intact.

A flame wavered on the flat mirror of the water. The god was close enough to touch. Quietly, he said, *Who are you now, Valerius, walker between the worlds? Julius Valerius was as fully of Rome as Bán was of the Eceni and neither will easily be laid to rest, however much you may seek to do so. Must you now renounce one to keep faith with the other? The choice is yours. No god can make it for you.*

Valerius had not come seeking choice, but an ending. For too long, he said nothing, staring at the iron staves and the stuttering candle. Then the quality of the silence changed and when he looked again the god was flowing into the fire and the fire into the water.

The loss was devastating. Abandoned, he sank to his knees and wept. Scalding tears melted tracks on his cheeks. He wanted urgently to swear fealty, all choices made, and could not; his voice was no longer at his command.

The coarse-pelted hound turned towards the lake and whined once, softly, then turned back and nudged Valerius' hand.

Through the echoing chamber of the cave, Mithras' voice reached him, softly. *Seek who it is that you have become, walker between the worlds. If you can find that, the peace of the gods will be open to you, and not only as you walk in the light of Nemain's moon.*

Valerius was alone, kneeling on the rock of the chamber's floor, shaking as badly as he ever did on ocean crossings. The hound made him sit up, made him stand, shoved at his leg so that he must brace against it or fall over. He wanted to be sick and did not dare so defile the god's cavern, however badly it had already been defiled.

The thought of that moved him. He had brought with him no tools, but he believed it possible that even empty-handed he could undo the worst of what men with tools had done.

The iron staves set around the lake were easiest to remove; the holes in which they were set were not deep, the mortar already rotten in the damp air. He raised them, one at a time, and stacked them against the wall near the tunnel that led to the outer world.

The altar was more complicated. It was not ugly; in the right place it might have been beautiful, but this was not the right place. Examining it, Valerius found that it had been made in sections, and so understood how it had been brought through the tunnel. The flat marble of the top lifted clear and the four walls were held by wooden pegs within.

It took some effort to prise it apart, but he had time and an energy that must be vented on something. The gold and frippery around the edges were easily removed. His only question was where to dispose of the pieces. He could not hurl them into the lake – of all the water in the world, this was not Nemain's – nor could he drag the marble out through the tunnel alone and without ropes or rollers.

The candles were nearly used up. He lit the third from the stump of the second and watched the two flames wind round each other in the loose air. They tipped to his left, towards the tunnel's mouth through which he had come, blown by a draught that came from the opposite side of the cavern. Valerius turned on one heel and stared at the wall of dark rock.

'So now, do you think I can go into the other cavern? The gods would not let me before.'

Valerius spoke to the hound, which gave no answer, but it did not hold him back when he lifted a bundle of iron stakes under one arm and searched for the mouth of the cave-within-cave that he had found once before. This opening had not been outlined in white lime. It was unlikely that the engineers with their drills and mortar had not seen it, but, like Valerius on his last visit, they may have been warned away by a power too great to be ignored.

The entrance looked no more inviting than it had done before. The candle drifted and spat and cast more shadows than it did light. Valerius squeezed himself sideways and slid his shoulders into the cleft that led to the new cave – and waited.

No voice came to stop him. The still place in his soul held no warning.

A greater draught blew out the candle.

Valerius was not afraid of the dark. He reminded himself of this fact three times as he propped the iron staves against the wall of the inner cavern and felt his way back whence he had come. His years in the legions had made him methodical if nothing else; the iron staves were stacked together in a row and he arranged the pieces of the altar in size order alongside. Carrying them into the inner cave was slow work, made slower by the lack of light and the need to feel his way, but Valerius became faster with practice so that the gold and icons of the altar pieces were easily taken further into the inner cavern and laid on ledges that he had come to know by touch.

He laid the last one in place and stood still, snuffing the air as a deer might do, scenting danger. He felt no threat, only a sense of great age and a watchfulness that was not his and a fainter touch of something that might have been a greeting, or at least an acknowledgement of his presence. There was a dryness to it that did not match the damp of the cavern but made him think of newly shed leaves before the rains of winter pulp them, or a snake skin, found soon after shedding.

He walked a little way forward, beyond the furthest point of his exploration, and let the draught lift the hair from his forehead.

'Thank you,' he said. 'I leave these in your care. They are not wrong in themselves, only in the wrong place for the wrong reasons. One day they may be right.'

The ancient, watching dark opened a little to drink in his words. He expected something to be given in return and was disappointed. The echo of Mithras' last words filtered faintly in the air, but the laden fragments of sound had shivered back and forth since the god departed and Valerius continued to ignore them. He had no intention of choosing anything until he had slept and eaten and was safely clear of the legions quartered in the valley below.

Without thinking, he pursed his lips and whistled gently for the hound as he used to do for Hail when he was a child. It nudged against his thigh, in the place it most belonged, and together they felt their way round Mithras' newly sanctified cavern to the mouth of the exit tunnel.

Collecting the stubs of his three candles, Valerius bowed towards the black-water lake. He felt a cleanliness that buoyed him and made less onerous the choices. Knowing the god-space twice filled laid on him a peace that was not, after all, only of Nemain.

Holding that thought, and the newness of it, he said, 'Thank you. I am grateful, always, for the gift of your presence. I will honour you, whatever happens.'

The god's echo enfolded him. *Choose well, Valerius.*

Emerging was the rebirth into joy that he had imagined at the ancestors' mound in Hibernia and had not experienced. Late morning sun blinded him, and the dazzle from the pool beneath the waterfall.

Thundering water and the scream of the buzzard swamped his ears and pierced his mind. Sharp air and sharper water shocked his face and he drank them all in and kept drinking, even as the men who sprang from the earth behind him took hold of his arms and crushed ropes on his wrists and kicked him twice in the belly so that he fell to the ground, sobbing for air, with dark and light and dark smashing through his closed eyes, and still a part of him was entranced by the morning and did not understand what was happening.

XXII

THE HOUND DID NOT STAY WITH VALERIUS AT HIS CAPTURE, NOR did it return as the four men, half a tent party of the XXth legion, beat him unconscious and then threw him in the pool beneath the waterfall to bring him round and then propped him between them, two in front, two behind, and marched him, with pauses to kick him again, down the mountain.

On the rare occasions when he could speak, Valerius called to the hound, sending it to find mac Calma, to keep it safe from harm, as if a god-given hound could be harmed by men. The rest of the time was lost to a sea of reddening pain, so that, in the end, he let go of his mind because it was easier to hide in the dark of unconsciousness and to trust his own body to ride the kicking as best it could without his interference.

There had been no need to ask where they were going; he had led these parties often enough himself. Perversely, he woke as they threw open the door to the inquisitors' chamber beneath the quartermaster's stores in the south-west corner of the barracks; the sound of unoiled hinges triggered too many memories for him to sink again into oblivion.

The room was built of coarse-hewn oak with a gravel floor and a single barred window to let in light and air. The fortress's grain store was directly above it, with spare harness stored in the loft above that. It was not noticeably worse than any other prison but the dreamers of the tribes brought here for questioning had feared this room more than they had feared the inquisitors and their irons.

Towards the end of his stay in the fortress, Valerius had known at least three who had broken simply as a result of having been left here overnight. He had always thought that it was the grain store that was the cause; that life in a roundhouse had left them unprepared for the skills of Rome's engineers and the realization that they were locked in a room with a year's supply of grain suspended above their heads had shattered their minds.

He could not have been more wrong. The reality was more disturbing and he discovered it as his captors opened the door and pitched him face first onto the gravel inside. As an officer in the legions, he had seen this place too often to count. He knew, as he had known his own quarters, the smell of old blood and vomit and stale urine and the old-meat stench of terror and capitulation.

Then, his rank had protected him, and the closed walls of his mind. Now he was no longer an officer and Nemain had opened all that had been closed. Sliding face first across the floor, he felt as if it were his own, the horror of every other dreamer, every other man and woman of the tribes who had lived and died in this place.

Some had been stronger at the start, some weaker, some given to gods other than Nemain, some trained in better ways to hold closed the floodgates of their minds so that the impact of their breaking would be less on those who came after.

None of them, however well schooled, had failed to add to the weight of horror and Valerius was only the latest in their line. The weight of their deaths fell on him like a sledgehammer and he screamed out the agony of it as the guards kicked him again in the guts for luck.

The kicking saved him. He crumpled, choking, into his own private hell of not-breathing and, briefly, the fight for air was too urgent and too overwhelming for the rest to swamp him. Clawing at the floor, fighting to hold the threads of mac Calma's teaching, he was able to find that part of the chaos that was only Valerius and hold it apart from the rest.

The guards let him alone while they undid his shackles. He lay prone, his cheek smeared with his own spit and tears and blood and dust, and fought to reason.

One fact rose late out of the rest: that they had brought him here, to this chamber, when they would have taken a serving officer, even a legionary, to the detention rooms in the south wing of the barracks. Thus they believed Valerius to be a tribesman and did not know his past identity. He clung to that, a spar in the ocean of his drowning.

The chamber was not a big place; the four guards barely fitted inside. They rolled him over and he could see them for the first time, at least with his left eye, which had not swollen shut. They were all young men, and strangers. None of them had seen service in the time of Scapula when the decurion of the First Thracian cavalry had led his troop across the river in a drive that had ultimately defeated Caradoc.

Even if they had been there, without his mount they would not have known Valerius. The Crow-horse had been his emblem, how-ever often he had painted the bull on his pennants. He had loved it and it had hated him, which was safest and best and he had loved it more for doing so. For one long, distracted moment, the loss of the Crow-horse mattered more to Valerius than the pressure of the inquisitors' room and the slow death that was to come. He called to the beast in Thracian and the four young men of the XXth thought he cried in Siluran and spat again, laughing.

The guards were young and lacked experience and left Valerius alone with his hands free while they turned to lock the door. Their blades hung at their hips, as open invitations. If he had been the warrior they believed him to be, he would have killed at least one of them, and then himself, in the time they took to fix the bolts.

Because he was not only a warrior, and did not intend to die, Valerius pushed himself upright and stood swaying in the centre of the room. His mouth was full of blood. He swallowed it rather than spit and, in the archaic Latin favoured by Claudius and still a sign of allegiance to the old emperor, said, 'You're supposed to strip me next. It's in the Order of Action: all clothing to be removed from the prisoner at the time of arrest. I think it's designed to deprive the warriors of warmth and dignity which rather presumes they have some dignity left to remove. Still, I think you should do it.'

Four men stared at him, aghast. One, black-haired, leaner and more intense than the rest, swore an oath in the name of Mithras.

Valerius had not made his choice in the cave, but he gave thanks in great profusion to the bull-god now, for the gift of this lean young man and the strength of his faith. Holding himself tall, he spoke the words of the Lion's invocation before the sun altar and watched the young initiate pale to the colour of grey parchment.

A well-tutored Siluran spy might, at a stretch, have known Claudian Latin and seen a copy of the Orders of Action, but only a man who had progressed high in the ranks of Mithras' priesthood could possibly know the Lion's invocation well enough to recite it aloud and such a man could never be of the tribes. The hierarchy of the bull-god was notoriously selective in its choice of those who held high order: with each passing word, Valerius proved not only that he was a Roman citizen who had seen service in the legions, but that he had been of the elite few who distinguished themselves so fully in battle that others might follow them who were not of their corps.

The silence that settled after he ended was brittle with fear. In the midst of it, the initiate of Mithras swore again, quietly, begging forgiveness of his god.

The youth was newly branded; every part of his bearing said so. Valerius leaned back against the wall and managed not to wince. He raised his arms so that his sleeves fell back to show the scars of the Lion's rank at his wrist, and placed his left thumb on the front of his tunic where it covered the old brand of Mithras that had been burned long ago on his chest: even the guards who had never been permitted within the cellars and caves of the bull-god could recognize that brand when they saw it.

'You really should strip me,' Valerius said, pleasantly. 'It will save us all time in the end although I'd be grateful if you could manage to do it without kicking me again. I'm not sure there's anywhere left that isn't going to take a month to heal.'

He thought he had pushed too far. All four of the legionaries gaped at him and the shape of their minds screamed of the need for help from a senior officer, preferably one branded for the god, ranked Lion or higher.

Very badly, Valerius did not want any of them to call for that help.

Looking past the young initiate, he caught instead the gaze of the armourer, who was the only officer among the four. He said, 'Your choices are simple: if I'm a warrior of the Silures, you have to strip me before the inquisitors come; it'll look bad otherwise. If I'm not, if I am, instead, what you see and hear . . .' he was not going to lay claim to the god aloud, but he touched again the brand of Mithras at his chest, 'then you'll pay for disobeying the order of a senior officer. I have ordered you to strip me. If you don't, I will report it. *Think*, man—' He snapped his fingers and felt four young men flinch. 'In battle, an officer who hesitates is dead, and his men with him. You know what—'

He would have had them. The young officer drew breath to give the order to strip him – and let it out again at the sound Valerius had heard half a heartbeat before and that had rendered all other arguments useless. Outside, a troop of auxiliary cavalry had just been ordered to stand to attention in rank formation in front of the door.

The help of a senior officer had arrived, unasked. The young officer blazed a smile, relief written bold across his face. Valerius smiled with him, and cursed in Hibernian, to hide the panic.

Once again, he could have armed himself; the guards wore their weapons with little care and all of their attention was on the officer outside. It would not have been hard to take a sword and sheathe it in his own chest. If he were prepared to risk being overwhelmed by the guards outside – or any other of the five thousand armed men in the fortress – he could probably have killed at least one of the young legionaries first and gone to the god with one last ghost waiting to greet him in the lands beyond life. He considered both of these in the time it took the newly arrived officer to march to the door and rap on it and demand to be admitted.

For the rest of his life, Valerius, once-decurion of the First Thracian Cavalry, believed that he had already decided to live – and not to kill – before he recognized the voice. Then the bolt was thrown back and the morning let in and Longinus Sdapeze, decurion of the first troop, the First Thracian Cavalry, took up all of the doorway.

Only because he was watching, and he knew Longinus exceptionally well, did Valerius see the in-breath of a suspicion confirmed and the consternation and the too-fast thinking that followed.

The rest saw the tall, much-garlanded officer of the Thracians sweep his helmet from his stag-red hair and toss it, grinning, to the prisoner, swearing a cheerful oath in Thracian and then again in

Gaulish and Latin. He clapped the young armourer of the XXth on the shoulder and, as one officer to another in the presence of the rabble said, 'Have you asked this idiot who he is or has he been too busy swearing by the bull-god to tell you?'

It was the luckiest of guesses, or Longinus had ways of hearing through wood. In that moment, Valerius believed each of these equally. He slid the cavalry helmet onto his head and if the rawly beaten parts of his skull throbbed hard against the metal, he was still glad of the protection.

He recognized all eight of the men waiting outside. The horse master, standing at the head of the troop, flicked his thumb in the sign that was life for a gladiator across the empire. For the men of the first troop of the Ala Prima Thracum, it had also signified their last decurion, who had ridden the mad, unrideable Crow-horse and had always led them into battle with the recklessness – and the luck – of the circus. Further back, a stout man with three of his four front teeth missing grinned unappealingly and winked.

The auxiliary did not foster an honour guard as the tribes did for their leaders, but such things came together of their own accord and these eight men, almost exactly, had been Valerius' honour guard for the last four years of his time with the legions. He knew them all; their names, their lovers' names, the names of their legitimate and illegitimate children. He knew their horses and how they rode and their courage, or lack of it, in battle and who could be relied upon to hold the left side of a line and who could best swim with a rope across a river at night and hold it fast, that the rest of the troop might follow.

They had been Valerius' men and were now Longinus', the wild Thracian horseman who had always loved and fought with a cheerful disdain for the risks. That these men had come to free Valerius was not in question, only whether, in all conscience, he could allow them to make the attempt.

The four ardent young officers of the XXth believed they had captured a Siluran warrior. Left alone, they would have questioned him as that and perhaps found, in the end, that he was given to Nemain and had lived some time on Mona. What they did not know, and might never find out, was that they had captured instead a former cavalry officer named traitor by the Emperor Nero, whose death in Rome would be worse, by far, than anything the inquisitors could inflict – and would be shared in kind with any others who had aided him at any point along the way.

Someone spoke over-loud nearby. Longinus leaned against the doorpost, holding open the door, all the while talking of Valerius, to Valerius, telling him what he needed to know.

'. . . the hell of it is, he's been so long among the natives that he's forgotten how to give his name in Latin. But he's the best pair of ears we've ever had inside the tribes. He got us news of Caradoc's trap at the Valley of the Lame Hind and he ran his mad bloody horse over the rampart at the revolt in Eceni lands when Scapula's son would have had us all killed. You should ask Priscus how he lost his teeth. You may think the Silurans are a bunch of wild bastards . . .'

Longinus turned and walked out of the door, sweeping the others with him. Most of what he said was true, and all of it was legend within the legions. The four youths of the XXth grinned, hearing in a new voice stories they already knew well.

'. . . hardest problem will be how to get him back out to the Silures without them realizing we've let him go deliberately. At least you've kicked him enough for it to look real. I'd say if we're quick, there's still time for him to "escape", if you see what I—'

Longinus was a cavalry man of exceptional valour but he had never been to Rome; he had not seen the circus, or helped to burn the bodies of the men branded traitor by an emperor. He had not seen the details of their dying, nor the exquisite care taken by men whose skill was in ensuring that those under their care did not die too early. Mercifully unaware, Longinus had no idea of the risk he took, for himself or those who served under him.

Valerius, who had done both, knew it exactly. In the time it took Longinus to sweep the ardent young officer of the XXth through the door, he saw, layered over the many deaths of the dreamers that haunted the inquisitor's chamber, nine more, slower and more bloody; of eight cavalrymen he cared for, and one he had loved.

Many times in his life, Valerius had sought his own destruction. Each time had been a denial of life, an escape from gods and men who had abandoned him. This time, in full awareness of what he did and for whom, he reached for Nemain, and was held by her, and for Mithras, and felt the savage understanding of the god. With that, he knew what he must do.

The lean, dark-haired initiate of Mithras had reached the doorway. As much as his comrades, he was entranced by Longinus' tales of past heroics, made drunk by his own close brush with danger, now passed, so that he laughed over-loud at the talk of war and battles and a life he feared and craved in equal measure.

Valerius put out an arm to block the young man's exit. 'When they find what I did to the god's cave on the mountain, they will skin you alive for letting me go. And that's nothing to what Mithras will do to you when you come to meet him at last with him clothed in flesh and you slim as a ghost.'

The youth stared at him, not daring to comprehend. Vicarious excitement evaporated as understanding came in spite of himself. Yellow with terror, he fought for words.

'What have you done?'

'Pulled out the eighteen iron staves that barred the way to the god's pool. Given to Nemain the offerings at the cave's mouth. Dismantled the altar and broken the—'

'For gods' sake, man, will you let go of your bloody tribal fantasies? You're among *friends*, and if we have to knock sense into your skull, to prove it, we'll do so with the greatest of pleasure . . .'

Longinus really had no idea what he risked. His life was too fully lived in the moment to encompass fear of sufficient magnitude.

Valerius had time to think exactly that much before his skull exploded into white light and unconsciousness claimed him.

XXIII

VALERIUS WOKE TO FIRELIGHT AND STARLIGHT AND THE CROP OF horses, grazing. The hound lay along his side, pressing against his damaged ribs. Its quiet, insistent whining held him awake.

He had forgotten what it was to wake stiff and sore and too afraid to begin to count the damage; his four years as a smith in Hibernia had been peacefully free of the bruises of battle.

He had a system that had always worked in the past and was worth the attempt. Inhaling deeply, he held the breath to test his ribs and decided that none of them was broken. He flexed his legs, just a little, and decided that his knee caps had probably not been cracked, nor his elbows or the parallel bones of his forearms. His skull ached fiercely, but was intact. Exploring beyond the flesh, he found that he was dressed and someone sat nearby holding a broth that smelled of mutton and bay leaves. He sat up, slowly.

A man coughed, not too far away. Another shifted so that his armour chinked. In this way, Valerius' former troop gave notice that they kept guard around him, without being obtrusive. If they still arranged themselves as he had taught them, four would be asleep and four on watch, spread out in a circle, leaving the officer in the centre to mind the fire.

That much was still true. Longinus sat on a half-log with the bowl of broth clasped in both hands and his hands between his knees. It was not clear if he could see the hound. His eyes were yellow in the firelight but then they would have been yellow in daylight, too; he had always had the gaze of a hawk. That gaze was hard now and incisive and neither felt comfortable for the man on whom it was trained.

Valerius pressed the heels of both hands to his eyes. When the world had gone black and then white again, he removed his hands and said, quietly, 'They'll flay you alive and make you wear a necklace of your eyes. Priscus and the others will die at your side. No officer of any worth takes that kind of risk with his troop.'

'Thank you. I am aware of that.' Longinus still did not smile, which was new; in the past, he had always been cheerful, even after Caradoc's capture when Valerius had taken refuge in wine and things had soured between them.

The Thracian dipped a finger in the broth and tested it, sucking the drips from his finger. 'Did you desecrate the bull-slayer's cave as you said?'

'It was desecrated when I arrived. I put it back as it was when we first saw it. You wouldn't have recognized it as it was yesterday, or approved.'

'Possibly not, but then what I think is hardly material. Did the god approve?'

'I believe so, but the new governor won't when he finds his alterations dismantled.'

'In that case it may be as well that it was not the new governor who ordered them, but the camp prefect of the Twentieth. Who is now dead.'

Valerius blinked. 'I see.'

'I'm not sure you do. In this particular legion, the prefect controlled the spies who report on the native councils, particularly those of the Silures. He was killed a month ago by three of their warriors who gave their lives to see him dead.'

'That was not my doing.'

'I didn't suggest it was. I only mention it because the last of the warriors brought flasks of oil and set fire to them in the prefect's lodgings and it was some time before the blaze was brought under control. As a result, the records of his agents and their activities are not as complete as they should be.'

Longinus smiled for the first time and it was the old smile, bright and alive and sharp with the challenge of a fine mind. It hurt in ways Valerius had not expected. He took in a slow breath and blew it out through the steeple of his fingers.

Thinking aloud, he said, 'Longinus, I'm wanted for treason. Nero signed the order personally on the day he was first hailed emperor. There's no way round that. You can tell the inquisitors that I've spied on every elder council held on Mona since the invasion and fed the details word-perfect to the governor himself and they'll still crucify you for letting me go.'

'Treason?' Longinus made a show of surprise. 'That was careless. I thought you were every emperor's favourite. Claudius clearly believed the gods walked in your shadow and even Caligula said you brought him luck. Whatever did you do to upset Nero so badly?'

Valerius grinned. Longinus had always cheered him. He said, 'I cut the throat of his favourite messenger. And I got Caradoc out of Rome when Claudius asked me to.'

'Ah. Was that you? I had wondered. News of that sort doesn't travel well; men don't pass on facts that might see them flogged for sedition.' Longinus dipped another finger in the broth and sucked it. 'Are you as hungry as you— Yes, clearly you are. Here . . . eat this and then I'll see if Priscus is still vain enough to carry a mirror.'

The broth was as good as it smelled. Valerius had forgotten what it was to eat in the company of men he could trust with his life. He was bruised and sore and battle-weary and still he relaxed as he had not done for years. A brittleness fell from him that he had not known he carried. The sensation was not unlike the first wave of peace he used to find in the wine. The pity of it had always been that it never lasted.

Longinus returned, holding a small circle of bronze.

Valerius paused with a spoon full of broth midway to his mouth. 'I take it that's Priscus' mirror. Apart from admiring the bruises, why would I need it?'

'Because I think you haven't used one recently. Come nearer the fire and see if you recognize what you see.'

Valerius had seen himself first as a child when the trader Arosted had brought a silver mirror for his mother. That had been fashioned for use as a gateway for the dreaming, as most mirrors

297

were, but three-year-old Bán had stolen a look and had been pleased with what he saw; he was a lot like his mother. He thought his eyes looked the same and his hair was as black, which was good, and the shape of his face was hers far more than his sister's had ever been.

For months afterwards, he had felt closer to his mother because of it although the mirror had been hidden amongst her secret things and he had not seen himself again until he was a slave in Gaul in a villa owned by a man notorious for his vanity whose residence was famed for the quantity and quality of its mirrors, none of which had been gateways to any dreaming.

Valerius had grown older by then, more than the sum of his years. Without choosing to look, he had seen himself too often. He had been leaner and the sharp angles of his cheeks had been made sharper by the dark thumbprints of exhaustion and despair beneath his eyes, but there had been an innocence, of sorts, as if he still believed that the gods and fate would be kind to him.

The Emperor Claudius had not favoured mirrors, nor had any of the governors, legates or tribunes under whom Valerius had served. Valerius had been in a tavern in Gaul when he had next seen himself and only by the sharp angles of his face and the blue-black of his hair had he recognized the man who stared at him from the smearings of poorly polished metal. He had lost all innocence by then.

He had lost it still, clearly. Priscus' mirror was no worse than the one in the tavern and if the surface was far from perfect, at least it was not spotted with fly stains. Valerius' eyes were harder than he remembered them; he no longer expected the gods to make life perfect. Beyond that, the mess of purpling bruises and welts on his face made it impossible to see anything of relevance.

Once more, the only way he recognized the man who stared at him in the fire-licked bronze was by the colour of his hair, which was as blue-black and straight as it had been in his childhood. He had always thought it his mother's gift, until Luain mac Calma had laid claim to be his father.

On reflection, Valerius realized that he looked a great deal like Luain mac Calma, which, if nothing else, explained a number of incidents in his past. He handed the mirror back to Longinus.

'Your point?' he asked.

'That we who share this fire know you because we spent ten years watching the hurt in your eyes, waiting for your patience to crack; a man remembers the things he's most afraid of. Only those of us who lived half our lives under the lash of your tongue would have the least idea that the prisoner brought in this morning is the man who was recalled to Rome by Claudius in the month before he was assassinated.

'Even if they guessed that much, there can't be more than three men in the province who knew you were named traitor by Nero and none of those is in the west. Your name will be in records somewhere, but our new governor, may the gods spit on his soul, is not a man to spend time or money searching through five-year-old papers for the half-ghosts of his predecessor's pasts.'

'Four,' said Valerius. 'It was four years ago.'

Longinus kicked a log into the fire, raising a shower of sparks. The movement carried all the tension he kept from his voice. 'Did you listen to anything I just said?'

'Yes. You were afraid of me. I thought you, of all men, knew me better.'

'Gods, man, you ordered me flogged once. Have you forgotten?'

'Did I?' Valerius had not thought he had lost so much to the wine. A memory returned, unsought, and others after. He found the fire required all his attention. Because it was easier than remembering, he said, 'I'm sure you deserved it.'

Valerius heard a breath sucked in tightly and waited for the explosion of its release. It never came. After a while, when nothing had happened, he looked up. The man who had shared his life, his bed and parts of his soul for nearly half a decade sat opposite with frustration and a desperate, sharp-edged irony painted in equal shades on his face. 'I don't think I did,' Longinus said eventually.

'Do you want to tell me what happened?'

'No. It's too long ago and if you truly don't remember, we should leave it that way. Now, all I want is for you to find your way to a boat that will carry you to Hibernia where you will be safe so that I can go back to the fortress and continue to take my place in the governor's planning meetings and strategy meetings and quarter-masters' meetings and armourers' meetings and all the other godforsaken meetings that are supposedly required to organize to the last iron boot stud and catapult bolt the new governor's invasion of Mona and the destruction of every dreamer left on the island. The governor will not be going back to Camulodunum for winter. Which other governor in your experience has spurned the hot baths and marble floors of the colony for a winter in a legionary fortress? He will attack as soon as the reserves arrive from the Rhine, and when he does, he won't stop until Mona is his.'

Longinus held Valerius' gaze through every word of the most blatant act of treason either of them had ever encountered – and never countenanced.

At the end, shamed in ways he could not name by the amber eyes, and the care and the flickering firelight within them, Valerius dropped his gaze to his hands. Words rolled over him, cold and unforgiving as a winter sea. *The governor will not be going back to Camulodunum for winter. He will attack . . . and when he does, he won't stop until Mona is his. The destruction of every dreamer left on the island.*

He closed his eyes. Within, the crowded god-space in his heart became a still, reflective sea, across which a hundred small boats sailed to freedom. Nemain held him, and Mithras stood at his shoulder, and both gave certainty to the vision, and the need for Luain mac Calma to hear of it.

Longinus was not a god, and had never sought to undermine Rome's advance. Dry-mouthed, Valerius asked, 'Why are you telling me this?'

The Thracian's smile was unreadable. His stag-red hair shone as copper in the firelight. 'Because I know you better than you think. Because you're the most stubborn, obstinate, mulish man in existence. Because I absolutely don't want to wade out of the sea on the headlands of Mona on the first day of next spring and find that I am fighting against you, and just at this moment I am very afraid that's exactly what's going to happen.'

'I couldn't kill you, Longinus. I'm not your decurion any longer.'

'No, you fool, I know that. My decurion would not have let himself be taken by four pasty-faced children late out of swaddling. You're a mess and I hope you are happy with it.'

'Then why . . .'

'Because I don't want to have to kill a man I still love. Now will you shut up and finish eating and we can think how best to get you and your half-hound to the coast in a way that will leave us all living?'

XXIV

THE AIR SMELLED OF WHITE LIME AND BEAR GREASE AND CUT PINE and fear. It was heavy with smoke and sweat and an aching desperation.

Cunomar mac Caradoc, son of the Boudica, first of the Eceni ever to give himself to the she-bear, stood in the doorway of the great-house he had built on the site of the spring and autumn horse fairs and defended it against attack.

Fifty-three times, a youth of the Eceni came at him. Fifty-three times, he raised the blade his mother had made for him and, in direct contravention of the laws of Rome, engaged in battle with the express intent of bringing a youth through the threshold to adulthood.

They did not fight to the death, but to first blood, which was his, so that the youths who came at him wielding sword-blades passed on as warriors, with their first battle cut on shoulders or chest. Four who dropped their guard early, the sooner to have it over, he struck on the upper arm with the flat of his blade and sent back out into the night. They came back later – much later – having passed again the earlier barriers held by Breaca and Ardacos.

If we had five hundred like you . . . even fifty . . . Breaca had said it in spring, wishing aloud on the bodies of the slain Coritani slave sellers, and then had spent the summer making the smaller wish real.

They were not like him, these desperate, terrified, hopeful children with their hair woven tight into warrior's braids and bear grease and the white lime bear-paint swirling across their beautiful, unmarked bodies; they had not spent nine days alone in a mid-winter cave with a sleeping she-bear learning the texture of their own silence as Cunomar had done, nor hunted, with only a knife, a bear known to kill men for sport, nor lived under the searing knives of the elders for three days afterwards, learning how un-ending, unendurable pain might open their souls.

More importantly, they had not spent nine months in solitary tuition, taught by the dozen finest minds of the Caledonii; such a luxury was not theirs to have in the lands of the Eceni, but they had spent two months of days building a great-house after the manner of their ancestors and of nights learning the ways of spear and blade as their parents had done and they themselves had never been allowed to do. In that was the beginning of their warrior's path.

A dark-haired girl came at him, her braid working loose and her lime paint smeared by sweat and exertion. Her eyes were white-rimmed and her nostrils flaring. She had a bruise on her right arm, up high, near the shoulder. If he tried, Cunomar could remember putting it there some time, long ago, at the beginning of the night.

If he thought about that, she would strike past his guard and cut him, which must not happen. He shifted his grip on his blade and raised it to block her strike and then cut past and blocked again and cut and moved into the rhythm of strikes he had taught her, waiting for the stillness to settle on her mind so that she might find the speed and surety to break out of the rhythm and put in a real attack.

The girl cut at his leg, and then the other, and then, as he raised his blade to match hers, she reversed her grip and used the hilt to strike his forearm. Pain made him grunt and he saw satisfaction and laughter flicker across her face but he had already moved to one side and used his elbow to shove her guard down and struck sideways, flicking his wrist so that the tip of his blade cut across her chest, high up, near the collarbone, in a long, slicing wound. She gasped aloud and stepped back and he saw on her face the same mix of pain and exultation he had seen on half a dozen of the others. These few were exceptional; the rest had shown pain and shock and a quieter satisfaction. If there were ever to be an elite within his honour guard, this girl and the handful like her would be it.

Unagh. Her name was Unagh, from the northern Wash, which had once been Efnís' home. Cunomar remembered it even as he lowered his blade and smeared the sweat from his palms and stepped aside saying, 'Warrior of the Eceni, you may pass.'

He thought she was the last, but was not certain. Tired, he leaned on the doorpost to the great-house, feeling newly planed wood smooth on his shoulder. Once, the building of such a place would have been planned ten years in advance, with the oaks that would make it marked and trained straight and the willow staves to bind the walls grown in place so that their roots would hold them secure and the reeds and straw for the thatch collected and dried in the height of summer.

Cunomar and his followers had made do with oak scavenged from the deeper forest and willow that must take root of its own accord later and more straw than reed for the thatch and most of that damp. It had survived the autumn gales and he wanted to believe it would survive the snows of winter, but was not certain.

There was snow in the air now; with the warriors gone he could smell it. He stretched an arm beyond the overhang of thatch at the doorway and felt the first feather touch of wetness, gone to nothing in a heartbeat on the heat of his hand.

Firelight from within caught the flash of a blade ahead of him. Straightening, he raised his own blade to guard. From the night, Breaca said, amused, 'If we are to fight, it should be in front of the elders. They would not want to miss that; the bear against the Boudica, they would talk of it for years, especially if one of us was hurt,' and then, coming close enough for him to see her, 'Did they all pass?'

'All.'

'Good. Then we can set them the spear-trial and hope they don't let the presence of their elders confuse them. You lead. This is your night. Ours comes after.'

The spear-trial of those who would join Cunomar's honour guard was held after the manner of the ancestors: indoors, sending the spears over thirty paces at targets of straw lit only by torchlight. The elders were drawn from their steadings and those nearby. Over a hundred had come; more than had gathered in the forest's heart two years before to determine the Boudica's future amongst the Eceni.

These were not youths who had grown under the yoke of Rome, but adults who had survived invasion and occupation and revolt and the savage reprisals that had followed it. These were the men and women who valued life above honour, or who felt that, in living, they served their people better. These were not ones who had stood and fought the legions, or spat on the auxiliary, or openly continued to act as dreamers for their communities in the face of Rome's ban.

Very few of them had been trained on Mona; they did not live in the dreaming as Airmid did, or know the winter tales and their hidden meanings as Dubornos had been taught. Even so, they had found the courage to travel at the end of the year, when the track-ways were hock deep in slick mud and Roman patrols still scoured them, and they remembered the spear-trials of old, and could bear witness to them, as was needful.

The young warriors threw in groups of four or five, lining them-selves along the mark, readying themselves as if they had trained for life, and not simply two months of evenings in the forest. Their blades caught the reddening light of the fire pits, making suns in the gloom. The song of the spears filled the great-house and became less, as each one sought to join with the soul of the warrior who held it.

'Just still the voice of your mind,' Breaca had said, long ago, and Eneit, who had understood the full measure of that, had said, 'Just?' and had done it even while he laughed at the impossibility.

The newly made warriors were not Eneit, but they gave all their hearts to try. Cunomar stood to one side, waiting to give the order to throw as his mother had done in the forest lifetimes ago, when, for him, the song of the spears had been impossible to hear.

Each time, with each new group, he felt the tension and nerves and growing calm as they strove to listen only to the voice of the spear, not the voice of their own fear and doubt. Each time, when he thought time had stretched too far and it was not possible to find the stillness, it crept on him and he said, 'Throw!' quietly and they did and their spears hit the targets as he had known they would do, except for four who would be allowed to try again in spring; they had not risked so much to fail this close to the end.

At the end, forty-nine warriors of the Eceni stood before Cunomar, in the presence of their elders, and swore oaths on their spears as had their ancestors, their lives for his, each life for the other, in the sight and care of the gods, for all time.

'Your son has come into his own. Responsibility has settled what the bear-dreamers began.'

'It would seem so. Through winter we will know for certain.' Breaca leaned on the oak post to one side of the threshold where the firelight caught her least. For now, it mattered that Cunomar hold the attention of the new warriors and their elders and that his mother keep to the shadows.

Ardacos crouched on the floor at her side, mending the binding on his spear. Their voices were lost in the rising murmur from the ranks of elders who lined the fire pits to the north side of the space. In the other half, the last of the newly made warriors rose to her feet and, defying the solemnity of her peers, raised her spear high above her head and spun it, whooping an old Eceni war cry. After a moment's shocked silence, those around her did the same. The roof thatch resounded to the high pitch of battle.

Ardacos turned to Breaca. 'She's like Braint. She fights like a wildcat. If she lives past her first battle, she will be good.'

'We have to bring them to battle for that to happen and we can't do that yet.' Breaca pushed herself away from the doorpost. All attention was on the howling youths and Cunomar, who, soberly, had stepped forward to calm them. In the time it took for silence to fall, Breaca walked round the side of the elders and reached her place at the far wall, opposite the door. There, a bundle of folded horse hides made a bench. A bronze shield hung on the wall behind, with the serpent-spear bold on its surface so that when she stood, the two heads of the spear seemed to emerge from her heart; if she sat, it crowned her.

She stood. Ardacos had followed her and now laid some wood in the nearest fire pit. Flames caught and grew and were caught in turn by the bronze of the shield and sent outwards by the curve of the metal so that, slowly, it became a second fire, and the iron of her drawn sword in the middle a star.

The attention of the elders came to her, drawn by the blaze of light and metal, by the white lime paint on her face and arms, by the warrior's braid, worn openly for the first time in the east, with the silver feather, black-quilled, for the uncounted numbers she had slain in battle.

Presently, when the sea of turned heads had become, instead, a sea of faces, of eyes reflecting the fire, Breaca nic Graine, first born of the royal line, said, 'Welcome, elders of the Eceni. Against Rome's edict, you have come here. There is not one of you who has not risked life to be present. Knowing that risk, you have borne witness to the first spear-trials to be held on Eceni land for seventeen years. Seventeen. Those who have today become warriors were not born when Rome's legions slaughtered their fathers and grandmothers, their aunts and cousins. If we allow another twenty years to pass, the children of these new-made warriors will grow in a land where the spear-trials are at best a memory, at worst, forgotten.'

They were hers, every part of their attention. She let them dwell on that, and signalled Cunomar. Smoothly, the product of much rehearsal, he led the forty-nine youths of his honour guard to make a curving line behind her.

She sat down, so that the bronze shield spilled red fire onto her hair, and flushed the skins of the nearest warriors. 'Tonight, an honour guard is born, of those whom you sent to us in the summer. They are not many, but given ten times as many we might bring the legions back to an eastern war . . .'

A dozen elders winced at the word. Those who had not sent youths, but might have done, sat stone-faced and dared her to continue.

'. . . but that war cannot begin without the express consent of the elder council. It has always been so and if we are to fight to preserve our heritage, we will not ignore the old ways. The time is not yet. Too many cleave to 'Tagos, who is held to rule us under Rome. The balance is fine. While he lives, we cannot openly raise warriors against Roman edict, and so—'

'Will you kill him?'

The question came from one of the strongest dissenters: a square-jawed man with greying hair who had shaken his head and murmured to his neighbour from the first moment the Boudica spoke of war. He was of Unagh's steading, the wild-cat girl with Braint's heart. She stood near Cunomar, a picture of mortified youth.

Breaca allowed time to consider the question. 'If he were dead, would you vote for war?' she asked.

'Not if you had killed him.'

'Which is one of the lesser reasons why I will not. Greater is that I have never and will never kill a man or woman of the Eceni simply because their beliefs do not match mine. 'Tagos believes the people are best served by their closeness to Rome. I believe that under the yoke of the legions, the Eceni will cease to exist. In this we are different, but the Ninth legion has its fortress a day's ride to the north and the Twentieth still has three thousand men at Camulodunum, and we cannot presume to defeat these two. I know this; I do not intend to bring our people to the brink of ruin. But it may be the gods will grant a time to act and we should prepare for that, or for ever regret its passing.'

The fire-shield weighed nothing; it had been made to honour the gods and the elders, not for battle. Breaca lifted it from the peg on the wall and hooked the strap over her shoulder, settling it in battle position. The flames at her feet were lower than they had been; the ashes glowed red on the shining metal. She tilted the shield so that light flowed down and she was in shadow, her voice flooding from darkness, with Mona's power behind.

'You have each risked your life to come here. The spear-trials are done and you are free to leave. But I invite you first to stay and to talk for as long as it takes, as we did in the elder councils of the days before Rome, to determine the case for war. If your decision is that we should fight, it will still not be easy, but we can begin, then, to determine how it may be done.'

'And if we decide against? Will you return to Mona as was asked of you by some of us two years ago?' Unagh's elder asked it, his face too masked to read.

'No. I am Eceni and my children with me. We will stay and we will act as the elder council requires of us. My son's honour guard will disband and the warriors will be offered the opportunity to follow their souls to the lands of the Caledonii or to return with you to their steadings.'

'Is that the view of you all?'

The Boudica stood again at the head of the council, with Ardacos and Cunomar beside her and the bronze shield at her back.

Her eyes were full of smoke and the grit of no-sleep. She ached to sit down, to lie down, to sleep and not to have to talk ever again of Rome and all it might bring, or the Eceni and what they might grow to be in a land free of occupation. Over the span of a day and a half, the gathered elders had talked and argued and talked and eaten and talked and slept and woken and gone outside to use the middens in twos and threes and talked and come back in again and talked further.

Others had found places for themselves among the fire pits and rolled in their cloaks and snored lightly for a time before their dreams and the talk around roused them once more. Cunomar and his newly made warriors had slept at the side through the first night, waking at dawn to bring wood for the fire pits, and to cook. Ardacos had left early and gone out into the forest to prepare for the last part of the new warriors' rites, which would come later.

Only the Boudica could not be seen to sleep, but rode like a skiff on the tide swell of their words and kept them ever moving forward.

Snow was falling outside when she took her place again at the shield and looked out over the weary, hoarse assembly of her people.

'Is that the view of you all?' she asked a second time. 'If there is one against, let that one speak now. We must have everyone, or we have no-one.'

At her side, Cunomar held his breath. Further along, she saw Unagh tense and then relax as the grey-haired elder from her steading shook his head. Around, others sat quietly. All dissent had been talked out of being, or was hidden, to raise its head another day.

Breaca let herself smile, careful not to break the mask of un-sleep. 'It is agreed, then, that you will spend the winter finding those men and women within your steadings and around who may have the heart for battle, and may answer a call without betraying us before we start. This is only the first step. While 'Tagos lives and stands against us, we cannot bring the warriors together. This is clear and I swear now before you all that his death will never be my doing. Even so, if we can begin to find those who have the will to fight, and to arm them, and to train them, when the gods send that the time is right, we can act. My thanks to you all.'

She stepped away from the shield and the council was over with no more ceremony, so that the elders began to rise and stretch and seek the door and find a way to fresh air and snow and to plan their journeys home.

The great-house had cleared by early afternoon, so that only the new warriors of Cunomar's honour guard were left. For a while, they had been rowdy with relief, taking their leave of the parting elders, but, as these thinned and were gone, the youths had become quiet again, awaiting their final test. If they wished to be reckoned amongst the warriors of the she-bear, not simply as Cunomar's honour guard, then they must follow Ardacos in a bear dance and for that even Breaca could not be present. Already the skull drums rattled inside the great-house. It was not a rhythm to hear long and stay sane.

Her horse was nearby, brought from the paddocks by Unagh, who had seen the need. Breaca struggled to fit the great bronze shield across her back and considered the effort of mounting and riding to 'Tagos' steading. Graine was there, and Airmid, and all comfort. If she rode sensibly, she should be there a little before nightfall; sooner if she rode stupidly fast, later if she slept and let the mare pick her own way through the dusk.

'Thank you. I'm glad that I—' She turned, looking down towards the trackway. 'That's Dubornos . . .'

She knew the horse; it was lame on the left fore, but not badly so, and Dubornos cared for it and would not set it aside. The sound of it ridden hard up the trackway was unmistakable, even with snow underfoot.

Ardacos came to her side, and then Cunomar abandoned his playing of the skull drums and joined her, so that they were all three together as Dubornos dragged his horse to a halt and did not dismount, but turned it, saying, 'The Latin slavers are at the steading. 'Tagos has offered them guest rights, and wine. They have already spoken twice to Graine. Airmid has her now, keeping her safe, but if they ask for her, 'Tagos may not stop them.'

Breaca stared at him, not hearing. 'To buy? That can't be. Even 'Tagos wouldn't—'

'Not to buy, not yet, but perhaps to make an offer, and they will know what they come for if they return in the spring.'

Breaca was already mounted. Sleep, so recently her only thought, was forgotten. Cunomar said, 'Wait. My horse isn't far. I'll come.'

Breaca's horse was already moving. 'No. Your warriors need you. This is the price of leadership, and in any case, this is not the time to let Rome know what we have. If we need you, I will send Dubornos back again.'

With that, she followed Dubornos, riding as she had never ridden before.

X X V

T HE SLAVER WHO BORE THE BADGE OF THE LEAPING SALMON HAD
never seen a warrior of the Eceni, dressed for battle, with her
hair braided at the side and a shield as wide as his arm across
her back and a spear in her hand, riding a horse black with sweat
and herself no cleaner.

He did his best; smiling a little stiffly and trying to hide his left
hand that made the sign against evil even as his right hand reached
to draw the legionary short sword from his belt. The ex-legionaries
who formed his bodyguard had less need to feign the courtesies of
guests; they drew their swords openly. One of those behind who
watched the wagons leaned in to take the reins of the dray
horses.

Breaca walked forward, catching her breath. It was a little before
nightfall, with the light less than perfect, but still, she knew how
she looked and she was not what a slaver valued in his wares. Led
by Dubornos, she had taken a shorter, uncleared path in the closing
parts of the ride; thorns had dragged at her, lacerating her arms.
Blood had mixed with the white lime paint so that she was marbled
in the colours of the gods. Her hair stood up stiffly in white spikes
at the front where she had swept it out of her eyes as she rode. She
stank of bear grease and sweat and raw blood and the slavers'
horses were terrified of her.

The conventions of Rome demanded other things from the wife

of a king. In a havoc of shattered propriety, 'Tagos stepped forward from the gates and took her arm, turning her at his side.

'Philus of Rome, allow me to present my wife, Breaca, mother to Graine, who will one day lead the Eceni.'

'Tagos was more of a diplomat than she had imagined. He spoke with aplomb in circumstances that begged for panic or ridicule and Philus could not but follow the lead he was given.

Sheathing his sword, the slaver bowed his head. 'My lady, you . . . I . . . that is, you . . .'

Breaca moved closer and words abandoned him, lost in a welter of sweat and the stinking remnants of bear grease.

With evident effort, he gathered himself, striving for courtesy. 'My lady, you find me at a loss. I had heard word of your skill as a smith and I have seen the exquisite beauty of your daughter, which was described by our late governor, may the gods rest his soul, but I had not expected her mother to be so . . . to have such . . . but I have no gifts left that would match you. I have given them all to the king, your husband.' His gaze shifted right and left, to his closest companions, who stared fixedly ahead and would not put up their weapons.

Breaca grinned artlessly. 'Your brooch is beautiful,' she said. 'I had imagined it Belgic when I first saw it, but now I see it closer, it is clearly not so. The Caledonii make the leaping salmon in such a fashion, with the small pieces of jet and the silver scales so perfectly set. Am I right? Is it one of theirs?'

She was within reach of the slaver's horse. It fought to step back so that Philus could barely hold it one-handed. He grimaced, sweating, caught between the opposing absolutes of diplomacy and his own clear need to keep the badge that was his symbol.

Breaca took the last step to his saddle horn and would have reached up, but that Graine ran forward from the gates and caught her hand. At eight years old, Breaca's daughter was no longer quite a child, but not yet nearly a woman. As either of these, she would have been beautiful. Hovering in the no-time between them, she captured and held the attention of the mercenaries as her mother had not done. She wrinkled her nose, theatrically.

'You smell of bear,' she said, 'Ardacos promised you wouldn't.' And then, with the wide-eyed innocence of the young, 'Philus says that I will be the talk of all Rome, that the emperor would wish me at his bedside.'

Graine had been trained in her dreaming by Airmid; she could put any meaning she chose into her words. With her voice, she conveyed the sense that she had been paid the greatest compliment of any child in the empire, while every adult present built an inner picture of the Emperor Nero's bedside and how a child might be treated there. The air closed tightly cold.

'Did he? Our guest thinks ahead of himself, it seems.' Breaca was not a dreamer, but she knew how to call death to walk in her shadow and to let the promise of it loose with her voice.

The slaver flushed scarlet and paled to an ugly, liverish yellow. His fingers fumbled at the clasp of his brooch.

'My lady, I spoke only to honour your daughter. I apologize for any misunderstanding. Perhaps you will do me the honour of accepting a gift in earnest of my good intentions towards you and your family?'

He was not a man used to pleading, the rustiness of his language said so, adding to the evident pain of losing his brooch as Breaca reached to take the salmon from his unwilling fingers.

'Thank you.' It was Caledonian, well fashioned and with a power of its own. She tossed it high, leaping silver in the watery light, and caught it one-handed. The flicker and flash and the suddenness of her reach upset the remaining horses. She saluted the slaver, using the Roman form, loading it with irony. 'I am overwhelmed. Anything held in such deep affection speaks greatly of the bearer. Come midwinter, the gods will take kindly to such a gift.'

The slaver knew enough of Eceni rites to see where she led; in his mind, he saw her cast his jewelled fish into the waters of the gods' pool, where no mortal man might find it again. Of all possibilities, that one had not occurred to him. She watched the pits of his eyes grow large and small again. If they had been in battle, he would have struck for her then, aiming to kill.

They were not in battle and Philus, former fish-bearer, had his eye set on the greater game. He forced a smile and put his closed fist over his heart, where the brooch had been. 'I am honoured, as will be those who made the fish when I tell them of your gift.'

He let his horse move at last, so that it spun on its hocks and kicked away from her. His parting words were shouted over his shoulder, muffled by the thunder of his retinue, 'My lady, I await the day of our next meeting. May it be soon.'

Breaca was laughing, weakly, for relief and the look on Philus' face when she took the fish badge, and the sudden release of terror. The world was lighter than it had been, with flashes of bright white at the margins of her vision and a reddening tunnel lined with night in the centre. She felt a small, cool hand press into her own and a thumb grind on her knuckle. Graine hissed at her, in the voice of the elder grandmother. 'They're watching. Stay awake. You can't fall now.'

'I wasn't going to fall.'

'I think you were. Your daughter is wiser than you know.' 'Tagos came to stand on her other side, completing the family. Between them, he and Graine held Breaca upright, while appearing to lean on her for support.

They stood like that, bonded in their need, until the last of the slavers' horses was too small to be seen. Graine stepped away first. 'The elder grandmother wishes you well,' she said.

Breaca pressed her palms to her eyes. The grit of the lime paint ground into her skin and did nothing to help her wake up. Slurring for lack of sleep, she said, 'Thank her for me. I'll do it myself later. For now, I need to wash and then to sleep.'

'Tagos caught at her arm. With an oddly brittle formality, he said, 'My bed is ready. I would be honoured if you would use it.'

She was sleeping already, clearly, and falling into disordered dreams. 'Tagos had not shared her bed since the end of Breaca's first winter in his steading. She slept in her own bed, in Airmid's hut on the western side of the compound. The prospect of falling into that bed, in that room, in that company, had sustained her through the last half-day of the elder council's deliberating.

She stared now at 'Tagos. He seemed sober, which surprised her. His eyes were open and dark and met hers without flinching. It occurred to her she might still be awake, and that the world, therefore, was not as she had left it. She said, 'I don't think I heard you correctly.'

'I think you did. I am inviting you to sleep in my room, which was once also yours. Only to sleep. Please. This time it matters.'

Graine said, 'Airmid is with a woman of the Trinovantes who gave birth three days ago and has milk fever. She will not return before tonight. Her fire is banked low and the hut's cold.'

'Is it?' Dawn had broken but the rising sun had not yet penetrated the cloud. If anything, the morning was colder than the night had been. Breaca was shivering and had not noticed. Frost bit at her feet. The air smelled of snow and storms.

'Tagos waited. He, too, needed to be moving. The tips of his ears were blue with cold and distress. For no better reason than that, Breaca made her decision. 'Is your fire lit?' she asked.

'Of course. Built high and hot.'

'Then I accept your offer. Thank you.'

'Tagos' room had changed since she was in it last. The coin chests were gone, all bar one, and the ornaments that had lain on them. A sword hung above the bed; not one of hers, but well made. The iron lay pale against the smoked wood of the wall and a vixen's mask had been worked in bronze on the pommel. She had not known 'Tagos still owned any blade, nor that he would dare to display it. The Roman ban on weapons was absolute and the penalty the same for a king as it had been for Eneit, a thirteen-year-old boy caught at a grave mound with a sword he did not know how to use.

She ran a finger across the edge to test the honing and found it battle-sharp. 'Did the governor give you dispensation to own this?'

'No. The governor is locked in the west planning his attack on Mona for the spring. Three cohorts of legionaries from the Rhine will overwinter at Camulodunum and when they march to join him, the attack will begin. I don't think whoever he has left in charge will venture north to see us, but if anyone comes, we will hear of it and I will take it down as I did when Philus was in here.'

'And put it back up again straight after. I see.'

Breaca sat heavily on the bed. She needed to sleep and she needed to think clearly and she could not do both at once. A window faced her, imperfectly covered. Daylight leaked through the thinning deer hide and splashed on the single wooden chest pushed against the wall. For no better reason than it was there, she kicked it. Emptiness rang through the room. 'Tagos flinched. With the fire hurling heat all around, his face was pinched and white.

He said, 'That's the first reason why I needed you here. I am no longer a rich man. We have to talk.'

Sleep mattered less than it had done. Breaca stood up and leaned against the wall beneath the sword. 'Tell me.'

'Tagos had the thoughts prepared, but not the words. His tongue was knotted and his throat too tight. He said, 'Philus takes his orders from Decianus Catus, the procurator of taxes who unveiled the old governor's memorial in the spring. Catus has a reputation for being harder and more brutal than any of his predecessors. And he has a wider remit: in addition to tax collection, this procurator has been ordered to recall the loans given by Claudius and Seneca to the eastern tribes at the time of the invasion.'

'What, all of them? The full amount? I thought it was to be repaid over decades.'

'So did I. So, I think, did Claudius when he lent it, but Nero is different. His exact orders to the procurator were to "drain the lifeblood from Britannia". They will take our gold, our corn, our cattle, our horses, our hounds. When we have nothing more to give, they will take us: the Eceni, the Trinovantes, the Coritani, the Catuvellauni – any man, woman or child who can walk and eat and be broken into slavery will be sold at profit in the markets of Rome. The rest they will kill.' The words came more smoothly now, drawn by their own momentum. In case there were any doubt, he lifted the lid of his single remaining coffer and kicked it onto its side. It was entirely empty.

. . . drain the lifeblood . . . Breaca stared into the flames. A dead standard-bearer saluted her from their depths. The ancestor-dreamer nodded and said nothing.

'Why has it come to this now?' Breaca asked.

'Philus has no idea. He doesn't care. His business is profit and we have become a source of it. Airmid has met with the physician from Athens, though, and he cares a great deal.'

'Theophilus? What did he say?'

'That Nero tires of the adventure that is Britannia. That the cost is greater than the benefit. That, of Rome's eleven legions, four are bogged down here and there is not one man amongst them who does not wish himself elsewhere. They die in their thousands in the wars in the west for no benefit and the emperor's advisers believe they should return to Rome. The governor was sent to subdue the west, or die in the attempt. Many believe he will die and those who rushed to give loans after the invasion expecting interest and profit are regretting their haste.'

The fire was too hot and the room lacked air. Breaca pressed her shoulders into the wall, seeking support for more than her body alone. From the measured mess of 'Tagos' words, one sentence emerged.

. . . the emperor's advisers believe they should return to Rome.

'Nero is thinking of recalling the legions from Britannia? Are you serious?'

'So Philus says, and he has no reason to lie. If the governor fails to subdue the west, every legionary and auxiliary cavalryman will have been recalled by next winter. But we may all be dead by then. They say, "Dead men pay no taxes" – that's why we have lived so far. When there are no more taxes to be collected, they have no reason to leave us alive.'

'Did Philus say that, too?'

'No. That was Theophilus. He is one who will leave willingly, and not because he fears us.'

'Theophilus wouldn't be here at all if he could leave with any honour.' Breaca ran a hand through her hair. Flakes of white lime paint made grit between her fingers. 'You said that was the first reason you needed me here. What else is there?'

'Tagos moved closer to the fire. Red light coloured his skin and hair equally. He was a man consumed as Breaca had never seen him. He stared into the flames. Presently, without turning back, he said, 'Philus sought my permission to trade in Eceni territory. The asking was a fiction; he has the permission – the orders – of the emperor to make as much profit as he can, he needs no word from me. As a test, he made me an offer. If I were to sell him Graine and Cygfa, he would write off our debt – the entire taxes of the Eceni nation, plus the loans from Claudius. Two children, even one a warrior, for more gold than either of us has ever seen.'

She could have killed him then, quite easily. The oath so easily sworn to the elders in the great-house taunted her. *His death will never be my doing.* She had not thought to add, 'Unless he sells my daughter into slavery, in which case his death will take the days of her life and he will regret every one of them.'

Holding fast to her anger, she said, 'Did you tell him you would die on the blades of your people did you even consider it?'

'No.' He turned and his smile was crooked, bouncing back on itself. 'I told him I would die by my own hand before I ever considered it. Do you really think I would have sold them? They may not be of my blood, but I care for them as if they were, and even if I hated the sight of them I am not so wedded to Rome that I believe anyone, child or adult, can be bought for gold. I don't dream as Airmid does, even as you do, but the gods speak to me in their fashion and they would never speak again if I had allowed that.'

'Except that Philus knows you can't stop him.'

'Exactly. He won't take Graine and Cygfa now, but he will in the spring. Even now, he may decide to "collect merchandise" from some of the smaller steadings as he returns to Camulodunum, knowing we can't stop him.'

'Tagos' skin was the colour of iron, grey and polished with sweat. Every part him craved wine. Breaca watched him meet the need and deny it. He pulled a dry log from the pile at the hearth and sat on it, wrapping his one arm around his knees. Speaking to the wall where his sword hung above her head, he said, 'I'm sorry. We should have raised an army when you first came. We would have died, but we would not have to watch as they bleed us dry.'

'Tagos stands against us.* She had said that to the elders, believing it.

Less certain now, she said, 'Cunomar and Ardacos are leading forty-nine warriors of the Eceni in a bear dancing. By midnight, we will have forty-nine new she-bears, the first of the Eceni, after Cunomar, to be so. With them, we could take on Philus now and kill him. Would you support that?'

He stared down at his one hand, crossed over his chest, holding the stump of the other. 'You forget that Philus has protection of the procurator. Rome knows he's here. If he fails to return, the legions will fall on us as they did in Scapula's time.' He raised his head. Horror and the memories of it showed on his face. 'You weren't here then. You didn't see the slaughter of Roman reprisals; the men and women hanged in rings around their steadings, with their children dead at their feet, all for the loss of a single legionary, for a stone thrown at an auxiliary. And Cygfa and Graine will be enslaved. Philus knows we value them; he will see that we know it as we die. If we fight, we will lose. Would you have me support that?'

Breaca said, 'If they are coming anyway, then yes, I would. Better to fight than to stand back and watch them bleed us white. And there is a chance we may win. It's already snowing; the legions won't leave their forts now. The gods have given us a winter to prepare and we will use it. The elders have gone home to find warriors with heart who may join us. If they find only ten each, we will have a thousand. If each of that thousand has the courage of Cunomar's new she-bears then, at the very least, we will give the legions something by which to remember us.'

'Cunomar has grown to be worthy of his father, then?'

'It would seem so. Certainly he has . . . the makings of a good leader.' She had been going to say that he had Caradoc's sway over those who followed him, and an added fire, but compassion stopped her.

'Tagos smiled, thinly. He looked as tired as she felt. 'You must be proud of your son. He's a credit to his parents.'

The pain in his voice cut through the clutter of half-hopes. Breaca wiped a hand across her eyes and looked at him properly for the first time in her life. For the first time in both their lives, 'Tagos met her gaze equally; a man driven to the edge of his being.

That edge was where she lived and he had never been. They faced each other across the room; the warrior and the never-warrior, mother and never-father, beloved and lover, but never loved.

'Tagos picked at the edge of his sleeve. 'I don't hate Caradoc,' he said presently. 'I never have done. I just wanted to be like him. Or to be him. If the dreamers had a way to change one man into the body of another, I would have traded places with Caradoc any day of our lives. Even now, when he is crippled and exiled in Gaul, I would do it, to have sired the children he has. His daughters shine as the sun and the moon, a warrior and a dreamer to cheer the singers for generations. It seems his son also is everything a man could ask for.'

They were not so far apart. Breaca reached a hand for his one arm and gripped it, briefly. 'Cunomar will be a credit to you, also. If he leads the warriors in the battles against Rome, it will be as your son that he is known to them.'

They were speaking with an honesty they had never found before. 'Tagos rubbed his hand across his eyes and they were red, not only from the smoke and the night with little sleep.

Breaca said, 'You do not have to live as if only a child could be your life's memorial. You are young; the loss of an arm is not the greatest loss. There is much you could do still and through winter we could plan that. It is not certain that we will die in spring. If the governor takes all the troops from Camulodunum, the veterans will not hold it alone, and if we take the city the Trinovantes will join us in rebellion. Mona's havoc could be our gain.' She tried to smile and could not make her mouth move properly. The ancestor-dreamer hovered close by, and the ghost of a slain standard-bearer. Fighting to see past them, she said, 'Even if we die in the first battle, death is not an ending. Ask the elder grandmother.'

'If I knew how, I might do that, but— Breaca!' He had hold of her shoulder, which was surprising given how far away he had been. 'Don't fall into the fire!' His face was very close indeed, and concerned. 'How long is it since you slept?'

'Three days? Four, I think. There were rites before the warrior-trials that must be honoured.'

'And no food for them either. You, too, do not have to prove yourself through the trials of your children.'

He sounded amused and worried together. Breaca tried to decide if she was being patronized and could not. She felt him lay her down on the bed and undress her and slide her under the sleeping-hides and did not flinch when he kissed her, chastely, on one cheek.

'Tagos had had the makings of a hero once. If Caradoc had not come to them, he would have shone amongst the warriors of the Eceni. The fire coloured him gold, meeting the daylight through the half-hidden window.

He bowed, drawing away, speaking softly. His words came thickly, through veils of sleep. 'If I knew how to speak to the dead, I would ask of the ancestors much of the lands beyond life. I can't, but am grateful that you can and that you bring back what you see.

Sleep well. There are battles to be fought that need you to lead them. You have a winter to raise your war host. In the spring, you can march to war.'

'If Philus has not taken our children into slavery and slain us as we sleep.'

'He won't. I give you my word on it.'

XXVI

'WHEN DID 'TAGOS LEAVE?'
  'Not long after the snow started. It was still light then.'

Breaca stood in swirling semi-dark. Flaring pine resin brands lit the ragged end of a blizzard. The worst had passed over as she slept, leaving snow to the height of her ankles; not too deep to ride or run, but enough to hide the gaps and ruts in the tracks and to make the going treacherous for fast horses.

Airmid, Cygfa and the singer Dubornos stood in an arc around her, protection against the worst of the wind. Dark hair, corn gold and red tangled in a line, made bright by the torchlight. They were tired, all three of them, as if the time between 'Tagos' leaving and their waking of the Boudica had been difficult and nothing had yet been resolved.

Breaca made herself step beyond their shelter. Cold, hard air embraced her, so that she could lean back against it and not fall. Her hair flew east, the way 'Tagos had gone.

'Is it certain that he followed Philus' slave band?' she asked.

Dubornos shrugged. 'No, but it's what he said he would do.'

Airmid said, 'He was a changed man after you spoke to him. Then his two men, Gaius and Titus, came back – he had sent them to follow the slavers. They brought bad news, or so it seemed. Before they left, all three broke the copper armbands that the governor gave them as guest-gifts.'

Cygfa smiled, sourly. 'I think our "king" wishes us to know that he is no longer Rome's whore, although whether he has the courage to inform the governor of this in the spring, of course, is another question. If he's lucky, the snow will close the tracks before any of his once-friends who still side with Rome can take horse and ride west with the news.'

'He'll still die for treason if anyone in Camulodunum hears of it, now or later.' Breaca turned side on to the wind. 'Airmid? Is there anything we can do?'

The dreamer had not moved. Her body leaned into the wind, as it did when she was least present. She shook her head. 'The gods have sent the snow to hold us safe from the legions. It doesn't matter to them if we don't find 'Tagos before he is slain by Philus.'

Breaca knelt and pressed her hands in the snow. Cold burned off the last remnants of sleep. 'It might do if, instead, he is captured alive and taken to Camulodunum for questioning – I told him about the she-bear dancing and Cunomar's honour guard and I would not like to depend on his ability to withstand the inquisitors. I think we should ride out to look for him.'

Airmid stood at her left shoulder, solid and safe. The other two were already armed. Blades of Breaca's making splintered the snowlight, dancing.

Cygfa said, 'So do we. That's why we woke you.'

They were four, three warriors and a dreamer, riding slowly, without light, through dense woodland with Cygfa as their scout. It was not true that she could see in the dark, but close enough to make no difference.

Snow drifted down through the trees, no longer driven by the wind. It was too deep now for easy travel; if the gods required them safe, they had achieved their aim. Their tracks closed over as they rode so that their passing left no trace.

Breaca was not yet fully awake. Fragmented dreams of the warrior-trials wove patterns across the unlit night, so that she saw Cunomar, endlessly, and the half-dozen of his honour guard who were exceptional. Skull drums tapped out their mind-eating rhythms and each of the white-painted warriors came at her, grinning, with bear claws instead of blades and she must match them with only her blade. In the dreams, as in the night through which she rode, she wished the sword in her hand were the one she had fought with all her life, not the substitute made in secret for the warrior-trials. With her father's blade, she could have set Cunomar at her right hand and Cygfa in the shield-place at her left and all Rome would not have—

A horse screamed in final agony and a man shouted and then he, too, screamed; another man howled an order in Latin.

Cygfa said, 'That's Philus,' and Airmid, 'The dead man is Gaius. 'Tagos has only Titus left to defend him.'

'So they are two against Philus' two dozen. And we are four so we—' Cygfa spun her horse on the snow. 'Gods . . . is that Cunomar?'

Breaca nodded. The havoc of the skull drums filled her mind, making it impossible to speak. The blade in her hand sang for the first time since its making. Neither of these could be heard by the others, but the distant sound of warriors running through a forest, and the high keening of the she-bears, was known to anyone who had fought alongside Ardacos in the west.

Dubornos, calm mind in battle, tilted his head to one side. 'Your son is close,' he said. 'If we wait, we will outnumber the slavers, but I think if we ride hard we may reach the battleground while they are still many to our few.'

They should have waited, all of them knew it, but a second horse screamed and Breaca recognized 'Tagos' bay mare, her gift to him in the summer, and, suddenly, for no clear reason, she knew that she did not want him dead, and that, very badly, she wanted to fight.

The scar on her palm seared as if newly cut; she had forgotten the joy buried in the pain. For the first time in three years, she felt the pull of true battle and it ran like fire in her veins. Her mare became harder to hold and she did not want to.

She glanced at Airmid, who could have stopped them and did not. Breaca said, 'We will be six against two dozen. If the gods did not condone this, they would have sent more snow to stop us, surely?'

'Surely.' The dreamer pointed up at the sky. 'The snow is on its way. If you must have your battle, have it quickly, else you will be fighting through white blindness.'

'Thank you. Keep yourself safe.'

Breaca let her mare have its head. Cygfa and Dubornos raced her across the untrampled snow.

Their horses were war trained; they ran towards the havoc of combat without urging. At a curve in the path, they came upon the slavers' camp, in which Philus, untimely, had ordered torches lit and the fire built up and the sudden rush of light showed trees and a small stream and a panic of slavers pressing their backs against the gully sides, facing a few who became less few and then, horrifyingly, too many.

The snow began slowly, the battle fast and hard. Cygfa fought on Breaca's left, in the shield-place of highest honour. Very soon – sooner than any of them had expected – Cunomar emerged from the trees to the right with the greater part of his honour guard around him. The rest, led by Ardacos, came at the slavers from the back, sweeping round in a bear's paw that crushed the enemy as a hammer crushes hot metal on an anvil.

Over half of Philus' men were battle-trained mercenaries. They had fought for the legions in Iberia, Mauretania and the Germanies against warriors who sucked the marrow from the bones of their still-living enemies. Instinct and long training served them well. They made a wedge without being ordered and then, when Ardacos' bear paw began to close, they made a square, turning about and about so that every man faced outwards and their small, round riding shields met at the edges with room to let their short swords stab out between.

At the back of the square, the slaughter had already begun. There, slavers who were not mercenaries and had no idea of how to conduct themselves in battle had sought protection behind wicker wattles left over from the high days of a herding summer. So doing, they had blocked the only route of escape. Ardacos sent six warriors against twelve men and could have sent half that number. The victory howls of the six youths rang above all the others sounds of carnage as each took life for the first time in the name of the bear.

The mercenaries knew already that escape was impossible. They could count and understood the odds and if they had not yet encountered the she-bear, they had faced other warriors of other nations who ran unclothed into battle with the veil of their gods about them and their courage bright for all to see. Every man chose one of those coming and spat on his blade, swearing to kill that one before he died.

Breaca saw her man. His eyes burned her. His short sword sang for her alone. Hers sang with a ferocity that matched the she-bear. She raised it, letting it taste the killing air, and was the Boudica again, and her world was perfect.

She urged her mare forward with her knees. She could not see Philus, either in the square or in the slaughter pen behind it, but there was no time to look properly; Cygfa had already pushed forward at an angle and cut down on her right to break the arm of a black-haired ex-legionary.

Blood sprayed from a split vessel and the man dropped to his knees, staring at his own leaking life. Breaca's man cursed and kicked the fallen body sideways, striving to close the gap in the shield wall.

Breaca pushed her mare into the space and drove her blade down, back-handed. She met iron, and twice again. Her opponent was good; he fought on foot against a warrior on horseback and gave no ground. Very quickly, he stopped trying to kill Breaca and strove instead to cripple her horse. He might have succeeded but that the mare had been trained by one who valued her mount's life as her own and the beast knew how to keep itself safe while seeking to give her rider a still point from which to strike. A strike from her forefoot ripped the man's helmet from his head and the Boudica's fourth cut, or her fifth, cracked through his skull to wedge on his upper teeth. She dragged the sword free as he fell.

The passing of his ghost distracted Breaca, so that she missed the moment when Cunomar, fighting for the first time in full battle, took his man. His battle yell scattered the ghosts and Breaca turned in time to see him stoop to plunge his hand in the blood of the fallen foe and print a bloody palm on his upper arm. He raised his head to cry again and his eyes met hers. His joy was Caradoc's, but sharper. He grinned and raised his red-stained palm. 'For father,' he yelled, 'and for Graine.'

Breaca made the salute of the warrior and saw his world, too, made perfect.

The din of battle abated. The legionaries' square was broken beyond redemption and the killing was faster now, as men saw their deaths and embraced them. Dubornos was nearby. Breaca caught at his arm, shouting, 'Where's 'Tagos? Where's Philus?'

'There. Together. Fighting.' He pointed with one elbow, swinging his horse round. 'Philus has the best of it.'

She was the Boudica; she had only to think and they followed her. Even as she turned, Cygfa took her place to the left. Cunomar was already running on her right. Dubornos grinned at the impatience of youth and held his horse in, awaiting her word.

The whisper of the skull drums still rang in her head. Snow melted on her naked arms. Breaca pointed her blade so that the light of Philus' torches flared along the metal. 'Help him.'

They were too late. She knew that as the mare sprang across the bloody slush. Philus heard them and chose not to turn. 'Tagos heard Cunomar's bear howl and the sheer power of it stole his attention.

He would have died, perhaps, in any case; he had never been a warrior of any great skill, but it hurt to see him cut down as the slavers had been, with a blow to the legs that he failed to block and then one to the shoulder of his bad arm that he could never have blocked, but that crushed his ribs and the lungs within them, and then a final one to the head, which did not land, because Philus should have looked, should have known that Dubornos, who was 'Tagos' cousin, was behind him and would never let the death of his blood kin pass unavenged.

Breaca heard Cunomar shout his congratulations and saw that he did not begrudge another man a kill that might have been his own. Truly, the world had changed.

Philus died more swiftly than 'Tagos, who lay, whistling bubbles of blood through a break in his nose. Breaca slid from her horse and knelt at his side in the thickening snow. Her children made an arc about her, with Dubornos, and Airmid, who had not fought but kept the night free from unwanted ghosts.

'Tagos' one hand was chilled, his palm slickly wet. He opened his mouth to speak and no sound came from his battered lungs. He closed his eyes and Breaca watched his brow furrow. With his eyes still shut, he said, 'Philus sent a messenger to Camulodunum . . . Sorry. They will know about Graine. Gaius followed him and came back. He should have—'

Breaca squeezed his hand. 'Gaius has crossed the river to Briga's care. Whatever he should have done, he knows now better than we do.'

'As I will. Soon.' A smile ghosted across his lips. 'The Eceni have a new ruler, one with the will for war. You can raise your war host when the snow clears and if the legions march west out of Camulodunum the city will be ripe for the taking. Lead your warriors well.'

'As long as I am able. 'Tagos, open your eyes.'

He did so, with effort. Breaca leaned over so that he could see her without turning his head, or his eyes. Bending, she kissed him on the mouth, dryly, tasting the blood on his breath.

Quietly, she said, 'Wait for me in the lands of the dead. Airmid and Caradoc will both live beyond us. There will be time enough then to find what we might have been.'

It was the greatest gift she could offer, freely given. He died with joy in his eyes and his grip firm on her hand.

IV

WINTER AD 59–EARLY
SPRING AD 60

XXVII

ON THE MORNING AFTER 'TAGOS' DEATH, BREACA TOOK BACK the ancestor-torc of the Eceni, that had been her mother's and her mother's mother's, back through the line for uncounted generations.

Nothing had changed and everything. 'Tagos lay dead, and Philus with him, and there was no going back. Breaca woke to the understanding of that, and lay listening to the wind drive the snow against the walls of Airmid's hut. She sent her mind forward to spring and what might be done and could see no way to keep the legions at bay while the war host was gathered that might defeat them.

She felt a draught and heard voices and knew that she was not fully awake. Fragments of dreams held her, of snow and torn flesh and the fading light in 'Tagos' eyes as he died. Struggling to bring herself into morning, she felt Airmid come close, and with her the ancient dark dryness of the ancestor-dreamer.

Too fast, she sat up, and opened her eyes to a dazzle of firelight on red Siluran gold. The torc of the ancestors took up all of her vision, a gift and a curse and alive with others' dreaming.

'Breaca?' Airmid was there, with a hand on her shoulder. 'What do you see?'

'That the ancestor-dreamer lives within the gold. I didn't know before.'

Breaca ran a finger along the cold metal, feeling the solid curve, shaped by centuries of wearing. Outwardly, it was the same as it had always been, a miracle of woven wires, with loops at the end pieces for the kill-feathers, after the manner of the ancestors.

She had worn it first as a child, when all that had mattered was that she felt royal and could seem so to others. Years after, on the battlefield of the Roman invasion, it had marked Macha's willing death and the sacrifice made so that others might live. Breaca had felt only grief and loneliness in taking it and later, passing it to Silla, had done her best to shield her younger sister from both of those. When 'Tagos had given the torc to Cygfa in the clearing, the dignity that passed with it had been obvious, but nothing else.

Only now, because she had known the ancestor-dreamer, did Breaca feel the rhythms of power woven into the gold. Stretching down from the past, they touched equally the shining battle soul within her and the darker core that had called once for vengeance for Caradoc, and, failing to call cleanly, had brought home Valerius instead.

The memory of that still haunted her nights. She said, 'Did my mother see it like this?'

Airmid sat on the end of the bed and laid the torc between them. 'No. Your mother's power was not of the serpent-spear, nor did she ever have need to call it. The ancestors come only to those who need them, and can stand firm in their presence.' She looked up, and was going to say something in jest and changed her mind and said, seriously, 'You can do that. It takes a different courage from battle, but you have it.'

'Maybe.' Memories of the ancestors' cave made cold the caverns of her mind. Breaca rose and began to dress, leaving the torc on the bed hides.

After a while, Airmid picked it up and laid it on the hearth stone by the fire. She took a twist of unwoven wool and dried it of snow. 'You are the Boudica,' she said. 'Today, after 'Tagos' death, you lead the Eceni in name as well as fact. It's not the torc that makes you either of these. You don't have to take it if you don't want to. We could lay it in the fire and melt it now and the spears would still give you their oaths in spring, the war host would still gather to the sign of the serpent-spear.'

'Which would be powerless.'

'Not entirely. You have your own power and it does not come only from the ancestors.'

'But I am not fighting this war only for myself.' Breaca came to sit on the opposite side of the fire. Flames spun in the draught and, fleetingly, took on the shapes of the dead: of Macha, of Silla, of 'Tagos, smiling as he died. She looked deeper, to the embers, and sought her own mother, who had worn the torc with dignity and untainted honour. No-one came, only a scattered childhood memory of the elder grandmother, whom she had loved, and the old woman's voice, lost in the crackles of the fire. *You won't lose me, I promise you that.*

She had not asked a clear question and it was not a clear answer but, quietly, as if from some distance away, Airmid said, 'Not all of the ancestors are dangerous. And the dark is unsafe only to the extent that we fear it.'

'And fear is the only enemy. You sound like Luain mac Calma.' Breaca reached for the torc and held it a moment near the flames. She was fully awake now, and the prickling danger of the ancestor was less than it had been, gone with the beads of snow-melt. The torc lay across her palms, quiet in its majesty. She said, 'It would be a pity to melt it. Graine should wear it one day, and her daughters. I would not leave it to them tainted with my own fears.' She looked up, and found she could smile, which was good. 'Do you know the words of the binding-oath?'

Airmid shook her head. 'Not well enough to speak them aloud, but I think they would be more for the witnesses than for you. The torc extracts its own oaths; taking it, knowing what you do, is enough.'

In the past, there would have been ceremony, and the full three hundred spears of her honour guard to witness the moment when Breaca, first born of the royal line, took back the torc of her ancestors. Dreamers sent from Mona would have offered speeches and told of their dreams. Her daughters would have pledged themselves to follow her, honouring all that she honoured.

On the day after 'Tagos' death, it felt better done in private, with Airmid alone to bear witness to the hesitation and the small act of courage that pushed her over yet another threshold so that, with her own hands, Breaca took the torc and fitted it to her neck. It lay solidly alive against her skin, cool and dry and serpentine. The fit was perfect, with the end pieces resting in the hollows below her collarbones and the weight set to the back so that her shoulders took the bulk of it. It had felt exactly the same when she was a child, and far smaller.

As a smith, she could admire the skill that had made it. As Breaca, as the Boudica, as first born of the royal line, come at last to her heritage, she sought to meet and to match what it might bring, and was surprised and a little disappointed to find no challenge or threat, but only a slight lurch in her abdomen and a sigh, as of a hound returning to the fireside.

Presently, when the ancestor did not come either to greet or to harangue, Breaca rose from the fire and lifted back the door-flap. Outside, the world was white; driven snow piled thigh high against the walls of the hut and the cold bit sharply.

Another threshold had been crossed. Nothing had changed, and everything. Airmid came to stand at her shoulder and it was good to remember those things that would never change.

To Airmid, staring out at the snow, Breaca said, 'You were right, the gods are with us. If Philus has been missed in Camulodunum, those left in charge will never risk sending a patrol out now to come and look for him. At the very least, we are safe until spring. We can use the time to think of ways to keep the legions at bay for longer.'

Snow fell for the remainder of the month, sealing the land in a blanket of ice so that the legions stayed in their winter billets and the tribes in their steadings and the land slept in a semblance of peace.

Three days before the year's-end, a month and a half before the winter solstice, the gods sent the easterly wind to blow southerly and warm, scouring the snow from the land. On the third day, when it was safe to ride, Breaca took a bay colt of Cygfa's, not long broken to saddle, and rode with Cunomar out to the gully in which Philus and his men had made their last, indefensible camp.

The snow lay thin and patchy, running to mud. The air smelled of damp and rotting leaves and, as they reached the valley, of meat hung past its best. The bay colt shied at the stench and had to be coaxed forward, but that was why he had been brought; a battle horse cannot fear the scents of carnage. Breaca tethered him to some willows, and followed Cunomar into the gully.

Winter had covered the corpses, keeping them whole so that only in the last days had the carrion feeders found them. Breaca had not made any conscious effort to remember the lie of the dead after the battle, but the pattern was easy enough to pace out: here, behind the wicker sheep folds, lay the twelve of Philus' merchants, all fallen face down and with wounds in the back or sides as they had tried to run; here in front, the mercenaries had died fighting. The black-haired one who went for Cygfa and lost his arm lay under his smaller, grey-haired companion, who had been Breaca's kill. Pulled tight by ice, their flesh had melted back onto their faces, and their blood had washed away with the snow, leaving them whitely sodden, as the leaf litter was sodden and the drips from the overhanging branches.

'He's here.' Cunomar crouched by a body a dozen paces away. 'You were right. He's not wearing the king-band.'

Breaca crossed to where 'Tagos lay in a puddle of melted snow. In death, he was composed and neat with his cloak wrapped about his shoulders and his one good arm across his chest, his blade still in his hand. A crow had taken his eyes and a fox had begun to feast on his face, but what was left held a peace that it had rarely done in life and it was still possible to see the authority and integrity of the man he might have been, and had tried to become.

Only his king-band was missing, the clamour of red gold, enamel and copper that Breaca had made for him in their first winter, the better to impress a governor with a taste for Eceni art. She knelt at his side and lifted the sodden wool of his cloak away from his one good arm. The band was gone and had been so while he still lived – anyone taking it from his corpse would have disturbed his peace too clearly.

Aloud, she said, 'It won't have fallen. He can only have given it away.'

'Philus is behind you,' Cunomar said, quietly.

Breaca turned. The slave trader lay as he had fallen, untidy and unmourned. His pack was not beside him, but she found it wedged in the roots of an oak, broken open by the weight of snow and stirred by rats and mice. She turned it upside down and the king-band spilled out, wrapped about in lamb's wool to keep it untarnished.

'Well done.' Cunomar grinned. 'I owe you a belt buckle.'

'Which you don't have to give me. I only bet because it was obvious.' Breaca picked up the cold metal and teased open the wool. 'No-one but Philus would have had the audacity to ask for this, and even if they had, 'Tagos would not have felt himself beholden to give it to anyone less threatening.'

Cunomar nodded. 'It's still the most beautiful thing you have made, and he treasured it. He would not have given it away if he had not felt it necessary.'

'I would like to think not.'

Unwrapped, the band lay across her hands, as bright as the day she had made it. Red gold caught the flat light of the morning, warming it; oval plates of blue enamel swam across like fish in summer water; copper roundels at the end pieces glimmered green in their fissures where sweat and man-heat had stained the metal. Lanolin greased her fingers, lightly pleasant, and made it easier to slip around 'Tagos' one good arm without tearing the fragile skin or flesh beneath. He looked more complete with it on, more obviously regal.

Breaca sat back on her heels and swept the sodden, crow-torn hair from his face. 'Made a king by gold and copper. He deserved better, at the end, at least.'

'If he serves us in death, he'll be glad of it.'

Cunomar spoke absently, his attention no longer on the dead, but on Cygfa's bay colt, which had been spooked by some crows. He was still dressed as he had been in the summer, in a sleeveless deerskin jerkin that made mockery of the cold and showed well the bear scars on his upper arms. At his left temple hung a hank of woven red horse hair with a single bear's tooth dangling, which had been a gift from Ardacos to mark the last day of the old year.

Breaca said, 'Cunomar? I, too, have a gift for you.'

He had not expected that, and was pleased. The elders of the Caledonii had taught him how to hide whatever he felt, but she saw the spark of surprise and the flush that followed and was glad she could still move him. She saw, too, and more openly, the consternation that followed. 'I brought nothing for you,' he said.

'I didn't expect you to. And you may not wish to accept what I offer, which is why we are speaking of it here, where we are overheard only by the dead. If you decide you don't want it, no-one living will know.'

That drew his full attention. Reaching into her belt pouch, she drew out a circlet of red gold, silver and copper. It was not exactly like 'Tagos' king-band, but so close that only a smith would know the difference.

'This is the first part,' she said. 'You should know that it was not only made for you. If we hadn't found 'Tagos' band, I would have given him this to hold in death through the winter; the Romans would never have known it wasn't his.' She held it out. 'Knowing that, if I offered it to you, would you still take it?'

'Gladly.' A smile lit his eyes so that, briefly, he was very much his father. 'I did say it was the most beautiful thing you ever made. I had always thought it wasted on 'Tagos.''

The band slid into place above his elbow. It was heavier than 'Tagos' and the end pieces were not enamelled discs, but fashioned in the shape of a bear's paw with room to fasten the kill-feathers, as had been done in the days of the far-distant ancestors.

Cunomar sat in silence as his mother fixed the five feathers of his kills on the left side. He would not look down when she had finished; he was too proud for that.

'You look more regal than 'Tagos has ever done,' Breaca said, and then, 'Cygfa painted and bound the feathers. Airmid helped me draw the wire. Graine carved the shapes for the end pieces. This is from all of us, to mark the start of a year that will be different from anything we have ever known. '

His head came up sharply. 'And so this is not the gift you feared I might turn down?'

'No.'

The wind was moving easterly again, and growing colder. Breaca blew on her hands to warm them.

Presently she said, 'After 'Tagos' death, it was agreed that we would wait until the bodies of the dead were found, and that I would go to Camulodunum in spring when the snow melts, to tell them of the tragedy of the king's death and how it has blighted our lives, to ask their help in returning his body so that we may mourn him properly, and to ask for their help in finding those responsible for his death. If the Romans believe us bereaved and not at fault, they will not send the legions to destroy the steading in revenge for Philus' death.'

Cunomar grinned, wryly. 'I don't think it was agreed. I think it was argued for three days and three nights and you had your way because you are the Boudica and even Ardacos, Cygfa, Dubornos and Airmid together cannot sway you when you set your mind to something so obviously dangerous.'

'You were the only one who didn't speak against it. Did you not agree with them?'

'Of course I agreed. It's madness you're going. If Rome does not believe you, you'll be the first to die and then who will lead the war host? Do you think the warriors will gather for Ardacos, or for the son of the Boudica whom they have never seen lead a single spear into battle? I don't. No king-band, however beautifully made, could make them trust me that much.'

He was not bitter, only speaking the truth as he saw it, and was probably right. He picked up a pebble and threw it at a crow that was teasing the bay colt. 'I would have argued against with the rest of them, but I'm your son. I can tell when your mind is set beyond changing. The Caledonii taught me never to waste my breath on arguments that couldn't be won.' He was not grinning any longer, and he did know her well. 'Is that your gift?' he asked. 'That you would not go?'

She nodded. 'That I would not go, and would ask you to go in my stead. You are the king's son. You speak Latin as well as I do. You have the courage and steadiness to say what is needful. If I can't go, and it does seem as if the gods and dreams – and common sense – are against it, then you are the best alternative. It may be that you were always the best anyway. If I asked it of you, would you risk your life in Camulodunum for us? For me?'

The elders of the Caledonii had done their job well. Only because he was her son did she see the blaze of unshaded joy behind Cunomar's eyes. Outwardly, his face was schooled to stillness, his answer measured. 'I would be more grateful than I have words to express,' he said. 'Can you tell me what made you change your mind?'

'Airmid. And then Ardacos, and then Dubornos and Cygfa together, and then Airmid again. They have all known me since before you were born, which perhaps gives them reason to believe that when my mind is set, it may still be altered.'

'Did they suggest I should go in your place?'

'Hardly. Each of them offered to do it alone, as I had done. It may be death, we all know that; no-one would ask that of anyone else. Except that now I ask it of you.'

'No. Now you offer it as the greatest gift you have ever given, or could give, to your son who still stands in the shadow of his parents and would prove himself a warrior. Which is why I accept, with great thanks.'

The rites of the year's-end passed quietly that year.

Once, the Eceni would have marked the end of autumn and the birth of the new child-winter with a killed ram and malted barley and games on river ice for the youths coming up to their long-nights and a ceremony afterwards in the roundhouse with all the dreamers and singers present to keep it safe.

'Tagos' steading – now Breaca's – had no roundhouse in which to gather and there had not been time to build one. It had also, by force of circumstance, become winter home to the forty-nine she-bear warriors who made Cunomar's new honour guard and even had they wished it, there was little food to spare for feasting. Thus, those who would fit gathered in Airmid's hut on the western edge of the steading, that was built most like a roundhouse and could take thirty seated if each did not mind rubbing knees tightly with the other.

They made a spiral, with Ardacos at the outer rim near the door, and Airmid in the centre by the only fire not yet extinguished. As the night progressed, the flames were allowed to die so that it seemed the dark leached in from the margins, pressing the light and the heat inwards and downwards to a dull, red glow in the base of the fire pit.

Close to midnight, Airmid cast a handful of leaves and roots on the embers, and more, until they smothered the last of the light and the harsh, heady smoke of their burning rose into the dark and spread out, touching the furthest of them, offering protection against the thinning boundaries of the night. When she spoke, her voice came from above, or behind, or echoed in both ears together.

'The year dies and is not yet reborn. In the space between is no-time, Briga's time, when she opens the gateways to the lands beyond life and the trackways from there to here lie clear. This night, of all nights, those who are gone may return without harm or censure, to meet again those who remain within life. Greet them, hear them, and, when the fire is relit, allow them to return whence they came.'

A collective shudder passed along the spiral, from centre to edge. The air became full, and emptied again, and where had been walls and a sense of safety was suddenly the hollowness of open space, as if each of those present had been walking in fog along a path, and had found themselves suddenly in clear skies on a narrow bridge across a mountain pass, with no handholds and a fathomless drop on either side to the ground below.

Breaca had met the dead too often to fear them, but on this night alone there was the chance she might find that Caradoc no longer lived, that he had died without her knowing and she would discover it only when his shade appeared, mourning the turning of her heart from the single-minded search for vengeance that had once consumed her. She feared that still, above many other things. Sitting in the black night with Graine pressed tight against her on one side, and sweat beading onto her arm from Cunomar on the other, she made herself breathe in Airmid's harsh smoke, the better to see the approaching dead.

The night remained empty. None of her dead appeared, not Caradoc, nor any of the ancestors who might have been drawn by the torc at her neck. Darkness stretched like a tunnel, punctuated by hollow inhalations of those who had been visited. In the dark, she heard someone say, 'Eneit?' and thought it was Lanis, until Cunomar shuddered and she realized that he was weeping, and was glad that he could do so.

No-one else spoke, neither human nor once-human, and, in time, the fire came again. At a signal felt but not heard, Cunomar cleared the embers of the last year's blaze and Graine, as youngest present, laid tinder on the stone base for the new one. Airmid struck a spark and fanned it and the flames ate shaved bark and dried grass and the hanks of ewe's wool and the tail hairs of brood mares that were sent to Briga to ask for good birthings.

Women who thought they might be pregnant, or who planned to become so that night, leaned forward and gave three of their own hairs to the fire. The men who thought they might father such children cut a nail paring from the first finger of each hand and gave that, to ask for health in their seed. There were many such pairings; a child conceived on the night of the un-year was fortunate. Born after midsummer, when the harvest had been taken in, it would find no hardship until winter when everyone suffered similarly – or might not, if the coming year turned as Breaca intended.

Airmid said, 'Next year's-end, we may see us free of Rome and all it carries,' and gave voice to everyone's thought.

Those gathered left soon after that, carrying lit torches of hawthorn staves dipped in sheep's fat, and shavings of oak bark and dried rowan leaves with which to start their own fires, never to let them out until the next year's turning.

Breaca alone remained behind. She banked the fire for morning, and called in Stone, who had been left outside for fear the dead would not approach him.

Airmid came back with the water carriers, and then both brought in the accumulation of urns and beakers and sealed jugs of plants and berries that had been moved outside, the better to accommodate the she-bears.

They sat a while by the firelight, not ready to sleep. The after-taste of dream smoke flavoured the air. Airmid cast on other leaves, sparingly; rosemary and sage and sharp mint, so that the scents freshened and the walls between the worlds began to feel secure again. She was wearing her neckpiece of silvered frog's bones that was older than Cunomar, older than Cygfa, older even than the presence of Rome. Smoke coiled about it, and her, so that she could have been a girl again, or infinitely old; a long-dead ancestor keeping care of the still-living.

She poured water, and something else, into a beaker and offered it across the fire to Breaca.

'Caradoc did not come to you?' she asked.

'No.' Only Airmid would ask, only Airmid could fully be answered. 'I would like to think that I would know before this if he were dead, but each year I am never sure until the night is over. Then I can forget for half a year, and worry again before the next time.' Breaca fed Stone the leavings of a roast hare and let him lick the grease from her fingers. He lay across her feet, a solid re-assurance. She said, 'Did Gwyddhien come for you?'

'Yes. She has come each year since her death. But less now than she did.'

There was pain in that, in the asking of it and hearing the answer. They both moved to lay a stick on the fire so that for a moment they were close. The light became a little stronger, the night a little warmer, the dead a little farther away.

After a while, Airmid said, 'Cunomar wears well his new arm-band. Did you ask him to go to Camulodunum in spring?'

'Yes, and he accepted.' Breaca drank the flavoured water Airmid had given her. It tasted of mugwort and burdock and melted snow. Letting the bitterness and the cold settle on her teeth, she said, 'He's the best choice, I do know that. He's the king's son, and such things matter to Rome. He speaks Latin well and has met the Emperor Claudius, which means he knows how the Romans conduct their formalities, and—'

'And the risk is enormous, and still you have to let him take it.' Airmid's foot reached to touch the side of her knee; a small thing, and a world of comfort. 'He's your son as much as Caradoc's. He has grown into what you both have given him, but he has things he needs to prove, to himself as much as to you.'

'I know. He said as much. But he's travelling and fighting alone, and shouldn't be. It's the care of the dreamer that makes the warrior. The elder grandmother taught us that and we have lived it since. Cunomar has no dreamer.'

'Graine would dream for him, willingly. She's almost old enough to sit her long-nights. It could be done in the spring and she could ride with him after.'

'Hardly.' Breaca laughed shortly. 'Graine hates violence. I can't imagine her riding into any battle willingly. In any case, Cunomar needs someone in whose shadow he has not spent his life.' The burdock was working its way into her blood, sharpening sight and sound and touch. She leaned back on a wall and felt the weave of her tunic as a lattice across her back, and the dry serpent's weight of the torc at her neck, and the press of Airmid's foot which was against her calf now, not her knee, because she had moved back.

She let her hand rest on the dreamer's ankle, feeling the small pulse across the top. It was regular and rhythmic and speeded a little under her touch. Not entirely steadily, she said, 'He needs someone who can be for him what you were to me. And have always been.'

From the dark, after a pause, Airmid said, 'Thank you.'

Suddenly, they were shy as children in each other's company, and had never been. Both stirred the fire and added wood, shifting the balance so that it had more fuel but burned less brightly.

Presently, because she needed to speak, Breaca said, 'Cygfa sleeps alone still. I had thought Braint might have been killed and might come to her as Eneit came to Cunomar, but there was no-one.'

Airmid said, 'Cygfa carries her wounds deeper than her brother. And Dubornos carries his wounds openly, the greatest of which is that he loves Cygfa and she does not love him. They lived closely together in Rome and she cares for him as she cares for Cunomar. I think she will not see him hurt further and so keeps chaste because of it.'

'And yet if she loved another, she would find ways not to hurt Dubornos. That alone would not stop her.'

'I know, but she doesn't allow herself to love. Cunomar is desperate for it, and seeks only one who can match him. Cygfa hurts still, deeply, and seeks no-one, believing herself stronger like that.'

'Could you heal her?'

Airmid grimaced. 'Only if she asked for it, and she will not. I spoke to her while we were on Mona, when you were hunting legionaries and we were alone. She walked away and I haven't tried again since. Her pain is her own, to heal as she chooses. As is ours.'

Such a small phrase, to open the world. The pulse under Breaca's fingers remained steady. The burdock had cleared the day's clutter from her mind, perhaps the year's clutter, or longer. For a night – for this night – she had no need to lie awake and plan the future. She poured some of the melt-water onto her cupped palms and rinsed her face with it, then set down the beaker, carefully, away from the fire.

Speaking slowly, navigating among the rocks of her words, she said, 'It was not to avoid hurting 'Tagos that I have slept alone these past years, but because of Caradoc.'

'I know.'

'And you the same because of Gwyddhien.'

'Yes.'

Through the three years since Gwyddhien's death, they had

never spoken of this. Breaca nudged a log deeper into the fire. Lit by new flames, she asked, 'Does she expect it of you still?'

'She has never expected it at all. As I am certain Caradoc never expected it of you.'

Airmid's eyes were entirely black. They searched Breaca's face, across and across. She said, 'It takes time to heal the pain of loss, and then it takes time to heal the memory of the pain, and the belief that honour requires us to hold that pain for ever. Then it takes more time to find that the loves of our past can still be loved, that something new – or something old, rewoven – does not diminish them. And then while we may know that to be true for others, while we see it in others and want to speak of it daily, it is harder to see it equally in ourselves.'

They had gone too far, now, to pretend. Breaca said, 'Did you think I should take someone else to bed after Caradoc?'

Airmid laughed. 'It surprises me daily that you have not.'

'But are you glad of it?'

That was when she knew, when she felt the steady beat of Airmid's pulse become unsteady, telling a truth that she might not have believed in words, or perhaps never dared to ask.

Shakily, Airmid said, 'Before tonight, I would have told myself not. Tonight I am very glad. Very glad indeed,' and reached a hand across the fire.

It was hard to breathe then, or to think with any clarity. The fire was between them, and then not between them, and then the beakers, so carefully put out of the way, were spilled onto the rushes of the floor, and neither of them cared because they were no longer dressed and cool water on one side balanced the heat of the fires from the other and in between was the endless mystery and wonder of touch, of skin on skin, of palms meeting, and hips and breasts and lips and teeth and hair and all of life resting in the blink of another's eye.

Breaca had forgotten how it could be, and, remembering, could not imagine how it had been possible to forget, as if the parched could forget water, or the starving forget the feast laid out for the taking. Her fingers traced contours her memory had long discarded, and brought them back again, renewed, with taste and touch and the heaviness of another body above her, and then below her, and the honey-salt slickness, binding them close.

They stayed awake through the night of the un-year, rediscovering what was old and inventing what could be new, and came to morning wound together like hound whelps among the sleeping-hides, drowsily.

Breaca drifted into sleep, and woke again and lay watching the thread of smoke coil up through the hole in the thatch, closing one eye and then the other, to make it shift back and forth, as her mind shifted with it, caught in the tangles of old images.

Airmid leaned over and kissed her. 'Good morning. May the year grow well within you.'

Breaca smiled into the kiss. 'And in you.' All lovers said that on the first morning of the child-year. Tradition demanded it.

Airmid laid her hand, splay-fingered, on Breaca's belly and tipped her head, as if listening. 'Something has taken seed in the night and it can't be a child, so it must be a dream. Can it be told?'

'Easily, but I'm not sure there's anything you can do.' Breaca took the hand and kissed the fingers, and then the knuckles, and then the soft place in the centre of the palm where her tongue stayed to trace shapes onto the lines the gods had put there. 'Unless you can become an iron-seeker and find me raw iron in Eceni lands and then learn to be a smith and help me turn the iron into blades for the war host, and can find a way to keep the legions from the great-house while we—'

'Breaca, stop. Don't think of that. Today, this morning, for now, don't think.' Airmid's hands gripped tight, folding fingers into fingers, holding her close. 'You are not alone in this. You don't have to fight the wars and arm the warriors and plan everything alone. You know that. Cunomar will go to Camulodunum and he will do well. We have ways to find iron and a smith and I can help with that. And for now, we have this, a gift of the gods. It doesn't have to be squandered.' Airmid kissed her forehead and her temples, and her eyelids, slowly, dizzyingly, with a different hunger from the night.

The last kiss landed carefully, placed in the hollow of her neck, where the two ends of the torc stood apart. 'Whatever happens, I will love you. For today, for now, can we let that be enough?'

XXVIII

'I BRING GIFTS. GIFTS FOR THE BOUDICA'S ARMY. LET ME IN!'

The hammering on the gates matched the hammering in the forge and it was only by chance that Graine passed the knot hole and saw the shape silhouetted against the snow outside. She hauled the oak bar from its sockets and stood back as a broad, grey-haired woman drove a team of five broad horses through the gates. Allowed to stop, the beasts stood buckle-kneed and steaming in the falling snow. The wagon they had drawn rolled half a hand forward and then sank to its axles in ground that was not overly soft.

'Thank you. I was beginning to think the Eceni had abandoned the guest laws in their quest to be free of Rome.'

The broad wagonwoman leered her thanks. Her face twisted unpleasantly and she swayed as she sat. When she threw the reins at the head of her lead horse and jumped down, she stumbled as she landed.

Not since the worst of 'Tagos' winters had Graine seen anyone walk abroad the worse for drink. The guest laws made no provision for a drunken woman driving her horses into the steading.

Chewing her lip, Graine looked at the ground, and then to the forge, but her mother was hammering sword blades and was too far away to reach. In any case, she was too busy to be disturbed by the minor difficulty of a drunken guest; they were two months from spring and the gathering of the war host and there was the limited stock of iron to be made into blades and the Boudica the only smith in the steading. She could not be called from the forge for anything less than the sight of a legion marching up the trackways.

The problem must be dealt with by other means, therefore. Looking again, Graine saw that the woman did not smell of either ale or wine, but of wet wool and wetter leather and spent, sweating horses. She leaned against the side of the wagon for support, holding it with her left hand. Her right hand, shoulder and hip were all crooked, as if they had once been broken and then set later, badly. Her hair was not entirely grey; threads ran through that were as richly red as the Boudica's.

Without the leer, her face would have been handsome. On the shoulder of her cloak, hidden in folds of sodden wool, was a brooch in the shape of the boar, the sign of the Dumnonii, who fought Rome in the far south-west with all the tenacity and savagery of the beast from which they took their mark.

Put together, all these things gave a name as clearly as if it had been spoken aloud. Graine felt herself flush. Shamefully late, she gave the salute of an apprentice to an elder dreamer of great power and said, 'Welcome to Gunovar, daughter to Gunovic, who gave his life for Macha at the invasion battles.'

The rest of what she knew ran silently in her mind, and doubtless could be read on her face: 'You were one of the foremost dreamers of your people until you spent four days under the care of the legions' inquisitors. Your warriors stormed the fortress to free you, losing half their number in the battle. The songs of that have reached us, but not the tales of how the legions acted afterwards, or of how you dream now, with your body broken.'

'Indeed.'

The woman's leer was weighted now with irony, all turned inward, none of it for Graine. It was not clear if she answered the salute, the welcome, or all that had not been said.

It was hard to look at her face, knowing how it might have been before the burns; easier to watch her eyes, where the pain and the humour met and each became more mellow. There was a great deal of humour. It occurred to Graine that Ardacos would like this woman, and not for the dryness of her humour alone.

Gunovar returned the dreamers' salute with some elegance,

managing in a single movement to acknowledge Graine's relative youth, while implying a depth of dreaming equal to her own.

She said, 'And you are Graine, hare-dreamer and daughter to the Boudica. I am honoured to meet you. Could you see to my horses while I talk to your mother? They've drawn me bravely for nearly a month and I would not have them die for lack of care now that— Ah, you're here, finally. I wondered how long it would take for you to notice you had company.'

Very few people spoke to the Boudica in that tone of voice. Fewer, since she had taken the torc after 'Tagos' death. Airmid might have done so still when they were alone, but nobody else that Graine knew of. She looked to her mother, and saw that she was grinning, and that the incomer, therefore, was that rarity to be treasured: a genuine friend.

'Did you? That would be why you announced yourself so fulsomely.' Breaca had reached the cart horses and was rubbing them behind the ears where the harness had chafed. Stooping, she ran her hand down the legs of the sweat-riven bay that was closest.

'I thought my daughter was greeting you admirably. She's too well mannered to tell you that you've ruined a good horse and it will take us until halfway through summer to heal it.'

'And you're not.'

Breaca hoisted herself up on the spoke of a wheel, reaching into the wagon. 'No. The draught horses of the Dumnonii are legend. What have you brought that makes it worth harming one of your greatest— Ah. Did the gods whisper in your ear or has news of our need reached the south-west?'

The sides of the cart were too tall for Graine to look inside directly. All she could see in those first moments after the oiled cover slid away was the wash of dull blue-grey reflected in her mother's eyes and the gratitude and reverent joy, as of a lifetime's prayers answered, in her voice. She did not have to be a dreamer to know what was inside.

Gunovar waved a hand lightly, as if driving a year's worth of iron across the land past two legions in the dead of winter were nothing of note. 'I'm not so closed to the dreaming as you might think. Airmid sent whisperings and I heard them, but in any case, word of war travels on the wind and the wind has been strong this winter. News of the Boudica's army has reached those who would support it. To fight Rome and win, you need iron; so much is obvious even had Nemain not walked through my nights. This is all we have. The rest we need for our own battles. Will it be enough?'

'I'll make it enough.' Breaca jumped down to stand in the wagon, ankle deep in iron. She lifted a bar and held it up to the wind and the snow, sighting along its length as if it were already a blade.

Gunovar stood by, watching, and was watched in her turn by Graine. The broad woman was broken and not fully mended, but she had the strength of mind and flesh to drive a wagon train through mud and ice alone. She had, in fact, the build of a smith.

Breaca already knew it. She crouched at the edge of the wagon and held the raw iron across her hands, like a blade. Passing it down to the woman below, she said, 'Gunovar, your father was one of the greatest smiths of his day. I have seen your work and you have his skill, if not more so. Will you stay and help me in the making? As much as iron, I need another smith. The legions slaughtered ours when they broke the blades in Scapula's time. I can't make all this into swords and spears before the fighting begins in spring.'

Gunovar smiled, and her face was almost even. 'If you listen to the hero tales, you could fashion an army of blades in one day from the fires of your forge and then fight Rome single-handed. Fortunately, I don't believe all of the tales, only those parts I hear first hand. Of course you can't arm your war host on your own. Why else do you think I have come?'

With Gunovar's help, the production of weapons resumed faster than before, although with pauses now to train the she-bears in their use. Graine had been right: Ardacos did like the broad woman with the broken body, and not only for the dryness of her wit. Together, these two took Cunomar's honour guard and began to fashion them into the core of an army.

Two months after the midwinter night of the all-dark, Breaca took a break from her hammering and called the honour guard into council. Forty-nine youths gathered in the great-house where they had taken their spear-trials, flushed with the promise of action. They were not disappointed when each was given an armband, made precisely to fit, with the she-bear stamped on one side and the serpent-spear that was the mark of the Boudica on the other. With this as their sign of surety, she sent each back to the village, steading or settlement that had once been home, and thence on to all those neighbouring.

Each bore the same message: 'Breaca nic Graine, first born of the royal line, summons the warriors of the Eceni nation to gather at the site of the horse fair by the first new moon after the spring equinox. The she-bears will guide those who do not know the way, or are wary of winter travel. Snow is your best protection. Travel early and in small numbers and pray that the winter holds and the legions do not move early from their forts.'

Thus was called into being the first war host of the Eceni to gather since the Roman invasion.

XXIX

IN THE WESTERN MOUNTAINS, CLOSE TO THE DREAMERS' ISLE OF Mona, the fighting began before the end of winter.

Snow lay knee deep; thicker in the valleys and thinner on the shoulders of the mountains where the wind carved it close. The peaks were frozen ice caps, inaccessible to man and beast. None of these prevented Rome's auxiliary cavalry from making increasingly wide-ranging forays into the mountain ranges west of their fortress base, or the warriors of Mona from attacking them whenever and wherever possible.

Wrapped in an oiled cloak for warmth, Valerius lay face down on packed ice under the notional cover of a wind-stripped hawthorn and looked down on the valley below where a Gaulish cavalry wing had made camp the night before. Dawn was breaking, bright and cold, so that the light was silver, with tints of blue and gold as the sun burned the horizon. A late mist rose and thinned and what had been a sea of grey became, slowly, lines of tents in perfect order, with two larger ones for the officers at one end.

At the end opposite these, nearer the neck of the valley, fifty riderless horses milled restlessly in a makeshift enclosure. To either side, small moments of violence made flurries in the mist and presently, when Valerius looked, two sentries of the Gaulish cavalry lay supine in the snow, leaking redly from throat and groin.

A white cloth flapped once near the tents behind the enclosure. To Valerius' left, a figure edged out from the lee of a boulder and lifted a knife blade high. There was barely light enough to see by; the polished iron flickered, greyly, but enough, signalling safety, and permission to proceed.

At the signal, two shapes darted forward from the tumble of rocks on the other side of the valley. The ropes of the makeshift corral sagged and separated where they had been cut. When a bundle of rotting wolf skin and fat was hurled into their midst, the entire herd had a clear route of escape. The panicked drum of their hooves filled the length of the valley and the mountains beyond.

No man could sleep through that, and the Gauls, if they had any sense, had been sleeping lightly and were not drunk. Within moments, the tents began to empty. On the hillside opposite, three warriors ran lightly up away from the enclosure and the bodies on either side. They were out of range long before the first javelins were hurled at them.

There was no need any longer for secrecy. The figure on Valerius' left was Braint of the Brigantes, in the Boudica's absence Warrior of Mona, leader of this raid and the half-dozen that had gone before.

She spat on the ground in thanks to the gods and squirmed backwards and out over the crest of the hill to where three other warriors waited at a small, smouldering fire. They left on her signal, skidding light-footed down the scree, bearing ropes of woven rawhide and pouches of winter stored corn and twists of salt with which to catch up the panicked cavalry horses when they tired and came to rest beyond the mouth of the valley.

None of them, neither Braint nor those who followed her, acknowledged Valerius' presence, nor did he expect them to. He stood up, shaking the snow from his cloak, and stretched, tentatively, easing cold joints.

His shoulders no longer hurt, which still amazed him. From the moment at the end of autumn when Longinus had sent him, broken and beaten, back to Mona, every part of him had screamed in pain. Bellos had taken charge of his healing, under instruction from Luain mac Calma. Through the slow months of foul infusions, sipped day and night, of poultices and bindings and the indignities of nursing, there had been a perverse satisfaction in finding first hand that he had been right and that, even blind, the Belgic youth made an exceptionally good healer.

Until midwinter, Valerius' bones had been so bruised and his muscles so torn that simply to sleep through the first part of the night without waking, weeping, had been an achievement. After the solstice, with the gradual lightening of the days, the breaks and the ripped ligaments had begun to heal so that if his sleep was broken, it was not by pain.

Even so, standing on the mountainside, the memory of the inquisitors' chamber sprang too readily to the surface of his mind. It was hard to look down on the gradually diminishing chaos among the cavalrymen in the valley, to hear the orders shouted in Latin and watch the men form a line and march forward, without feeling again the cringing concussion of fists and feet and staves that made him want to curl into a ball and hide.

He made himself stand and watch, and not flinch as the Gaulish cavalrymen, deprived of their horses, walked towards but not into the ambush set at the narrow neck of the valley where the wide plain became a gully. They stopped in a huddle, waiting. They were not stupid; the question was not whether an ambush had been laid, only by how many they were outnumbered and whether the natives had confined themselves to spears and boulders, or whether they kept slingers among them, against whom there was no real defence except distance.

There were slingers; Valerius had watched them leave Mona and had a fair idea of where they were stationed in the snowy scrub of the gully's walls. Even as the officers conferred, the first slingstone cracked down from the high ground and the first of the auxiliaries died. The sound came after the sight, blustered by the wind, so that the man had already fallen and his ghost walked loose before the sharp peal of his cry floated up to the high ground above.

Valerius turned away, reluctant to watch yet another ghost wander lost through the heather; the world was too full of those, and the gods within him had not yet shown how they might all be laid to rest. Alone, he caught up his horse and set her gently down the mountain towards the ferry. A stone rattled after him on the scree and might have been an accident, not a slingstone sent to unseat him.

*

355

'Efnís, it's not going to work. I am not impugning Braint's courage, or the willingness of Mona's warriors to fight, I am simply adding up numbers. Suetonius Paulinus was made governor precisely because he knows about mountain warfare. He has been told to make safe the west or die in the attempt and he doesn't intend to die. He has two legions and all their cavalry: about thirteen thousand men, every one of whom will lay down his own life to save their governor's skin. You have a little short of four thousand warriors, six if every dreamer and child over the age of five picks up a weapon. In the past month, Braint's raids have killed fifty-three auxiliaries, for the loss of six warriors. This is good. It is laudable. It is great credit to the courage of your Warrior and those she leads. It is not enough.'

'Did I ask for your opinion?'

Uniquely, Efnís was alone in Mona's great-house, standing semi-naked in the waist-deep trench of a fire pit, digging out a winter's ash. Luain mac Calma, yet again, had taken ship for Hibernia, or perhaps Gaul, nobody knew which. In his absence, Efnís was Elder. His word was law on Mona and throughout the lands where dreamers still held sway. That he took it upon himself to clean out the winter's leavings said more about him than he chose to believe.

Without being asked, Valerius shed his tunic and jumped into the trench. He lifted clear a charred hawthorn log and laid it to one side.

When he was not expressly invited to leave, he said, 'You have never asked for my opinion. But Luain mac Calma wishes me to be on Mona and so I am on Mona. If I am to stay here, I would rather not die in a pointless battle against men I once led.'

'Because you still care for them?' Efnís did not spit, but might as well have done.

Valerius paused for a moment, his cupped palms full of ash. Even in the poor light, his face was unusually bland. He said, 'I do care for them, yes; they were good men. But more because I know how they are trained and what they can do and I know that, however great the courage of Braint's warriors, however profound the dreaming you build, you cannot stop fifteen thousand trained infantry from marching over the whole of Mona and killing every living thing they meet. If you attempt it simply to prove me wrong, the deaths of your people will lie on your conscience. Their ghosts will wait for yours when the inquisitors finally let you die.'

It was the first time he had been so plain. Efnís turned to stare at him. His eyes raked across the scars, new and old, on the other's body as if they spoke a truth his words did not. 'What would you have us do?' he asked.

In the god-space of Valerius' heart was the image that had rested there since Longinus had spoken his treachery: of dreamers and children on ships on a quiet sea. He had spoken of it to mac Calma, and urged him to act, and, instead, the Elder had taken ship at midwinter, when no sane man sailed, and had not come home. He had not, apparently, thought to share the vision with Efnís before he left.

Valerius said, 'I would beg, borrow and steal every ship that can hold more than five people and start evacuating the entire population of Mona to Hibernia.'

'What?' Efnís' laugh was lost in the vast space of the great-house. 'Don't be ridiculous. Where in Hibernia could be put six thousand people? What are we supposed to feed them? Where will they sleep?'

They were standing at either end of the trench, with only white ash between them. Valerius leaned back and dusted the crumbs from his hands. 'What will you feed them and where will they sleep when the legions have razed Mona to the ground? Start calling in merchant ships from Hibernia; they owe you their livelihood, they'll come if you ask it. You can take the seed corn, the cattle, the in-lamb ewes you would have kept here. Hibernia has land to spare and you can produce more corn than you eat. You will be taking the full elder council of Mona, with two thousand dreamers, healers and singers and as many trained warriors as survive. For that, the Hibernians will welcome you as their brothers and sisters.'

'What of the great-house? It has stood since before the time of the ancestors. If we leave, it will be destroyed.'

'Then it can be rebuilt after Rome has gone.'

Valerius spoke the greatest sacrilege in the place of greatest sanctity and the gods did not strike him dumb. Efnís stared and opened his mouth and shut it again.

Gently, Valerius said, 'Efnís – think. Luain mac Calma isn't here and you have people to protect. Paulinus is massing an army on the mainland that is almost as big as the one that invaded Britannia nearly twenty years ago. When they have taken the western mountains, they will commandeer every floating craft to make a way across the straits. You don't have the luxury of time.'

Pulling himself out of the pit, Valerius stepped round to Efnís' side. The wall behind was alive with carvings of other ages. The newest was his, the outline of a hound with the wood still white beneath. His hound rarely showed itself fully on Mona; the carving carried the essence of it, so that his hands felt more alive if he touched it. To abandon it, to feel it burn in the legions' conflagration, would hurt more than he cared to imagine.

Efnís was still in the trench, his head lower than a child's. Crouching down, so that their eyes were level and soul could meet soul, Valerius said gently, 'It's the elders who make the house great, not the wood or the thatch or even the carvings along the roof beams. I can carve another hound. I can't teach the lore of Mona to a new generation of dreamers because I don't know it. If you're dead, and the great-house still stands, will the gods thank you for it, do you think?'

They had been friends once, long ago, when the Eceni had been all of the world and Rome a name to frighten children. Beneath all the taints of betrayal and the vengeful dead, a thread remained to let Valerius read in Efnís' eyes the moment when the impossible became not only possible, but unavoidable.

It took longer for Efnís to acknowledge, and longer still for him to speak aloud. When he did, it was with the desperation of one cornered, who still has the power to hurt.

'Braint will never agree to withdraw the warriors,' he said, at last. 'She will die defending Mona and those who follow her will stand over her body until the last of them is cut down. They would have done the same for your sister. They still will, if the Boudica ever returns to take her place amongst them.'

'BRAINT'S GONE. HER HORSE CAME BACK WITHOUT HER. WE searched for her body all morning and couldn't find it.'

The news was delivered by the slinger who had led the ambush Valerius had watched. A blunt, broad-shouldered Siluran youth, he looked barely old enough to lift a spear and yet bore the scars of five years' fighting. He stood on the jetty with the ferry rope still in his hand and only the teeth bitten hard into his lower lip kept him from weeping.

Half a month had passed since the dawn raid on the cavalry horses and Valerius' conversation with Efnís that had followed. In that time, the calm life of Mona had disintegrated into barely ordered chaos.

Luain mac Calma had returned from Hibernia, bringing with him a small flotilla of fishing boats, as if Valerius' suggested evacuation had been planned in detail since the autumn. The process of moving entire families, with their goods, horses, sheep and cattle, stretched the organizational powers of the elders beyond all sanity, but a third of the population had made the crossing and been welcomed by the Hibernians and the ships were sailing twice daily with full payloads to make safe the rest as fast as wind and water would allow.

There was no guarantee that they would be in time. Spring had come early to the west, on the back of a warm westerly wind blown in off the sea that had scoured the snow from all but the highest peaks. Across the straits on the mainland, the meticulous preparations of Suetonius Paulinus, by Nero's pleasure fifth governor of Britannia, were reaching a culmination, watched with increasing anxiety by the scouts.

Most recently, two wings of auxiliary cavalry had made camp closer to the straits than any had dared come before. Spies reported that their orders were to flush out of the mountain passes all the warriors of Mona, and kill them. In the first, at least, they were succeeding.

Luain mac Calma picked up a stone from the shore and sent it skipping across the choppy water of the strait. It bounced five times and sank. If the gods spoke in its movement, only he could read it. Grimacing, he turned to his left. 'Valerius? What will they do with her?'

'Take her to the inquisitors at the fortress, unless their orders are otherwise.'

Valerius stared over the water and ran his fingers through the coarse pelt of his hound. The beast had returned as the first boats were leaving for Hibernia, as if it were required to witness the departure of the people from Mona. Whatever the reason for its return, Valerius had greeted it as he would have done Hail and revelled for a while in its company as a friend among the unfriendly. Still, it had brought also a sense of foreboding that he could not shake off.

Walking with it openly at heel as the evacuations progressed, he had felt increasingly hollow, as he used to do in the days before battle. Because of it, he had been watching the strait for Braint's homecoming and so had been first to see the warriors race down the slopes to the ferry and then first again to see that Braint's horse was with them but carried no rider. What had surprised him most was that he cared.

The sea ruffled under the breeze. The ferry jigged at its mooring, held fast by Sorcha, the ferrywoman, who had seen too many warriors ride out and not come back to let it touch her now. A wave of nausea hit the back of Valerius' throat, and was not only premature seasickness. Over the winter, while his body had healed, mac Calma had taught Valerius how better to hear the many whispers of Nemain. He felt her touch now, in the closeness of the hound and the stillness of the day, but it was the sudden presence of Mithras in his mind that brought the sickness.

To the young Siluran slinger, he said, 'How was she taken, can you tell me exactly?'

The boy fell gladly into talking, as if by speaking aloud he could rewrite the past. 'A wing of cavalry was camped at the head of the long pass on the other side of the mountains there—' His arm waved behind to the taller peaks hidden in morning mist. 'We were cutting loose their horses as we always do and Braint was on the hillside. She never gave the signal for the ambush so we didn't attack. In any case, the horses we set loose were not the cavalry's best. They had kept those hidden in their tents and mounted as soon as they heard the others run off. Even if Braint had given the signal we could not have attacked; they came through us too fast. Then she didn't meet us at the hawthorns as she should have done and when we went to look for her, her horse was there but she was gone.'

The boy pressed the heels of his hands together and stared at the them. He said, 'They haven't taken her anywhere yet. They rode straight back to the camp. Limarnos is watching. He'll set fire to the heather as a signal if they leave and she is with them.'

A watch fire would be seen equally by both sides, and be equally plain in its meaning. As if he were the commanding officer, and the boy a new recruit in need of encouragement, Valerius said, 'That was well done. Which troop were the auxiliaries? Did you see a standard?'

The youth was too young to know the details of Valerius' treachery. He frowned and thought for a moment and then, 'They were Thracian. The leader rode under the standard of the bull, like the mark of the ancestors, but painted in red on a grey ground, Mona's colour.'

'Thank you.' The mark had been Valerius' once, and kept by Longinus. The war hound pressed against Valerius' thigh and he laid his hand on its head for comfort.

Before the pain of the following silence became too great, mac Calma said, quietly, 'They were trained by the best, to be the best, that's why Paulinus is using them now. Will they question Braint themselves?'

Valerius looked up at the high peaks on the far side of the strait. After a while, he said, 'Not unless they have changed beyond recognition since I led them. Longinus would never offer violence to a woman, except if she came at him in battle. In normal circumstances, they would take her back to the fortress for questioning by the inquisitors. If they have not done so yet, it is because they have orders to hold her here, where we might attempt a rescue.'

'Good. I had hoped that might be the case. Thank you.'

A second stone skipped across the water. It bounced nine times and the spray of its last dash floated high after it had sunk. Luain mac Calma, Elder of Mona, watched as Manannan's white horses closed over the place where it had been.

Slipping his hands in the folds of his cloak, he turned away from the water. His eyes sought Valerius' and held them, and he was Nemain and Mithras together, and something deeper than both, with more pain.

He said, 'It seems we have a moment's grace, a gift of the gods, in which to act. The governor must not find out about the evacuation of our people to Hibernia. It would be best if Braint could be returned to us whole and unhurt, but if that is not possible, better for her and for us that she not reach the fortress of the Twentieth alive. Valerius, will you take what warriors you need and see to it?'

The choosing of the Warrior of Mona was a lengthy process, traditionally overseen by the full elder council. The position was not given on a whim to a man who had betrayed, slain and delivered into questioning more warriors and dreamers than he or anyone else chose to count.

Nevertheless, Luain mac Calma was sworn Elder of Mona and his word was law. If he chose to give leadership of the warriors to a man who had once led the enemy cavalry, if he chose to make this man, in effect, Warrior-in-waiting without consultation or explanation, no other could gainsay him. That did not mean that the remaining spears, blades and slingers of Mona had to give such a man their trust or their care. Only the hope of returning Braint alive led them to accept Valerius' command and that hope was far from certain.

The morning fell to frantic planning during which Valerius found that he knew more warriors by name and ability than he would have imagined. More important, he was coming to know which would follow him grudgingly, but well, and which would try to kill him out of hand at the first opportunity. The hound walked at his side as he strode from the great-house to the armouries and back again. Those warriors who acknowledged it were, he found, those he could trust most. The few who made the ward against evil were the most dangerous.

Just after noon, he called a meeting in the great-house, summoning the captains of the shield-groups, so that each warrior was represented, even if the place could not house them all. He had the door hides pegged back and the wall wattles lifted. Light streamed in, brighter than the fires.

He could have walked among them; Breaca would certainly have done so. Valerius, the ex-auxiliary officer, chose to stand on a levelled oak stump, so that he was lifted head and shoulders above the rest and could be seen from the back. He wore chain mail and an old cavalry cloak, stolen in Caradoc's time and used in ambushes, and his banner hung behind him on the wall. He had painted the mark of the war hound on cloth in the red of unclotted blood on a grey background and had hung it between two willow stalks so that it could be seen from all parts of the great-house.

If the shape had been a little different, it would have matched exactly the red bull of the Thracian cavalry under which Valerius had once fought for Rome. When he mounted his podium, he met a silence so heavy the air was poisoned. Not one warrior present doubted who he had been; they had not expected him so to revel in it.

Valerius had addressed troops before battles greater than this one; he knew how to touch them, however much they loathed him. Casting his voice to the outer edges of the gathering, he said, 'You know who I have been. You know also what the Elder has made me. I am sworn to him as you are; we have no choice in this. Until Braint returns to take her place as Warrior – and I wish that as much as you do – you are oath-bound to follow me.'

So much they already knew. Valerius watched how they reacted and revised again his notion of whom he could trust.

He said, 'Braint is taken and must not reach the fortress of the Twentieth alive. We bring her back, or we leave her dead. Those are our choices.'

They must have known that as well, but they did not want to hear it from him. If their wishing it could have killed him, Valerius would have fallen dead.

It did not, and he went on. 'The cavalry wing is not camped in the long pass by accident. This is a trap and only the first half has been sprung. They were the bait that captured Braint, and she is the bait for a greater prize – which is you. The governor knows the courage and honour of the sworn spears of Mona and he seeks to destroy you so that he may take the island safely.'

Valerius flattered them and they despised him the more for it. He said, 'They will, therefore, be waiting for us – but perhaps not only them. It may be that this is the greatest trap of all. We have to consider that this may be the beginning of the final assault on Mona: that the governor seeks to draw the entire mass of our warriors out into a single pass, allowing the legions to march on Mona unopposed. I do not intend to let that happen.'

One or two of those listening had considered this, most had not. Valerius felt the texture of the air change. The hound came to his side and more of them acknowledged it than before.

Valerius put his hands behind his back. As Caesar addressing his troops, he said, 'There are three paths clear before us: first, we can bring Braint back alive, which is the best we can hope for. If that fails, then second, we can kill her and know she died cleanly, which would not be good, but would also not be the worst that could happen. Or, third, we could abandon her and instead expend our lives in the defence of this island and all that is on it, allowing the evacuation to continue until it is complete or the last of us falls, whichever comes first.'

He spoke at the end, not into uproar – such a thing could not happen in the great-house of Mona – but into such exhalations of distress that his last words were as lost as if they had shouted him down.

When the space was quiet he spoke again, dropping his voice so that they had to strain to hear, and the last of those shuffling was forced into silence.

'There is a fourth choice: that we divide the warriors of Mona, that the greater part of you remain here, defending the strait against the legions. If we do this, then a smaller party of only six hundred warriors will ride with me to the valley where Braint is held, offering the cavalry full battle. With your help, this is the path I intend to take.'

He had them now, as the hare has the hound, focused beyond all distraction. The quality of their attention could not have been more different. Valerius raised his hand and lowered it stiffly like a blade. The edge split the air in front of him, making a line through their ranks. Unconsciously they swayed aside from it with the greater part to his right.

He addressed himself first to this larger part. 'You have the defence of Mona. I leave you under the command of Tethis of the Caledonii. Tethis, both sides of the strait must be protected. How you achieve that is up to you.'

It was a popular choice. Tethis was widely believed to be Braint's natural successor, the Warrior-in-waiting whose position Valerius had usurped. He would have liked to have kept her with him, but she was one of the few who could be trusted to balance courage with pragmatism in defence of the island. Tethis would not waste lives in pointless charges or hopeless acts of heroism, but she would still send warriors to their deaths if it meant defeating the enemy in the end.

For a moment, the floor was hers. She commanded her warriors neatly, drawing order from the havoc. She chose for her shield-mate a squat woman of the Cornovii whose brothers had died at Valerius' hand and who would have flayed him and kept his body living for a month sealed in clay, feeding him daily to prolong his death, if only the Elder had given her the chance. Too many of her kind still abounded in the six hundred Valerius had kept for his own troop, but if he had left them all behind, he would have been left to charge the auxiliary camp with half a hundred spears.

Presently, when Tethis and her warriors had departed, he addressed the six hundred who remained. His speech to them was short, detailing his battle plan with riding order, weapons and battle calls given crisply, as if they were a cavalry wing long under his command. They hated him for that, too, but could find no fault with it. At the end, he led them outside and stuck his standard in the ground, scoring a mark on the earth to the north-east of its shadow.

'It is now shortly after noon. We meet when the shadow hits the mark. Make what preparations you need, say whatever goodbyes are useful. I am not going to squander your lives, nor am I going to give you the opportunity to be heroes. We will outnumber the auxiliaries by one hundred horse which means we should not fail, but still, some of you will die and some will fall and so will also die. Be clear on that: I do not intend to mount a second rescue mission. We leave no-one, *no-one*, alive on the field when we retreat. I will not have the details of the evacuation of Mona given to the inquisitors of Rome. Anyone who cannot be brought back will bleed their last on mountain soil.'

He looked around. Nobody moved. 'Good. Those who are not here at the meeting of the shadows will be left behind. If you find that, after all, you cannot stomach my command, you can choose to remain with Tethis. The rest, I will see here shortly.'

Three warriors out of six hundred chose to remain with Tethis and take part in the defence of Mona. The remainder crossed the straits to the mainland with Valerius. Mounted on the far side, they ranged behind him in close order and kept his war-hound banner in view, but they lacked the order and discipline of the Roman cavalry and Valerius yearned for the clear battlefield communications of his past.

The bay mare he rode was one of their best, for which he was grateful. An ex-cavalry mount stolen in an earlier raid, she stretched her back and came lightly into hand and pricked her ears towards the campfire smoke in the distance. She had the feel of speed and a love of battle and Valerius loved her for it.

He crooned and scratched her neck for encouragement and pushed her forward up the first real incline of the mountain. The afternoon yawned towards evening, warm for the time of year. The morning's mist had lifted. Heather, not yet in bloom, covered the steepening slope. Below a certain line, the ferns unfurled, ready for spring. A skylark lifted high above the rock-strewn peak of the mountain, singing into the waiting silence.

The *waiting* silence.

Valerius slowed the mare and lifted his hand. The young Siluran slinger who had first brought news of Braint's capture rode at his right hand, bearing the banner.

Valerius said, 'We split the force here. Can you remember the signal?'

'Of course.' The boy was named Huw. He was related distantly to Caradoc on his mother's side, and tetchily proud of it.

The signal was a simple one; a youth could not learn the complex signalling of the Roman cavalry in a morning. Huw waved the banner once, sunwise. The grey of its background merged with the grey of the sky so that the war hound spun and danced as if alive.

At the sight of it, Valerius' group divided into two; the larger part rode on under the command of a badger-haired warrior of the Durotriges, heavy with kill-feathers and the marks of war. Breaking into a canter, they passed along the foot of the mountain, in a line that would bring them, curving, to the valley's mouth.

Thirty warriors remained with Valerius. At least in part, they made an effort to conceal themselves.

'Have they seen us?'

Whatever his heritage, Huw was anxious and trying to conceal it. His were the skills of ambush, not open warfare.

Valerius' attention had been on his hound, which ranged a little ahead. Still watching it, he said, 'Of course. They are meant to. If we're lucky, I have been recognized. If we're twice lucky, a man I once knew is still leading the Ala Prima Thracum. If we are lucky beyond all reason, he will remember a tactic I once used to rescue a standard-bearer who had been taken captive by the Silures in the southern mountains.'

'Then if he remembers it . . . ?'

'He may believe that I will use it a second time here. In which case, we can tell where he will direct his men. Or he may be more clever than that, in which case we are all riding to our deaths. Did you want to turn back?'

'No!' The boy flushed hotly. 'I would never turn back.'

'Unless I order it, which I may well do . . .' Valerius narrowed his eyes, shielding them against the watery sun. 'Do you suppose that's a signal fire up on the hillside, or just the mist setting early for evening?'

It was a signal fire, seen equally by both sides, but, with luck, not read equally by each.

The valley in which Braint was held was arrow-shaped, with its tip to the north. There, two steep-sided mountain ridges came together to form the blind end of the arrow's point. At its southern end, the mouth was wide enough to take a hundred horsemen ranged in a line abreast, with a spear's length between.

Between, the land was flat, as if a river had once scoured it, and almost clear of boulders, so that horsemen could gallop hard without fear for the safety of their mounts. Longinus had picked his site well and had camped in the open where no troops could come at him without warning. Throughout the morning, Mona's scouts had reported that the auxiliaries' tents were huddled in a cluster one third of the way in from the wider, southern end as they had been at Braint's capture. Amongst other things, the signal fire confirmed them still there.

Valerius urged his cavalry mare up the hill towards the northern point of the valley. His band of thirty followed in single file, leaving a gap from nose to tail. From above, for those expecting to see it, they could look like a cavalry patrol, riding under column orders, making every effort not to be seen.

A rockfall blocked the path. Valerius halted in the shelter of it, unable to see the mountaintop, or be seen from it.

Huw was at his side, pale and very still. His sling hung from his hand, a forgotten appendage. His pouch of pebbles bulged.

Valerius said, 'Braint has been seen and is alive; the smoke would have been black if she were dead. So we go on, as we planned. Huw, give the standard to me and your horse to Nydd.'

Nydd was of the Ordovices and several years older than Huw, but his hair was the same dense, highland black and his tunic, by design, carried the same green flash at the shoulders and hem.

The horse that changed hands was a flashy grey with black points; by far the most easily noticed by watching cavalry riders who valued horses above gold or women. Eceni-bred, it was branded on the off-side shoulder with the mark of the serpent-spear. If Longinus still retained the services of the Batavian scout who could read the battle honours on a legionary standard at a thousand paces, then he would know that the warriors who rode with Valerius' standard were all mounted on the best that Mona could provide. If he remembered anything, he would remember the reasons for that.

'Huw, do you remember the signals and how to act on them?'

'Of course.'

'What do you do if the enemy cavalry attack you before we have freed Braint?'

'I run back to here, take the spare horse and escape. Under no circumstances must I allow myself to be caught because you don't want to have to do all this again tomorrow for a slinger whose courage exceeds his discretion.' He was a good mimic; he sounded almost like Valerius. Anger and affronted pride had brought the colour back to his cheeks, and he looked less sick.

Valerius smiled. 'Very good. Braint's life depends on you. I trust you can do it.'

The Silures were renowned for their skills as trackers and hunters. Huw set his jaw and wrapped the strings of his sling more carefully round his wrist. 'I know what you did and who you were,' he said. 'I am doing this for Braint. I won't fail her.'

The boy became a smudge of green and brown among the heather and then less than that. A short, sweating wait later, a small stone, less than might have been dislodged by a settling crow, cracked onto the rocks above Valerius' head to show he was in place and had, if nothing else, remembered the first of his orders.

Nydd held the standard. To him, Valerius said, 'Keep beside me, ride where I ride. If we are attacked, I will defend you. If the war hound falls, we have no way to signal to Huw and he will die. If he dies, Braint dies to the inquisitors at the fortress. Do you understand?'

Nydd was older than Huw, and had fought more battles. He did not flush. 'I have killed enough Roman standard-bearers. I know what happens when they fall.'

'Good. Let's go.'

Valerius led his column out from the rock cover and felt the watching eyes more keenly than before. There was satisfaction in their touch, tinged with disappointment that he should repeat old manoeuvres; Longinus expected better of him than that.

They climbed steeply north along a goat track too narrow for any sane rider. At a certain point, where the bracken ceased to unfurl, they dismounted and led the horses over rock that even the goats chose not to attempt. Two of the older Silures had lived in these mountains as children; their memories of youthful dares were the foundation of Valerius' plan. His relief in finding their memories sound lasted him most of the climb up the mountain.

They reached the top, where the two ridges met at the valley's point, and, for the first time, looked down into the open plain spread out below. The path down was as unappealing as the one up and the drops on either side were terrifying in their steepness.

When all thirty warriors had joined him and remounted Valerius said, 'Nydd, let the standard fall to the east and then bring it up again. Make it look as if it has slipped and you have caught it.'

The standard-bearer did as he was bid, neatly. For the space of ten breaths, there was peace. The horses shifted a little under their riders, finding safer footing. A crow circled and landed on a stunted, wind-blown oak. Valerius' war hound whined and snuffed the air. Then a horse screamed, not one of Mona's, and out of the peace came, briefly, chaos, and then pandemonium.

At the far southern end of the pass, nearly six hundred warriors rode line abreast into the mouth of the valley. Because Longinus had, indeed, remembered the strategy of the past, a full wing of five hundred Thracian cavalry were waiting for them. The clash as the two came together carried across the straits to Mona.

On the high mountain, above the carnage but not beyond the noise, Valerius raised his hand. He waited a moment, offering prayers to both of the gods who held his heart, and swung it down.

'Let's go.'

Above everything else, the warriors of Mona knew how to ride. Their horses were as sure-footed as any in the world and they lived for war. If need demanded, they could gallop down a mountain and not break a leg. Valerius' bay cavalry mare was branded from Iberia, and she was as good. He set her to the steep slope down and, for a while, there was nothing to be done but lose himself in the vertiginous incline of the path and the need for speed and the improbability of reaching the valley's floor alive. The closer they came to the foot of the mountain, the fewer stones blocked their path and the faster they were able to go until all thirty were riding line abreast along the valley's floor, far behind the lines of battle, and the horses were racing for the joy of it.

Valerius pushed his mare until her mane flagged back in his face and his eyes streamed with the wild wind of their running. His heart matched the rhythm of the gallop, wild with elation, and he shouted encouragement, reminding the mare of the greatness of her forebears and of the foals she would one day carry. Once, as a child, he had dreamed of this, or something close, and the exultation filled him each time. However jaded, however drunk, however careworn or weighed with responsibility, for the duration of each battle's ride Valerius of the Eceni was free and the world was at war without him.

The tents of the cavalry were ahead, five lines with the officers' tents closest to the mouth of the valley. The scouts believed that Braint was held in one of them, but none had seen which.

Valerius had dismounted before his mare had stopped running. His blade was already naked in his hand.

Warriors ran to join him, ready to kill the guards. There were none; Longinus rarely squandered the lives of his men. Valerius used his belt-knife to cut the side of the largest of the officers' tents, slicing up and across so that a triangle of white fell inwards and he could step through. The inside was not lit; he stepped out of daylight into gloom. There were no guards here, either, which surprised him.

A figure lay prone against the far side, chained at wrist and ankle with the loops fixed to an oak log too heavy for two men to lift.

'Braint?'

Valerius ran to her, and knelt. She turned her head, stiffly. They had not beaten her as he had been beaten, but she had fought them and someone had used the flat edge of his blade on her face; the angry cut sliced up and across and would scar her for life, if she lived long enough for it to heal that far. Afterwards, they had knocked her unconscious at least once. An angry bruise grew from the side of her temple, and closed her left eye

Unthinking, Valerius reached out to touch it. She jerked back out of his reach. Her open eye raked him, full of scorn. 'You! I thought Tethis might come. I'm glad she has more sense. It's a trap, do you not know that?'

Valerius nodded cheerfully. Here, in the heart of action, he was free and could carry the sting of her hate. 'Of course. I would be disappointed if it weren't. Longinus was always the best mind in the cavalry.'

He looked up. A smith of the Cornovii had followed him in, bearing a hammer and forged chisel with the point hardened in charcoal fires. To him, Valerius said, 'Cut the staple at the log. The manacles will take too long.'

Any time was too long and waiting was torture. The sound of the hammer chimed over the more distant turmoil resounding from the mouth of the valley – and then changed, suddenly. The smith grunted satisfaction.

'Gone.'

He was a big man. He lifted Braint as if she were a child. Her chains clattered around her, still tying her wrists and ankles. She twisted her head to look back.

'Valerius, you can't—' Never in the history of Mona had the Warrior been carried alive from the field of battle. Better to die than be so dishonoured.

Valerius said, 'There's no time to cut you free. You can go out across the horse. Nydd will take you to safety. If you have to go to Mona like this, at least you're still alive.'

Nydd was outside, holding the reins of the bay cavalry mare alongside his own grey. These two were the best horses on Mona; solid and fast and able to take care of a rider. Without ceremony, the smith slung Braint across the bay's saddle.

Valerius said, 'Hold the girth strap if you have to. It'll be a fast ride out.'

Braint spat at him. 'If I die like this, unable to fight, I'll wait for you for all time in the lands of the dead.'

'You won't be alone.'

Valerius lifted his hand to slap the bay mare's rump – and stopped, as a flash of sun on armour caught his eye.

He turned. South, the valley was a mass of several hundred cavalry riders who had suddenly found themselves alone on a battlefield that had once been thick with warriors. As fast as they had come, the warriors of Mona who had charged the valley's mouth had melted back into the mist and the heather and the scrubby oak thickets. Fearful of ambush, the cavalry had not ridden out, but had turned back, to close for a second time the trap they thought secure. These were men who knew how to make a line and hold it, without being ordered. They rode slowly and steadily towards their own tents, a solid bank of horseflesh and metal.

'They're coming.' Nydd said it quietly. His gaze flicked back and forth. 'They're blocking the valley all the way across.'

'I know. But they think you're going to try to break through the line and go south and you're not. Ride north and don't look back. Your horse can make it back up that hill; most of theirs can't. And whatever you do, don't drop the standard. We need to know when you're safe.'

Valerius slapped both horses and felt them start away from him, like the first strides in a race. On either side, two dozen warriors hesitated, watching the incoming cavalry; they were not used to being told to flee in the face of the enemy.

Valerius swung his arm forward as he had done so often, leading a cavalry charge. 'Go! All of you. To the north and to Mona. *Go!*'

The two dozen warriors kicked their mounts from a standstill to a gallop. Circling Nydd, Braint and the smith, they raced north, to freedom, using their bodies as living shields. Their horses were not racing for honour and victory now, but for their lives, flat to the ground, as fast as blood and straining flesh could take them. They knew the route, having ridden it in; each warrior had marked a clear path out and was committed to ride it or die.

Two died, caught by thrown spears. Valerius heard them fall and chose to believe that neither was Nydd or Braint; he had no time to look. He was left with six warriors and they faced the advancing wall of Thracian cavalrymen.

Valerius watched them come, counting the heartbeats. Twenty for Nydd and Braint to reach the foothills of the mountain. A dozen more for the blood-red banner of the war hound to be high enough that Huw might see it and use his sling to signal once again. Less than that for the auxiliary to reach him. Braint was no longer their first concern. They were watching Valerius. He was unmounted, an easy target.

'Here. Valerius. Get up.'

He had asked for a loose horse to be caught without expecting it to happen. Nevertheless, someone passed him the reins of a roan gelding that had run from the carnage at the valley's mouth. It was black with sweat and bleeding from a shallow wound to its chest, but still willing.

With his eyes on the oncoming riders, Valerius whistled to make it run and the six warriors who followed him and the hundreds of auxiliaries he had once commanded watched him make the cavalry mount from the ground onto a running horse and were reminded that here was something exceptional.

Then, doubting their senses, the horsemen of the Ala Prima Thracum saw their former commander swing his arm high and bring it down and heard the war cry of Mona howl from his throat as he led his handful of warriors directly towards them.

We will be the distraction that allows Braint to escape. If we make the arrow of Mona and ride hard, we may break through their line, but I make no promises. Those who remain with me are least likely of all to survive.

So Valerius had said before they left Mona and, against all expectation, four women and two men had offered to remain with him while Braint was taken to safety. They followed him now, as tightly disciplined as any Roman-trained cavalry, and he led them towards the only weak spot in the enemy line, a gap of less than a horse's width between the standard-bearer and the armourer, whom he recognized of old: the man had never yet ridden sober into combat.

This one man's inattention let them through. Horseflesh cannoned on horseflesh as the broad edge of Valerius' living wedge met the line of the enemy. Blades struck blades and iron sang and sparks crested high above and two men died and neither a warrior of Mona. They burst into open ground and Valerius swung his arm and they moved into line abreast and raced south, for their lives, and the open mouth of the valley.

Which was no longer open, and perhaps had never been. Long before they reached it, Longinus was there, with the other half of his troop, closing the trap on the trap on the trap. A string of cavalry was lined up across the valley. They were more than a hundred with less than a spear's length between them and each man was stone cold sober; not one of these was about to let him through.

'Halt!' Forgetting himself, Valerius flung up his arm. Responding to a cavalry command they had seen but never learned, six warriors pulled their sweating, blowing horses to a halt.

'Valerius! Their officer is riding your horse!'

It was Madb who spoke, a wild Hibernian woman with slate-grey hair and the bright eyes of a jackdaw who fought for Mona because she chose to, not because her land was under threat. The spare horse had come from her, and the protection now at Valerius' back. He had never fought at her side before and regretted it.

Valerius held his new mount steady and looked where her blade pointed. He had seen it already, had known it, possibly, for months, but it did no harm to look as if the news were fresh and welcome.

The other five warriors held their horses steady to watch. They were outnumbered hundreds to one and there was nowhere to go and, in any case, the notoriety of the pied horse that had been Valerius' mount had reached far beyond the ranks of the cavalry. Its anger and ferocity in combat were legend, vented as much against its rider as against the enemy, except at the peak of battle when horse and rider fought as one. It emerged from the mass of the oncoming cavalry, running hard towards Valerius. Madb's indrawn breath was only the closest, not the loudest or the most heartfelt.

What could be said of the Crow-horse but that it was perfection on four legs? Splashed white on black, it was as if the gods had poured liquid snow onto the blanket of the night and both were perfect in their purity. Cleaned now for battle, it ran for Longinus with the same bloody-minded dedication as it had for Valerius, and for the first time the man who had thought himself its only master saw how it must have looked to others, and was left silent and unwatchful in the heart of the enemy, disabled by the pain of its loss.

Aloud, he said, 'I have your mother. She is on Mona, in foal one last time to a sire who might be the match of yours. She would be proud of you.'

'*Move!*'

Madb pushed him, and so saved his life. The spear that had been aimed for his throat clattered spent on the ground and skidded into a tent.

'Hold!' Longinus, too, threw up his arm and the singularius who had hurled the spear lowered his second weapon, slowly.

'Valerius! I wasn't sure you'd come.' Longinus clicked his tongue and the Crow-horse trotted forward, as if on parade. It had always loathed parades. Brought neatly to a halt, it stood squarely between the cavalry and the warriors of Mona, facing Valerius. Foam dripped from its bit and its white-rimmed eyes were full of hate, but they had been like that since it was a weanling. Valerius had no idea if it knew who he was.

Longinus, of all men, knew exactly who he was, all the many layers that made him. He himself was unchanged; still the reckless, god-blessed officer who had risked his life to free his soul-friend from the inquisitors, the man who had ridden alongside Valerius in battle for ten years, the man with whom he had bet and won and lost too often to count, the man who rode helmetless into battle with his tawny hair flying free to his shoulders, russet as a rutting stag. His eyes were the striking amber of a hawk and as piercing. There was warmth in them still, amongst the disappointment and impending loss.

Once, when their friendship was new, Valerius had bet this man that he could not stand on rotting ice for fifty heartbeats. They had counted by Longinus' heart, which had beat faster, and so he had won. Valerius' heart beat the faster now. His borrowed horse, quivering, felt it and was ready.

Sixty heartbeats had passed since Nydd had reached the summit of the ridge and dipped the standard towards the setting sun. Nothing had come of it yet, and may never do.

'Congratulations. I never thought you'd find the courage to ride my horse. Has he ever bitten your shoulder?' Valerius eased his own mount forward, close enough almost to touch. On either side, eight auxiliaries unsheathed their blades and made it clear that a further step towards their decurion would be Valerius' last on this earth.

The remaining warriors of Mona grouped together, except for Madb who kept at Valerius' side, grinning. He felt safe in her presence. She had an instinct for danger that kept more than just herself alive in battle.

She pressed close to Valerius' left shoulder and, as his heart beat for the hundredth time since Nydd had spun the standard, he felt her stiffen and turn her head a fraction to the left. Too low for anyone else to hear, she said, 'They're here. Well done. I thought they'd leave you.'

'They might yet. Don't look up.' Valerius took care not to raise his eyes. Louder, to Longinus, he said, 'You are about to ask for our surrender?'

'I would if I didn't think I'd be wasting my breath. Would you give it?'

'Six of us against five hundred is not encouraging odds, but then certain death in battle might be preferable to imprisonment at the hands of Rome, particularly for a traitor who is known to have spent the winter on Mona.'

'It certainly would. You should have escaped with the woman you freed.'

'Possibly, but then I would not have seen you ride the Crow-horse and my life would be the poorer for it. What would you do in my place?'

Longinus grinned. Always, in his smile, there had been challenge and invitation. He reached for his sword and held it out flat. The weapon was Gaulish, made for his reach and his weight, with the crescent moon of the Thracian god embedded in silver in the hilt and the blade worked in the old style, with sinuous lines of blued iron weaving down its length. In the haze of the evening, it glimmered like flat water under moonlight.

Raising his brows, Longinus said, 'I would fight – what else are we for?' His blade was his invitation. 'We have never truly tested each other and it seems to me that you are no longer the mess I believed you to be last summer. My men won't interfere if you want to test your blade against mine this one last time. You never know, you might win.'

Valerius made a half-salute. 'I would accept, but if you lift your blade further, you will die, which would be a pity. The warriors behind you on the mountain are the best slingers of Mona and you are easily within range. I'm sorry; their orders were clear and I have no way to change them from here. If you surrender now, you will not be harmed. Otherwise they will target the first to raise a blade against us.'

He spoke in Latin, loud enough for at least the front ranks of the cavalry to hear. Men who had been relaxed, awaiting the ritual of single combat, looked up and to both sides. Coarse curses in Latin and Thracian scattered through the first ranks and then those behind until, abandoning discipline, the whole wing had spun to face the valley walls.

Valerius raised his arm in one final signal and a glittering wave of sunlit armour appeared on either side as warrior after warrior moved their mounts to the crests of the mountains. They were the greater mass of Valerius' warriors, less only those who had died in the first clash at the valley's mouth. Melting back from the battle, they had taken new positions, awaiting the small signal of a slung pebble to say that Braint was free. Receiving it, they followed the last of their orders so that, like crows on a tree, silently, they lined the ridges from north to south on both sides of the valley without a break. Across the valley's mouth, ranks of waiting warriors made a wall as solid as any rock.

Longinus alone did not look up. The yellow hawk's eyes fixed pensively on Valerius. 'How many?' he asked.

'Six hundred. We outnumber you by one hundred horse. I thought it enough. They command the valley; there is no way out. You're surrounded and outnumbered. In such circumstances, there's no dishonour in surrender and we have no inquisitors on Mona. You will be given the option to fight for us if you wish. Already, we have a handful of Batavians and a Gaul who ride at our side. If you do not wish to join them, your deaths will be clean and fast.'

Longinus had never lacked courage. Grinning, he said, 'So you are really not the mess we both thought. I'm glad.'

'Longinus, that's not the point, you have to choose. Your men will do as you do, you know that. If you— *No!*'

Lightning fast, the moon-marked blade struck for Valerius' head. By instinct alone, he blocked it, and felt the shock run through him to his horse. Iron sang on iron as he ripped his own blade sideways. Sparks flew, lighting the air. A dozen slingstones showered around him and two auxiliaries fell. 'Longinus! Don't be a fool. You can't run from a sling— Ah, gods, why did I ever leave you my horse? Let's go.'

He spoke above a hammering of running horses. The Crow-horse had never allowed its rider to be bested in battle. With or without Longinus' command, it had spun on its hocks, high out of danger, and sprung away, heading south. True to their training, the men and mounts of the Ala Prima Thracum followed it.

Valerius followed, on a horse that was slower and already wounded, but still gave him its heart. Madb urged her mount alongside his, making of herself the shield at his shoulder, and together they hurtled south, following the fleeing Longinus who was heading directly for a solid wall of Mona's warriors, led by Nydd, who had remembered everything he had been told.

XXXI

THE CLASH OF IRON AND HORSEFLESH AND HUMAN BLOOD AND
bone shook the earth to the nape of the valley.

Valerius of the Eceni, once decurion of the Ala Prima
Thracum, had lived through many nightmares and found each to
be less than the fear he had built. Fighting hand to hand, blade to
blade, against men he had led and for whom he had cared, was not
the least of these, but also not the greatest. As ever, the exhilaration
of battle fired him; the power of the moment and the overwhelming need to survive did not allow time for regret. As never before,
he rode understanding the gods who filled him; Nemain's clarity
joined with Mithras' savage power and he loved them both and his
life within them and knew that if he died now, he could be at peace.

He fought, too, with Madb, a shield-mate who kept him safe and
for whose life he cared and that was something he had missed for
so long he had forgotten how it felt. He raised his borrowed blade
and pushed his borrowed horse forward and the war hound ran at
his side as it was born to do and he remembered that he, who
would be a dreamer, was nevertheless a warrior and that life would
not be complete without both.

The air was dense with man-sweat and woman-sweat and horse-
sweat and spittle and soon with an ocean of blood and sliding guts
that made the footing unsafe and required a new dimension of
watchfulness. Valerius chose his man: a stranger with one blue eye

and one brown who rode a bay mare that was trained to strike. It aimed for Valerius' roan, who jinked sideways, leaving the mare off balance and the rider with it, so that Valerius could strike for the gap beneath the rim of his helmet and cleave open a living brow to the dying brain beneath. He had time to wrench his blade clear of the toppling body, and the roan horse clear of the mare's next strike, before the battle moved on.

On his right, Madb wounded a Thracian whom Valerius thought he recognized. To his left, the shield side, a woman of the Coritani with the kill-feathers bunched heavy in her hair missed her stroke and was nearly beheaded by a man Valerius *did* know. She fell from her horse, dead before she could scream. Priscus, keeper of mirrors, grinned savagely and turned on Valerius and was, in turn, slain by the woman's lover, who, howling, drove his horse broadside into the cavalryman's gelding, crushing its ribs. His blade shattered Priscus' helmet with the force of his strike.

Valerius felt his horse rise under him and made it come down because the cavalry were trained to gut horses that rose high to strike and it was not a time to lose his mount. He struck back-handed at the man who was already leaning down to cut at the blue roan's belly. He felt the blow land unevenly and then his hand became weightless as his borrowed sword broke. Cursing, he dragged his horse back.

'Here!'

The lover of the dead Coritani dipped down from his saddle, grasped her blade and threw it in one movement. Yesterday, he would have gutted Valerius with it, tomorrow he might do so again; today, they fought together against a greater enemy. Valerius caught the hilt and saluted and took a swipe under his arm for his inattention so that only his horse's jink to the left kept him alive and let Madb kill his attacker.

'We should strike down their standard!'

The Hibernian woman howled it over the tumult of battle. As much as Valerius, she was enjoying herself. She grinned and struck and forced her mount into the place where the fallen man had been.

Ahead, in the heart of the maelstrom, the red bull standard of the Ala Prima Thracum lolled on an idle breeze. Longinus fought nearby, riding tall on the Crow-horse, safe in the god-haven where mount and rider have long since become one. If he died now, he would count himself blessed. Valerius, who had been in his place, knew it.

'Come on!'

The gap was closing and Valerius not yet through. Madb drove for the fluttering standard. She was his shield-mate; honour demanded Valerius follow. He sent his horse forward half-heartedly.

In battle, the half-hearted are soon dead. Three men, seeing his inattention, struck for Valerius' unwary guard so that only a life-time of reflexes saved him – and Braint, freed from her fetters and riding a rip tide of battle rage that scattered all before her.

With Nydd at her side, she burst through on Valerius' right, killing with the recklessness of one who no longer cares for life or love. Her aim, very plainly, was Longinus; the man who had taken her captive. She wanted his life above all others.

There was no way to stop them. Valerius had only time to lift a hand to his mouth and shout, *'Longinus!'* so that at least the man would see whence came his death, and then they were on him, one from either side, freshly mounted and freshly armed, fighting a man who was neither of these and bound to be slower because of it, however great his skill and his horse.

The Crow-horse believed itself immortal, and may have been right. Valerius was not the only one to pause and watch as it rose, screaming, to meet Braint's mount. The mind-splitting noise of its cry, the sheer undiluted hatred, stopped men and women in their own private battles.

For a moment, there was quiet in the carnage, long enough for Valerius to see the Crow-horse rear and swing and strike and Longinus to follow the flow of it with a beauty to awe the gods; for him to see Braint evade the strike with heart-breaking ease and then to see her strike in return, and to hear the unmistakable clash of iron on mail with the crush of bone beneath.

'Longinus!' Valerius screamed it alone as the battle was re-joined around him. The sound was lost; one more note in a tumult of shouting, screaming beasts and warriors, and Valerius did not know he had uttered it until Madb threw him a fresh shield, taken from a dying warrior, and shouted, 'You'll have him yet! They can't get to his body. Your mad bloody horse won't let them near.'

381

It might have been true. Valerius neither knew nor had the energy to care. He fought because he must, because it was what he was born for, because his gods, both Nemain and Mithras, demanded it of him and he was not yet ready to face them having failed to honour their requests, but the day had become dust-driven and shrunken and he killed without joy, heartlessly, and hated it.

The warriors of Mona outnumbered the cavalrymen of the Prima Thracum by one hundred horse and they were buoyed by Braint's return in exactly the same measure as the Thracians were demoralized by Longinus' fall. The battle was brutal and short and forty-eight living Thracians surrendered their weapons at the end.

Valerius took no part in the securing of the prisoners or the stripping of the dead. Before the battle ended, he had dismounted and stood ankle deep in heather just beyond range of the Crow-horse. White with sweat and bleeding from half a dozen shallow wounds, the pied horse still stood over Longinus' prostrate form as a hound stands over a fallen warrior, and would let no-one near.

'You'll have to kill the beast if you want your man's body.'

Madb sat her horse nearby, keeping watch on Valerius' back. She had saved him twice towards the end of the battle and he had not yet thanked her. A part of him knew that time was passing and it would soon be too late to do so with any integrity. The greater part of him had eyes only for the pied horse standing opposite, and the man lying half prone beneath its feet.

He had seen a movement of Longinus' chest; only once and not recently, but enough to hang hope on. He found himself praying to Briga, to whom he was not and had never been given, but who ruled the deaths of battle. Crows took his words and carried them and he felt himself heard.

Madb was still watching him. She said, 'Valerius, did you hear me? The horse is mad, or inspired by the gods. You're going to have to cut its throat if you want to get close to your friend.'

'If you think you can get near enough to kill it, you're welcome.'

The woman barked a laugh. Her voice was deep and rich and resonant and the sound was strange in all the death and wounding. She said, 'Do I look as if I want to die? I was thinking you could ask Huw to use his sling. He's strangely in awe of you; he'd probably do it.'

'Would a stone kill him?' Valerius stooped for a pebble and tossed it close to Longinus. The Crow-horse snaked its head at him, ears flat and mouth wide. It ignored the pebble. Stepping a half-stride closer, Valerius said, 'It might work, but Huw's too soft to do it. He'd spend the rest of his life reliving the day he killed the greatest war mount ever to set foot on the earth. I wouldn't ask that of any man. They sing of this horse as they sing of Hail. I know. I've heard the songs.'

Madb said, 'So have I. They say it's evil.'

She was testing him, as she had tested him in the battle. Her jackdaw's eyes watched him, brightly. Valerius shook his head. 'No. They say the man who rode it is evil.'

'Are they right?'

'I don't know. You spent the afternoon's battle saving his life.' Valerius dragged his gaze from the horse. 'Did you know who I was?'

He had not looked at her properly since the end of battle. She was bruised down one side of her face where the edge of a shield had caught her. It would blacken overnight and leave her half dark for a month. Her left wrist was swollen enough to be sprained and would need binding soon if it were not to stiffen. She sat her horse as if each of these was normal for her, and looked down at him pensively.

'Of course I knew. How could I not? You don't need a red hound painted on grey to show who you are, it's stamped on every part of you. "Valerius of the Eceni." The man who fights for both sides and loves neither. Except it seems he does love one part of one side after all. Did he know?'

'Longinus? Possibly once. Not now.'

'Then you'd best get to him to tell him before Braint decides four dozen live Thracians are not enough of a prize and she wants a head on a stake to show Rome what fate awaits it.' Madb pursed her lips, appraising. 'I saw you show off your skill at the warrior's mount very prettily this afternoon. It's easy on a willing horse, harder on one trying to kill you. Could you do it now, do you think, if I had the beast's attention?'

'We could find out.'

It was the only real chance and Valerius had been working towards exactly that since the battle ended. Spoken openly, it

383

became harder to think of. His palms were wet. He rubbed them dry on his tunic.

The Crow-horse felt the sharpening of his attention and spun fully to face him. Its flanks heaved and its nostrils flared scarlet, dragging in air. Its tail slashed, violent as a wildcat's. Its eyes were red-rimmed with dust and rage and the loathing of being surrounded. More than any other living beast, it understood the ebb and flow of battle. Never while Valerius rode it had it been on the losing side in more than a skirmish and never in all of its life had it been taken captive.

Valerius would not believe that it was evil, only that it hated him. He wanted to believe that it had hated Longinus as deeply and, by the same token, that it would have protected Valerius as savagely if he had ever fallen in battle. He began to speak to it in the language of the ancestors, that he had used in the beginning when he and the beast had newly met, when he had first made the warrior's mount in front of a blood-hungry circus crowd, with it the freshly broken colt brought in for barter and he the slave-boy trying to escape. He had loved the beast then, and had thought it could come to love him. Half his life had passed waiting for that to happen.

He tossed another pebble and the horse ignored it entirely. He cast a handful towards Longinus' fallen body and was sure he saw a shudder. Valerius wrapped the thread of his hope around that certainty and, with every fraction of his attention on the beast that sought his life, he edged inwards, speaking lullabies in the tongue of the ancestors. Halfway through, in Hibernian, he said, 'I need it to turn to my right and take a step forward.'

Madb was a moving thing on the edge of his vision. Her voice was a rolling wave on the sea. She said, 'Does it know what a spear is?'

'It did when I rode it.'

'Good. *Here then, horse of all hate, shall we see now, are you all that they say?*'

The blur of her movement wove into the screaming spin of the Crow-horse as it flung itself towards the new danger – and drew Valerius with it, as a wind draws leaves. Sucked by its power, pulled by the lock of his attention, he leaped forward and up for the saddle horn, throwing himself up on the rise of its rise, swinging up and over and down to land square in the saddle, his hands already reaching for the reins.

The Crow-horse felt him and knew itself cheated. Forgetting Madb, it threw itself into a screaming, rearing, bucking frenzy. On the first day he rode it, Valerius had watched a man nearly lose his life to its rage. It was older now and fitter and more practised in dislodging its riders. He felt the bunched muscle beneath him explode into action, felt his body wrenched and his teeth clash and blood gush from his tongue and knew that if it really tried, the beast could crush him to pulp.

The horse felt the same, and knew how. It came back to earth and there was a moment's stillness as it gathered itself inwards. Valerius thought it might buck and grabbed a handful of mane to hold himself by. Then he felt the hindquarters gather and thought it might bolt and then the ground fell away and the sky tilted and it was rearing high enough to touch the clouds, high enough to throw itself backwards and crush the man on its back even if it broke its own spine in the attempt.

It screamed as it had screamed at Braint so that the sound shattered the sky and Valerius, knowing himself about to die, screamed with it, giving vent to all a lifetime's pain and frustration and exhilaration and devastation that no amount of killing in battle, no depth of dreaming to the gods, would ever drain dry.

The sky did not fall. The horse did not topple and kill them both. The birds of Briga, circling, cawed thrice and flew west and did not take the souls of either man or horse.

The Crow-horse came back down to stand still on the earth, shaking its head, and Valerius, deafened, sat on it drawing breath after breath of sharp mountain air with tears scalding his face and pooling in the crook of his collarbone and no idea why he shed them.

He became aware, slowly, that others were close. Madb was in front of him, her spear held in a clear salute. Braint was with her, fierce-eyed and silent, and Nydd and Huw and the smith and others whose names he had once known and might know again, but for now could not begin to remember.

To Madb, he said, 'Is Longinus still alive?'

'Of course. Would you not know if he were dead?'

'I thought perhaps I wept for him.'

'Did you so? Then you are more of a fool than I took you for.

He is alive and awake and his eyes are open. Get off your god-riven horse and talk to him. And when you are finished, you can talk to those who fought for you, not against you. You were right; this was a diversion. Mona is under attack and Tethis holds the straits with three thousand against four times that number. Only the water and the good will of the gods keep Rome from the island. Neither will last for ever.'

Some time later, Longinus Sdapeze, former decurion of the Ala Prima Thracum, woke with a crashing headache.

Presently, when it became clear he was not about to die, he felt about him and then opened his eyes. The covered top of a wagon swayed pleasingly above his head, lit by a dawn sky. A brindled war hound lay at his side, peaceably watchful. A lean, dark-haired man sat on the sprung seat of the wagon, blocking most of the light.

Longinus lay a while, studying the familiar, stubborn set of the back so that he knew the moment when his scrutiny had been felt. He considered sitting up to ask at least one of the several pressing questions rocking against the walls of his head, but the hound stared at him until he thought better of it.

He slept a while and ate and was sick and drank water and slept again. When he woke, it was dusk and the hound had gone. The sway of the wagon was the sway of the cradle and it was hard to stay awake. Forcing himself to sit, Longinus reached up to touch the shoulder of the man who had saved his life. 'Where are we going?'

'East.'

'Why?'

'Because your brains are turned to milk in your head and you won't be fit to sit on a horse until they curdle again to the broth you were born with.'

His brains had turned to milk and they made him sleep again, unquestioning, so that it was halfway through the night before he realized he had not been given an answer. The hound lay with him then, keeping him warm.

At dawn, when they had not stopped, he asked, 'Valerius, where's your horse?'

'What do you think is taking you forward?'

Longinus laughed and it hurt so he stopped. 'You're making the *Crow-horse* pull a wagon? Valerius! Are you entirely mad?'

'He's good at it. And I have the roan and your mare as well. Two pull at any one time and one walks behind. In any case, I couldn't leave him. Braint would have tried to ride him and he'd have killed her, which would not have been good. She's needed to lead the warriors in the defence of Mona.'

Sobered, Longinus said, 'They can't win, your warriors. Suetonius Paulinus may be an appalling governor, but he's an excellent general. He wouldn't have attacked if there were the slightest chance he would lose.'

'He will gain Mona eventually,' agreed Valerius. 'It won't be this month, or possibly even next; the Silures and Ordovices have rallied and are attacking him from the rear, so that he can't throw his weight at the straits, but still, I think you are right. He will have the island by midsummer at the latest. He will not, however, walk to it on the blood and flesh of those who have lived there. It's the people that matter; the elders to hold the wisdom and the children to hear it. Where they are, so is Mona, and they can be saved. All we need is time. Braint and her warriors are buying that time with their flesh and blood.'

Longinus was watching the planes of his face. He knew Valerius as well as any man, possibly better than Valerius himself. At length, with compassion, he said, 'And do you not want to be with the warriors of Mona as they mount their defence?'

Valerius stared at his hound a while, and then at the horses pulling the wagon and the path ahead. The soft rhythm of footfalls might have lulled Longinus into sleep, but that the answer mattered too much to both of them for that. Eventually, 'I want to be with them more than I can possibly express,' Valerius said.

Longinus pushed himself forward, against nausea and the resistance of his friend, to sit on the bench where the hound had been. The Crow-horse was, indeed, pulling the wagon, which was, if nothing else, a sign of its rider's desperate need to be moving. 'So let me ask again. Why are we going east?'

Valerius sighed and pinched the bridge of his nose in the way Corvus used to do when pressed beyond endurance. Without looking to the side, he said, 'I am going because Luain mac Calma, the man who claims to be my father and is Elder of Mona, has ordered that I take word to my sister that it would be to the great benefit of the gods and their people if the eastern tribes were to rise in revolt while the assault on Mona is under way. I am sworn to follow his wishes, or die in the attempt. You are going because I am going and I was not prepared to leave you behind.'

They were close enough to feel each other's warmth and each became aware of it. The wagon faltered and moved on again; the Crow-horse had been ridden by both, and knew what moved them. After a long while, Longinus said, 'And will we die in the attempt?'

At last, Valerius turned to face him. Surprisingly, his eyes were at peace, and had room for the old, dry humour.

'I may do. You won't unless everything I have done or can do fails. You kept the Crow-horse safe for me. Getting you killed would be a poor repayment.'

XXXII

THE TOMBSTONE WAS DELIVERED EARLY, BEFORE FIRST LIGHT. THE factor of the prefect's household was woken by a night slave and, blearily irritable, ordered it left in the spartan enclave of his master's office.

Quintus Valerius Corvus, prefect of the Ala Quinta Gallorum and acting commander of Camulodunum, found it shortly after dawn as he came to his paperwork, seeking an hour's peace before the debilitating trivia of colonial governance began to take its toll.

He had heard the watch called twice before he thought to inspect the stone he had so recently commissioned. He was studying it still, an hour later, when his first visitor called.

'What do you think of it?'

Clean and sharp and scurrilous, the stone leaned against the farther wall. The sackcloth hung over one edge; the prefect's usually scrupulous tidiness had, this once, abandoned him.

Corvus spoke Alexandrian, for privacy and out of courtesy for his guest and friend, the physician Theophilus, late of Rome, the Germanies, Athens and Cos, and now of Britannia. Theophilus had seen too many tombstones of late to find them absorbing and his eyesight was not as good as it had once been. Still, for his friend's sake, he leaned forward to study it.

After a while, he leaned back again. 'It's very . . . striking. What would you like me to think of it?'

'That Longinus would appreciate the humour, that it suits the man as we knew him and that it will serve him well in death as he served well in life.'

Theophilus nodded, sagely. 'Then, indeed, for your sake as much as his, that is what I will think.' He crouched more closely and read the lines incised on the stone. ' "*Longinus Sdapeze, son of Matycus, duplicarius of the first squadron, the Ala Prima Thracum*, et cetera, et cetera . . . *His heirs had this erected in accordance with his will.*" Did they indeed?' He looked up. 'I hadn't realized you were one of his heirs. Who was the other?'

Corvus pinched the bridge of his nose. 'Valerius. Who else?'

'I see.' The physician's eyes were watery and kind, and still sharp enough to see the gaps in another man's soul. Gently, he said, 'So, in effect, you are the sole inheritor. Did our departed friend leave you anything of worth?'

'Enough gold to have this monstrosity made – he picked the mason so we can only assume he knew what was coming, which is more than I did – and a certain pied war horse, if it survived him, if I can find it amidst the wreckage of the governor's war when I finally march west to join him, if, having found the beast, I can get near it and if, having done all of these, I am stupid or reckless enough to try to mount it.'

Theophilus rose with a creak of arthritic knees and came to stand behind the prefect, kneading the man's shoulders with bony fingers. The muscles softened, but not enough to diminish the headache he could see growing before his eyes. He said, 'As your physician, I would strongly recommend that you have that particular horse poleaxed the moment you lay eyes on it, but I don't expect that you will. Do I gather that you are going west soon?'

'Very soon.' Corvus stretched his neck. 'Now that the snow is clearing, I am ordered to take the three cohorts of new recruits and my cavalry wing west "with all possible facility". I gather the war is not going to the governor's satisfaction. We should have continued training here for another month. As it is, I'll leave the day after tomorrow at dawn, if the weather holds.'

'Are they ready?'

'The men? No, but they're as ready as anyone ever is who has never seen a dead man with his gonads cut from his groin and jammed between his teeth and the kill-marks of Mona cut on his brow and chest.' Corvus smiled savagely. 'The governor needs help and we are all that he has. He'll win in the end, but he will lose more than Longinus in doing so. Our Trinovante mason, meanwhile, occupies himself in making tombstones of striking vivacity, if limited taste. If you look carefully at this morning's gift, you'll see the cowering native under the feet of Longinus' horse is possessed of a fully erect phallus.'

'And the smile of a man somewhat less than cowed. Thank you. I rather thought it better not to notice either of those. The horse is good, though; whatever else may be said of them, the natives have a good eye for a horse.' Theophilus dropped the cover back over the stone. 'You need fresh air. Shall we go— Ah, alas not.' He tilted his head in the direction of the disturbance at the doorway. 'Would that be the procurator?'

Corvus' face took on the weariness of a man under siege. 'Who else, making that much noise at this time in the morning? Will you stay? I might need a witness when I kill him, to say that I was driven to it out of fear for my own sanity.'

'Willingly.'

Theophilus settled himself to wait. In his opinion, Decianus Catus, procurator of all Britannia, was a clerk and a money-counter who would not have rated a second glance had not the emperor chosen to make of him the second most powerful man in Britannia. Only the governor had powers of absolute veto over the procurator's actions and even those were used with discretion. Each of these two, governor and procurator, had orders to succeed or die in the taming of Britannia, and neither man was prepared have it said afterwards in the senate that the other had hindered his efforts.

For a while, Theophilus had found it amusing to watch the governor, leader of armies and subduer of nations, hedging round a counting clerk as if the poisonous little man were a senator on the road to the imperial throne. Watching Corvus forced into increasingly harassed retreat by a man who should have drowned in his mother's birth fluids and saved the world from his presence was not amusing at all.

The physician turned from his inspection of the wall mosaics to hear the end of a sentence.

'. . . fully aware of the unfortunate disappearance of the

merchant Philus. However, until we either find him alive, or come across his body, it is impossible to say how he died.'

'He was slain by Prasutagos and his barbarian filth.' The procurator spoke with the hoarse, whispering force of one who has coughed too much in early life.

Corvus was leaning on his desk, staring down at the splayed whiteness of his fingers. 'Procurator Catus, the King Prasutagos has been loyal since the first moment the Divine Claudius set foot in this province. He escorted the imperial cavalcade personally into Camulodunum. In any case, the Eceni were disarmed by force over a decade ago. I think it highly unlikely that even their king could rouse them to attack a group of armed slavers.'

'No?' The procurator's eyes flew wide. 'Then you are more of a fool than I thought. If I didn't have an armed escort, I would have died ten times over in the first month I was here. Everywhere we go, they raise their "skinning knives" and look down the blades to see if they are sharp enough to kill a man.'

'Everywhere *you* go, I'm sure they do.' Theophilus said it in Alexandrian, peering at the bronze statuette of Horus on the small shelf above the brazier as if he commented on the workmanship. He saw a muscle in Corvus' cheek twitch and smiled, blandly.

A little hollowly, Corvus said, 'My point entirely, procurator. The peace here is tenuous at best. We cannot begin to destroy entire villages without due recourse to law. The emperor will not thank me for setting alight the tinderbox of the east for the sake of a man who has been mauled by a bear.'

'He was not mauled by a bear.'

'So you say. But if you wish me to act, you must find me not only Philus' body, but also proof beyond doubt that he was killed by human agency.'

'Of course.' The procurator smiled at the prefect and his friend, the Greek physician. His voice slid over them both. 'Prefect, if you will step outside? And you, physician? I believe your skills will provide the proof the prefect needs.'

They should have seen it coming. Perhaps Corvus had, but there was nothing he could have done to reverse it.

Outside, an unhitched ox cart waited in the part-thaw of morning, shrouded against prying eyes. It smelled, not unpleasantly, of earth and melted ice and a little of hound's urine, as if a wandering cur had lately marked the wheels. A century of armed men stood behind it in military order: the procurator's veteran mercenaries.

The procurator stepped up on the wheel spokes with a surprising agility and balanced on the edge of the cart, giving himself the advantage of height. He stared down at Corvus, stone-faced. 'You will recall that the merchant Philus and two of those closest to him wore at all times the badge of the leaping fish. Is that correct?'

'It is.'

Corvus was an officer of the cavalry. He had fought and killed better men than this. Theophilus watched him set aside his headache, which must by then have been fierce, and engage instead an enquiring smile. 'You have located that badge?' he asked.

'Not the one belonging to Philus, but then it was of silver and had some worth. But we have two others of copper and iron, which were missed by the looters. They were found amongst the remains of the men-at-arms who served Philus and died in an effort to save his life. We were not able to bring them all back, but each is accounted for, sworn in the presence of my men.'

A retired legionary whom Theophilus remembered as viciously unsuited to leading any group of armed men stepped forward in a clash of over-polished mail, saluted and, without request or permission, said, 'Forty-three different bodies found. One dozen natives, twenty-seven men-at-arms, four unidentifiable on account of . . .'

Corvus' smile acquired the edge that any man who had ever served under him should recognize. The legionary stuttered to a close. Corvus' nod was devastatingly crisp. 'Thank you, Driscus, we can imagine the rest.' Speaking over the man's head, he said, 'Procurator, you have the bodies with you?'

'Of course. I could not expect you to take my word for something of this magnitude.'

The procurator had a liking for theatre and his men had been drilled to the point of automation. He stepped down from the wheel as neatly as he had stepped up. At his nod, Driscus clashed forward to lift one corner of the canvas. Three others came to help. The stripping away of the wagon's cover was achieved in a single, clean manoeuvre. The procurator's men, it was to be understood, were as finely disciplined as any still serving in the legions, if not more so.

Theophilus had spent large parts of his career watching men like Driscus uncover wagonloads of slain. Wearily, he waited for the wall of stench to reach him – and waited – and presently realized that it had done so and that he could relax because winter and the carrion beasts had softened the smell to something mouldily sweet and almost pleasant.

He leaned over the edge for a better look. Yellowing bones and fragmented skulls lay joined and disjoined in a child's game of tangled ligaments and dried, stringy human hide. Tatters of clothing stuck here and there where the natives, the winter beasts and the spring birds had not yet found better use for them. On the top, lying ostentatiously on the curve of a clean-picked ribcage, lay two leaping salmon, brilliant with rust and verdigris, so that only the jewelled eyes were clean.

As was intended, they caught Theophilus' attention, so that it took a moment to look beyond, and see the thing that mattered more. He looked up. Corvus caught his gaze and shook his head so that the physician closed his mouth over what he had been about to say and waited for a better time.

The procurator stood over them both. His breath smelled of old shellfish and was worse than the winter-cleansed dead. With the air of one educating infants, he said, 'I believe this . . .' he prodded with a sheathed knife at a body, 'was Philus. His fish badge is gone, but the skeleton has the small finger missing on its left hand, and a healed break on the ankle, as he did. As to the rest, you will observe that the bodies are unclothed. More importantly, no mail or weapons were found in the clearing.' He grinned. His men grinned with him, knowingly. They had heard this speech before, more than once. 'In my experience, bears rarely make the effort to strip their kills. Native insurgents always do.'

Corvus did not grin. Distractedly, he said, 'As do bandits and thieves. Theophilus, I will need details of how these men died, as far as it can be ascertained from their bones.' He had mounted the wagon's tailgate, the better to study its contents. The act gave him back his advantage of height. 'Procurator, until we have a full inventory of the bodies, including the means of death and as much identification as we—'

'How much more identification can you need? Do you deny that this is Philus?'

'. . . until we have full identification of the bodies that are not Roman, until we have found the nature of the injuries to the dead and had an opportunity to establish the identity of their assailants—'

'Prefect, this is nonsense. Philus was last known to be with Prasutagos. He is dead and all his men with him. At Driscus' best estimate, there are at least two dozen sets of sword, shield and mail unaccounted for. Therefore we not only have a nest of killers festering in the stinking midden of "King" Prasutagos' steading, but the beginnings of insurrection. How could you believe otherwise?'

'Because Prasutagos, too, is dead.'

Rain had begun to fall. The patter of it on the roof tiles ripped the silence. Corvus' smile was carefully neutral.

The procurator blinked at him, slowly. The white margins of his nostrils became yellow with the pressure of his breathing. He said, 'How can you be sure?'

'I am sure of nothing, which is why I have requested that our physician make an inventory, but I know of no other man who wore the king-band of the Eceni on his only arm.' Corvus stepped back a little. 'Theophilus? Would you confirm for me that the skeleton lying behind Philus has had the right arm amputated above the elbow in early adulthood, and that until very recently, something with bronze or copper end pieces lay about the remaining left arm?'

A minor miracle enabled Theophilus to keep his face straight. He murmured, 'Nicely done,' in Alexandrian, and then leaned forward to smear a finger across the copper-green stains on the upper arm of 'Tagos' skeleton and then again on the ribcage against which that arm had rested. Even those at the margins of the crowd could see the green on his finger when he held up his hand.

'The band was removed after the last fall of rain,' he said, 'which was yesterday. Native craftwork of this quality would fetch a small ransom in Rome. I expect one of the procurator's men is holding it in safe keeping, which would be wise; it could too easily have fallen from the wagon. Procurator?'

The procurator could cheerfully have killed him. Failing that, he was almost certainly going to come very close to killing the man who had taken the king-band. The threat of a flogging hung ripe in the air and several men in the procurator's retinue had become distinctly unhappy.

Corvus cleared his throat. 'Thank you, Theophilus. I think we should perhaps—'

For the fourth time that morning, the prefect was interrupted; not, this time, by the procurator, but by the sound of horses approaching at speed.

The morning was quiet and the clatter of many horses carried clearly from the eastern gates. When the gates opened, the in-comers had formed an ordered block, flanked on both sides by the gate officers in an escort which was at once a guard of honour and an arrest party.

They rode sedately along the via praetoria, as measured as any delegation from Rome. The guards' horses were restive, sidling sideways under hands that held them too hard, and men who were unsure of their position. The nine incomers they escorted were all native youths, mounted on matching chestnut geldings and dressed alike in short riding cloaks of Eceni blue, with elabo-rate weavings at hem and neckline. Each bore ornaments of bear's teeth woven at the hair of their temples and a gold brooch was pinned at each shoulder, shaped as the running horse of the Eceni.

The tallest of them rode in the centre. His hair was the gold of summer corn and his eyes amber and he wore a king-band on his upper arm that matched, and perhaps exceeded, the magnificence of the one that had once graced the arm of Prasutagos, dead king of the Eceni.

Theophilus watched the procurator assess the value of that band, and of the brooches worn by the other eight riders, and of the horses they rode, and was about to step forward to intervene in what might well have been a diplomatic disaster when Corvus caught his arm and, in Alexandrian, murmured, 'No. He knows. Watch,' and Theophilus did watch, with rising delight, as the young warrior broke away from his guard and his retinue and pushed his horse to a hand gallop, heading directly for the procurator.

The guards were slow and had only time to shout alarm, not to act. The procurator's mercenaries were caught equally unprepared and failed to throw themselves bodily in front of their employer as would have been proper. Only a Coritani scout who had attached himself to the procurator's retinue had the presence of mind to step forward, knife in hand, to face the incoming warrior and he stepped back again soon enough as the young man in the Eceni cloak brought his horse crisply to a halt and flung himself from the saddle to kneel at the feet of the second most powerful man in Britannia.

'Decianus Catus, procurator of all Britannia, Breaca of the Eceni bids you greetings and her regret that, after the death of her husband, she is in mourning and unable to leave her steading. I come in her place, her son and his, to offer you the gift of the Eceni, and our plea that you help us recover the body of our king, who was slain at the start of winter defending the life of the slave trader Philus, may the gods deal justly with them both.'

His delivery was perfect, with the cadence and clarity of a court herald. As the words fell to the echo amongst the copper-roofed villas of Rome's first city, he unpinned the brooch from his shoulder, letting the blue cloak fall to the ground at his heels, and held out the running horse in solid gold that was worth half the annual salary of any man in the procurator's pay. Beneath, he was naked to the waist, with scars of war or ritual about his body that made Theophilus wince and left the procurator speechless.

'The gift of the Eceni,' said the youth, smiling. 'With our honour for your position and our earnest desire to see returned the body of our murdered king.'

Naked to the waist, with the bear marks showing clear on his shoulders and back, Cunomar knelt in the filthy slush of Camulodunum's main street and watched the procurator of all Britannia consider and discard three different responses to his gift and the request that accompanied it.

The man was a sucking leech, and to be despised, but he was not the governor and for that Cunomar was grateful. He had practised the speech through winter until he could, and did, recite it in his sleep. Clots of Latin crowded his dreams like crows at a battlefield and he had been inordinately grateful when the thaw came, and the time to act.

It had not been possible to know beforehand who would be in command of the city's garrison when the thaw came and, faced with two alternatives, the decision to kneel before the procurator had been a late one, prompted by instinct: Corvus was not so lost in pride that he would object to being passed by, and the procurator was dangerous, and must be won over, or at least bound by some semblance of honour.

Watching now, Cunomar saw his guess proved right. Before the procurator could collect himself, Corvus stepped forward and, offering Cunomar his hand, helped him to rise.

'Welcome to Camulodunum, Cunomar, son of Breaca and heir to Prasutagos, king of the Eceni. We regret deeply the death of your king and offer our condolences to your mother and family. In the emperor's name, we will return to you Prasutagos' body as soon as we are able. In the meantime, it has been a long ride; you must be weary. If you would care to bring your honour guard and join us, we might offer you our city's hospitality?'

It was neatly done. No man, however powerful, could readily countermand an offer made in the name of his emperor.

Cunomar bowed, as he had once seen an emperor's son do in Rome, 'Thank you. In the name of my people I—'

'No.' The procurator had recovered his voice. 'Of course the king's body must be returned, but before that we must examine his will, which became law on his death and has been allowed to go unattended. A copy is kept under guard at the governor's residence. It should be read immediately to determine the size of the estate and the names of the beneficiaries.'

. . . the size of the estate and the names of the beneficiaries. Ghost winds spread down Cunomar's spine. Through all the winter, that had been the one thing about which they knew nothing: no-one, in the steading or beyond it, had any idea of the content of 'Tagos' will, or of how it might be enacted on his death.

Nor, it seemed, had Corvus, although he read the undercurrents in the procurator's tone as easily as had Cunomar, and liked them as little.

'What hurry, Catus? If the king has been dead since the start of winter, then half a day more will not matter, and we have a guest who should be welcomed and made comfortable after his journey, before he escorts his father's remains to their last rest. Would you have our visitors believe Rome incapable of the simple courtesies that are commonplace amongst the tribes?'

As skilfully as any strategist of war, the procurator closed the trap he had opened and none had foreseen. 'On the contrary, prefect, I am doing my best for our young guest and he will be grateful. If the king has been dead that long, then there will be six months' interest to pay on the monies due to the emperor. Would you deprive the imperial coffers of their due? Or impose on the king's son any greater burden than the one under which he already suffers? If so, you have only to say. I defer, always, to your rank.'

That was risible. The procurator, clearly, deferred to no-one. Cunomar watched as the prefect pinched the bridge of his nose. He looked like a man fighting a monumental headache. 'No,' he said. 'I believe we should bow in this case to your greater wisdom. The records are kept under seal in the governor's office. If you would care to lead the way?'

There was white marble on the floor of the office of the governor's clerk, and on the walls and across the roof. The desk at which sat the governor's clerk was of black marble and the candlesticks thereon were of solid gold, shaped like the heads of elephants, with the tallow tapers held in their coiled trunks.

Cunomar, who had spent two months as a prisoner in Rome and attended an audience with the emperor, recognized the ostentation of it, and the intent to impress. It was not a beautiful room, but the scent of money leaked from it, of a weight to stun the senses, so that anyone brought there would know that here was the wealth of Britannia openly displayed, and that this was only the clerk's cold, stone-lined office, which was the least of Rome's property.

The clerk himself was the smallest man in the room by a hand's breadth, but he commanded the space as if he were the officer and the others in his service. Cunomar had watched as he winnowed down the accumulating throng of the venal, the fearful and the merely curious to those who had either the authority to insist, or an unimpeachable reason for entering his domain.

There were four in the end. The prefect was the governor's highest representative and could not be dismissed. The procurator answered only to Nero and possibly outranked the prefect; certainly he outranked a clerk, however stately his office. Theophilus was present because the physician had cured the clerk's gallstones in the winter and the man had not the will to send him out.

That left only Cunomar, who was a barbarian and should not have been allowed into the office in the first place and would have been left to wait in the antechamber with his warriors, but that he was also the son of the late king and had a right to hear the reading of his father's will. He had smiled at the clerk, who was not used to dealing with the natives in any capacity, never to semi-naked young men with ornaments in their hair and scars across their bodies who smiled at him and flexed their shoulders so that the beast marks came momentarily alive. He had flushed darkly at the base of his throat, more as Cunomar's smile broadened, and abandoned his carefully structured protest.

Thus four men stood like errant children before the marble desk as the clerk searched for, found and read the roll of parchment that Prasutagos, by the emperor's grace king of the Eceni, had signed in front of witnesses on the day Eneit had died.

A part of Cunomar lived for ever in the elder cave of the Caledonii where he had first met the she-bear. There, lying under hot knives for three days, he had learned what it was to school his mind and his body to the service of the gods.

That knowledge served him well in the chilled marble office of the governor's clerk. It blurred his senses and resharpened them so that he could smell the almost-victory in the procurator, and the wary honesty of Corvus, the prefect, and the more pragmatic despair of the physician. The bear marks on his shoulders burned as if newly made and his guts churned with the prospect of a battle he did not fully know how to fight, but could not afford to lose.

Believing him the best, his mother had sent him, and, believing himself the best, Cunomar had accepted the gift of her trust and come. He believed it still, depending on his bear-honed instincts to tell him how to act when the time came. All that was required of him in the waiting between was that he hold himself ready and not give way to his fear. He eased his shoulders up and back, spreading the tension. The clerk looked up as he did it, and the black points of his eyes flared open.

The man swallowed, drily, and, slowly, as if to an idiot, said, 'You are the king's son?'

Cunomar smiled purely to see the man flush again and said, in faultless Latin, 'I am his son in name only. I am not of his blood.'

'I see. That would explain it.' In the chill of early spring, in a room clothed in stone, the clerk was sweating lightly. His gaze flickered from the procurator to the prefect and back. It was not clear whose patience would fray first, only that neither man was inclined to be kept waiting any longer.

Corvus spoke first. 'Clerk, if we could have the detail of the king's bequest, without any of the interjections to gods or emperor, we would be more speedily gone from your office.'

The clerk hesitated, weighing the needs of the law against the more urgent need to be rid of the men who had invaded his office. At length, dropping his eyes to the document in front of him, he said, 'Leaving out the lists of horses and gold and land and subjects, it is clear that the king makes no mention of his son in his will as would have been proper, but instead leaves half of his estate to the emperor, long may he be blessed, and the other half . . . to his two daughters.'

Cunomar had not expected to be mentioned. A part of him exulted in the honouring of Graine and Cygfa while the rest began to plan how it might be possible to keep 'Tagos' 'estate' to a minimum. Too late, he felt the procurator's silent triumph on one side and Corvus' equal despair on the other.

Looking up, he saw something unspoken but tangible pass between Corvus and Theophilus, the physician. They both turned to face him and he read pity in their eyes, and a wish to help and no way to do it.

Theophilus nudged him. The procurator was speaking and Cunomar had not heard. 'I'm sorry?' he said.

The man spoke again, in a child's easy Latin, spacing the words. 'Your sisters, the daughters of the king, are they married?'

Within the space of a sentence, they were in combat, as plainly as if the blades were already blooded. Because the gods loved only the truth, Cunomar said, 'The Eceni do not marry. We see no value in it.'

The marbled silence fell apart. A single tear of wax dripped from one of the elephant-borne candles onto the clerk's table. The noise it made was less than the falling of a feather and sounded loud to them all. Corvus winced. Theophilus shut his eyes and tapped his forefingers to his lips.

Decianus Catus, procurator of all goods and monies owing to

the emperor, and Nero's civil representative in the province of Britannia, laughed openly.

'Then they are orphaned and must, of course, be made wards of the emperor who will undertake the onerous burden of managing their goods and property. He will be happy to find suitable husbands for them in Rome. Many men, I am sure, would be glad to wed the daughter of a barbarian king, if the dowry be large enough. A portion of the Eceni revenues would persuade even the dullest of senator's sons to— No!' The procurator stepped back, cracking his hip on the clerk's table. Shrilly, 'Would you offer violence in front of a prefect?'

'I offer you no violence.'

It was true; Cunomar had not moved. Three days under the bear knives of the Caledonii kept him still against every fibre of instinct and the hot, curdling need to kill that he had seen in his mother and never yet felt in himself. That it had showed, however briefly, in his eyes, or on his face, was regrettable. He did what he could to find the quiet in his soul.

In that, he had help. Theophilus was behind him; he could feel the physician's hand in the small of his back and hear in Eceni the soft murmurings of the invocations to Nemain that came before battle. Corvus, too, was closer than he had been, so that his shoulder met Cunomar's and his weight kept him steady. The prefect said, 'If he had made a move, I would arrest him. He has not moved.'

'He is a barbarian and knows no civility.' The procurator would have died in battle; his fear showed too openly. Sweating, he said, 'They kill without care for the consequences. Philus is proof of that. The emperor's property must be recovered with all speed or they will secrete it. Prefect, if it is to be done swiftly, I will need armed support.'

'Which you have. As you were careful to show us earlier.'

'A single century of former legionaries is not sufficient.'

'I would beg to differ.' Corvus was frigidly polite. 'The king's son has listened to you traduce his sisters and has shown admirable restraint. However, if you believe you need additional men to approach his mother in her mourning, then you will have to recruit them. I have three cohorts of men at my command and have orders to lead them west to the governor's aid. Titus Aquilius, primus

402

pilus of the Twentieth legion, will remain here with a single century at his disposal. There is no question but that you outrank him. If you wish to order his troops to escort you north, leaving him with no-one with whom to police the affairs of Camulodunum, then you must of course do so. I will advise him to require that you sign a memorandum of your order in front of witnesses so that if and when the veterans run amok, or one of the natives drinks over-much and cannot be restrained, it is clear why he was left unable to act.'

Corvus leaned against the clerk's marble desk and toyed with the soft, pooling wax beneath the elephant's head. In Eceni, thought-fully, as if reciting a litany, he said, 'Son of the Boudica, I can do no more. Keep safe your father's legacy. Do not throw away your life, as he did not.'

Looking up, he said in more formal Latin, 'Cunomar, I am sorry for the behaviour of my countryman. The offer of our city's hospitality remains, for you and your honour guard, while the procurator arranges his affairs. I believe you should travel north with him, and that he would want that.'

'He would indeed. He will, in fact, insist that the "king's son" and his rabble be kept under armed guard until we can take them back whence they came. If you wish to feed them as they wait, you may do so, but if you let even one of them go, you will answer to the emperor for it.'

The procurator pushed past and opened the door. Outside, Unagh and the other seven of Cunomar's honour guard waited in the cold marble space of the antechamber. Beyond that, in the square that surrounded the governor's residence, eighty armed men of the procurator's command waited on his word.

Left with Corvus and Theophilus in the clerk's office, Cunomar examined and then discarded all the possible paths of action. Every one of them led to disaster; for himself, for his she-bears, for his mother, for the war host that, even now, she was raising.

Keep safe your father's legacy. Do not throw away your life, as he did not. Corvus was as much a warrior as Cunomar; he had seen the paths and the deaths at the end of each and had tried, in his own way, to avert catastrophe. He had failed.

Cunomar had watched the dignity with which his father faced his own death in Rome. As the procurator's men formed into a line and eight of them came into the office to escort him out, he found something close to that dignity within himself so that he could bow and say to Corvus, 'Thank you. The prefect has always been a friend to the Eceni. My mother holds you close and will continue to do so, whatever now befalls our people.'

XXXIII

THE GOD CAME TO VALERIUS IN THE SHAPE OF A BLACK BULL, holding the moon between its horns, or perhaps as the moon, holding fast a bull on the sickle edge of its blade.

He saw it by the light of the fire, standing near the edge of the field. It stayed there as he got up and went to find what had drawn him out. The hound walked at his side, more substantial under the old moon than the new.

The bull was a solid thing of flesh and blood, alive with the power and passions of spring. It ambled over to the thorn hedge and snuffed at Valerius' hand and curled a long tongue round the edge of his palm for the taste of his salt sweat.

He stayed with it a while, listening to the wind in the hawthorns and the whisper of the gods, and then went back to the fire and roused Longinus who rolled over sleepily and, much as the bull had done, caught his wrist and kissed the heel of his hand.

'You smell of cattle.'

'There's a bull in the field.'

'Ah.' Longinus tried to turn round and could not. 'Is it red?'

'No, black. And real, but we need to move.'

'Why does that not surprise me?' Awake now, Longinus sat up. Through ten days of travel, he had regained most of the weight he had lost after the battle and the haggard press of pain was gone from his eyes. He shook the sleep from his head and drank from the beaker of water that Valerius offered him.

He looked over the hedge at the bull, which looked back. 'I didn't know the bull-god still spoke to you since you desecrated his shrine.'

'I restored it. That's different. And it may not be Mithras. We're in Eceni territory now. The ancestors of this land knew the god in the form of a bull long before the legions brought their All-father from Persia. At least you can stand; that's good. Can you run, do you think?'

'If I must. It was my head that was injured, not my legs. Where are we going?'

'To find ourselves weapons not made by Rome. We're not going far, but we need to be back here before dawn.'

'Why can't we ride?'

'The place we're going is guarded. The horses can't go there.'

Longinus shivered. Nothing of man would guard a place against horses, but not men. 'But we are invited?' he asked.

'I hope so.'

They ran and then walked and then ran again. The moon rose high in the sky and the night was no longer young.

Valerius felt a tremor through the soles of his feet, the whisper of Nemain made manifest, tinged with undercurrents far older. He followed it forward, letting it guide his reason. Falling behind, Longinus stumbled on a thorn root. He was slowing and clearly in pain.

Valerius pushed through a thicket of briars and berry bushes with an open landscape beyond, cast in muted silver and black. It looked as he imagined the lands of the dead, which was not a good thing to think of.

He stopped by a solitary birch and waited. 'I'm sorry. I hadn't realized it was so far. We can rest for the day once we've got the blades and are back at the fire.'

Longinus reached him, breathing hard and holding his side. He grinned, tightly. 'Don't apologize. If we're going to fight, I need to be fit.' He closed his eyes and leaned back against the birch. 'I take it we are going to fight?'

Valerius' attention was on the hound, which had gone ahead, down a track made by another moon than the one that lit the night. Without thinking greatly, he said, 'It would seem so. If we need blades, it must be to fight. Not tonight, but soon.' The tremor beneath his feet steadied and became more certain. Leaving the birch, he followed it forward and left, between two boulders.

Longinus' voice sought him out. 'Have your gods told you which side we'll be on?'

'Not yet. Have yours?'

'Hardly.' Longinus barked a short, pained laugh. 'Mine are too busy trying to keep me alive to be concerned with minor details like which side of a foreign war I might be asked to fight for.' He pushed himself forward as far as the boulders. 'We should run again. Dawn is not so far and I have no wish to find out what happens if we are not back by the fire before daylight.'

'I think we're here. Come and look.'

Had the hound and the thrumming of the gods not guided him, Valerius would never have found the grave mound. Even standing a spear's length from the opening, he was not certain what it was, except that he could hear voices that were not in his ears, nor even in his head, but in the far corners of his soul. They were angry, but not with him, or perhaps he was simply so used to the anger of the dead that he had become inured to the power of it. He tilted his head, trying to hear beyond the wash of noise to what lay beneath.

Longinus reached him, and regretted it. 'Gods, Valerius . . .' The Thracian had forgotten his pain. He gripped the hilt of the blade at his side, which was a good, solid Roman cavalry blade and of no worth at all against those already dead. He took in the grave mound, and its opening. 'It's very small,' he said faintly.

Despite himself, Valerius laughed. 'The dead do not need great space.'

'Nor light, I should think. Did you bring a flame?'

'I did.' Since his time in the god's cave, Valerius had carried the means to make light everywhere; tinder and a candle and a small rod dipped in a mix of pine resin and sheep fat that flared and held a larger flame than the candle might have done. He lit it now and carried it in his sword hand, as an act of trust. 'I won't make you come, but I think you should.'

'So do I.' Longinus was hoarse with nerves. 'I'll go where the light goes. Just don't let it go out.'

*

Longinus was right; the mound was small. Valerius crawled through an opening that would have been cramped for a child, and on through a tunnel that came out, at length, into a chamber far smaller than the one inside the dreaming mound of the ancestors on Hibernia.

His pine resin flame flickered on rock and bones and dried turf. He could feel others around him: Cunomar, the spoiled child; Cygfa, the warrior who was Caradoc reborn as woman and terrifying for it; Valerius' own father, not Luain mac Calma, but Eburovic, master bladesmith of the Eceni, whom he had known as father for all of his childhood. Above them all, stronger, nearer, so close he could touch her, was Breaca.

She was not here. She could not be here; the space in the mound did not allow it, but she had been, and left a part of herself behind. Valerius made himself look beyond the shifting shadows to the flame and all it touched on, to the rock and old bones and mouse droppings and then, blindingly – how could he not have seen them at the start? – to the five blades that lay on ledges cut into the walls.

The pressure in his head was astonishing; not in the ancestors' mound in Hibernia or in Mithras' cave in the western mountains had he felt so closely the presence of the dead, or their certain intent to kill. Theirs was a serpent's hiss that filled his mind, designed to steal his soul and drive him empty back into the night to die. Uniquely, their hatred seemed impersonal; they did not loathe Valerius for who he was or what he had been, simply for being there, and for having come uninvited.

He had been invited; he believed that with all that he knew to be true. Closing his eyes, he sought the same thread of the moon and the direction of the bull that bore the moon between its horns, and found it, and stepped forward to meet what was there, less inimical than the rest.

Slowly, the world became iron, woven and beaten and woven again, and bronze molten and flowing, red as life blood, cast into the shape of a feeding she-bear that rose on her hind legs to look at him. It spoke in the voice of Eburovic, not-father to Valerius, who had spent the whole of one spring in the making of just this one blade.

Take it, blade of my soul. Keep it safe. You will know what must be done with it and when.

Through all the years of his haunting, in the uncountable taunts of the dead, Eburovic had never hated his son, nor wished him ill. Valerius asked, 'Why now?' and heard nothing.

'We shouldn't be here.' Longinus said it, whispering. His voice was lost in the spitting havoc of the dead.

My son, lift the bear from the stone. It is yours by right.

'You are not my father.' It was true. When had he come truly to believe it? Sometime on Mona, when yet another dreamer had mistaken him for the Elder and regretted it after. 'Luain mac Calma sired me.'

Nevertheless, I give you the blade of my making to hold and to keep until I ask that you relinquish it.

'What of the others? Not all five blades were made by you.'

No, but still, they are good. Take them. In the war that is coming, they will be needed. Too few are left that carry the good-will of the dead.

'Valerius, we should . . .' Longinus, living, was less tangible than the dead.

The ghost was the centre of the world, all-powerful and all-knowing, as Eburovic had seemed to the child Bán, who grew to be Valerius. It made the salute of one warrior to another and then of the warrior to the dreamer. It formed its left hand into the crescent of Nemain, that could have been the horns of a bull. *Please?* It spoke, earnestly. *As the one who was your father in all but blood, I ask it of you. More lives than yours depend on it.*

No ghost had ever pleaded with Valerius. He had been threatened, barracked, promised death and an eternity of others' vengeance in the lands beyond life, but never had any one of them asked him for a favour.

The novelty of it shocked him, and the sudden clarity, as of fog lifting with the dawn; this once in his life, he understood exactly what he must do – and could do it.

He said, 'Longinus, if you trust me at all, help me carry the blades. Choose whichever suits you best, except this one, and keep it. The rest we will keep in our riding packs. Do it now, without thinking. Or if you must think, think of the Crow-horse and what it was like to ride him, not the shadows that would bring you to ruin. Think of the Crow-horse, think of what it is to hold him when he is in full flight . . . Good man, well done. Now follow me

409

out. If you can run, we will run. If not, we will walk. If we are back at the fire before daylight, we will be safe.'

'I can run.' Longinus was behind him, step for step and breath for breath, crawling out through the entrance into the night and back down the track along which they had come. 'You wouldn't believe how fast I can run.'

XXXIV

THE SOUND OF HAMMERED METAL MARKED TIME AT THE SITE OF
the Eceni horse fairs.

For lack of anything better to pass the time, Breaca beat
out the tang of a sword blade in the new forge, built by the she-
bears next to the great-house.

The day was sharp with frost and potential. A brisk wind sent
clouds in the shape of herons across the sky; a thrush clucked in
the trees behind the forge, not quite in time with her hammer;
across the clearing, six new warriors arrived as a group, bright in
their blue Eceni cloaks, with the clan marks of the fox about the
hems and sleeves.

Through the making of the tang, they were greeted by the she-
bears assigned to that day, helped to settle in the great-house,
shown what food and weapons and armour was available, and
showed in turn what they had brought on their pack horses, which
was considerable; for a people starved through winter, the incoming warriors had brought more than any of Breaca's group had
imagined. Over the half-month since the snows had begun to melt,
the stores of grain, of dried meat, of oat bannocks baked for the
journey, had grown as the stocks of blades and spear-heads fell.

They were not many yet, the warriors who flocked to her call,
but they were the beginnings of a war host. On the day Cunomar
left to take his message to Camulodunum, one hundred and eighty

warriors had already gathered. By the day after, when he had still not returned, that number had risen by sixty and continued to rise through the morning.

Breaca watched as each new group were not only given weapons and shown the beginnings of how to use them, but were also instructed in how best to evacuate the great-house. Gunovar did it, crouching on the sandy soil, drawing maps with the point of her knife and showing the waymarkers used by the she-bears: the black-painted staves and bear-claw marks slashed on trees that would show the warriors the way out of the clearing to the forest and, perhaps, back in again.

They were not sent away; an army forced into retreat before it has ever formed is one crippled from the start. Still, no-one doubted it would happen if Cunomar failed.

He would not fail. Breaca needed to believe that, and had made herself do so, through the evening and sleepless night after his leaving and again as the new day dawned and he had not yet returned. She calculated three times the time it might take him to reach the city, give his news and return. At her best estimate, he could appear any time after noon on the day following his departure. She marked it in her mind and then forgot it: counting the heartbeats did not make the time move faster.

Halfway to noon, with nothing else to do, she began work on a fresh sword-blade. Elsewhere, others found their own occupations. Graine sat cradling the head of a heavily pregnant hound bitch who lay in the spring sun in front of the smithy, enjoying the warmth from the fires; Airmid spoke to the dozen or so dreamers who had come with their warriors, as had always been the case in the old days: one dreamer for every warrior, to keep their heart in battle; Dubornos and Gunovar began schooling the incomers in use of sword and spear; Ardacos stood at the roasting pits, seeing to Cunomar's hunted deer; and Cygfa . . . finally Cygfa came, who had been keeping watch on the southern trackway to Camulodunum.

She came in too fast on a foundering horse and threw herself to the ground outside the forge. 'Theophilus of Athens and Cos sends a message: "Your son is not dead. They have not put him to the question. But the procurator is bringing him north at speed, with three hundred mercenary veterans behind him. Put your affairs in order, and hide whatever you would not wish him to seize in the name of the emperor." '

Breaca laid down the half-made blade. 'Did Theophilus meet you himself?'

'No. He sent a messenger who turned back; he did not wish to be seen by the procurator, but he brought this, as evidence of his good faith.' Cygfa opened her hand. A staff of applewood spanned her palm, wound about with two snakes in the sign of the caduceus that was the physician's personal mark. She said. 'He's telling the truth. I saw a cavalcade of horsemen riding hard on the track north from Camulodunum. They have wagons in train, which slows them, but they will still reach 'Tagos' steading by midday.'

The morning became very still. With exaggerated care, Breaca placed her hammer across the anvil, as if the angle of it mattered and must be got right.

It was not like battle, this destruction of a vision; there was no fire in her soul, or clash of blades, or swing and strike that might lead equally to life or death but would at least be action.

Outwardly, nothing had changed. The wind still blew from the east, sending clouds in the shape of herons to spear across the snow-thin sky. The same thrush chucked in the thorns on the edge of the clearing. Stone lay at her side and she could still feel the easy rhythm of his breathing against her shin, although he had lifted his head and was looking at her, cross-browed, as if she had spoken his name and then nothing more.

Reaching down to rub his ears on his skull, she said, 'And if they find the steading empty, they will set their Coritani tracker to find us. We have hidden the tracks to here well enough to keep away the legions, but not one of our own.'

Others had gathered; those who mattered, so that she was not alone. Ardacos came from the roasting pits, and Dubornos from the warrior-training. Gunovar was close, and Airmid, who stood now at her left side, and held Graine's hand. The she-bears and the new warriors of her war host who had trekked through melting snow and knee-deep mud to come to her grouped in a half-circle a short distance away from the forge, and made a show of not listening.

Looking out at them, Cygfa said, 'How many have we?'

Breaca shook her head. 'Not enough to face three centuries

of time-served veterans who scent gold and slaves for the taking.'

Quietly, Ardacos said, 'Of those who have come, less than a dozen have lived through war. The rest are as untrained as the she-bears were before winter. They need half a month, at the very least, to learn how to hold themselves in battle or they will die to no cause.'

He spoke aloud what they all knew. The choices were clear and well rehearsed; they had talked of little else since midwinter, so that the paths forward had become tales for the telling, like the hero tales of the singers.

Because it needed to be spoken aloud, Breaca said, 'We could wait for them here and fight, and lose everything. Or we few can take half of Cunomar's she-bears and meet the procurator where he expects to find us at 'Tagos' steading and delay them at least until the remaining warriors have had time to disperse. It is not what we dreamed. It's not in any way what we prayed for, but it was always the risk and we cannot, with any honour, endanger the lives of those we have called here. If they can be sent to safety, to fight at another time, we have to make it possible. Dubornos, I want you to—'

'No. Lanis can do it. I won't leave you.'

Breaca's mind had already run ahead. Shocked, she brought it back. Dubornos was smiling at her. There was more humour in his gaze than she had seen in all their joint adulthood.

He said, 'Caradoc tried much the same and gave in. I won't leave you and you haven't time to waste trying to make me. Lanis knows the land here better than I do. She's a dreamer; the warriors will listen to her. She can organize the evacuation.'

'She can, yes, but she has not given me an oath to protect the Boudica's children or die in the attempt. Would you not honour it now that we have most need of you?'

Breaca would have softened that, but there was so little time. Dubornos flushed and then paled. Stiffly, he said, 'What would you have me do?'

'Take Graine and—'

'No!' Graine broke free of Airmid's grasp and stood on her own in the doorway. She glared at her mother, making a straight line of lips that wavered. With the sun behind and the fire in front, held between two lights, she looked more ethereal than she had ever done. 'I'm not going away without you. If you leave without me, I'll follow you, and you won't be able to stop me.'

There was no time to make it easier for her, either; every heart-beat, now, brought them closer to disaster.

'Forgive me,' said Breaca, 'I love you,' and, taking her knife from her belt, she struck her daughter on the head with the back end of the hilt near the temple, where the damage would be least after-wards when she came to her senses.

Graine moaned and crumpled to the floor, blue-lipped and twitching. Dubornos knelt and gathered her, carefully.

'Wait.' Breaca put her hands to the torc at her neck. She had worn it since the day after 'Tagos' death when Cygfa had first handed it to her, and had felt nothing more than the warmth and weight of its metal. Any power it might have had seemed to have waned. 'She should have this. You will need to hold it until she is of age—'

She stopped, because she could no longer speak. The woven gold had become thick, corded snake coils that writhed under her hand, pressing on the vessels of her neck. In the caverns of her mind, a gap opened, and a mountain wind blew through. She could have fought it, possibly she would have done, but Airmid's hand on her wrist stopped her, and Airmid's voice, carefully guarded, said, 'Breaca, you are still first born of the Eceni. Don't discard that now.'

She took her hand away. The pressure around her neck eased. The wind died in her mind.

Dubornos stood waiting, cradling Graine's broken head against his shoulder. Her daughter should have something to carry through her life apart from memories. The brooch of the serpent spear with its tags of black wool was pinned to Breaca's shoulder, as it had been since the day Caradoc had sent it as his gift from Gaul.

'You are my first thought and my last, for all time.' Caradoc had sent the message then and Breaca said it now, quietly, as she unpinned the brooch and set it on Graine's tunic, a gift from both parents that would go with her into adulthood.

Dubornos understood, and could explain it when the child was old enough. His black eyes thanked her.

Breaca leaned forward and kissed her daughter and then, to his surprise, Dubornos. 'Protect her for me,' she said.

'With my life.'

She had never seen him weep. Tears smeared his cheeks as he nodded to those who were left, to Ardacos, Airmid, Gunovar, and last to Cygfa, to whom he had given the spark of his soul knowing she could never return it, and carried his too-light burden from the smithy.

There was quiet after he had gone, as there might have been before battle, if the body of a slain scout had been found and the strength of the enemy tested and found real.

Breaca said, 'We need someone to hide the blades. I have not worked all winter to lose them now. Gunovar, you can—'

'I can come with you and see what your son has made of himself in the company of Rome. The warriors can take the weapons made so far. The unworked iron will have to stay here; there isn't time to bury it. And don't try to hit me as you did your daughter. I'm too old for that, and you don't have time to lose fighting me instead of Rome.'

Starkly, Breaca said, 'You know how we may die?'

The broken dreamer splayed her hand flat across the scars of her face. Her crooked mouth twisted, accentuating the scars. 'Do you doubt it?'

'No. Of course not. I'm sorry. Your life is yours to cast to the gods as you wish.'

The rest gathered round: Cygfa who had been to Rome and stood in the shadow of her own crucifix and kept her damage to herself; Ardacos, who could yet go north and be an elder amongst the Caledonii; Airmid, heart of her heart, soul of her soul, who could have been Elder of Mona and taken the dreaming west to Hibernia.

Breaca said, 'I would prefer that all of you left, now, with Dubornos and Lanis and the warriors, but I don't have the power to compel you.'

They all knew it, and struggled to find the words. In the end, it was Cygfa who said lightly, 'I don't think the procurator would stop long at the steading if he found only one woman within it.'

Which was why, in a shorter time than any of them imagined possible, Breaca of the Eceni led half of her son's honour guard and all but two of the men and women who held the strings of her heart down to the steading to which she had brought them two years before.

Shortly thereafter, as the trackway trembled to the hammer of incoming horses, she led them out again to stand before the emperor's procurator of taxes and his three hundred mercenary veterans.

She left Stone at the gates so that he might not scent the enemy and attack them out of hand and rode the grey battle mare because it was the most reliable of all her horses, and dressed in a new tunic of Eceni blue with a knotwork of muted grey bordering the sleeves and neck and hem, because it looked least warlike. She left her hair unbraided to hang to her shoulder and her shield hidden and outwardly bore no knife nor anything edged that might conceivably be considered a weapon, nor any armbands that might show undue wealth, but only the corded gold torc of the Eceni that weighed like rope about her neck.

As she rode her mare forward to greet the head of the incoming riders, she sought through the voids of all-time for the grandmother, the ancestor, or Nemain. All were silent.

'It does us no honour and I regret it deeply, but we cannot feed three hundred men. Winter has left our stores empty and the trading has not yet begun.'

It was true, after its fashion. Certainly the steading had little by way of provisions and the two dozen she-bear warriors who had followed Breaca from the great-house had brought only enough from the great-house to feed themselves. As befitted a settlement in mourning, the she-bears wore tunics tied with unmade rawhide belts and no gold and their belt-knives were short and could not be challenged under Roman law. They occupied themselves with tending the horses or the fields and none welcomed the procurator, or invited him in.

Later, if they had to fight, there would be no risk that any of them had broken the guest laws and incurred the gods' disfavour.

'Thank you. We bring our own provisions.'

Breaca had addressed the procurator in Latin and he replied to her in Eceni, through a youth of the Trinovantes who wound a finger in his hair and stared at the ground and would not look up.

Without waiting for the boy to finish, the procurator pushed his flea-bitten grey gelding through the gates. He was a man in a hurry; his eyes fed on the gold at the Boudica's neck, not the quiet wool of her tunic or the carefully combed sheen of her hair. His men followed him, orderly as any legion.

Cunomar and his eight she-bears were in the second century, flanked by veterans from Camulodunum, men whom Breaca recognized by sight but not by name. She had traded with them in the time before Eneit's death, swapping belt buckles for raw bronze, or an armband for iron; two had been present in the theatre to witness the spear contest with the former governor.

One of these nudged his neighbour and said something coarse in gutter Latin but Breaca's attention had already passed behind to the rear of the column where rode a Coritani youth who bore in his topknot the trio of red kite feathers that marked him as a scout of the legions, and, more importantly, displayed openly the warrior marks of a fire lizard on his arms.

Each was both a warning and a declaration of enmity and each was unnecessary; his face, seen in profile, was a younger stamp of the slave seller Breaca and Cunomar had killed in the forest beyond the horse fair and she would have seen that in him any-where, without need for reminders.

He rode at the tail of the second century and made no effort to hide himself; quite the reverse. Passing by, his eyes met Breaca's, and he nodded a greeting that carried more threat in its cool, quiet understanding than all the procurator's mercenaries put together. Because it mattered not to show the depth of her shock, she saluted him after the manner of the Coritani warriors and was surprised when he returned it.

A standard-bearer rode to the front of the column, holding aloft a banner on which weighing scales stitched in silver graced a scarlet background. He signalled with it and the rearmost century stepped out of line and encircled the steading. It was done smoothly, the product of much practice.

The remaining two centuries divided into eights; one group to guard Cunomar, another for all of his she-bears, a third to watch over Breaca and her family, except for Ardacos, who was a grown man and clearly a warrior and so warranted another eight guards on his own.

Those not called to guard duty spread out into a line that ran from one edge of the steading to the other. The standard-bearer signalled and they walked forward in perfect step. One man in every eight was armed with a stylus and tablet.

'The men will prepare an inventory. You will remain with us while it is done. Afterwards, you will be required to confirm it.'

The procurator spoke in Latin and the Trinovante youth translated into stilted Eceni and in either language what he said was unacceptable. Nevertheless, in the time it took to speak it, and to repeat it, another thirty warriors had run another hundred paces further away from this man and his mercenaries and all the machinery of Rome.

Breaca nodded and said to the youth, 'If the procurator would care to wait in the king's chamber? It has not been used since his death, but I can light the fire and the damp will clear.'

The procurator was not comfortable in the chill damp of an unaired, unheated room. He chose to remain in the king's chamber only for the time it took to overturn the coin-chest and reveal it empty.

'You have hidden his money. Where?'

'Why would I hide what we have to pay in taxes? If we had it, you could take it now.'

'Then how will you pay if you have nothing?'

The procurator was a man for whom food was never short over winter, and his life depended on making Britannia pay; she had to remember that.

Breaca said, 'The money is not due until midsummer. By then, we will have traded enough horses and hounds to pay. I have a bitch due to whelp that will—'

'You would pay the emperor's dues with *hounds*?'

'If the procurator had ever hunted, he would know the value of Eceni hounds.' The young Coritani hawk-scout leaned against the doorpost. He had been there from the start, an unobtrusive observer. He said, 'My father's people would pay the worth of a war-trained colt for a brood bitch of the Eceni. You should remember that in your inventories.'

She had killed his father and he knew it; how could he not when word of the Boudica's kill had spread through every steading of every tribe in the east? There was, therefore, no reason for him to help her. Breaca nodded her thanks and it was gracefully received and her nerves jangled; an enemy who offers help is twice dangerous.

There was nothing she could do and the procurator was the present danger. He was staring at the wall where the king's sword had once hung. The wood was paler by a whisper where it had been.

'Prasutagos was fighting with a weapon not legal under law,' he said. 'Where did he get it?'

He was guessing. 'Tagos' blade was with Breaca's, hidden in the smithy by the great-house where only a search of utter destruction could find it; he could not possibly know its length. Even so, it did no harm to talk. Each passing moment was its own victory.

Breaca waited for the interpreter and said, 'I have no idea what length his blade might have been or where he might have got it. He was the king. He did not share such knowledge with me and he is dead, and so cannot be asked. If you have the weapon, you could read the smith marks on it to find the source.'

The procurator stared at her and smiled, thinly. His lips were the bluish purple of a bad heart and his skin the sallow of an over-taxed liver. Without the legions of Rome to give him power, he would have made his money writing wills for small-town merchants and spent it in a brothel. 'Later,' he said. 'When the inventory is done.'

The air in the king's chamber was musted from a winter of no use; they did not tarry there long. Outside, the line of walking mercenaries had crossed the steading. Half of them turned back through the gates and were working their way up through the horse paddocks, past the in-foal brood mares to the youngstock and geldings, to the three breeding horses kept apart on the slopes of the hill.

The last son of the grey battle mare was up there, product of a lifetime's breeding. His sire had died, killed under Braint on Mona before he could truly be tested. The son he had left was not yet trained for battle, but had raced twice in the autumn and won. His first foals were due in the spring and would outrun the best of the best. He stood in the highest field and screamed at the strangers, who were not horsemen and dared not go close.

Next to Stone, who stood with his shoulder pressed to her knee, the grey mare's son had been Breaca's greatest beacon of how life had once been and might yet be when the legions had been destroyed. She was surprised, amidst all the turmoil, how much the sight of him lifted her, and the thought of losing him hurt.

Even so, it was important to keep speaking. 'The horses are poor after a winter with little fodder,' she said. 'They will be fit again in time for the autumn horse fair.'

The procurator did not break his gaze from the hillside. 'By autumn, that will no longer be your concern.' The Trinovante interpreter could not bring himself to translate. Breaca did not remind him.

Another warrior another spear length away. It mattered not to rise to this. It mattered, instead, to know where each member of her family was, and to account for them, moment by moment, until the time came to act.

Cunomar was sitting on a log in the middle of the steading with his eight guards around him. He caught his mother's eye and pressed his hand to his arm. He wore no tunic and so had no knife concealed beneath his sleeve, but he had seen, or guessed, where Breaca kept hers, far longer than was legal, bound to the inside shaft of her left forearm. He was unarmed, but he was a she-bear and could kill without weapons. She had seen Ardacos do so often.

Airmid, Cygfa and Gunovar were held apart, just outside 'Tagos' chamber. Above everything else, it mattered not to be taken too far from them; Airmid bore no knife and could not be left alive for long when the fighting started. More than anything else, Breaca was grateful that she had not let Graine come.

'You have more horses than this.'

A man less desperate might have made it a question. There was no clear reason that Breaca could see why the procurator of the emperor's taxes should be so driven, unless, unwitting, he felt the urgency in her.

Striving for calm, she said, 'Through the winter, the horse herds are spread out across the land, to give least burden to each steading. We bring them in again after foaling in the spring.'

That made sense, at least. The procurator pursed his lips and said, 'In that case, how many head have you altogether, that were the property of the king?'

'The king had no interest in horses. None of these were his.'

'Who owns them, then?'

'I do.'

'You are his wife.' The procurator looked at her flatly. 'Therefore they were his and are now the emperor's. How many?'

Breaca had been an elder in the council of Mona, she could school her face to her will whatever the chaos within. She said, 'After the winter we have had? It's hard to tell. If the mares have lived and carry foals to term, if the foaling goes well and the youngstock thrive, then, including the foals, we will tally over one thousand. If the foaling goes poorly and we lose mares and foals as we have done in some years, perhaps as low as seven hundred. Such things are in the hands of the gods.'

'From today, they are in the hands of the emperor,' said the procurator, 'which is more certain than any god.' He turned on his heel, still counting numbers. His eyes fell on Stone who lay at her side. 'If the hounds are of value, we should include them. How many have you?'

She could school her face from a Roman, not her soul from her hound. Stone was dangerous when he growled, but lethal when silent. He rose to his feet now, without a sound. Breaca laid a hand on his neck and felt his mane grow stiff along the length of his spine. She said, 'The hounds of the Eceni are traded only at need, and only those surplus to our own breeding. Until the whelping is over, there are none to spare.'

The procurator ran his tongue round the upper arcade of his teeth and a vein pulsed at his temple. He spoke crisply to the interpreter. 'Ask again. She does not understand. How many hounds were in the king's household? How many in the outlying lands?'

Sometime in the past few breaths, it had become clear that battle, and death, were inevitable. If she were going to die, Breaca wished it to be over something worthwhile. Before the interpreter had taken breath, she said in Latin, 'I understood fully. The hounds of the Eceni are not for sale, nor will they be given in payment of tax.'

The procurator answered her directly this time, and it pained him to do it. Spacing his words, he said, 'You do not understand. This is not a tax. This is an assessment of the emperor's property. Your king is dead. What was the king's has become the emperor's: his lands, his wealth, his horses, his hounds, his wife and his daughters. Everything that was Eceni is now of Rome.' He smiled, tightly. 'It is of no consequence to me whether you answer freely or under duress, but you will answer. I will ask you once more, and only once; how many hounds?'

If she remembered the thrush that had woken her in the morning, she might remain sane. Breaca said, 'The king wrote a will. It was witnessed by the last governor.' Out of the corner of her eye, she saw Cunomar shake his head.

The procurator saw it too, and claimed his victory. 'Your king left half of his estate to his emperor, as is proper. The other half he left to his daughters, clearly intended as dowry.' His gaze roamed to Cygfa and back. 'I am told that one of the king's daughters is a child and yet I see no children. Where is she?'

Too many people held their breaths. Locked in a wasteland of false calm, Breaca said, 'The king's daughter died over winter, of cold and hunger and grief at her father's death. I could take you to her grave, if you required to see it.'

The procurator pursed his lips and studied her and could not find the hole in the lie. 'No matter. That saves some senator's son from the duty of taking a native to wife, although I have been told that the savages of the north mature early and it would have been— *No!*'

It was not Cygfa who broke, or even Cunomar; not Gunovar or Airmid or Ardacos and the she-bears, but Breaca. It must have been her, however hard she tried to hold it, because Stone lived to serve her and it was Stone who attacked the procurator first, and it may have been that Cunomar was trying to pull the hound back, not to further the attack, but the mercenaries were not paid to watch and report what may or may not have happened, only to keep order and collect gold and goods and, at all costs, to protect the life and person of the man who paid them.

Stone was struck and then Cunomar was struck and then the she-bears, howling, were uncontrollable, which had always been the risk when they were there and Cunomar was in danger.

They fought better than Breaca had imagined. Against overwhelming numbers, armed with knives barely long enough to cut through a cheese, with woollen tunics as their only protection they hurled themselves at the veterans of the colony of Camulodunum in their legionary mail and leather armour and oval cavalry shields and the short blades of their days in service, which sang gladly to their hands and made short work of killing.

Eight Eceni died in as many heartbeats and three others were clubbed unconscious and Breaca had barely time to crack the point of her elbow against the nose of the veteran to her left and bring the long-bladed knife from its place on her arm, had not begun to think if there was time to kill the procurator or any of his men before she must turn it on Airmid, when she heard Cygfa shout the war cry of Mona and someone else scream in a voice she had never heard before, splitting the air with his pain.

She killed the veteran who stood to her right, because he was closest and the scream had taken his attention, and by the time her knife was free of his throat it was clear that it was not Cygfa or Airmid who had been taken, but Cunomar, who had fought without weapons and lost. Her son was held between two men, with his ear cut from his head and blood sheeting down the left half of his face.

'*Stop!* Stop now. His life is mine. Do you know how long a man may take to die?'

The shout was in perfect Eceni, not from any of the mercenaries, or the Trinovante interpreter, but from the Coritani scout who bore the mark of the fire lizard crawling up his arms, and who brandished Cunomar's severed ear on the tip of his knife.

'Don't stop!' Cunomar kicked and fought the two men who held him, and half a dozen of the she-bears took him at his word, but the momentum had gone from the bulk of them and another of the veterans took hold of Airmid and pressed the tip of his sword to her eye and that brought everyone to a halt.

There was a crystalline moment in which Breaca could have stepped forward and rammed her knife to the hilt in the living flesh of her dreamer's heart and Airmid, holding her gaze over the cold iron of the blade, would not have stopped her; only somewhere quite close, a thrush chucked in the thorns as it had in the morning and the space in her mind that the torc had newly opened was open again, and filled with a certainty that stopped her.

Then the moment was gone, and the shuddering release of violence and the promise of a clean death was lost, taking with it all hope of victory.

The procurator stood before Breaca, shaking. He was not a man used to battle and the closeness of his own death terrified him. He wiped both hands up his cheeks, kneading the flesh, and swept a trembling arm across his brow.

When he had done, and his features had settled, if not the palsy in his limbs, he spoke to her, drawing power from the armed men around him.

'You did not understand. Now you will do so. Before, you were the emperor's property. Now, you are his prisoners, taken in the act of assaulting his officers in the province of Britannia. The charge is insurrection and murder for which the penalty is death. When we have searched the steading and have garnered the additional evidence – because there *will* be some, you *did* kill Philus – then we will conduct a trial and pass sentence and you will have time, as you die, to reflect that life as the wife of a senator's third son in Rome might not have been so bad for any of you.'

XXXV

GRAINE WAS GONE TO SAFETY. THAT MUCH WAS GOOD.
The other news came in piecemeal, as the evening drew
darker and groups of mercenaries came to the procurator
to report, or simply showed what they had found. Those ordered
to search the steading did so as they had in the days when Valerius
led them: violently, destroying anything that might have held a
weapon. They found the shields hidden in the roof thatch, which
had never been in doubt, and a spear, which had been hidden long
ago and forgotten and was rusted beyond any reasonable use.

The Coritani scout helped those searching outside to find the
tracks leading to the great-house and there they discovered
the cache of unworked iron, which Breaca had hoped would not
happen, but was inevitable. Looking further, they found the tracks
leading away from the great-house but did not find any warriors,
or children; nor, as dusk began to fall, did they dare send out
trackers to look for them.

Except for Cunomar and Ardacos who were considered
dangerous and kept apart, the family of the dead king were im-
prisoned overnight in his chamber, after the bed had been taken out
and burned and the chest that had once held money. A small
bronze horse lay in one corner, unwanted and ignored.

Breaca had never been held captive. The possibility had always
been present; before every night-time foray in the west, before

every battle, she had schooled herself to imagine imprisonment and what would inevitably follow.

The reality was infinitely harder than she had imagined; not impossible, but close to it. Her respect for Cygfa and Cunomar, who had survived months in prison in Rome, with death waiting at each turn, rose with every passing heartbeat.

Lacking a fire, 'Tagos' chamber was a dark and airless place. Breaca stood leaning against the wall for a while, and then sat on the floor, pulling her knees to her chest so that her feet, outstretched, might not entangle the feet of another, intruding on their privacy. Privacy was important, she discovered, balancing the strength in not being alone.

She knew without asking where the others were sitting around her. Airmid kept close, so that they could feel each other's heartbeats; privacy did not matter there. Cygfa was directly opposite, with Gunovar a little to her left, each keeping silent, because that way lay strength; not-talking, they could maintain the illusion of not-fear. Only if they touched, or tried to speak, did it become clear that each of them was shaking, a small, continuous tremor that could not be controlled, but only contained, and experienced, so that by morning, perhaps, it could be damped and not shown to the world.

It did not help to think of the morning. Breaca pressed her spine hard into the wooden wall and turned her mind away from the future. She thought instead of food and water and the need to urinate and the cold of the wall and the weight of the ancestor-torc around her neck. She regretted not having given it to Dubornos to keep safe for Graine and the future however much the ancestor had railed against it. The procurator would take it now, before or after her death. Melted to gold, it would pay half a century for half a year. Or a century for a quarter-year. Or a single tent party of eight men for—

'Why would they bother with a trial?' Gunovar asked it, from somewhere nearby in the darkness. Her voice was quite steady.

Breaca said, 'For the records. We are a king's family. They will want it to be seen to be legal. Small men with small gods rarely do anything that is not accountable. Cygfa, was it like this in Rome?'

'If you discount the half-month in the hold of a ship spent getting there, and the physicians who insisted on physical examinations afterwards, and the two months of waiting while they tortured Caradoc and Dubornos, yes, it was quite like this. They fed us in Rome, and gave us water. We would have died else.' Cygfa contrived to sound drily amused. 'The shaking stops, eventually, after the second month. A body can only hold so much terror before it overflows.'

There was, it seemed, no harm in talking after all. A fear made open became less. Breaca said, 'With luck, we should have joined the grandmothers in Briga's care long before that.'

Cygfa snorted mild amusement. 'We can hope so. Julius Caesar kept Vercingetorix, war leader of the Gauls, in prison for seven years before he had him slain. I don't think our procurator has that much patience.'

'Or this emperor.'

Gunovar said, 'No. Although it would be better if he did not find you are the Boudica. His patience might be greater then, and you – and we – might live longer, and regret it more deeply.'

There was a short, shocked silence. Breaca said, 'Thank you. It might be a good thing to forget. I imagine they will not ask questions, unless they believe we have answers to hide.'

Gunovar said, 'And if they ask, seek death in the manner of their asking. Your body will try to live, but the ways to death will be open if you can embrace them.'

'We can try.'

The worst had been named aloud, and they were no worse for it. After that, they spoke of Rome, and Gunovar talked of her time under questioning in the fortress of the IInd legion in the southwest and there was a strange comfort in the memory of pain that is over and the reminder that everything passes in time; it is only that the waiting is tedious.

Only Airmid did not speak. She sat so close that Breaca could feel the lift and fall of her breathing, which was slower than sleep and faster than death, but only just, and meant that she was dreaming, which was good; any escape from the present was good.

Cygfa had begun to tell of the procession in Rome, led by Valerius, who had once been Bán, and how the ghosts of his past assailed him and were invisible to the legions, when Airmid breathed in hard and fast and let it out again, harshly.

'She's coming.'

'Who is?'

'Now. They're bringing her here. Do you still have your knife?'

It was the worst of warnings, and the best there could be, sent from deep within the dream, and it gave Breaca time to pull herself clear of the gaping hole that exploded in her chest, to school her features and to lift herself from the floor and appear composed as the sound of booted feet came closer, and the light of a brand lit the doorframe and then the doorway as the door was flung open to reveal hair the colour of ox blood, ragged now with human blood and sweat and tied tight with a cloth that wrapped the small mouth so she could not have screamed to warn her mother.

Graine was not safe.

She fell to the floor of Prasutagos' chamber, twisting to keep her face from the dirt. Her hands were tied behind and her tunic was filthy, with a triangular tear where the serpent-spear brooch had been ripped away.

'Your daughter died of hunger and grief in the winter.' The procurator stood in the doorway. 'You will therefore have no objections if we put this child to the question in the morning, to find the names of her parents and where they are hidden.'

'This is my daughter.' Breaca was weeping and did not care. What use composure? The torc became tight around her neck, or her throat had swollen with grief; either was possible and she had not time or strength to find out which. Through a blur of sweat and otherness, she said, 'I lied. Clearly my daughter did not die. I can point out those amongst your men who saw us together at the signing of the late king's will and can attest to it. If you have issue with that, the fault is mine.'

She knelt and lifted her daughter, light of her soul, to her breast, and pulled the gag from her mouth. Graine pressed her face into the crook of her mother's neck, sliming her skin with tears and her running nose.

There, too muffled to be clearly heard, she said, 'I'm sorry, it's my fault. I wanted to come back and prayed to Nemain to find a way but she wouldn't give it so I prayed to the ancestor-dreamer who holds the serpent-spear and then Dubornos fell asleep and I took his horse and it knew the way home and then I fell off and someone found me and it's my fault. I'm sorry.'

'It's not your fault. It's not . . . I love you. It's my fault. I shouldn't have sent you away. I'm sorry, so sorry . . .'

Breaca spoke Eceni at first, slipping back into the language of the ancestors, which was the only one with the words to hold her grief and not let it destroy them both. She became aware, through blinding tears, that the procurator was still in the doorway, watching.

He caught her eye and nodded. 'A delightful child.' He tilted the light so that it fell on mother and daughter together. 'I am sure the senator's sons would have been glad of her. She has not, I take it, borne a child of her own?'

'She's eight years old!'

'Yes, of course. The prefect, Corvus, said as much in Camulodunum. He cares for her also, it seems. A pity he has been called west to reinforce the governor's war. And you—' He moved the brand so the light fell on Cygfa. 'They tell me the Eceni do not marry, but I do not believe you live chaste. Have you ever borne a child?'

Cygfa was white, very suddenly. Her knuckles were yellow where she gripped them together. Not understanding, Breaca answered for her, 'No, Cygfa has never borne children.'

She is her father's daughter, the passion of fire made living, but she has never taken a lover, because to do so would have damaged Dubornos beyond all telling and she cares too much for him to do that.

'My mother is telling the truth.' Very softly, with a venom born of fear, Cygfa said, 'You could, of course, have your physician confirm it.'

The procurator stared at her. He wet his lips, thoughtfully. 'I don't believe we shall need to. I am happy to take your mother's word.'

He closed the door and the world was black again.

'Cygfa?' Cygfa was weeping, violently, trying to be quiet and failing. Gunovar was closest and held her, while Breaca struggled with the knots that bound Graine's hands and mouth. 'Cygfa? What is it?'

Gunovar answered for her. 'They cannot execute a virgin. It offends their gods and so their laws.'

'What? What difference does it . . . ? But then, if it's true, Graine and Cygfa must be . . .'

'Must no longer be intact when they come to die. It is not hard for a company of men to ensure that a girl is no longer chaste before she dies. They would do it anyway, only this way they do it with the full consent of the law.' Gunovar's voice was hollow, shorn of the irony that usually gave it life. The words were poison and she spoke them, because somebody must.

Cygfa made herself quiet and drew a breath and said, 'I'm sorry. It should not matter. It doesn't matter. In everything else, it is one more thing, of no moment. I will be ready by morning.'

'*Cygfa?*' Breaca whispered it, because the understanding was too sudden and too great to give it sound. For ten years, she had believed that Cygfa had taken no lovers out of compassion for Dubornos, when the truth was unthinkable: that Caradoc's daughter had lived three months as a prisoner in Rome lying nightly awake, making herself ready for a morning that must come.

It had not come, but the waiting alone had broken her, and the probing examinations of men who had trained to heal, and had been made to maim. *You could, of course, have your physician confirm it.* As had the physicians of Rome.

The decision, then, was easy. Once, in a cave, the ancestor-dreamer had made a promise. *I promise you nothing. Only that I will be with you, and that if you ask it, I can give you death, which you may crave, or my aid to live, which you may not.* It was time to accept that offer, if not for herself, then for others.

'You will not be ready by morning. There is no need and no point.'

Breaca stood up. Graine's knots were undone. The swelling on her left temple where the Boudica's knife had struck her was the size of a blackbird's egg and hot to the touch. She was fevered and clung to her mother with small, frantic hands. The patter of her heart beat erratically against Breaca's chest and she wept herself into incoherence, repeating only the words of earlier, 'I'm sorry. I'm sorry. I'm sorry . . .'

'Don't be sorry. It's good you're here. I love you. And we are not powerless.' Breaca smoothed the hot, damp hair out of her daughter's eyes and kissed her eyelids, one at a time. It was dark, and she did not have to school her face, only her voice, that she might seem not to be panicked, or desperate.

In truth, she was neither of these, only tired and worn thin with grief so that it was hard to reach for the place inside where the ancestor had taken up residence, to ask now for the strength to do what must be done. It had seemed easier when she had considered this before in Camulodunum, in daylight, with men and women and the façades of Rome all around. Then, Graine had stopped her, and Corvus, in friendship, and the ancestor-dreamer had taken no part.

Breaca slid her fingers up her daughter's spine, to the crook at the back of her neck where her head was set on, and tried to keep breathing, to seem calm. To the space in her soul where the wind of the gods blew most strongly, she said, *I ask your aid, as you wanted me to. And I accept your offer of death.*

She did not think she had spoken aloud, but Airmid took hold of her wrist. 'Breaca, you cannot ask that for another. Each of us must make our own peace with the gods if we wish to die.'

'Even Graine?'

'Especially Graine. Listen to what the ancestor says.'

Breaca tried and heard nothing except the clamour of grief and desperation and the nearness of a panic that had never touched her in battle, nor even when Caradoc was lost. She said, 'Can't we— Ah, gods, will they not leave us alone?'

Outside, guards were running, with lit brands. A voice – Cunomar's? – was shouting. The door hammered open in a blaze of torch-fire. The procurator stood on the threshold, lit on all sides by flaring torches.

Peering in, he said, 'Still alive? And the child? Good.' He waved in men who came with ropes. 'Bind them. Take the child. Quickly.'

It was only a small room, too crowded, too soon. Three men came for Breaca. She fought them, seeking her own death and Graine's. *The ways to death will be open if you can embrace them.* Her forearm crushed a man's windpipe and she was clawing for living eyes when lightning broke through her skull and exploded into dark and the ground and the wall crashed up against her and the weight that was Graine was gone.

Unkind hands rolled her onto her belly, tying her wrists, and turned her back. The procurator stood at her shoulder, looking down into her face. 'Our Coritani scout has excelled himself. He has a reason to hate you, I believe, and to seek vengeance, which I have promised him. He claims you were once a warrior of some renown?'

It would be better if he did not find you are the Boudica. One by one the safe barriers of her life were shattered. She spat at the man standing over her.

The procurator stepped back a pace and so was not marked. He said, 'The scout claimed that, left alone, you would kill the child, and perhaps the others. I am relieved that you are less of a warrior than he believed.'

He stood aside to let out the guards who had tied and gagged the others and held Graine, howling, between them. Pleasantly, he said, 'It will be over soon. Tomorrow. Or perhaps the day after. I have had to send to Camulodunum for the timber with which to raise you. Foolish of me, I should have thought to bring some with me.'

He stepped back, wiping his fingers on his tunic. The door closed behind him. Breaca lay half conscious in the swimming, in-commodious dark, lost to the pain in her head and her ribs and her kidneys, battered over and over by the sound of her daughter screaming her name and the sudden stop as someone held shut her mouth.

She made no effort to reach the ancestor, or to find a way now to meet death early. Graine was not safe. Nothing else mattered.

XXXVI

THE DOOR DID NOT OPEN IN THE MORNING, OR AT MIDDAY, BUT in the late afternoon.

Daylight revealed Airmid, Gunovar and Cygfa as they had been through the night; lying tied on the floor, sleepless and bruised and consumed, as Breaca was, by hunger and thirst and the need to urinate without soiling herself, which was trivial and born of pride and would, presumably, cease to consume her at all before the end of the day.

They supported each other with their eyes and chose not to notice the shaking, which had not stopped.

They were not fed, but washed and given the chance to use the midden and to drink, because, as the mercenary said, who had made the sign of Nemain, 'A body can last longer than you'd ever believe without food, but keep your captives short of water and they're dead before you know it.'

He had said it after Breaca had drunk, or she would have refused. He had grinned knowingly, and poured the remaining, precious, contents of his water carrier on his cupped palms and washed his face with it.

Outside, the reason for the delay was clear. Breaca stood in the open ground in the centre of the steading watching the lower edge of the sun drop towards the horizon, and to her left were dug, but not yet filled, the post holes for half a dozen crosses. *I have had to send to Camulodunum for the timber.*

Two stanchions of oak had been erected, made of wood scavenged from the houses. Cunomar and Ardacos were tied to one, three of the she-bears to the other.

Graine was not there. It was all that mattered.

Breaca could look or not look. She could fight to contain the shaking, so that she might not appear afraid, or abandon the attempt, and stand white and wide-eyed. None of it was noticed, or made any difference.

The procurator emerged from a tent that had been erected on the northern face of the steading and surveyed them with satisfaction. 'I have news from Camulodunum that the wagons will leave with the timber by tomorrow's dawn. They will be here by late morning, which gives us time to complete the inventories and the other preparations. There is the matter first of the king's daughters, who must be attended to, and of the men, who have caused trouble in the night.'

She had heard Cunomar's shout and had failed to help him. In the litany of her failings, it was not the greatest, but by far not the least. The signs of it showed on the men, already stripped for flogging. Cunomar's face was bloody where his ear had gone. Ardacos was bruised down the full length of his torso, but no worse than after battle. His eyes were swollen and blackened. He stared at Breaca through one and was trying to tell her something. She shook her head. *I can't hear.* He grimaced and turned his face to the wood.

'You are charged with insurrection, with murder of the following named legionaries . . .'

This, then, was the trial. The procurator stood on a small podium of nailed planks. The cache of raw iron had been brought down from the smithy by the great-house and lay bundled at his feet. Breaca's own blade was laid to the side, with Ardacos' and Cygfa's; to find them, the forge must have been destroyed.

The procurator's voice was a meaningless hum, joining the greater noise of the steading. Breaca watched a crow pick a straw from the torn thatch of the hut that she had shared with Airmid and fly with it to the lightning-struck oak in the lower horse paddocks. The Sun Hound had flayed his errant dreamers and hung them from oaks such as that. Only Rome needed to kill a tree to kill a man.

'. . . or we could ask your daughter. The younger one. Would you prefer that?'

Airmid was leaning on her shoulder, trying to bring her back to the present. The procurator's mouth was moving and the sound reached her, and the meaning some time after.

'Ask her what?' said Breaca. She looked about again. Graine was not there. The aching space where she should have been was empty and had not been filled.

The procurator said, 'Where is the army for whom this iron would have made the weapons?' He asked it slowly, spacing the words.

Breaca looked at him. He was a clerk; he had no understanding of warfare. She said, 'It doesn't exist yet. The weather has not allowed it.'

'You're lying.'

'No. If each of those bars were made to a blade, and each had a warrior to wield it, would we be standing here now? You have three centuries of men. We could have armed twice that many easily. If they were here, we would have done so. There is no army. Those who had already gathered will have dispersed to the north and safety, or back to their steadings. They will never gather again when we are gone.'

'Indeed? Who would have led them?'

'I would.' Cunomar answered before Breaca could. 'I was the king's son, given to the bear in the northern forests, the better to gather a war host in the south.'

The procurator took some time to move his gaze from Breaca to her son. Even then, he stared past him, to Ardacos. 'And this man, he is your father by blood?'

'No. My father is in exile in Gaul.' Cunomar had come through the night better than the others, high-headed, kept ablaze by the arrogance of youth, or by the bear. She could hope so, while praying that pain and despair had not turned him back to who he had been.

Breaca stared at him, much as Airmid had earlier stared at her, trying to speak into his mind. *Cunomar, Cunomar, tell them nothing they could not find out by other means.*

Cunomar was not looking at her, but at the Coritani scout who stood amongst the mercenaries. His every glance was a challenge. He said, 'When your governor has lost his war in the west, then my father will return and lead the warriors of Mona west to break open Camulodunum. Then the iron my mother has gathered will be made to blades and used by those with the honour and courage to use them.'

'Your *mother* made these?' The procurator's gaze switched back to Breaca. 'You are a smith?'

'Yes.'

'And you made these. Of course, of course . . .' He kicked sideways at a bundle of spear-heads. They clattered to the ground, breaking free of the rawhide thong that bound them. 'A woman of the Eceni who makes spears, and perhaps throws them.' Walking close, he took her chin and forced her to face him. 'Was it you who killed the governor with your witch-spears?'

No, Airmid did that. It is the dreamer who makes the warrior, not the reverse.

Breaca said, 'Yes.'

The procurator gazed at her in appalled fascination. 'You know the penalty for being a dreamer?'

'It is much the same, I believe, as the penalty for insurrection.'

'Almost. The rebel is flogged before hanging, the dreamer often not. You admit to both?'

She was tired of the farce of the trial and all that went with it. She should have spat in his face again, or railed against his nation's invasion of her land. Instead, wearily, she said, 'Why deny it? I am what the gods made of me. It is under your laws, not theirs or mine, that I am guilty of wrong.'

They flogged Cunomar, Ardacos, and the three she-bears who had each killed a mercenary. It was done thoroughly, by men who had been flogged many times themselves in their twenty-five years in the legions. It was not easy to witness, but not impossible.

If Breaca watched the sun, and the crow that collected thatch straw in spite of the noise, if she gave attention to the trail of ants across the beaten earth of the steading, if she rested her mind in the net of the ancestor-torc, which was silent, as if waiting, then it was possible to bear witness, to honour the courage and not the pain.

It was not necessarily worse than battle, and wounds taken now would hasten death later, which was not a bad thing.

After a while, she gave her attention to Cygfa, who was shaking uncontrollably, and tried to think of something that might help. 'They may be armed,' she said, quietly. 'It may be possible to take a knife and turn it inwards.'

With appalling certainty, Cygfa said, 'They won't be. They have done this before. They will take no risks.'

'I'm sorry.'

There was nothing to say then, but to watch the ground and the single file of marching ants and ask again of the silent ancestor why every part of her vision should be extinguished like this, when there had been so much to hope for.

It ended, in time, because all sport ends, and there was more to come, which might be better entertainment.

Then it was impossible to watch the ants, because Graine was there at last, dazed and silent and unsteady on her feet, pushed out of the hut that had been Airmid's, where the crows drew straws from the thatch.

The child had been cleaned, and fed, and had been sick, and that, too, had been cleaned, and someone, Briga maim them and hold them for ever in pain, had combed her hair and set a circlet of woven oak leaves about it, and a filament of gold about her neck, so that her beauty was beyond doubt, and her chastity.

She was small and alone and terrified and beyond the ability to be brave. Her eyes sought her mother's and found no comfort there. She opened her mouth to speak and shut it again. She was weeping, and had been so and would continue for ever and there was nothing that could be done.

In her head, silently, over and over, Breaca said, *Graine, I'm sorry*, and heard the voice of her daughter, earnest and desperate, saying, *It's my fault. Dubornos fell asleep . . .*

Cygfa was cursing, rigidly, a long continuous hiss that called on all that was darkest of Briga and Nemain to aid her and blight the men who came for her. They laughed, and hit her and closed her mouth with a rag. She did not have to look beautiful.

Then the nightmare began, and it was impossible to witness it and remain sane.

Near the beginning, Breaca was sick; a pathetic puking of bile and spit that retched her empty and inside out. No-one came to clean her. Airmid leaned on her one arm and Gunovar on her other and between them they kept her upright.

Airmid said, 'Don't look,' and she did not look but it was impossible not to listen, not to hear the annihilation of Graine, the delicate, beautiful child who held the strings of her heart, and of Cygfa, who was Caradoc reborn as woman, and more vulnerable for it, as man after man of the procurator's guard, by daylight and then by firelight, ensured beyond all possible doubt that neither was chaste and that their executions in the morning would not offend the Roman gods, or break the laws of Rome.

Through it all, the torc remained silent and empty; the ancestor-dreamer offered no aid and could not be reached to ask for it, or Breaca would have done so, if only for herself. There was nothing, ever, that could be done to repair the destruction.

Cunomar lay on his side in the bloodied dirt in the place where the mercenaries had left him, which may have been his own room, that he had once shared with Eneit and now shared with Ardacos and three of the she-bears.

They had been kept there the night before and had scraped a latrine in the corner and used it, not expecting to come back. The stench mingled with the hammering pain of his head where his ear had once been and his back, which no longer bore skin, and his arms where the weight of hanging on the ties at the stanchion had pulled at his shoulders.

There was no way to lie that did not send fire through his body, and so no way to sleep. He lay in the dark and felt Ardacos' shoulder pressed on the heel of his foot; a steady presence that gave more comfort than words could do. The three she-bears lay about him, holding steady their breathing as he was steadying his. It was the best he could do; a final attempt not to crumble to weeping distraction, while in his head all he could hear was the inhuman croak of Graine screaming and screaming, and then not screaming, which was worse.

All through his childhood, when he had envied his sister's delicacy and beauty and the affection of their mother and her place in Airmid's heart, and Sorcha's, and her easy way with Stone and her growing power, Cunomar had never wished her dead. He did so now, passionately, for her sake. Lying on the cold floor with no feeling in his fingers where the ties had cut the blood from his wrists, and too much in his head, his arms and his back, he prayed to the nameless bear who lived within him that Graine's silence meant she had found release in death.

Later, colder, he wished the same for himself, and the others.

Later still, shuddering uncontrollably and on the verge of weeping, he remembered what Ardacos had said before it started. *Think of the bear-marking, and of what it made you.* Then again, afterwards, as they were carried back to the hut. *Think of the bear-marking. It was worse than this.*

It might have been worse, it was hard to remember. Pain passed is easily forgotten, except in the sense of triumph at having survived it. Certainly the bear-marking had gone on for longer; the flogging had lasted barely an afternoon while his time in the bear's cave under the care of the elders of the Caledonii had lasted from dusk of the first day to dusk of the fourth and every moment between had been agony.

He thought they had used heated flint blades to make the scars on his shoulders and back, but had never been sure. At the time, it had been too dark and he had been too lost, too locked into each breath, to care. Afterwards, it had been part of the magic and important not to know how it was done.

Breathe. Dive into the breath. Let it carry you to the core of yourself, where your strength lies.

The elders had said it, over and over, and time had warped so that it seemed he had taken days, months, years of fighting his body, of fighting not to scream, of fighting not to fight, but to lie still under the searing, cutting, nagging knives, before the words had made sense and he had begun to dive with each breath, deeper, further into the core of himself, to where he had found the wellspring of his own endurance.

More, he had found within that place a gateway to the infinite. Beyond the pain were avenues that ran among the stars. There, Cunomar had walked with the spirits of the bear he had slain and the beaver that had been his first kill for the elders, and beyond them he had met the panoply of gods: Briga and Nemain, Camul the war god of the Trinovantes, and Belin, the sun. Each of them separately had given him a glimpse of what it was to be a dreamer.

He had risen, bear-marked, with two gifts; the first and most palpable was the knowledge of the strength he bore at the core of himself. Beyond that, the gift that bore aloft his soul was the crack that had opened in the firmament and let him see through, as a dreamer sees, to a possible future.

I wish to be a warrior to surpass my mother and my father, of a stature to lead the rout of Rome. In the presence of the bear-dancers of the Caledonii, Cunomar had spoken aloud the wish of his heart and the elders had sent him back to his people, full of hope and promise. Lying in the dirt and blood and sweat of his own failure, the irony of that, the hubris and the gods' reckoning after, hit him, as suddenly and as hard as the veteran's lash through the afternoon: a true dreamer would have seen what was coming and would have avoided it, or would at least know how to find again the crack between the worlds that let his soul walk through.

That place still remained. If he could reach it, he might find sanity and a way to survive the morning, but to do that he had to find a way through the sound of Graine screaming herself hoarse that filled his head.

He rolled over and lay on his stomach. *Breathe. Dive into the breath. Let it carry you—*

'Drink. Drink and then wake. Come *on*. Drink, and wake. It was not so bad, and nothing to tomorrow . . .'

The voice broke through the shell he was building and would not leave. It dragged him protesting back to pain and the memory of Graine's voice. Cold splashed on his lips and into his gullet and he would have choked, but a cool hand sealed his mouth and a thumb ran down the side of his throat and he was silent and coughed hard through his nose.

'Cunomar. Wake. Listen to me. You must wake . . .'

He knew the voice, distantly. 'Eneit?' No, Eneit was dead, given a clean death by his mother. He had understood it at the time and still hated her for it. Now, he hated the arrogance of who he had been.

Not Eneit, then. A cold certainty made him open his eyes, and it was not, after all, too dark to see. The door to the hut was ajar and firelight played at the rim, bright enough to show the feathers in the hair of the Coritani hawk-scout bending over him, and the white scars of the fire-lizard branding crawling up his arm.

Cunomar had forgotten what it was truly to hate, to immerse himself in the all-consuming passion of loathing. He remembered now. His hatred of the procurator, who was a weak man and had never known honour, was a ghosted marsh-flame compared to the burning inferno he felt for the traitor of the Coritani who had found Graine lost on the trackway outside the steading and delivered her alive to the procurator.

Pushing himself to sitting, he said, 'The mercenaries sang that you returned my sister to them for their pleasure. For that, I will wait for you for ever in the lands beyond life, and you will know no rest.' His voice was rusty. His breath was meant for other things. He coughed and had to wait until the pain had passed before he could be heard.

The scout shook his head. 'I went beyond honour. I'm sorry. I did not know they would . . . do what they did. The Coritani might spear a child taken in war, or cut her throat, but it would be done cleanly. Never . . . that.'

Cunomar despised him, openly. 'Why are you here?'

'To tell you that. To apologize, so that you go to your death tomorrow and pass on afterwards and do not wait for me with hate in your heart in the lands beyond life. The Boudica and her son slew my father; that is well known and you have not denied it. Your deaths will avenge him, but I swear to you on my father's life that I did not intend what happened to the child.'

'Then get her free.'

'I can't. I have tried to see her, to give her the peace of death, but the procurator's men are guarding her too closely and they have seen how I feel. I am not trusted any longer near either of the king's daughters. I'm sorry. On my honour as one who bears the lizard brands, I have tried.'

The scout made to rise. The bear god spoke clearly for once and Cunomar grabbed the man's wrist, surprising them both. 'Then try harder. Find Corvus, the prefect who greeted me in Camulodunum. He can't stop them from hanging us, we killed the procurator's men and must die for it, but he cares for Graine and could save her yet. He's leading three cohorts west towards Mona. They can't have marched far if they've left at all. Find him, tell him what's happened. Bring him here.'

There was a wait, and a changing tension in the arm that he

held, then, 'Perhaps. If there is a way it can be done, I may try.'

The scout pushed back on his heels and upright. He thought for a moment, then said, 'I have not told them the other name of your mother, nor will I.'

They must not know she is the Boudica. Ardacos had said it, very early, and Cunomar had said, *The hawk-scout knows. It is there to be read on his face. He'll tell them.*

Against all expectation, he had not. Unwilling, Cunomar said, 'Thank you,' and meant it.

'There would have been no honour in telling it. What they do is enough.' The scout paused in the doorway. He said, 'Your mother has honour. It shows, and the men of Rome are afraid of her for it. In the morning they will do to her as they have done to you. Don't try to stop them. It will help her to die faster afterwards.'

In the morning they will do to her as they have done to you. Don't try to stop them.

Cunomar could not have stopped them, and would not waste his pride trying, for her sake; only bear witness, as she had done, and do what he could to give her strength.

The thought roused him early, so that he was ready when the guard came to the door, bringing slave chains from the wagons to bind them. He had not found the core of his own peace in the night after the hawk-scout had left, nor, he thought, had any of the others; the pain was too great, and the fear of what dawn would bring.

Blinking and haggard, chained to Ardacos on one side and the she-bears on the other, he shuffled into the morning.

And stopped.

The timber wagons had arrived from Camulodunum. The post holes dug by the mercenaries had been filled.

Six crosses ranged from east to west across the steading, for the family of the former king and those closest to them. A gibbet, heavy with ropes, awaited the she-bears.

Cunomar was not sick, but one of the bear-warriors chained at his left retched violently, and he heard, and then smelled, a long, fluid fart as the guts of another gave way. He had only his experience in Rome to thank that he did not similarly disgrace himself. That same experience told him that he would do so eventually, and that by then he would no longer care.

His mother was there. After the crosses, he saw her. She was fixed to the oak stanchion in the centre of the steading, where Cunomar had been tied the day before; dishonoured and alone in the place that should have given birth to her dream.

She was still the Boudica; every line of her said so. More than anything else now, it mattered that the procurator not find out her identity, but it was hard to see how he could not when it shone from her so clearly: from the copper river of her hair, tied up by the legionaries in a parody of the warrior's knot, to keep it from her back; from the battle scars that laced every part of her body; from the raging calm in her eyes, that despised the men who held her captive, and stood above them, and beyond.

Cunomar felt the same twist in his heart he had felt when Eneit stood ready to die and knew without doubt that he loved her and was proud of her and it was too late to say so. He would have taken all the horror for her, but could not find a way to do that, or even to help her to do it herself.

That was a new thought and it scared him as much as the crosses had done. Breaca had not been marked for the bear; her long-nights had been quieter and she had come home afterwards unscarred. For all her time in battle, leading the warriors or hunting alone amongst the mountains, Cunomar was not convinced that his mother knew how best to keep hold of her sanity in the face of what they would do to her.

Breathe. He wanted to shout it and could not, because if he was deemed to help her, they would harm him, and that would make it worse for her. *Dive with the breath, let it carry you inwards. Find the place inside that cannot be broken.*

She must have heard something, or felt it. Her forehead came away from the oak and her eyes rested on him and, for an astonishing, blissful moment, he was her son, the bear-dancer, whole and free, and she was the Boudica, given for ever to victory, and nothing could step between them; she loved him and he knew it, and she knew that he loved her and he could dive into the unquiet love of her soul and drown and be happy.

A guard jerked the shackles at his wrists and pain lanced through his body so that he had to shut his eyes to stay on his feet. When he could look again, his mother's gaze was gone, turned back into the oak and herself. The procurator had mounted his podium.

'You are charged with being both a dreamer and an insurgent. Do you deny that you are both?'

'No.' She lied to protect Airmid. It was the only gift she could give and they would still die together.

'Good.' The procurator nodded to the leader of the mercenaries who stood behind her. 'Begin.'

XXXVII

THE HOUND WAS FIRST TO WARN VALERIUS OF THE STRANGER hidden on the margins of the coppice, and then the Crow-horse, less subtly.

Valerius slid from the saddle and made a knot of the reins round the pommel of his saddle that they might not get underfoot.

'Go on,' he said to Longinus, who had stopped. 'Keep going until you get through the wood. If you reach the edge and I haven't rejoined you, stop as if you've dropped something. Keep talking. If you can, make my voice, too.'

Longinus was fit to ride by then, leading the pack horses. The wagon which had borne him from the battlefield was far behind, hidden in a thicket in the pleasant pretence that they might live to return one day and find it and have use of it again.

Walking beside the Crow-horse, Valerius shrugged out of his mail shirt and hooked it with his helmet across his saddle-pack. His cloak was already there, slip-tied so he could reach it at need. They were travelling in the uniform of Roman scouts, with mail and helmet and the sky-blue shoulder cloaks. It was safer than travelling as warriors and as plausible as any cover. Amidst the anarchy of the western battles, they could quite easily have been sent east to Camulodunum with orders for whoever was acting governor. It was safe as long as they avoided any legionary patrols and they had seen none of those; the snow had not lifted

446

long enough to let them forage freely out of their winter billets.

The thicket was small, less than three spear casts long, of beech and birch and small, shrunken oaks. The trees were damp, hung with old rain and new cobwebs, only barely coming to life; birds gathered in them, but not the nests and young there should have been. Valerius sought for and found a deer track, which was wide enough to take him if he dropped to all fours and crawled. The hound led the way and he followed it, silently.

The warrior waiting at the tree's edge had heard the horses; it would have been impossible for him not to. Longinus did a good job of carrying on a conversation in two voices and four languages so that anyone listening would need to know Latin, Thracian, Gaulish and a smattering of Eceni to fit the flow of it together.

The listener was young, dark-haired and dark-skinned, and armed with a hunting knife far beyond the legal length for anyone not employed directly by the legions. Three red kite feathers fluttering limply from his topknot marked him as a legionary scout and his belt was buckled with the medallion given to those who have excelled themselves; the eagle sparked gold in the weak morning sun.

The youth moved from the rock behind which he had hidden, to a place at the edge of the thicket, whence he could see, but not be seen by, the men who rode along the path.

A mail shirt hit the ground in a chiming slither of iron, shattering a flock of sparrows from the trees.

'Damn it, Valerius. It's gone into the thorn bush. Did you see where it went?'

Longinus was querulous and slurred a little, as if not yet recovered from last night's wine. He dismounted heavily and went in search of that which had fallen, catching his sword in the undergrowth and cursing in Thracian and Eceni.

The scout shook his head at the weakness of the wine-sodden invaders, huffed through rigid nostrils and relaxed his stance.

Valerius grabbed the thick lock of his hair and hauled back on it, kneed him in the small of the back and pushed him over, kneeling on his shoulder to trap his knife hand.

It was too easy. The scouts who worked for the legions now were young and had not been born to war. Reaching round, Valerius slid the edge of his blade across the boy's throat, enough to bring the blood leaking from the skin, but not from the great vessels that contained his life.

'Breathe carefully,' he said, 'if you wish to breathe at all.'

Dark eyes glanced at him sideways, their rims white as a hunted doe. In Latin, the youth said, 'I am a scout for the Twentieth legion, stationed at Camulodunum. I am seeking Corvus, prefect of the Twentieth—'

Valerius shook his head. 'Wrong guess,' he said softly, and leaned on the blade.

'. . . Boudica . . .'

The word was a hiss, in the face of dying. Flesh trembled under Valerius' hand and it was hard not to kill out of instinct. Longinus was there. He put a hand on his friend's shoulder. 'Steady.'

Both of those were not enough. What stayed his hand was the sight of the brooch pinned to the boy's cloak: a serpent-spear cast in silver, with three threads of blackened wool hanging from the lower loop.

Biting his lip, Valerius eased back on the knife's pressure. 'That brooch,' he said. 'Where did you get it?'

'Boudica's . . . daughter.' The scout's windpipe was part severed. Blood foamed at the cut. 'I . . . hold the life of . . . the Boudica's child.'

'How?'

Dark eyes closed and opened again. 'My life for hers. Your oath on it.' A whisper, sprayed red.

Valerius laughed. He moved his knife up and back, to rest below the scout's lip. Against corded, futile resistance, he pushed down with his other hand on the back of the boy's head, forcing him slowly forward until the tip of his knife met the solid stop of bone. The youth groaned through tight teeth as the acolytes of Mithras used to do at their first branding.

Blood pulsed freely onto the back of Valerius' hand. 'You haven't been long with the legions, have you?' he said. 'Information comes free to whomsoever holds the knife. I think we might have it without the oaths.'

'No time . . .' The boy's eyes grew wide at the centres. Astonishingly, a spark of humour lingered in their core. 'I will die and she will die. Her death . . . will be worse.'

He might have died then for the sheer effrontery of it, but the hound came to lick the blood from his lip and he saw it and jerked away as he had not done from the knife, terror naked on his face.

Longinus said, quietly, 'Valerius, he can see your hound.'

'I noticed.' Valerius drew back his hand. His knife was level with the boy's eye. It, too, was beyond the legal length and honed back at the blade, like the skinning knives of the dreamers, that they used to find the truth. The scout recognized that, too, and it scared him almost as much as the hound.

Valerius said, 'I will know if you lie to me. Do you believe that?'

'Yes.'

They made him sit and bound his hands and ankles. He was no longer bleeding from his throat, but his lower lip had swollen to the size of a slingstone where Valerius had cut it and the blood had pooled beneath the skin.

Valerius crouched in front of him, holding the knife. 'Talk to me.'

Heron-clouds speared the sky, pushed by an easterly breeze.

Breaca could not see them, only feel them, as if they reached down to her, with memories of the wind.

Memories; nothing seen. It was a long time since she had seen anything but oak and lately not that. Darkness was better, although sweat stung her eyes and the light hurt when she blinked it away. That was a new kind of pain, a layer on the other layers, one that could be made better when the rest could not.

Nothing made better the pain in her back, her shoulders, her arms. Breathing hurt and not breathing hurt and cursing and not cursing. She had not yet found if screaming made any difference, but would do so, soon. In the beginning, a small part of her had wanted to scream, to rage against the shock, the indignity, the stripping of her pride, but her pride was the greater part and had not allowed it. Now, the greater part of her needed release and only a small, waning kernel of something not yet broken kept her silent.

Soon she would break, but not yet. Not yet. *Not yet*. The voice in her head, which had once been at least partly her own, was now entirely the ancestor-dreamer's. It kept up the litany.

Not yet. This is the beginning. The rest will be worse; don't bring it sooner.

She could not imagine worse. This much was more than she

could bear. She opened her mouth and breathed in hot, sweating air and—

Not yet.

She closed her mouth and choked on sweat and old spit and somewhere, somebody laughed and she remembered that they could see her and for a moment, she took the weight on her legs, not her arms, and pressed her forehead to the oak and made the feel of it count against the stunning, blinding, nauseating, endless, endless, endless pain.

A blaze of lightning struck her arms, above her head, and she forgot about her weight and slumped against the ties and the lightning struck her back again, adding pain to infinite pain and the oak was gone and all sense of safety and she opened her mouth and took a breath—

Not yet.

—and closed it again.

Not yet. You have too much pride. You should listen to me.

'I did listen to you. I came east to lead the war host as you told me. I am here now because of it.'

The torc lay like an iron clamp on her neck. She had thought the procurator would take it; certainly he had fingered it, had estimated its value as she had: melted to gold it would pay a century of men for a summer of months, or a half-century for—

That way out did not work any longer. The lightning strikes across her back did not allow it. The ancestor-dreamer stood by and watched.

Breaca said, 'Why did you lie to me? You promised a war host, and freedom.'

No. I promised only that I would be with you, which I am, and that I would give you death if you asked it. Do you ask it?

'No. Never.' It was good to rage at something other than the pain, however unreasonably. 'You give nothing freely and I will not pay your price.'

Not even to save the life of your daughter?

There was darkness, and a blink of salted pain, and the lightning strikes and all of it was lost in the memory of Graine's voice, and the silence when it had ended. Breaca said, 'You did not come to me last night when I sought you.'

And instead, I come to you now.

450

'What do you offer?'

The life of your child.

'What do you ask?'

What I have always asked, that you come to me shorn of your arrogance, that you abandon the walls you have built about yourself and see what there is to see behind them.

'What point, when I am about to die?'

Would you go ignorant to the lands beyond life, never knowing who you were born to? Would you— The pain pressed on her, driving her into darkness. It was difficult to hear anything clearly, even the voice in her head.

The black became darker, muddier, the ancestor more urgent. *Come to me, bringer of victory. Come. I am not so far away now.*

Come to me. *Come to me. Come to . . .* And breathe. Only breathe, because someone had emptied a bucket of water on her head and the cold was as shocking as the lightning strikes and it was all she could do to take a breath and open her mouth and—

Not yet. Come to me. Follow the dark.

There was no dark. Only the lightning, which was red, and the hurtful blink of an eye.

Come to me. I am here to hold you. Only follow the dark.

Something had to break; the small kernel of pride was too small to survive. Caught in the vortex of the lightning, broken by the agony in her arms, Breaca of the Eceni, bearer of the serpent-spear, let go of her pride and, for the sake of her daughter, followed the thread of a voice she did not trust into the dark.

She was in a cave and the ancestor was in the cave with her and it was not the cave of rock and running water in the high mountains east of Mona, but a safe place, where the kernel of herself might shelter against assault and not break, at least for a while.

Welcome. The ancestor was old beyond all imagining and the serpent of her dreaming lived within her. She was vast, and made herself small, that she might be approached without terror. *Welcome. We could both wish you had come to me sooner.*

'I did not know how. And had not the need.'

The laugh became part of her. *You have had the need since you were a child, only that your pride would not allow it.*

At another time, she might have argued against that, but her pride had got in the way of too many things to catalogue and there was not time to list them now. Caught in the quiet cave, in a miracle of no-pain, or of a pain so entirely consuming that it had swamped her and she was already dying, she reached out to the ancient past.

'What must I do?'

Come to know who you are. What else is there anyone can do?

Cunomar watched his mother lose consciousness the first time, and be made to feel again with the water, and then slump again soon after.

He thought she might have died, and prayed for it, but the staggered rise and fall of her chest said that she had only gone for a time beyond reach and could be brought back again with more water. The mercenaries thought the same. One took the bucket to the horse trough and filled it and would have dashed it on her as he had before, but the procurator stepped forward and stayed his arm.

'Stop. Enough. If she dies now . . .' He tapped his forefingers to his lips, thinking, then said, 'Cut her down. Lie flat the crosses for the others. If she hears her daughters raised up she will wake. Bring them—'

A horse, ridden hard, came up the trackway. Two horses; a second followed, with three others, so five altogether. It helped to count things, to keep his attention elsewhere; Cunomar was learning that.

The first of the incomers swung through the gates, turning too tightly for safety. A normal horse, pulled round so hard, might have fallen. This one gathered itself on the turn and stopped where was needful, in front of the stanchion, missing by a hand's breadth the fallen body of the woman lying limp on the ground.

Cunomar gaped and closed his eyes and opened them and stared again. The horse was pied, the two colours of a frost-laden night. The rider bore the leather armour and blue cloak of a Roman messenger, with the oak leaf in gold pinned under his chin that said he came from the governor. He swept off his helmet and the hair beneath was black and the profile could have been Luain mac Calma's made younger and harder and assailed more by life.

Cunomar closed his mouth and swallowed, drily. His mind caught up late with his memories. Hoarsely, he said, 'Valerius?'

'What? Gods, it is.' Ardacos jerked in the shackles, sending a ripple down the line of men.

Ardacos never showed surprise, or fear, or anger, or pride, or hate; until now when the loathing in his voice would have stripped a lesser man to the skin. 'Traitor. He's come to gloat.' He shouted it aloud. *'Traitor!'*

The she-bears took up the shout, and Gunovar; none of them knew who the stranger was, only that life was ending and this man had come to watch it and Ardacos, whom they revered, clearly hated him.

Airmid looked on, distractedly, as if recently woken from dreaming, or perhaps not woken at all. She said three words to Gunovar and both of them shouted it. 'Traitor! Nemain bind you!' Their trained voices carried over the she-bears' and roused more amusement in the men guarding them, which was understandable; they had shouted in Latin.

The messenger – Valerius – ignored them as he had ignored the bleeding body of the Boudica lying prone beneath his horse's feet. Without dismounting, he presented himself as was proper to the procurator, neatly and only a little out of breath.

'The governor sends his greetings and his word.' The message satchel at his shoulder was sealed with wax and the elephant-seal of Britannia, that it was death to break unbidden. 'If you would care to read the message privately?'

'Thank you.' The procurator clearly did not care to do so at all if it interrupted his morning, but could not be seen to say so. He delayed, while the messenger's companion ploughed through the gateway leading three pack horses. The newcomer swept off his helmet to reveal a mass of astonishingly rich russet hair.

The veterans made space for the incomer, pleasantly jocular, and there was a small moment of chaos when too many horses took up too much space and Valerius' horse, which had been ridden hardest, threw its head restlessly against the hold of the reins and jumped sideways, so that it jostled the procurator.

The emperor's collector of taxes was not used to being jostled, and was deeply afraid of the horse. He ducked sideways, swearing. 'Carefully, man. Can't you get that beast—'

The sword-blade that rested along his throat was polished and honed and it had already broken his skin. The black eyes of

453

the man above it were the epitome of vicious, lethal arrogance. The man in messenger's dress, who had just this moment been so polite, said with freezing clarity, 'My horse is battle trained. If you move, I will have him kill you. It will be spectacular, and faster than you deserve, but . . . I really don't think so. Driscus, call your men into order. You will die first if they assault us. Thank you, Longinus . . .'

For this last, he cast his voice past the procurator to the mercenary veterans gathered beyond the stanchion. Not quite fast enough, they had seen the risk to their patron and would have come to his aid, but for the fact that Driscus, their leader, had also moved too slowly and had been relieved of his sword in a single swift manoeuvre by the cavalryman with the russet hair and was staring at the point of it, a little cross-eyed. Blood drizzled from a horizontal cut on his forehead. His men shifted uneasily, and waited for an order.

'Better.' Valerius nodded, pleasantly. As if the procurator did not exist, he looked past the empty stanchion to the swordless mercenary. 'Driscus, I may have grown my hair since you last saw me, in which case you are forgiven for not remembering the man who had you flogged three times in one winter for being drunk on duty, but I am devastated that you don't remember the horse that took the better half out of your sword arm and put you under the care of Theophilus for a month.'

The man Driscus stared and frowned and stared, then, 'Valerius? It can't be. You're dead. You died in Gaul. Corvus told us. I paid two sesterces towards your memorial.'

'You flatter my memory.' Valerius sketched a salute. 'Even so, I am not dead. Anyone who wishes to risk losing their arm to the Crow-horse can come close to test it. Or you could make better use of the time and pack whatever gold you have collected and leave now for Camulodunum.'

'Why?'

'Because the prefect, Corvus, of the Ala Quinta Gallorum, is on his way with three cohorts of legionaries and he is not at all happy at having to break his journey west to deal with a tax collector who has grossly exceeded his powers. This—' He swept his blade in a horizontal arc. A dozen mercenaries ducked, unconsciously. '—is the family of a king. They have done nothing but properly mourn the death of the man who ruled them.'

'They attacked the proc—'

'They were goaded. We have a witness who will swear to it on his life.'

'They have arms. We have—'

'Yes, I saw. They have iron bars, Driscus. Every steading from here to the far southern coast has a cache of iron bars. They trade with them, they turn them into hoes and bridle bits and the pathetic cheese knives we let them hunt with. If you're going to name as traitor every smith who keeps a stock of iron bars, we are going to be excessively busy this spring, and frankly, I think the Governor has bigger things in mind.'

Affronted, Driscus said, 'They killed Strignus. And Titus Castellius.'

Valerius laughed. 'And is that supposed to be somebody's loss? A child with a bent twig could have killed Strignus on his better days. And Castellius was probably raping their children, in which case he is very much better dead than he would be when I'd finished with him.'

There was a dry, aching pause, as several dozen mercenaries remembered very well exactly how Valerius had treated men who raped the native children, and each held his breath and prayed to all the gods that his neighbour would not choose to say something foolish.

'Yes. Right.' Driscus cleared his throat. 'So then what should we—'

'He's lying. Are you insane? He's lying and he has no power to enforce any of this. In the name of the emperor, I order you to disarm him. The man's quite clearly—' The procurator had found his voice. He lost it again on the point of Valerius' sword, and the hard black eyes above it.

Valerius said, 'Lie down. Face down, and don't move.'

Very few men had the mettle to ignore that voice and the procurator was not one of them. Even had he been, the order was underscored by the unmistakable sound of a troop of horses riding hard along the trackway, coming closer.

'That will be Corvus,' said Valerius pleasantly. 'And his personal cavalry troop. You can, of course, accuse him also of lying. I will be pleased to bear witness to it later at your trial. In the meantime, you will lie down and you will not speak unless spoken to.'

The procurator lay down.

Very shortly, Corvus rode in through the gates at the head of his personal troop of cavalry, living proof that Valerius had not been lying. He brought with him the Coritani hawk-scout, who had a wrap of bloodied wool around his throat and a blackened swelling at his lip and would not look at Valerius. Cunomar should have been amused by that, and did not have the strength, or the breath to spare that was not used for praying.

The prefect had pushed his horse easily as hard as Valerius had done ahead of him. He led his small troop of twenty hand-picked riders into a compound thronged by newly nervous mercenaries and their silent, watchful prisoners. His men had been given prior orders. They rode in double file through the gates and divided on entry, half to the left, half to the right, forming a semicircle of armoured iron that blocked the exit from the steading. Every second man dismounted and handed his reins to the rider on his right.

Corvus' attention was on Valerius, and had been since he rode in. They faced each other as stags might, meeting on the boundaries of the rut; or as enemies on a battlefield, who have fought for years without meeting, and, having finally done so, find each other not as they supposed.

Without shifting his gaze, Corvus said to his men, 'Find their packs and search them.'

The mercenary veterans of Camulodunum had been promised wealth to excess if they marched to the aid of their procurator. The steading of the late king of the Eceni had not proved as rich as they might have expected, but, as was normal on any campaign, they had taken a judicious share before submitting the rest to the inventory.

Emptied onto the beaten earth of the compound, their packs revealed a magpie's horde of gold and silver, of enamelled arm-bands that would fetch a good price in the markets of Rome, of brooches and god-offerings and necklaces and, in one, a child's brooch of a wren, wrapped in wool for safe keeping.

The search of the few buildings still upright revealed also the presence of the king's two daughters, who were in urgent need of a physician's care – if they were not deemed traitors, in which case they could hang and finish what had been started.

The captain of the cavalry said as much to his prefect, who nodded and pinched the bridge of his nose, and with his gaze still on Valerius, said, 'Driscus, you were a bad armourer and you make a worse centurion but sadly that's not a capital offence, unlike theft of the emperor's property, which most certainly is. It is your great fortune that I have a war to attend and do not have the time to hang you and your rabble personally. You have until the remainder of my cohorts arrive to marshal your men and leave. I suggest you do so with more professionalism than you demonstrated on leaving Camulodunum.'

Addressing the mercenaries, Valerius had spoken the soldiers' patois, the loose, louche language of the legions, broadened with Gaulish and Thracian and the throaty Batavian of the crack cavalry units. Corvus spoke the senate's Latin, that made gutter scum of all beneath it, and did as much damage to the veterans as the words. Driscus had coloured, deeply, long before the prefect finished speaking, and was twisting the leather end of his belt in his hand by the end.

Given leave to move, the leader of the procurator's three veteran centuries had things to prove, and he did his best. The order with which his men marched out of the Eceni steading was not militarily perfect, but it was considerably sharper than when they had marched in.

A number of small things happened as the last of them left. The Coritani scout was sent to take water and what help he could offer to the king's daughters. The captain of the prefect's cavalry, who had been with them, remounted his horse and ordered his men to do likewise. Twenty seasoned troopers gathered on restless horses and rode out through the gate, to wait on the far side. Jarred into action, Corvus finally wrested his gaze from Valerius and looked down at the woman who, since his arrival, he had sheltered beneath the feet of his horse.

'Breaca?'

She was dead; Cunomar was certain of it. From the moment the prefect had first ridden in, she had not moved, and the rise of her breathing could no longer be seen, obvious or not.

'Breaca?' Urgently now, Corvus dismounted and knelt beside her and pressed his fingers to the side of her neck and then stood and drew his own water canister from the side of his saddle and dribbled a little into the corner of her mouth. 'Breaca?'

She coughed, and so was alive.

Cunomar swayed in the chains that held him. At his side, Ardacos cursed and was weeping. Airmid took the last of three steps forward and dropped to her knees at Breaca's head and took the water skin that was offered her and poured it more carefully now, so that the water was swallowed, and spoke and was answered, in a whisper too hoarse to carry across the compound, so that only the word 'Graine?' could be heard with any clarity and Airmid's answer was lost in the further coughing fit that followed.

'Valerius?' Corvus had stepped back and remounted.

Valerius' black eyes were unreadable. He said, 'Thank you. I wasn't sure you would come. This is more than I can repay.'

Corvus said, 'I came for Breaca. And her daughters. In the minds of the legions, you are dead. It would be best if you remained so.'

'Then you have helped a ghost find solace, for which he is grateful.' Very slowly, Valerius leaned forward and offered his arm in the soldiers' greeting, that is at the same time a farewell, and an encouragement to battle. 'I am sorry to have brought this on you,' he said.

After a brief pause, stiffly, Corvus took the offered arm. 'True solace?' he asked.

'As much as the gods ever give it. I have missed you. I will miss you still.'

'And I.'

They would not weep, either of them, and the air cracked for need of it. Cunomar wept for them, through the pounding pain in his head and the rawness of his throat, and did not know why he did so.

A crow called and they broke apart, as if ordered. Corvus swung his horse. He paused at the gates to salute the cavalryman with the russet hair and said, 'Longinus, I have your memorial stone. If you ever wish to see it, you have only to re-present yourself to your quartermaster as living.'

The cavalryman saluted in his turn. 'If I ever find the company of ghosts displeasing, I will do so. Thank you.'

At no time did Corvus mention, talk to, or even acknowledge, the procurator, lying rigidly terrified beneath the Crow-horse's front feet.

Nobody moved, nobody spoke. Slowly, the sound of cavalry horses, ridden hard, became quieter.

Cunomar stood still, so very, very still, so that not one link of the chains that bound him chimed against another.

Still they waited, until the sound of the crow gathering thatch from the broken roof of Airmid's hut was louder than the staccato whisper of distant horses, and then a little longer, until eventually Valerius said something in a language that was neither Eceni, nor Latin, nor Gaulish, and the cavalryman with the russet hair nodded and walked to Gunovar and freed her.

She was a smith and had not been badly harmed. With the cavalryman's help, she began to work her way round and strike off the slave fetters that held the she-bears.

Dazed, and still not entirely believing, Cunomar put his wrists together and shuffled forward. He leaned his forehead on Ardacos' shoulder, because he could, and he loved him, and he was too tired to stand unsupported and all of these things were entirely acceptable, and he was utterly unprepared for the violence that erupted beyond the stanchion.

'No!' The procurator's scream was higher than a child's, and as futile.

He was not appealing to a human agency, with heart and soul and mind that could be moved. Valerius' pied horse had lifted its forelegs from the ground and reared high and stood there for a moment, taller than any man; the embodiment of vengeance, driven by the warrior who sat erect on its back and, with a quiet word and a touch of his heel, brought the beast down again, hard, onto the Roman scrabbling to escape beneath its feet.

Valerius' one word was the last quiet and the steady rear the last thing that was steady. The horse's feet smashed into the procurator and the man screamed and the sound and the feel triggered an explosion of savagery that eclipsed any seen that morning.

Moved by a hatred that went beyond anything of man, the pied beast threw itself high to the sky and came down again on the bleeding body and again and again and again, screaming its passion so that the procurator's voice was lost, as his body was lost in the chaos of bones and flesh and teeth until nothing was left of the man who had ordered the flogging of the Boudica and the rape of her daughters but a carrion-mess of bloody viscera and the white fragments of skull within it.

'Valerius, stop. Stop. It's over. You can stop.'

The russet-haired cavalryman had more courage than Cunomar. He stepped in close beside the raging horse and reached up to its rider, holding his arm in the brief moment when the beast was down, before it threw itself up again.

'Stop. Your sister needs your help. The children need your help. This isn't helping.'

The horse became still and stood sweat-washed and shuddering as if it had raced and won. Valerius was not sweating, or shaking, but sitting very still, white-faced, looking beyond Cunomar to the hawk-scout, who had come out of the hut that sheltered the Boudica's daughters, and then to Airmid, who still knelt beside Breaca.

Something he read in her face reached him. He dismounted and knelt, finally, at the side of his sister, who lay within a spear's length of the horse that could have killed her. He laid a hand to her head, and then to her heart, and then bent to press his ear to her chest.

Rising he said, 'Longinus, get water. Hawk, get whoever is free and can walk and seal the gates and bring the crosses down and use them to build a barricade. If Driscus has second thoughts and marches back up from Camulodunum, I'd like to believe we have a whisper of protection.'

Valerius knelt then, in the filth beside the woman against whom he had fought for so long, and lifted her in his arms with the care of a lover and stood and looked around to find some building that had not been destroyed, and took her at last to Airmid's hut on the western side of the clearing where, if nothing else, there was water from the stream, and shelter under the broken thatch.

'Is Breaca awake?'

'I hope not.'

Yes.

She wanted to speak, but her mouth would not move to the commands of her mind.

Airmid was close by, and had been since the first touch of her hands beneath the stanchion and her voice which had said all that was necessary: 'Graine is alive. Corvus is here. All will be well,' so that it was not necessary for Breaca to climb out of the well of peace she had found.

The blackness came and went. Hands wrapped her hands, cleaning each finger of the dirt and blood that had become ingrained. Later, someone laid something cool and wet across the ruined flesh of her back. She flinched violently and groaned aloud, not finding words, nor even seeking them, and the cool went away, but not the wet. More of it dribbled on, slowly, so that each drop warmed and soothed before the next came and in time the steady patter became bearable.

Above, voices rolled back and forth. She listened to the tone if not the words until it was clear that Airmid had asked a question, but not who had answered, except that it was a man, and that he cared for her.

Some time later, when the sun had moved and there was less heat in her back, the same man said, 'She needs to move as Cunomar and the others who were flogged with him are moving.'

Airmid said, 'She's not ready.'

Patiently, 'Then we have to make her ready. If she lies as she is, her back will stiffen as it heals and she'll be hindered as a warrior.'

A new voice, gruffly male, asked, 'Will she care?'

'I believe so. You could always ask her.'

'It's not my business. I only came to see how you were. I'll be outside, helping with the others. Find me when you're done.' A memory came of a cavalry officer with russet hair, who had stood beside her, watchfully, while there was still danger. He was a good man, and he cared deeply, but not for her.

With him gone, the texture of the voices changed and a voice in her ear said, 'Breaca? If you're awake, just nod. You don't have to speak.'

She nodded.

'I need to move you. Is that all right?'

She nodded again and steady hands turned her head and someone dribbled water into the side of her mouth and she swallowed it without coughing and thought that she had lain long enough like a helpless infant and could move by herself, and did move; and stopped moving, abruptly.

When she could breathe again, she said, 'Why do I have to move?' Her voice wavered, weakly.

'Because your back will heal into something like wood and you will never swing a sword again, nor cast a slingstone, nor throw a spear. If you can keep moving now, then it will heal freely and you will only have more scars, not a body that fails to answer your bidding.'

A long time ago, in her childhood, her father had taken a bone splinter out of her hand. The pain then had seemed as bad as anything could ever be. The man sitting at her bedside sounded exactly as Eburovic had then, or Luain mac Calma at other times with other wounds: benignly reasonable when pain was coming and there was nothing to be done about it.

She swivelled her head round to look. He sat near her shoulder, holding her hand. He had cleaned her fingers and he was mac Calma, Elder of Mona, more exhausted than she had known him, and with a new edge of irony, turned in on himself, and a hound at his side that looked very like Hail.

Hoarsely, she said, 'I thought you were on Mona?'

Surprised, he raised a brow. 'I was.'

'What brought you here?'

'Luain mac Calma sent me. He thought you should be encouraged to raise the tribes in rebellion while the governor is busy in the west. That was what he said at the time. I suspect his true motives may have been different.'

Luain mac Calma sent me. That made no sense. She closed her eyes, the better to think. The hound stood very close to him, as Stone would do for her, except that Stone was a hound of flesh and blood and this hound was not.

Luain mac Calma's dream was the heron. He did not have a hound that would cross from death to life to find him, nor a russet-haired cavalry officer with a gruff voice who cared for him with single-minded intensity; nor, if she thought about it, had he ever ridden a horse that could kill a man on command, nor ever had the need to find one.

Breaca opened her eyes.

'*Bán?*'

It was not the right name. Her brother flinched as if struck and the strange, dry humour of his gaze died to bleakness. Without it,

462

exhaustion showed, and the bottomless well of pain to which his horse had given such shattering voice in the morning. Suddenly, he looked very much as he had done on the boat returning from Gaul, brought close to destruction by the ghosts of his own despair. He had used another name then, perhaps not only to taunt her.

Guessing, Breaca said, 'Valerius, then. If it fits better.'

He looked down, and seemed to be searching for words. When he looked up, he had found the humour again, however shakily.

'I think it does. I had hoped not, even prayed not, but the gods are wiser. Bán died a long time ago, and cannot be brought back now. In his place, you have Valerius of Nemain and Mithras, a dreamer with some facility as a warrior, who offers you his service, if you wish it.'

There was too much in that to deal with at once. She said, 'Of Nemain and Mithras? Can you serve both?'

'It would seem so. I had thought there would be space for only one, but apparently not. We have reached an . . . accommodation. It serves us all well, and could serve you, if you wish it.'

He had said the same, exactly, a moment ago. Breaca held her breath against the pain and made herself sit up. 'Why might I not?'

He looked at her, and through her, to all that was beyond. 'When we met last, on a ship, mac Calma stopped you from killing me. He said you would have need of me. He did not tell you that he was my father, and that he had that much reason to keep me alive.'

The brother she once knew would have given that news more tightly. The man sitting by her bedside might have done, she thought, if he had remembered what it was to be gentle with himself.

Misreading her silence, he said, 'Mac Calma is not here now. I would imagine that is by design, not accident.'

'So that I could kill you now if I chose?' She laughed, which hurt them both. 'I'm hardly in any condition to kill anyone.'

'Which is not the point.'

He was not smiling; even the irony, which had seemed so habitual, was gone. His eyes devoured her and his soul lay open, so that she could see the dark corners of it much as the ancestor had shown her the darkness in her own heart. Before, she would have been appalled, and might indeed have turned him away. Now, knowing herself as she had never done, she saw past the dark to the god-space, and the passion that fired it, and had given him the strength to serve two gods and not split apart.

He dropped his gaze, hiding himself. His hands lay flat on the pallet, scarred and sun-worn, with the nails pared tight and the tendons like ropes on the backs, from years of wielding a sword. They shook, lightly, and would not be stilled.

The silence stretched and he would not break it. He was offering his soul and her response mattered to him, as much as anything, as much, possibly, as the parting from Corvus.

Breaca had heard that, lying beneath the stanchion, and the words neither had said. She had not known who he was then, only felt the raw currents that had tugged at them, and she knew, if no-one else, that the explosion of grief that had come afterwards and had slain the procurator had not all been for the sake of the children.

He was her brother, and they shared no blood, except that their mothers had been sisters. Unknowing, she had grown to adulthood and beyond, had become Warrior of Mona and then the Boudica, and each battle had been fought with this man in her heart, believing him brother, believing him dead, wanting him to know that she loved him.

Still he did not know it.

She made herself move, slowly, carefully, until she could grasp both of his hands between her own, and feel the shaking, and still it. She said, 'A long time ago, I made an oath to the serpent-dreamer of the ancestors that I would do whatever it took to protect my family. I renewed that oath now, at the stanchion, understanding more of what it meant. Whatever your blood, you are part of my family. On the boat from Gaul, I had forgotten that. It was a mistake. Will you forgive me?'

He was weeping and had been for some time. She held his hand and waited and watched and he forced himself not to flinch this time but sustained her scrutiny for as long as either of them could bear, and then broke away and looked down again at her hands holding his.

He said, 'It's not for me to forgive. So much of what I have done is unforgivable and there is no going back. But we can go forward, and perhaps not make the same mistakes again. Airmid says you are looking for warriors to drive the legions back to the sea. I am not the warrior to lead the final rout of Rome, but rather a dreamer who has lived the past twenty years as a warrior, and can still fight if I have to. If I offered to fight for you, would you accept it?'

The world held its breath, and the ancestor, who was within her.

Breaca made the moment last, because it was a good one, and few things in the recent past had been good. Then she pulled his hands to hers and kissed them and then reached up and kissed his cheek; he was her brother, whatever his blood, and he needed to know it.

'Yes, of course,' she said. 'With great gratitude, I will accept and return it; my life for yours, for all time.'

EPILOGUE

TWO HAMMERS RANG ON THEIR ANVILS, RHYTHMICALLY.

Breaca woke and lay for a while staring at the striated thatch-shadows spread across the wall to her left. The noise made its own stripes, matching the light-and-dark. She lost herself in them for a while, working up to moving. It was important to move; Valerius had said so and had come to remind her three times each day for the past five days. 'It's the old rule of the legions: keep moving your back while a flogging heals, else the flesh will stiffen for ever. It hurts for now, but it'll be worth it later, I promise.'

He was a man who did not cast his promises lightly, she was coming to know that. Experimentally, she brought her knees to her chest and away again. It was possible to do it now without holding her breath to keep from swearing. She did it again, more smoothly.

'Mother?'

Breaca jerked upright, forgetting the pain. 'Graine? I thought you were asleep?'

'No. Don't want to sleep. It hurts.' Graine lay an arm's reach away and had done for two days, since Airmid had said she was well enough to be carried the distance across the steading from one hut to the other. She lay now in the striped sunlight, insubstantial as a ghost, with her white skin stretched tight over the battered bones of her skull and the bruises fading on her face and the blue-black shadows beneath her eyes not fading at all.

Breaca made herself stand, slowly. 'Airmid left something for you to drink. It might help. Do you want it?'

'No.' Graine made a face, and turned away, rubbing her eyes with the backs of her hands, like an infant.

'I have some milk, then, and some cheese. They have no poppy in them, or anything that will make you dream. Would you eat them with me?'

Breaca sat on the edge of the piled sheepskins and crumbled the white goat's cheese and found a wrinkled apple that one of the incoming warriors must have brought. She bit away a half-moon portion and held it out. 'Graine? Love of life, can you eat?'

'A bit.' They sat up together, both of them broken, and ate slowly, pushing food past the nausea and fear.

Graine chewed, slowly, mechanically, as if it were a duty, un-willingly met. She stared out of the door to the steading beyond. 'Who's making the noise?'

'The hammering? That's Gunovar and Valerius, my brother. They're making weapons for the new warriors.'

There were a great many new warriors. In the days she had been bedridden, the war host had grown to over a thousand, and was growing still. Ardacos had charge of it, with Dubornos. It mattered to keep Dubornos busy; he was alive only because Graine was still alive. If she had died, he would have laid himself on her grave and followed her into the lands beyond life. Breaca had absolved him of all fault, openly and before witnesses, and he had not believed her.

'Will there be war?' Graine was still looking out of the door.

'Yes. Very soon.'

'If you're still sick, will Valerius lead it?'

'Maybe. If the others will follow him. He knows most about Rome. If the legions come, which they must do now, then he knows best how to fight against them.'

'Cunomar hates him.'

Breaca laid down her cheese, unable to eat. Graine was so small, and had been so sick, and Breaca had thought her asleep when Cunomar had carried her into the hut, and found Valerius already there, and refused to acknowledge him. It had only lasted a moment; Valerius had gone out, as if it were right that he do so.

Breaca had not stopped him. It was the first time she had seen Cunomar since he had stood in slave chains beneath the cross on which he was about to die and it had taken all her self-control simply to lie still and look at her son and not show anything, or speak.

Cunomar had laid Graine on the sheepskins piled along the wall and, straightening, had said, 'It doesn't matter. An ear's a small price to pay for living.'

Breaca had nodded, speechless. Her beautiful, gold-haired warrior son was beautiful no longer. Sometime during the day, he had shaved the hair at his temples and back along the sides of his head, so that his one ear stood proud and unhidden, and the other, which had gone, showed a black clot of old blood and the hole in the centre of it that Airmid had packed with rolled leaves to keep it open. He had been beautiful, and was damaged beyond all repair, and knew it.

'It doesn't matter,' he had said, again. 'We're alive. We have a war to fight and to win. If this is the worst of what happens, we will be happy at the end of it.'

He was right, for himself if not for Graine, the child-dreamer who feared to sleep, who cried out at night and made herself wake and then lay rigidly still, staring into the dark. She found no safety or help in the things that would have held her before; she could not call on the elder grandmother, nor hear the ancestor-dreamer, and the hare that ran through her dreams was gone.

Privately, Airmid had said the dreaming could have been driven out of her for ever or could return later, stronger; that it would be impossible to tell until all the pieces of her that had been broken were mended, and that such a healing could not be hurried and might take days or months or years or pass beyond this lifetime.

'There's nothing any of us can do, except care for her,' she had said, and Breaca had stared at the wall and bitten her lip and said nothing. As she was, there was nothing she could do about anything, and the frustration of that was driving her to distraction.

Now, she made herself walk from the bed to the door and back again. Outside, a fire burned, fragrantly. The wind tugged strands of smoke into the hut. Graine sniffed and smiled thinly and took a crumb of cheese, as if that might make the walk back to the bed easier.

'Cygfa likes him,' Graine said, 'your brother. Ardacos told me. She's training her horse to be like his Crow-horse.'

'Is she? I don't think it's possible to train a horse to be like that. Can you drink this?' Breaca held a beaker of milk and helped Graine to drink it, and then stayed at her side, holding her small shoulders, trying to find some comfort. 'Is Cygfa well enough to ride?'

'Not really. But she won't listen to Airmid. She said she would rest but she got up and spent the morning training with the new warriors and the afternoon talking to your brother about his horse. He's a dreamer, isn't he, not a warrior or a smith?'

'Valerius? He's all of those things, but he's a dreamer before everything else, yes. How do you know?'

'His hound walks in his soul. Like Airmid's frog, and your serpent-spear.' Graine tilted her head back and studied her mother curiously. 'That's new,' she said. 'Stronger.' She continued to look. Her face blurred, as if sleep-drenched, and then cleared again. Her eyes lost some of their haunting. 'Cunomar doesn't have a bear like that. He is given to it, but it doesn't live in him. Is that why he hates your brother?'

'I think so.' Breaca bent her neck against the stiffness in her back and pressed her lips to her daughter's sweated hair. She breathed in the smell, the sharpness of pain and fear and hurt and the aching absence of dreaming. She reached inside for the ancestor, and found her, quietly watchful.

I promised you her life, said the ancestor. *You did not ask that she be whole. I could not have made her that.*

'I know. Nobody could. But she sees Valerius' dream-hound; she cannot, then, be for ever cut off from her dreaming?'

No more than you were.

Once, she would have railed against so ambiguous an answer. Now, she nodded and kissed Graine again and said aloud, 'Since I first came from the ancestor's cave, Cunomar has wanted to be the one to lead the rout of Rome. He is afraid now that Valerius will take his place. I have said that only the gods can know who will be alive to fight and that we should all be ready but he is still afraid.'

'What does the ancestor say?' Graine squirmed round to see her properly.

'Nothing. She will speak when it matters and not before. For the moment, all that matters is that you get well again. Can you drink some more milk, do you think?'

They drank, and finished the apple and the cheese and a haunch of roast hare that Airmid had cooked and wrapped in leaves and infused with the faintest taint of poppy, and other things that might bring dreamless sleep.

Breaca lifted Graine and carried her back to the pile of hides that was her own bed and they lay in it together, carefully, curling round to find the places of least discomfort that still let them lie together, skin on skin, finding a semblance of peace in a world racing to war.

Later, when Graine slept, and her breathing was even, Breaca lay quietly awake. She ran her fingers through the ox-blood hair and bent forward, painfully, and kissed the place at the back, in the middle, where a small arrow-head of rich red hairs came together.

'You're alive,' she said to the child, and the listening gods. 'It was all I asked for. For today, that's enough. Tomorrow, or the day after, we can give thanks that everyone else is alive and then we can raise and arm every warrior of every tribe and push Rome and its legions back into the sea.'

AUTHOR'S NOTE

THOSE WHO KNOW ANYTHING OF BOUDICA'S STORY, FROM SCHOOL OR modern media histories, know that she was flogged and her daughters were raped and that this was the spark that lit the fires of her revolt against Roman occupation. It makes romantic reading and gave our Victorian forebears an understandable excuse for why and how a woman might have had the opportunity and ability to lead an armed war host in a series of successful military actions; the 'wronged matron' fighting to avenge the assault on her daughters ruffles no feathers.

In reality, the atrocities committed by the Roman authorities in the wake of Prasutagos' death were the end point of a cumulating oppression and, it seems to me, were more likely in retribution for the beginnings of insurrection that was already under way than the trigger that began it. We have no exact date to pinpoint the start of this uprising but it came at a time when Suetonius Paulinus was attacking the druidic island of Mona (now known as Anglesey) and we can assume that he attacked early in the battle season, simply to give himself time to complete his actions before the autumn. We also know from Tacitus that the tribes '. . . had been careless in sowing corn, people of every age having gone to war . . .' from which we can assume that the revolt was under way at the time of the spring plantings – not long after the winter thaw.

If we put these facts together, we have a spring uprising, in which a number of well-armed tribal warriors conducted at least two well-planned raids, which took full advantage of the governor's preoccupation in the west of the country. It seems to me unlikely that whoever ruled the Eceni could have mustered a war host from amongst a defeated, disarmed nation without some degree of preparation and warning and, given the restrictions of winter, that this preparation had been under way since at least the previous autumn.

If this is the case, then Prasutagos' death – the timing of which is also inexact – is likely to have come towards the end of those preparations.

Tacitus' eloquent description of the abuse of the native tribes by the Roman colonists of Camulodunum makes stark reading. A single paragraph summarizes the conditions that led to war:

> It was against the veterans that [the rebelling tribes'] hatred was most intense. For these new settlers in the colony of Camulodunum drove people out of their houses, ejected them from their farms, called them captives and slaves and the lawlessness of the veterans was encouraged by the soldiers, who lived a similar life and hoped for similar licence. A temple also erected to the Divine Claudius was ever before their eyes, a citadel, as it seemed, of perpetual tyranny.

Thus we have the Trinovantes in Camulodunum being treated as are all natives by the occupying power: with contempt and little observation of the law. We have also from Suetonius in his *Lives of the Caesars* the fact that Nero – a profligate spender even by Roman imperial standards – had considered withdrawing his troops from Britain. This in itself might not have caused panic, but Dio Cassius tells us that the imperial adviser Seneca

> . . . in the hope of receiving a good rate of interest, had lent to the islanders 40,000,000 sesterces that they did not want, and had afterwards called in this loan all at once and had resorted to severe measures in exacting it.

The tribes of the east, therefore, were under immense social and political pressure. It is not hard to imagine each new insult pushing them closer to the edge of war and the Eceni were well placed to spark a rebellion. They had been party to a fairly effective armed revolt in AD 47 and they were not immediately under the thumb of the veterans in Camulodunum as were their neighbours, the Trinovantes. Their king, Prasutagos, however, was a client king, installed by Claudius and presumably considered a loyal Roman subject, unlikely to rebel.

We know very little of Prasutagos other than that he was 'famed for his long prosperity' and that he died having made one of the most insane wills in history, which named his two daughters as co-inheritors with the emperor.

It is hard to imagine why he did this. Possibilities range from his signing a document he could not read, to his signing a document that was given to him with little option; a case of 'sign this and we might honour it; don't sign and we'll take everything anyway.'

The question of the rights of women to inherit at this point is open. Cicero reports that the 'Lex Vocania' broadly forbade any man 'included in the census' to make a woman his heir. This was transmuted by Augustus who ruled instead that women might inherit if they had given birth to three children if they were Roman citizens; four if they were freeborn Latins; or five if they were not citizens. This would suggest that girls too young to conceive, or who had failed to marry or to bear children, could not inherit.

This brings us, then, to Prasutagos' daughters about which precisely nothing is known except that they were 'outraged' by the centurions sent to take possession of the entirety of his inheritance at the same time as their mother, the Boudica, was 'scourged'.

Here, Tacitus is our only source, but he is fairly specific that it was the king's daughters who were raped and his wife who was flogged. One wonders – at least I wonder – why a group of armed men with nothing whatsoever to lose chose not to rape the wife as well, but paused in their blood-frenzy for long enough to organize a flogging – which is hardly the most spontaneous of events – and then neither raped the Boudica nor slaughtered the entire family afterwards.

Two things seem relevant here, both minor points of Roman law. Elsewhere in Tacitus is a vivid description of the revenge meted out to the family of the traitor Sejanus at the time of Tiberius, roughly half a century before the Boudican revolt. In this, we hear of Sejanus' young daughter who is dragged off to execution, entirely too young to understand what is going on or why. 'Historians of the time tell us that, as there was no precedent for the capital punishment of a virgin, she was violated by the executioner, with the rope on her neck.' Much later, in the fourth century AD, the young woman who became St Agnes was also 'violated' before her execution on the grounds that she was a virgin and it was illegal to execute a girl who had yet to lose her chastity.

If we add to that the very well documented fact that flogging was routinely practised against insurgents prior to their crucifixion (Christ is the obvious case in point) then we have the possibility that the rapes of the girls and the flogging of the Boudica were not simply the acts of men out of control, but the planned prelude to a judicial execution of a family caught in the act of rebellion.

The question remains as to why that execution failed to take place and for that we have no reasons, except that, like its successor, the Spanish Inquisition, Rome was a punctilious observer of the rule of law and the execution of a king's family was not something to be taken lightly by anyone less than an emperor. A governor might have the necessary authority to carry out such an act, but we know that Paulinus was otherwise occupied in the assault on Mona. Thus whoever acted in the east was almost certainly overstepping his powers and a senior officer might reasonably be assumed to have stepped in to stop it.

These, then, are the written historical grounds for this book. The rest is built around my interpretation of the archaeology. One piece is relatively unaltered: a tombstone was found in Colchester dating from the period of the Boudican revolt. It was dedicated to a man named 'Longinus Sdapeze' who had fought with the First Thracian Cavalry. The tombstone and the wording thereon are almost exactly as described in the text.

For the rest, as ever, the fiction outweighs the fact although I have tried to build on a skeleton of what is known or can be inferred from the existing data. The structure of tribal society is my own, based around a relatively flimsy skeleton of archaeology and later records of Celtic Ireland, which was never invaded by Rome. One of the most concrete 'facts' is the annual calendar followed by Breaca and her people which is based on a Gaulish remnant carved on stone. For the Gauls, certainly, and I believe the tribal Britons, the day began at dusk so that night preceded day, and the year began at the start of winter on what is now called Samhain, or 1 November. The night before, 31 October, is still the time when the veils between the worlds are thinnest.

The depth and colour are added to the characters and their journeys by the dreaming, which drives and enhances their lives. As with the previous volumes, the dreaming of this book has mirrored my own dreaming and the journeys of those who have joined it. This has no particular basis in what we might call ordinary consensus reality, but is based on an increasingly concrete experience of various non-ordinary realities that impinge on it.

For those who enjoy exploring the geography of these things, the caves of Mithras in which Valerius meets his god are fictional, but the Passage Tombs in Ireland in which he comes to know himself are very real and are almost exactly as described. These seem to me to have been designed expressly as dreaming chambers, although by a civilization far older than the late pre-Roman Iron Age of these novels. The rest, as ever, is as possible now as it was then, if we only set our intent sufficiently clearly and open to the possibility that the world is rarely as concrete as we would like to believe.

The author's website, http://www.mandascott.co.uk, carries details of contemporary dreaming workshops, recommended reading and other resources.

THE LANGUAGE OF THE PRE-ROMAN TRIBES IS LOST TO US; WE HAVE NO means of knowing the exact pronunciations although linguists make brave attempts, based on known living and dead languages, particularly modern and medieval Breton, Cornish and Welsh. The following are my best attempts at accuracy. You are free to make your own. The names of characters based in history are marked with an asterisk.

Tribal characters

Airmid of Nemain – Air-med. Frog-dreamer, former lover to Breaca. Airmid is one of the Irish names of the goddess.

Ardacos – Ar-dah-kos. She-bear warrior of the Caledones. Former lover to Breaca.

Bán – Breaca's half-brother, son of Macha. The 'á' is pronounced rather like the 'o' in bonfire. It means 'white'.

Bellos – Bell-oss. Former slave boy of the Belgae, and companion of Valerius in Hibernia.

*Breaca – Bray-ah-ca. Also known as the Boudica, from the old word 'Boudeg' meaning Bringer of Victory, thus 'She who Brings Victory'. Breaca is a derivative of the goddess Briga.

*Caradoc – Kar-a-dok. Lover to Breaca, father to Cygfa and Cunomar. Co-leader of the western resistance against Rome.

*Cunobelin – Koon-oh-bel-in. Father to Caradoc, now dead. Cun – 'hound', Belin, the sun god. Hence, Hound of the Sun or Sun Hound.

Cunomar – Koon-oh-mar. Son of Breaca and Caradoc. His name means 'hound of the sea'.

Cygfa – Sig-va. Daughter of Caradoc and Cwmfen, half-sister to Cunomar.

Dubornos – Doob-ohr-nos. Singer and warrior of the Eceni, childhood companion to Breaca and Bán.

Eburovic – Eh-boor-oh-vik. Father to Breaca and Bán, now dead.

Efnís – Eff-neesh. Dreamer of the Eceni.

Eneit – Enate. Soul-friend of Cunomar. His name means 'spirit'.

Graine – Granya; the first 'a' is pronounced like the 'o' in bonfire. Daughter of Breaca and Caradoc.

Gunovar – Goonavar. Daughter of Gunovic and a dreamer of the Dumnonii.

Gwyddhien – G-with-i-enne. Warrior of the Silures, lover to Airmid.

Iccius – Ikk-i-ooss. Belgic slave-boy killed in an accident while enslaved by Amminios. Friend and soul-mate to Bán, now dead.

Lanis – Lan-is. Mother of Eneit, and a dreamer of the Eceni.

Luain mac Calma – Luw-ain mak Kalma. Elder of Mona and heron-dreamer. A prince of Hibernia.

Macha – Mach-ah. The 'ch' is soft as in Scottish 'loch'. Bán's mother, now dead. Macha is a derivative of the horse goddess.

Madb – Maeve. A warrior of the Hibernians.

Roman characters

Latin is rather closer to our language, although we would pronounce the letter 'J' as equivalent to the current 'Y', 'V' would be 'W' and 'C' would be a hard 'K' in all cases. However, this is so rarely used that it is simpler to retain standard modern pronunciation of these letters.

*Decianus Catus – procurator of all Britannia under Nero.

Julius Valerius – officer in the auxiliary cavalry, originally with the Ala Quinta Gallorum, later the Ala Prima Thracum.

*Longinus Sdapeze – officer with the Ala Prima Thracum.

*Lucius Domitius Ahenobarbus, a.k.a. Nero, emperor of Rome.

Quintus Valerius Corvus – prefect of the Ala Quinta Gallorum.

*Quintus Veranius – fourth governor of Britannia, AD 57–58.

*Seneca – adviser to Nero, emperor of Rome.

*Suetonius Paulinus – governor of all Britannia.